HARDBOILED &
HIGH HEELED

HARDBOILED &
HIGH HEELED

The Woman Detective
in Popular Culture

Linda Mizejewski

ROUTLEDGE
NEW YORK & LONDON

Published in 2004 by
Routledge
29 West 35th Street
New York, NY 10001
www.routledge-ny.com

Published in Great Britain by
Routledge
11 New Fetter Lane
London EC4P 4EE
www.routledge.co.uk

Routledge is an imprint of the Taylor & Francis Group.

Printed in the United States of America on acid-free paper.

10 9 8 7 6 5 4 3 2 1

Cataloging-in-Publication data available from the Library of Congress upon request.
ISBN 0-415-96970-0 (alk. paper)
ISBN 0-415-96971-9 (pbk: alk. paper)

For my mystery-loving women friends

CONTENTS

ACKNOWLEDGMENTS

I am grateful to many people who helped me picture this book and made it possible—and fun—to write. Thanks especially to my friends who share my enthusiasm for the woman-detective character: Judith Mayne, Debra Moddelmog, Terry Moore, Meg Gerlach Laker, Jan Polek, and Jeanne Neff. They're the ones who handed me books, emailed me lists and recommendations, rehashed *X-Files* episodes, and indulged me with fan gossip. Thanks also to Pamela R. Matthews, Mary Ann O'Farrell, Jeanine Basinger, and Priscilla L. Walton for encouragement and inspiration. All of them are first-rate investigating women in their own right. Also big thanks to Marilyn Brownstein, Debra Bruce, Elizabeth Davis, Rita Mayer, Carolyn Rhodes, and Charlotte Stovall, who may not be fans of this genre but have helped me through life's other mysteries.

I'm also thankful to Jean Redmann for her kindness in giving me interview time and to Sue Grafton for generously answering queries. Thanks also to Richard Thomas for friendship and support. As always, my family was the reliable backup so critical for the woman investigator on the case: the Mizejewskis, Komars, Pokrywkas, Edward Vargas, and especially my mother, Ann Mizejewski, who was surely a hardboiled, high-heeled detective in another lifetime. Most of all, I owe big thanks to George Cowmeadow Bauman, who lived through this project day by day and was ceaselessly patient, loving, and good humored.

I also received generous support for this project from the Ohio State University. The Department of Women's Studies awarded me a Coca-Cola Critical Difference for Women Grant, which made it possible for me to travel to archives. The English Department under the chairship of Jim Phelan supported my sabbatical time and other release time so I could complete this manuscript. Grants-in-Aid from the College of

Humanities and research funding from the Department of Women's Studies supported final costs of manuscript preparation. The English Department's First Draft Writing Group saw several of these chapters and gave me good advice. My thanks also go to my excellent research assistants Yi Zhong and Min Sook Heo, and especially to Melanie Maltry and Clarissa Moore for their tireless work in the last stages of the project. For their help and patience in the final stages of manuscript preparation, I owe many thanks to the Women's Studies staff: Ada Draughon, Linda O'Brien, and especially to Melinda Bogarty for her keen eye and interest. I also want to thank all four anonymous press readers, whose suggestions guided me in revisions, and Matt Byrnie, Emily Vail, Alan Kaplan, and Erin E. McElroy at Routledge. Finally, I'm grateful to Elizabeth Johnson for poring over every sentence and making good suggestions.

Earlier versions of portions of this book have appeared in the following publications: *South Central Review* (2001), *Journal of Film and Video* (1993), and *Keyframes: Popular Cinema and Cultural Studies*, edited by Matthew Tinkcom and Amy Villarejo, 2001.

1

WATCHING THE WOMEN DETECTIVES

FANS AND FANTASIES

In Thomas Harris's 1988 novel *The Silence of the Lambs*, the cannibal-psychiatrist Hannibal Lecter quizzes rookie FBI agent Clarice Starling about how we acquire our tastes. Lecter is trying to put her into the mind of the serial killer known as Buffalo Bill, who is a discriminating consumer, collecting fabrics for a wardrobe made from human skin. There may be no accounting for taste, but Lecter wants Clarice to understand that consumers desire the things that are dangled in front of them. "We begin by coveting what we see everyday," he tells her, and goes on to remind her of the desiring eyes she feels on her own body as she goes about her work.[1]

This conversation also appears in Jonathan Demme's 1991 film version of the book, with Anthony Hopkins delivering the lecture, his unblinking gaze trained on Jodie Foster's Clarice. In light of his own tastes, Lecter's mini-lesson and his focus on Clarice pack a chill. As a mass murderer, Lecter is actually less predictable and more imaginative than serial killers, who tend to repeat the same scenario in compulsive ways, hoping to fulfill a fantasy that's never quite satisfied. But when Lecter stalks Clarice in the sequel, *Hannibal*, he becomes obsessive. At one point he breaks into her car simply to sniff the air. With Clarice, Lecter begins to resemble smitten fans who pursue stars and celebrities, hoping for contact, manipulating a scenario for a fantasy come true. Most of us are far less frightening as fans of our favorite stars, writers, and stories, but the marketers of these commodities hope that we, like Hannibal Lecter, are insatiable consumers.

By the end of the 1990s, the woman detective character had become a commodity with a hungry fan base, eager for the next Patricia Cornwell book and the next installment of Sue Grafton's alphabet series. Bookstores by that time carried more than a hundred crime series featuring heroines who were private investigators, cops, sheriffs, forensics experts, constables, or federal agents. In the summer of 2003, women were regular members of investigating teams on nine network and cable television series, including the Nielsen ratings' number-one hit *CSI: Crime Scene Investigation* (2000–). And within a two-year span Sandra Bullock, one of the top-grossing actresses in Hollywood, played an investigator in *Miss Congeniality* (2000) and *Murder by Numbers* (2002).

The amateur female sleuth—Nancy Drew in her roadster, Miss Marple in her rocker—has been a staple of mystery novels for generations. In fact, sleuthing women have appeared in literature since the middle of the nineteenth century.[2] But the *professional* female character is an exhilarating newcomer to a market long dominated by men. Asked to imagine a private investigator (P.I.), most people will still picture Peter Falk as Columbo or Humphrey Bogart as Sam Spade in a rumpled trench coat and two-days' growth of beard. For better or worse, cultural ideas about detectives are welded to the books, films, and television programs that shape our assumptions about crime investigation: what bodies are in these places, how they're dressed, how they stride into the police station or end in the morgue in very specific shoes—perhaps heels.

My book about picturing women investigators begins with Clarice Starling because her stories in *The Silence of the Lambs* and *Hannibal*, as books and movies, have been widely pictured, dangled in front of us, through the 1990s and into the first years of the new century. Clarice Starling may not be an "everyday" image, but she's been offered to readers and audiences as a coveted commodity, made familiar through book-movie connections, stardom, ads, talk-show promotions, magazine covers, late-show parodies, and feature-story journalism.

The Clarice character also poses a mystery at the heart of my own investigation. Jodie Foster won an Academy Award for her role in *The Silence of the Lambs*, an enormously profitable and high-profile movie that ends with Clarice still in pursuit of Hannibal Lecter, leaving audiences to drool for the sequel. Given the Hollywood penchant for imitating box-office hits—the slasher trend following *Halloween* (1978), the action-hero movies following *Die Hard* (1988)—you would expect a dozen wanna-be Clarices or even trashy FBI babes populating scripts for the next several years. Instead, scarcely a handful of woman-investigator movies appeared over the next decade. Especially considering the woman-detective boom in the publishing industry, why has this character's career in Hollywood and on prime-time television been slower and spottier? There's no single answer or smoking gun, but this question has turned up a rich history of stardom, marketing, fan bases, television trends, and Internet fictions—all part of the picturing of this character in the media and in the imagination of her fans.

I'm one of those fans, and my imaginary connection to Clarice is another reason her story frames this book. In *The Silence of the Lambs* Clarice gets her most important break in the case when she goes back to the gray river town where Buffalo Bill's first victim had lived. In the victim's bedroom, Clarice sees the importance of a fact the FBI guys wouldn't know: working-class women often sew their own clothes. Interviewing Stacy, the victim's best friend, Clarice asks questions about sewing that quickly take her to the murderer and his horrific basement lair.

In the novel, the scene with Stacy takes place in an office, but in the film version, it takes place in Moxley's Drugstore. Though the film identifies the location as Belvedere, Ohio, Moxley's is actually in my hometown of Homestead, Pennsylvania, in the Pittsburgh area, where most of *The Silence of the Lambs* was filmed. Jodie Foster and Lauren Roselli, the actress who plays Stacy, sit at the soda counter where I spent many of my teenage hours after school and on Saturday afternoons.

Through the 1960s Moxley's served vanilla fountain Cokes and lime rickeys. My girlfriends and I would order these exotic concoctions and linger on the padded green stools, chatting and dreaming of the days when we'd leave Homestead, which has always been a gray, working-class river town, but which was once a thriving one, in the days of the steel mills. "Is that a good job, FBI agent?" Stacy asks in the movie. "Get to travel around and stuff? I mean, better places than this?" A lot of the young women in my high school were Stacy. Their parents believed college was a waste of money for girls, who could always get jobs as clerks or secretaries in the steel mills.

Across from the soda counter, a mirror ran the length of the wall, and we would stare into it to imagine ourselves in a glamorous future away from the noxious industrial air of Homestead, our skin and minds clarified at last. When I saw *The Silence of the Lambs* for the first time, the Moxley's scene had the dizzying impact of time-travel back to those days of adolescent mysteries. For a moment, the movie screen became the familiar public mirror at Moxley's in which—a fan's dream scenario come true!—Jodie Foster appears instead of my skinny, bouffant-haired high-school self.

Moxley's Drugstore, like most of the main drag in Homestead, is closed up now, but when I go home to visit my family, I usually stop and peer in the dirty window so I can see the counter where, I imagine, Jodie Foster, Clarice Starling, and I have met through Stacy. I've daydreamed that the abandoned furnishings will come up for auction one day so I can purchase the counter and stools to keep as a private museum of fiction, fans, stardom, and fantasy—all of which are topics of this book.

Even some of us who did leave Homestead are apparently still tied there. Clarice breaks the case, after all, by going back to a working-class locale she already knows. The woman detective character has an ambivalent relationship to class. Police work is inherently a working-class scene—low-paying, physical, no college education required. Private investigators get their own offices, but no steady paychecks. Even the prestigious job of Special Agent in the FBI isn't imagined in these stories as an upper-class life. With seven years of service in the Bureau, Clarice Starling lives modestly in a blue-collar neighborhood, according to Harris's sequel novel *Hannibal*. The same is true of *The X-Files'* Dana Scully, *Prime Suspect's* Jane Tennison, and Cagney and Lacey, who don't have chic apartments, designer wardrobes, and to-die-for cars. The perks of life as a female investigator are less tangible. Instead of Dior bags and BMWs, these heroines have adventures, a commitment to justice, and a license to do what's usually done by men. Movies like *Blue Steel* (1990) highlight the enticement of police work for women as empowerment and equalization. And freedom—the detective earns her own paycheck but isn't tied down to a desk, computer, cubicle, kitchen, or nursery.

Yet these stories always entail the minute details of what these women wear, eat, and window shop. In *Fatal Beauty* (1987), Whoopi Goldberg as an undercover cop is stopped in her tracks by a $5,000 evening gown in a display window. On *The X-Files* (1993–2002), Dana Scully's pantsuits improved with the series' ratings. Carol O'Connell's cop heroine Kathleen Mallory wears cashmere blazers and $200-an-ounce fragrances. In the sequel to *The Silence of the Lambs*, Hannibal sends Clarice a pair of red Gucci pumps in a sly reference to his first cruel assessment of her origins and accessories—her failure to buy good shoes.[3]

But whatever they wear, these heroines dress to please *themselves*. Their job isn't to look good, but to do the looking. And this delicious in-your-face freedom is what all the investigating-women scenarios have in common. In its leanest form, the fantasy is Sue Grafton's heroine Kinsey Millhone in her tidy cottage, the owner of one dress and a dozen interchangeable turtlenecks and jeans, happily immune to the lures of products and clothes attached to her wealthier clients. If Hannibal Lecter presented her with red Guccis, she would use their pointy little toes to kick him out the door. In its more pampered version, the fantasy is Patricia Cornwell's Kay Scarpetta, who rises from a poor childhood to her palatial manse in a gated neighborhood. She already owns closetfuls of Guccis, and so would likewise be indifferent to Lecter's gift. Among female investigators, the upscale Scarpetta is the exception rather than the norm, and she's on the best-seller list for good reason as the flip side of Kinsey's spartan life in jeans.

Clarice Starling, poised midway between these two fantasies, evokes all these elements at once: the Appalachian background, the scholarship girl with aspirations, the cruelties of the bureaucracy, and the temptation of the Gucci heels. As women who show up asking questions, flashing a license or diploma, professional women are likely to identify with this story's mixed bag of ambition, disappointments, successes, and carefully chosen accessories.

Readers of women's mystery fiction can easily picture versions of themselves as the main characters, but once we move from book to movie, the picturing of this character gets more complicated. The character that appears at Moxley's is played by Jodie Foster, who attracts her own mix of diverse audience fantasies to this story. Foster's public images have included precocious child star, sexual child/woman, authoritative director, and lesbian icon. The reception of the film *The Silence of the Lambs* illustrates the contradictory effects of her casting. When gay protesters accused the film of a homophobic portrayal of Buffalo Bill, Foster was outed and attacked as a political traitor. But other audiences insisted her casting made it possible to read Clarice Starling as a lesbian, and for this group, Foster was a political groundbreaker.[4] In short, the picturing of the woman detective onscreen always involves an actress, stardom, and its baggage. Readers might imagine policewoman Amelia Sachs in Jeffery Deaver's novel *The Bone Collector* in a number of ways, but once she's portrayed by Angelina Jolie, she comes with pouting lips. a bad-girl reputation, and the psycho intensity of her previous film, *Girl, Interrupted* (1999).

The picturing also entails the conventions of how women are usually filmed and portrayed in mainstream movies. For a character as nonconformist as the woman detective—a woman whose story doesn't lead to love and marriage—the easiest way to assure audiences she's straight is to glamorize her, give her a male cop partner, or put her into a bikini and high heels, as television did with Angie Dickinson in *Police Woman* (1974–78), with plenty of silhouette-profile shots. Demme's film version of *Silence of the Lambs* worked hard to avoid that route. Unlike the Harris novel from which it was adapted, the film makes no reference to Clarice in relation to dating or a boyfriend. The casting of Jodie Foster, Foster's costuming, and the shot compositions further removed the character from girlie or glamorous clichés. Yet the entire

Fig. 1 Jodie Foster as Clarice Starling among the FBI boys in *The Silence of the Lambs* (1991). Courtesy of Photofest.

film revolves around questions of how Clarice is *seen* and scrutinized by her superiors and by Hannibal Lecter, and eventually how she's seen through the deadly vision of Buffalo Bill's night goggles in the basement from hell.[5]

I discuss *The Silence of the Lambs* in more detail in chapter 7, but it's worth pausing here to consider two images early in this film because they sum up the problems of picturing the woman investigator. Shortly after the opening credit sequence at FBI headquarters in Quantico, a medium shot shows the petite Clarice in an elevator full of her towering male colleagues. Since she'd been summoned from her run on an obstacle course, she's still wearing a formless, sweaty shirt, no makeup, her hair carelessly pulled back—certainly not a feminine outfit. Yet when she enters the elevator and takes a position among the beefy guys, she suddenly looks delicate, vulnerable, and pretty despite the sweaty gym clothes. The emphatic effect is *difference*, not just the gender difference of her longer hair, but difference of the *body*, a reminder that the FBI is not just a prestigious, dominant organization but a predominantly *male* one—and a conservative one at that.

A little later in *The Silence of the Lambs*, another brief shot zeros in on the film's self-consciousness about the female body. We see Clarice and her roommate on the running track, themselves being tracked by the admiring glances of their male cohorts even though the women themselves are oblivious to those gazes. This shot of fairly innocuous looking and being-looked-at neatly sums up a long visual history of gender from the art nude through the chorus girl and *Playboy* playmate.

The running-track shot in *Silence of the Lambs* also reminds us that issues of *looking* are central to the detective story. The detective is classically the character who sees what others miss and even sees what's missing. "There used to be a painting on that wall," mumbles Columbo. Sherlock Holmes is always chiding Watson to do more active and deductive observing. "That walking stick belongs to a man who owns a large dog," Holmes announces to his colleague in the film version of *The Hound of the Baskervilles* (1939). Significantly, one of the formula repetitions of the early *X-Files* seasons was that Dana Scully typically arrived on the scene a moment too late, just missing what her partner Fox Mulder was able to see.[6]

Feminist film theory makes a persuasive argument that much of traditional Hollywood cinema has been unconsciously organized along these lines: men looking and taking action, women being looked at. The conventions of framing, lighting, and editing women's bodies and faces all play to these dynamics. The "male gaze" argument about Hollywood cinema has been thoroughly debated and criticized for its limitations, but its general truths surface in the continual complaints from actresses about the scarcity of good roles for women. *The X-Files* eventually developed Scully's character so that she equaled Mulder's. But the more typical Hollywood setup through most of the twentieth century was the James Bond or Indiana Jones quest, in which the "action" heroine mostly screams, writhes, entices, and wears flirty little outfits. Even in the later Bond films in which the gal-pal knows her tae kwon do, it's still *his* story and her good looks that matter.

How is it, then, that women have always enjoyed these films and still take great pleasure in women's action films such as *Charlie's Angels: Full Throttle* (2003), in which good looks and tight framings of sleek leather pants still matter? Through the 1990s, feminist film critics became more skeptical about pleasurable movie viewing being strictly divided into gendered lines. The concept that's proven more useful, and the phrase I've been using in this chapter, is *fantasy*, which is a far more fluid and ambiguous model of how movies and our responses to them might work.[7]

In fantasy, identification isn't necessarily attached to one character or point of view, but might fluctuate among several. For instance, in my fantasy scenario at the soda counter in Moxley's, I'm sometimes the young girl from Homestead who has turned into Clarice Starling, but sometimes I imagine being in the place of Stacy, thrilled to be sitting next to Clarice, or thrilled to be sitting next to Jodie Foster. Or I'm looking into the mirror and seeing Clarice or Foster. Or I'm present but happily watching the scene with all of us/them in place. The excitement is the scenario itself, at once both familiar (the drugstore on Eighth Avenue) and heightened in drama (A hunt for a serial murderer! A movie made in Homestead!).

As this suggests, fantasy scenarios aren't logical and can in fact embrace contradictions and contradictory attitudes and desires. The class fantasies about the professional woman investigator include both Kinsey Millhone's cotton turtlenecks and Kathy Mallory's cashmere blazers. It's the scenario that matters—the heady freedom of choice, the refusal of these women to dress for men.

The fluidity of fantasy also explains the striking overlap of straight women and lesbians as fans of woman detective fictions. Many lesbian detective novels are marketed and sold to a wider (not exclusively lesbian-identified) audience. Writers like Katherine V. Forrest, Laurie R. King, J.M. Redmann, and Mary Wings have all published their lesbian detective novels with mainstream presses.[8]

And the straight/gay crossover appeal of the woman detective has a huge impact on the *picturing* of this character onscreen and on television. A June 2003 essay in the lesbian magazine *Curve* argued that characters on the television series *CSI*, or *Crossing Jordan*, or *Fastlane* don't have to be *written* as lesbian in order to be interpreted that way. "What makes more sense than an ass-kicking lesbian?" a quoted critic points out. As the *Curve* article and my own Moxley's fantasy suggest, fans are *active* consumers, not passive recipients of intended meanings. Over and over in this book, fans show up as powerful creators of their own meanings. Fans of Sue Grafton imagine and discuss who would star in a movie that will never be made. Fans of *The X-Files* provided Dana Scully with hundreds of fictional back stories and spinoffs. Fan groups of Jodie Foster and Patricia Cornwell imagine the private lives of the star and author in ways that give their fictions different meanings.[9]

My point is that the woman detective character provokes a wide range of fans and fantasies. Nor are these fantasies limited to what actually happens in the book, movie, or television series. In the television programs described in the *Curve* essay, the women characters sometimes have romances with men, and some of the episodes and plots are more heterosexual than others. But that's not to say women viewers, and men viewers for that matter, are neatly aligned into gay or straight readings of these shows.

Consider the slippery building blocks of the maverick woman-investigator character. Her story doesn't depend on her looks, her adventures aren't geared toward marriage, and her loyalties to the macho police or FBI will always be tested by cruel reminders that she's an outsider. These very qualities of the outsider, the eternal bachelor, and the adventurer make the traditional *male* hero appealing. But the same traits in a woman give her a different flavor.

Straight women insisting that this spunky, independent woman doesn't *have* to be gay are absolutely right. But she doesn't *have* to be straight, either. Gay readings of this character in film and on television can quickly reveal "something queer here," as Alexander Doty has put it, and can celebrate the ambiguity of certain scripts and performances—Jodie Foster as Clarice, Betty Thomas as the plucky police-woman on *Hill Street Blues*.[10] But less generous, outright homophobic suspicions of "something queer here" can come from other quarters. The most publicized example is the early reception of *Cagney & Lacey* (1982–88), described in detail in chapter 3. This series was plagued by right-wing protests and network anxieties about the lesbian overtones of two aggressive women in a man's job, despite their overtly straight characterization. In response, the network replaced actress Meg Foster, who looked too "butch," with more conventionally "feminine" Sharon Gless—who promptly became a cult lesbian favorite.

For producers and sponsors, the possibility of this kind of "slippage" from heterosexuality creates the need to appease one faction of the audience and tease another. The result is often deliberately mixed signals. In an intriguing 2002 television episode of *Crossing Jordan*, Mariel Hemingway guest-starred as a lesbian radio psychologist who's befriended by forensics expert Jordan (Jill Hennessy) during a murder investigation. Both Hemingway and Hennessy had previously played film roles as lesbians, so for some audiences there was already a meaningful history in this casting.[11] In the *Jordan* script, written by gay executive story editor Elizabeth Sarnoff, sparks fly. The women are clearly attracted to each other, and supporting characters knowingly nod their heads about Jordan's orientation. Inevitably, Jordan withdraws from the would-be romance, but the episode was surprising in its frankness about Jordan's less-than-bulletproof heterosexuality and in the casual comments of her coworkers about it. Less surprising was that the previews for the following week's episode pointedly focused on Jordan kissing a male costar, a blunt assurance by the network that no more funny business was at hand.

Picturing the woman detective always involves a bottom line, and the sexually subversive nuances of this character make her more of an

Fig. 2 Jill Hennessy as forensic investigator Jordan Cavanaugh on *Crossing Jordan* (NBC, 2001–). Courtesy of Photofest.

economic risk for television and movies than for publishing. In the 1990s, publishing technology became cheaper because of digital cameras that produce high-quality products, so smaller ventures such as the Mysterious Press and the Poisoned Pen Press thrived in that decade with a list of detective titles. For the major publishers, the cheaper technology also encouraged novelty. While they could issue multimillion dollar contracts to their mass-market superstars, they could also take low-cost risks on first-time writers. In 1996 Patricia Cornwell was paid $24 million for a three-book contract, but her first novel was purchased in 1990 by Scribner's for $6,000. At the end of the 1990s, the major houses reported bigger budgets for fewer best-seller authors, but the result was that many more authors were picked up by smaller publishers.

While publishing has become less costly, television and film production costs keep going up. Television series are actually more flexible than movies because television has the ability to develop a character and even to make changes within one season to accommodate audience responses. So television has been relatively adventurous about portraying professional women investigators, even during the 1970s, long before Hollywood did so. It's true that the female detective on television—unlike her male counterparts Columbo or Mannix or the boys at

Sunset Strip—had to endure some flimsy packaging as pinup or as part of a romantic couple. Yet television is exactly the place where we see how forcefully the female investigator has become part of our cultural "central casting," gradually infiltrating the all-boys crime shows. As this book was going to press, two new woman-investigator shows premiered on the Fall 2003 network television lineup. *Cold Case* (CBS) features a Philadelphia homicide detective played by Kathryn Morris, and *Karen Sisco* (ABC) stars Carla Gugino as a federal marshal. The Morris and Gugino characters are sexy but sturdy, and abrasive when they need to be. Clearly, the networks think a quick-thinking woman with a license and gun is a good prime-time risk.

Films are far steeper investment risks. Unlike television, a film has no system of revision or long-term development after its release. All of its characterization takes place within a two-hour span, and its popularity depends on reviews and box-office returns within its first week of distribution. The video release will bring in more profits, but its returns usually reflect early reviews. The financial stakes are enormous. At the end of the 1990s, the budget for a first-run film, including marketing, typically ran $80 million; costs for a first-run low-budget film (no big-name stars, limited shooting time, modest production costs) ran about $5 million.[12]

Given these numbers, the spreadsheets for romantic comedies and male-buddy action films will always look like safer bets. In the either-or sexual logic of Hollywood, if the heroine isn't part of a straight couple or doesn't look likely to be, then she's a lesbian, possibly offensive to large segments of the audience and a threat to the male privileges and romantic codes of Hollywood stories. This anxiety about the woman detective's sexuality is played out in the 1990 cop film *Internal Affairs*, which starred Andy Garcia and featured a humorless lesbian police detective played by Laurie Metcalf. Metcalf's character, coldly referred to as "the dyke" by the guys on the force, is the film's tough moral center, the only one who's motivated by a sense of justice and the law. But her all-business, no-warmth character is also the least fleshed-out in the script.[13] Proof of her expendability is that she's shot and put into an ambulance at the end of the film, and we never learn what happened to her! She's sharp, brave, not interested in men, and apparently way too scary for a 1990 audience.

Internal Affairs is preoccupied with the theme of the cop as a criminal at heart, which is also the prickly subtext of most detective stories. The traditional male detective's resemblances to the bad guys, his attraction to crime and to bad neighborhoods, got him in the business in the first place. The ability to think like the bad guys is the ability to catch them. This secret-outlaw theme continues with the woman detective. Any reader of Sue Grafton or J.M. Redmann remembers the ease (and even glee) with which their women P.I.s tell lies, impersonate authorities, and engage in minor breaking and entering in their pursuit of the case.

The catch is that lesbians have also been characterized as secret outlaws, often in a far less playful way. Some critics argue that the "hidden history" of lesbianism—that is, lesbianism before the category was named and medicalized in the late nineteenth century—can be more easily found in histories of so-called unnatural women who were aggressive, violent, or hostile to men.[14] Also, as Kathleen Gregory Klein has pointed out, the stereotype of the lesbian as "unnatural woman" or the woman-who-is-not-a-woman is particularly resonant in the detective genre. Crime stories usually push the guys and the girls into separate niches—male villains and investigators, on the one hand, and female victims and *fatales* on the other.[15] The lesbian as "not really female" in cultural terms (refusing heterosexual definitions and relations) fits the job description of female detective: the wrong body in the expected place.

The kick of the woman detective story is actually how it flirts with this dynamic by bucking the system, especially the system convincing women that marriage and romance are our only stories. The romance story in all its forms works hard to gloss over the bumps and pitfalls of heterosexuality. But the female-detective genre actually *depends* on these tensions to sustain the story. When romance does occur in the popular series by Janet Evanovich, Cornwell, and Grafton, it's bound to be a problem, not a solution, in this way remarkably akin to real life. Evanovich begins her first Stephanie Plum novel with a succinct description of the cop who will be Stephanie's on-again off-again lover in the series: "There are some men who enter a woman's life and screw it up forever."[16]

Of the scores of detective heroines in print, a few are married, but 98 percent are single, divorced, or widowed. Nor are these heroines actively hunting husbands. "I love being single," says Kinsey Millhone in *D Is for Deadbeat*. "It's almost like being rich." Or as she puts it more defiantly in *B Is for Burglar*, "I don't experience myself as lonely, incomplete, or unfulfilled, but I don't talk about that much. It seems to piss people off—especially men."[17] Stephanie Plum and the sexy cop actually edge toward marriage, but at the end of the sixth novel in the series, *Hot Six*, Stephanie has said no to the cop and is in bed with another man. The traditional story for women doesn't end this way, on the note of female pleasure without security, promises, and long-term commitment.

Yet what adult woman doesn't know the grim actuarial statistics about that traditional happy ending? The appeal of the female detective story to heterosexual women readers probably resides in its crankiness and suspicions about men. The heroines imagined by the likes of Grafton, Cornwell, and Sara Paretsky are women who love and sleep with men, but who also face stubborn sexism in their fields, abusive men in the world at large, and patterns of violence that are often directed at women.[18] Why would the detective heroine, besieged by sexist institutions and violent men, trust any man enough for a long-term commitment? How does any real-life heterosexual woman do so? As Sandra Scoppettone's lesbian P.I. says in *My Sweet Untraceable You*, "Why should *we* hate men? We don't have to sleep with them."[19]

To some extent, the woman investigator will always be a rebuke to traditional and even physical ways of imagining both women and detectives. In 1999 Robert B. Parker—famous for his hardboiled Spenser character—introduced a new P.I. series with a woman detective, Sunny Randall. Sunny's first-person narration begins with her complaint that once she went from uniformed cop to undercover work, she had no convenient place to keep her gun on her body or in her attire: "A shoulder holster is uncomfortable, and looks terrible under clothes."[20] She chooses a short-barrel .38 special so it will fit on a belt under her jacket, but the lesson and metaphor are clear. To *look* right and *feel* right, the woman P.I. packs a smaller piece.

The following year, Donald Petrie's movie *Miss Congeniality* registered the same complaint, in a comic mode, when tomboy FBI agent Gracie Hart (Sandra Bullock) needs to go undercover as a beauty-queen contestant. Looking at the photos of the women in evening gowns and swimsuits, she cries out in dismay, "Where do I put my gun?!" The comedy of *Miss Congeniality* stems from turning Gracie from "one of the boys" into a girl. A generation ago, that movie would have ended with Gracie giving up life in the Bureau for life with a beau. In turn-of-the-twenty-first-century Hollywood, with a full decade of woman investigators elbowing their way onto the screen, Gracie is allowed both.

Yet the entire premise of *Miss Congeniality*—the makeover of a tomboy FBI agent into a swimsuit contestant—poses anatomy and fashion as combined problems for this relatively new Hollywood character, the professional woman investigator, not just a dame with a gun, but a licensed woman in a hardboiled tradition: in short, the female dick.

BODIES OF EVIDENCE

A recurring scenario in current female crime novels is the new client who's surprised by the gender of the private investigator found in the phone book—Paretsky's V.I. Warshawski or Redmann's Micky Knight or Grafton's Kinsey Millhone. In J.M. Redmann's *Death by the River-side*, Micky gives an ambiguous answer to a prospective client on the phone. "I didn't tell her there was no Mr. Knight. She would know that soon enough. Besides, once she made the trip all the way down to this section of town, she would be less likely to dance off to some all-male dick shop. I needed the business." As one critic has put it, the private detective in American culture is a "visual cliché" that means "sexed male."[21]

Female detective fiction is highly conscious of the body switch that's occurred in the story, in the investigation business, and even in the word *detective*, which is itself pictured and sexed by its slang term, *dick*. For centuries, this slang word meant "fellow" or "man," but was also used as a verb meaning "to watch." In the late nineteenth century, the word came into vulgar usage as both "penis" and "police officer/detective" (the man who watches, or the man on the watch).

By the latter part of the twentieth century, the older meaning of *dick*—"to watch"—was lost, and it was more difficult to shake off the sexual meanings of the term, as made clear by Bruce Jay Friedman's humorous 1970 novel *The Dick*, about a sexually neurotic detective. As a metaphor, the "dick" pictures investigation work as male power and pleasure. It also hints at the more ambiguous qualities associated with modern detectives, including moral confusion ("thinking with his dick"), existential angst ("he doesn't know dick"), and the anxieties of sexual identification ("dicking around").

The detective story is all about bodies, usually beginning with homicide, the disturbing discovery of the body, a threat to meaning and order. The goal is to restore order through the justice system. But the usual machineries of justice—investigators, police, the legal system—are overwhelmingly filled with masculine, white, heterosexual bodies—an old-boys network, shot through with suspicion of women. When she does appear in the traditional story, the woman shows up as *a body*—if not the victim, then the seductress or suspect. The interrogation scene in *Basic Instinct* (1992) says it all—a roomful of guys and the lethal blonde in a skirt who uncrosses her legs.

So when the detective genre switches gender, when it's a woman doing business at the dick shop, the shockwave is visceral, physical, sexual. "Whatsa matter," Kathleen Turner smirks in the movie *V.I. Warshawski* (1991), "haven't you ever seen a female dick?" The effect can be campy, as was intended in this movie version of the Paretsky character, or it can be threatening or monstrous. Some of the screen pictures of the woman investigator—*Blue Steel* and to some extent, *The Silence of the Lambs*—toy with the freakish nature of this character, her "unnatural" qualities, at the same time as they cheer her gutsy turnaround of the hardboiled tradition. The very concept of the "female dick" asks us to *reimagine* sex, bodies, and gender, at least in detective fiction. And as a gender and sexual outlaw, the female dick will be a more complicated case to picture onscreen, less straightforward, more conflicted than her male counterparts Sherlock Holmes, Lieutenant Columbo, or Sam Spade.[22]

As all this suggests, popular genres are gold mines for cultural studies because they tap into our fantasies and assumptions about gender, power, and sexuality. A genre like the crime story works only so long as there are readers and audiences literally willing to buy into it. Publishers' best-seller lists, box-office returns, and Nielsen ratings are the heart monitors of these formulas. They're popular because they appeal to and usually confirm mainstream values and ideas about the family (melodrama), sexuality (romance), and the nation (the Western).[23] Popular romance stories, for example, persuade us that marriage is worthwhile, even though the plot stops just short of showing the hard work of living together.

Yet these formula Westerns, romances, and soaps about a white, heterosexual America are shot through with suspicions and doubts about these values and ideals. In that most classic of Westerns, John Ford's 1939 *Stagecoach*, John Wayne and the settlers escape the supposedly savage Indians only to ride into a shabby, honky-tonk white folks settlement blighting the wilderness. The achingly beautiful landscape and its sad ruination by a perfectly likable John Wayne sum up the Western's contradictions and melancholy soul.

Also, while their formulas remain the same, genres change with the times. A good example is the horror genre, which has always been preoccupied with sex—Dr. Frankenstein reproducing without a woman, Dracula's bedside suckings, and so on. But since the development of the slasher movie in the late 1970s, just after the sexual revolutions of the 1960s, questions of violence and sexuality have exploded in this story. Film scholars claim horror always entails questions of both normalcy and monstrous bodies, so it's the genre where anxieties about sex and gender are most likely to register.[24] Generally, the literatures and entertainments that we take least seriously—soap opera, horror, comedy—have been taken most seriously by critics as chronicles of how we think about ourselves as women and men.[25]

So it's inevitable that the woman detective character has arrived on the crime scene where bodies, blood, serial killers, and sexual violence abound. She's also a character who crisscrosses mysteries, medical forensics, police dramas, and thrillers. Patricia Cornwell has complained that her crime novels about a woman medical examiner are often mistakenly termed "mysteries," a technical difference of formula.[26] Yet the confusion of terms shows that readers aren't as concerned with the formula as with a type of character and story. Retail marketers know this, too. If you order Cornwell's books on Amazon.com, the website cheerfully makes pop-up suggestions of the female mystery novels from which Cornwell apparently wanted to be disassociated.[27]

Crossovers among media and types of stories are also a good example of how popular culture gels. When *The X-Files* debuted on television in 1993, reviewers commented on the similarities between FBI agent Dana Scully and the FBI rookie Clarice Starling of *The Silence of the Lambs*. Actually, the television series was as much science fiction as investigation drama, and it relied on a more conventional structure—a male and female pair of investigators—as opposed to the lone rookie Starling. Despite these differences, viewers were predisposed to think of the television heroine in light of the female FBI character who had so recently attracted national attention.[28] Meanwhile, by 1992, when the *X-Files* series was being written, Cornwell's early crime novels had hit the best-seller list. Coincidentally or not, the Scully character is a doctor as well as an agent, and her frequent assignments to autopsies are strikingly similar to those of Patricia Cornwell's doctor/lawyer heroine, Kay Scarpetta. And by 1994, Cornwell's heroine was working as a consultant for the FBI.

In this early 1990s constellation of *The Silence of the Lambs*, *The X-Files*, and Cornwell, we can trace a story and character that captured the cultural imagination. The hook of this story is a body switch (a savvy woman shows up instead of a man) at a crime scene focused on bodies. It's a macabre metaphor about professional women, women as authorities, women in places as macho and prestigious as the FBI. Pop culture doesn't register the facts so much as cultural interest in the facts. As one critic has pointed out, women and minorities altogether made up only 20 percent of the FBI in the 1990s, but in movies and television shows of the era, women made up almost 50 percent of this federal force.[29] So the characters Scully, Starling, and Scarpetta with their FBI associations aren't useful measures of social change, but they're good measures of social fantasy—in this case, fantasy about the place of women in high-level law enforcement, at the forensic autopsy or with a giant flashlight in the labyrinth.

DAMES TO DICKS: A BRIEF HISTORY

The detective story is as much about male bonding as about bodies. In Edgar Allen Poe's 1841 tale "Murders in the Rue Morgue," widely acknowledged as the first mystery story, the victims are two women described only as mangled bodies. The detective is Chevalier C. Auguste

Dupin, the astute inspector who prowls the Paris nights with his male housemate/narrator. And the prototype detective is of course Sir Arthur Conan Doyle's Sherlock Holmes, who first appeared in 1887, with his confidante Watson. Watson marries and drifts from Sherlock briefly, only to return for further adventures with his buddy. Poe and Doyle established the brilliant detective hero who relied more on brain than brawn to solve the crime—the armchair detective.

Yet women were very much present in the genre both as writers and protagonists. The beloved sleuths of Agatha Christie (Miss Marple, Hercule Poirot) and Dorothy Sayers (Harriet Vane and Lord Peter Wimsey) were part of the so-called golden age of the detective genre, roughly the period up until World War I, which also included distinguished writers such as Ngaio Marsh and Margery Allingham. And if the female sleuth was most typically the curious old lady, the spunky spinster, or someone's girlfriend, this was mostly due to real-world constraints. The professional woman investigator was a historical rarity until the 1970s.

The detective story was Americanized and masculinized in the same breath, with the innovation of the rough-edged crime story in the pulp magazine *Black Mask* in the early 1920s. *Black Mask* introduced the writer Dashiell Hammett, a former Pinkerton detective determined to bust the polite conventions of the British-style detective yarn. Hammett's hardboiled hero was the backlash to the intellectual, sometimes effete detective exemplified by Wimsey or Poirot. The new American detective was smart but, more important, street-smart, a tough action hero. Hammett and his colleagues Raymond Chandler, Erle Stanley Gardner, James M. Cain, and Cornwell Woolrich embellished the mystery story with violence, cynicism, and infamous mean streets.[30] The antisocial inclinations of Poe's Monsieur Dupin and the substance abuse of Sherlock Holmes were amplified and even romanticized in the new detective heroes, as were their suspicions of women, the seductive *femmes fatales*. Danger, deadly women, tests of wit, and macho personas—add guns, booze, and reckless bravado, and the testosterone-driven model of this hero is complete.

Scholars love to talk about detective stories as low-brow versions of high-brow ideas. The detective is Oedipus, the secret killer who keeps tripping on his own guilty past. Or the detective is Freud, the transgressive hunter of troubling secrets. So despite its low-brow status, the detective story, like the Western, has also gotten considerable respect and attention as contemporary male epic.[31] Women are right to be skeptical because we know this story all too well: male sexuality as power, knowledge, entitlement; the female body as the site of seduction and death.

In more graphic terms, at the end of John Huston's *The Maltese Falcon* (1941), the smug Humphrey Bogart as Sam Spade carries away the little plaster bird, having disposed of both the dame and the trio of exotic gay men who had confused the symbol for the larger power structure, in which they would always be marginalized.[32] Spade, on the other hand, has solved two murders, made some money, and enjoyed the woman before handing her over to the legal authorities, probably to be hanged. Little wonder the detective has been associated with Oedipus and Freud, and characterized as a guilty and brutal investigator of secrets. Kyle MacLachlan as the voyeur-snoop of *Blue Velvet* (1986) spies on Isabella Rossellini from her closet. Jack Nicholson slaps the terrible truth out of Faye Dunaway in *Chinatown* (1974). In both movies, the investigator's discovery of white, privileged corruption and sexual wrongdoing involve his journey into a bad neighborhood, bound by class or racial taboos. Along the way, he meets his own dark capacities for violence against women. Blonde aristocrat or forbidden dark lady, she's the mystery to be penetrated and exposed.[33]

The gender stereotypes of the detective story are tied to the history of professional law enforcement, which, until the early 1970s, was in fact mostly male. In the United States, women comprised only *1 percent* of federal agents and state/local police until 1972. That year, federal legislation prohibited discrimination in law-enforcement hiring at all levels, and the percentage of women in police and government agencies slowly began to increase to 5 percent in 1980 and 9.1 percent in 1995.[34] Statistics on women private investigators are more difficult to track down, but considering that most people in that profession are former police or federal agents, it's safe to say that professional, licensed women investigators of all kinds became a presence, though a minority one, only in the last two decades of the twentieth century.

Yet through much of that century, girls grew up reading and idolizing the amateur girl sleuths of adolescent literature. These widely read series emerged in 1929 and continue in updated forms today. Nancy Drew, Cherry Ames, and other young heroines were clues to the fabulous future awaiting this character and her professionalized, post-1970s fans. These series provided an alternative fantasy for the young girl, who for most of the century had been offered books with either romantic heroines (even Jo March eventually marries), or endless guy-adventure heroes, Odysseus through Hawkeye and Huck, whose war stories and frontier adventures were taught as universal experience. The thrill of Nancy Drew or Trixie Beldon was their mobility, their capacity to follow their curiosity on forbidden nondomestic and nonromantic quests. Even though the girl sleuth might flirt with her beau, she ended her adventure snaring a criminal rather than a husband.

As Bobbie Ann Mason points out in her loving tribute to these old series, the unspeakable subtext in these innocent teenage adventures was sex. "Mysteries are a substitute for sex," she writes, "since sex is the greatest mystery of all."[35] Nancy Drew, Trixie Beldon, and Judy Bolton show no signs of the obsessive Oedipal anxieties of the adult male detective, but surely their appeal to young women was the similar lure of knowledge and power. Sexual knowledge hovered at the boundaries of these stories—the intimacies with girl pals, the attractions to the young men and to adult danger.

Many critics believe the mystery novel is the popular niche in which 1960s–70s feminism most clearly made its mark, with a heroine who's defined by her work rather than by her looks.[36] After 1980, baby-boomer women, even the ones who distanced themselves from feminism, began to expect the bottom line of the women's movement—equal opportunity, economic independence, and stories of their own. For this grown-up readership, the Nancy Drew template already had it all: a recognizable world of clothes and cars; a network of reliable girlfriends; the exuberant power of mobility and curiosity; and sexual exploration without need for commitment. All this heroine needed was a gun, a divorce, and a private investigator license.

The first serious professional women investigators began to appear in mainstream fiction in the early 1970s, but fans claim the turning point was 1982, when Sue Grafton and Sara Paretsky introduced their female P.I. series. That was also the year Marcia Muller followed up her 1977 P.I. novel with a sequel that—like Grafton's and Paretsky's books—would become part of a long-running series.[37] The heroines of Grafton, Paretsky, and Muller's stories were hard-working women with domestic and financial problems. They were loners, wise about taking care of themselves, skilled with a gun and ready to use it if necessary. Grafton ends the first novel in her series, *A Is for Alibi*, with the violent confrontation between the P.I. and the villain, a handsome *homme fatale* with whom she's already done the dirty. The last line of the book is, "I blew him away."[38]

Blown away, too, were the trade-book industry's previous assumptions about crime and mystery fiction. The market that had been primarily male in its heroes and topics blossomed into what fans and publishers called a new golden age of the detective genre in the 1990s, reinvigorated by women authors, characters, and fans. The number of female-investigator novels published in the United States has tripled every five years since 1985.[39] The tough-guy heroes of Ed McBain,

Mickey Spillane, Lawrence Block, and so on continue to flourish and sell, but they've been joined by a throng of top-selling crime heroines who now regularly inhabit the *New York Times* and publishers' best-seller lists: Grafton, Cornwell, Paretsky, but also Janet Evanovich, Nevada Barr, and Linda Barnes. Nor are the mainstream-press detectives of either sex necessarily white and/or straight, as seen in the work of Valerie Wilson Wesley, J.M. Redmann, Leslie Glass, Sandra Scoppetone, Walter Mosley, Barbara Neely, and Tony Hillerman.

With robust sales charts, publishers have been eager to endorse even the women detective stories with a dark side, like the plucky 1990s "Tart Noir" mysteries by Lauren Henderson and Katy Munger. Marketing strategies often focus on tough women characters themselves, such as Hyperion's 1999 ad campaign around Linda Barnes's attractive but formidable female P.I., a six-feet-one-inch cab driver and ex-cop. The same year, HarperCollins promoted Barbara Seranella's heroine, parolee/auto-mechanic Munch Mancini, by handing out screwdrivers (the tools, not the drinks) at book events. The 1999 and 2000 mystery roundups by *Publishers Weekly* reported these tactics as investments for a market that remained steadily hot through the 1990s, with women's series consistently ringing up as best-sellers on their lists.[40]

When Grafton, Paretsky, and Muller introduced their female detective series in 1982, their heroines—neither gorgeous blonde policewomen in bikinis nor curvaceous angels in cleavage—were emphatically unlike the ones television had offered in the previous decade. The influence of the new fiction market hit Hollywood in the late 1980s, but there was no woman-investigator film that was a box-office hit until *The Silence of the Lambs* in 1991, and even then, Jodie Foster's Clarice shared the top billing with Anthony Hopkins's Hannibal. So far in film history, there has been no female equivalent to Basil Rathbone's Holmes or Bogart's Spade, or Mickey Spillane's Mike Hammer, who has appeared in seven films, four television series, and five made-for-TV movies. Nor has television produced the equivalent of a female Mannix, Columbo, or Kojak.

Given this uneven media history, the female FBI agent made over into *Miss Congeniality* suggests a lingering anxiety about how to picture this character—hardboiled but high heeled. Bullock's line about where to wear her gun is a cheap shot, but that's because it short-circuits the more interesting issues involved in picturing the woman investigator, from bikini-clad policewomen on television to the pregnant sheriff of *Fargo* (1996) to Sue Grafton's mug on a coffee mug at Barnes and Noble. This book is an investigation of those pictures, their meanings, and their sources.

2

PICTURING THE BEST-SELLER LIST
Sue Grafton and Patricia Cornwell

CELEBRITIES AND THE F-WORD

Detective novels have enjoyed a lurid association with fabulously cheesy pulp-fiction art. In its glory days, the 1930s–50s paperback covers featured platinum blonde lushes and throbbing, grimacing heroes in rumpled white shirts and disheveled ties. They were corrupt cops or restless accountants lured into shady schemes, with their bad-girl companions in push-up bras, all of them evoked with garish ink strokes and rusty shades of blood.[1]

Given the tawdry pulp-fiction graphics associated with the detective genre, it's remarkable that through the latter part of the 1990s, the most familiar icon of current detective novels was the smiling pixie face of Sue Grafton, one of the literary faces used by Barnes and Noble on their coffee-mug series and on the large banners decorating their store walls in malls all over the United States. Grafton, creator of the best-selling and high-profile alphabet series, is herself a high-profile figure in pop culture, showing up not just on bookstore décor, but also in spreads ranging from *People* magazine to *Architectural Digest*.

While cover art and ad illustrations are still important marketing tools for popular novels, the usage of the author herself has become more common for trade-book marketing since the 1980s. It's now an accepted practice for publishers to promote the writer not only in the photograph on the back of the book, but also through reading tours, interviews, and television appearances. The point is to associate the book with a face, voice, and personality. This is hardly a new promotion tactic, if we think about nineteenth-century author-lecture tours by Charles Dickens and Mark Twain (whose faces accompany Grafton's on the walls at Barnes and Noble). The difference is that technology now makes the writer a multimedia presence. Popular authors are expected to be available to fans not just in occasional print and television interviews, but on regularly updated Web pages, many of which offer an email address for feedback or interaction. Best-selling mystery writers such as Lawrence Block, Dick Francis, Robert B. Parker, Rex Stout, Joan Hess, and Carolyn Hart may not get their faces on coffee mugs, but each is a well-known persona within the book trade, kept in circulation through the machineries of marketing.

Even more aggressively, some popular writers have pushed an identification with their trademark characters—most notably, Mickey Spillane, who actually played the part of his tough-guy Mike Hammer in one of the film adaptations (*The Girl Hunters*, 1963). So when authors such as Sue Grafton, Linda Barnes, and Sara Paretsky appear in book jacket photographs with props suggesting their female P.I. characters, they're part of a larger commercial scene involving writers as celebrities. And in this celebrity-driven culture, the meaning of the book is inevitably enmeshed with the "meaning" of the author.[2]

Of all the woman-detective-writer celebrities, the most main-streamed and high-profile are Sue Grafton and Patricia Cornwell. Certainly many other writers appear on book jacket photographs and in interviews, on tours, and on websites. From the best-seller list, Sara Paretsky is famous for her in-depth interviews, and Janet Evanovich draws huge crowds for her good-humored readings of the adventures of Stephanie Plum. But neither author has attained the *personal* popularity of Grafton and Cornwell, who by the end of the 1990s regularly appeared on television talk shows and in magazines found at the hair salon.

These media appearances are mostly tied to promotions of new books, but are often focused on the writers themselves, with behind-the-scenes details implying the "truth" about the fictions. Yes, Cornwell really pilots a helicopter and knows her way around a morgue. Yes, Grafton really jogs on the beach at dawn and owns a VW Beetle with the license plate KINSEY. Both writers have appeared as experts in feature articles on crime and investigation: Cornwell answered questions about law enforcement in a *New York Times Magazine* article "What are Cops Afraid Of?" and Grafton advised "How to Be Your Own Private Detective" in *McCall's*.[3]

Grafton and Cornwell weren't invented as celebrities by their publishers, but their exceptional off-the-shelf lives make canny matches with their fictions. Their celebrity also tells us something about the appeal of their series to mainstream fantasies, different though these may be. Grafton's character owns one dress and a beat-up 1970s VW bug, keeps neither pets nor houseplants, and rents a streamlined garage-turned-bungalow in a California seaside town. Cornwell's character is a doctor, lawyer, gourmet chef, and wine connoisseur who drives a customized Mercedes and lives in a gated community in Richmond, Virginia.[4]

As female fantasies, these are class-specific versions of Virginia Woolf's room of one's own—the basics of the professional woman who needs space, time, silence, and control of her own agenda. Yet these are also specifically American fantasies about autonomy and self-determination. The respective ideals of simplicity and power, California cottage and gated estate, are flip versions of Emersonian self-reliance.

Woolf's point was that a woman is less likely than a man to be entitled to close the door, shut out the whining family, and claim time to herself. Sure enough, the Grafton and Cornwell heroines both resist family ties in order to pursue the lonely work of investigation. Grafton's detective, orphaned at a very young age, is horrified to discover, halfway through the series, a bevy of long-lost female cousins attempting to claim her into family dynamics she thought she'd avoided. Cornwell's investigator keeps a nagging mother and man-clinging sister out of sight in Florida.

Still, the theme of both heroines is self-identification not tied to roles of daughter, mother, or wife. Although their romantic relationships are doomed to failure, these women are otherwise successful, self-sufficient, and respected even by those they irritate.

So is this the feminist heroine for the turn of the twenty-first century? The refusal of wife/mother roles certainly aligns them with nontraditional women's stories. But other aspects of these characters could as well align them with conventional and even right-wing thinking. The successful loner, the gritty nonconformist, the stubborn individualist who's licensed to carry a gun—these are figures more likely to be found in the NRA than in NOW. Cornwell's heroine, Kay Scarpetta, makes conspicuously Republican comments about law-and-order issues and reveres a character named Senator Lord who's an obvious fictionalization of Orrin Hatch, Republican Senator from Utah.

The Grafton and Cornwell series in some ways exemplify the 1970s tough-chic school of feminism, in which women succeed on male turf without changing the rules of the game. But they might also exemplify the residue of mainstream feminism *and* its backlash at the end of the twentieth century. After all, both sides can claim this strong female character as their own. She can be proof that women can succeed without the help of a cause or politics; and she can be proof that 1970s feminism *did* succeed, with the result that this character is now possible. That's why critics who debate the politics of the woman detective character often use the same evidence to come to different conclusions, a clue about why this character has such wide appeal.[5]

Grafton and Cornwell can also be located within the larger map of female crime-novel politics. The most explicitly feminist themes can be found in the lesbian detective series of writers like Barbara Wilson, J.M. Redmann, Katherine V. Forrest, Mary Wings, Ellen Hart, and Deborah Powell, whose heroines often encounter the poisonous common grounds of misogyny and homophobia. Barbara Wilson's lesbian investigator Pam Nilsen is among the most self-conscious of these heroines, exploring the political implications of detective work in *Murder in the Collective* (1984) and *Sisters of the Road* (1986). J.M. Redmann's P.I. Micky Knight grows from a promiscuous, hard-drinking troublemaker to a more thoughtful and politically aware detective in the course of the series, as made clear by the title of one of the later novels—*The Intersection of Law and Desire* (1995).[6]

A review blurb from *The Nation* on the dust jacket of Redmann's next book, *Lost Daughters* (1999), likewise indicates crossover marketing and also some of the more subtle appeal of this marketing: "Imagine Kinsey Millhone as a lesbian and you've got Micky Knight." As I pointed out in chapter 1, the incitement to "imagine Kinsey Millhone as a lesbian" is the trick or treat of the woman investigator story, depending on your point of view. A crossover fantasy that could provide a thrill for some readers of both Grafton and Redmann could also work another way, as a backlash mechanism for identifying Kinsey Millhone as a feminist (or as a secret lesbian) and condemning her for it.

The 1960–70s feminist movement often distanced itself from lesbians, carefully switching its public face from Kate Millett to Gloria Steinem and middle-class *Ms.* magazine. Its 1960s icon Betty Friedan was criticized for homophobic remarks. But it's also true that lesbians supported and staffed many feminist political activities through the 1970s and 1980s, such as rape prevention and awareness campaigns, women's shelters, child-care centers, and education in self-defense, health, and workers' rights.[7] These are exactly the issues that are often featured in the plots of lesbian mysteries, even though these issues aren't limited to either gay or straight women.

Also, the overtones of female bonding and loyalty, even in supposedly "straight" scenarios in women detective stories, can have lesbian overtones, as some critics have pointed out regarding Sara Paretsky's V.I. Warshawski series, which features a devout network of female support.[8] Paretsky's (heterosexual) heroine is one of the few blatantly feminist women detectives who have been mainstream and popular for almost two decades. Self-identified as a feminist in numerous interviews, Paretsky focuses her V.I. Warshawski plots on bureaucratic injustice and white-collar crime, clearly implicating and criticizing big power structures. Nor is Paretsky the only popular female detective with an edgy, liberal conscience. Marcia Muller, respected as the "mother" of the American female detective series, sets her Sharon Mc-Cone stories in a lawyers' co-op in San Francisco, where the woman detective is part of a low-cost legal services team, keenly aware of the economic injustices of the legal system.

Despite many conservative trends and nervous backlashes against feminism since the 1980s, both Paretsky and Muller have retained their popularity and solid sales in mystery fiction, holding on to their fans and loyal followings. But as it turns out, these authors are also less iconic than Grafton and Cornwell, less visible in popular venues. Sharon McCone in her liberal legal co-op and the undistilled V.I. Warshawski remain at one end of the political spectrum in this genre, just left of center. As I point out in chapter 5, the film adaptation of Warshawski moved her into safer, traditional images, a clue about the political revamping of the woman detective for movies.

GRAFTON AND CORNWELL: SNAPSHOTS

Grafton and Cornwell have not only negotiated this minefield of politics, sex, and gumshoes, but have saturated the area with their images, just as Mickey Spillane had done for an earlier gumshoe generation. Patricia Cornwell rose from her position as a newcomer at Scribner's in 1990 to a dynasty unto herself just eight years later. Sue Grafton's celebrity has been more slowly developed, emerging in 1989 only after her alphabet series, which debuted in 1982, had won a number of book awards and had proven itself in sales through the first five novels. The difference shows the more welcoming climate for women investigators in the 1990s publishing world. Their more significant difference, though, is in their public images, the orchestrated picturing of their lives as the "real" women behind the fantasy characters.

These writer celebrities are the *public* figures of the writers, not to be confused with the "real" Cornwell and Grafton, although the two sides overlap. When Cornwell appears on the *Today* show, or when Grafton is interviewed in *Architectural Digest*, the details that turn up are fairly well controlled by the format and by publicity agents. Even when a curious reporter digs up less flattering stories and pictures, some editor decides which details will sell a magazine or appeal to a wide audience. Either way, media coverage delivers a set of images and issues the public is willing to buy into at a given moment.

Patricia Cornwell has been a startling, controversial public figure since the mid-1990s. As a former reporter with a good instinct for grabby headlines and photos, Cornwell has eagerly shown journalists her personal arsenal of guns and the designer brand labels of her wardrobe. In a glossy spread in a 1996 *New York Times Magazine*, she posed beside a laboratory skeleton, its brittle arm slung intimately around her shoulder. In a 1997 Annie Leibovitz photo for *Vanity Fair*, Cornwell stands covered with blood at an autopsy table, a cigarette dangling from her mouth, camping it up "in the guise of her character," as the caption explains.[9] The innuendoes are playful but sharp: is it Cornwell or her character Scarpetta who is in love with death, obsessed with violence, dangerously at ease with blood?

Other innuendoes have been even more titillating. Despite her silence on the matter, Cornwell has attracted a substantial lesbian following, fueled by rumors and the intriguing butch book-jacket photographs of the author in a punky leather jacket or piloting a helicopter. Also, the author's persona in many ways matches her heroine, Kay Scarpetta, who's similarly obsessive about her work and her cooking. But the Cornwell persona also matches another character who grows more important in each Scarpetta novel, the beautiful lesbian niece Lucy, who is as impetuous and difficult as Cornwell is rumored to be.

In 1996 her public images prompted more serious insinuations. After a hostage situation and shoot-out involving an estranged couple, both former FBI agents, Cornwell was named as the wife's lover and cause of the conflict. In a *Vanity Fair* article the following year, Cornwell confessed to a "very brief" affair with the woman in question, but in that interview and all subsequent ones, Cornwell refuses to be identified as a lesbian. That doesn't stop fans from fantasizing about the photos of Cornwell with Billie Jean King that appeared on her official website, for example, or about the 1997 essay in *Esquire* that described the writer's "obsessed" desire to meet Jodie Foster and presumably have the actress portray Scarpetta in a film project.[10]

The fusion of author and character is intended to seem cozy and whimsical in the little Christmas book, *Scarpetta's Winter Table* (1998), with Scarpetta offering favorite recipes that are obviously Cornwell's. But the fusion appears in darker ways elsewhere. "She's either become Scarpetta or Scarpetta's become her," one friend reports in the *Vanity Fair* article, with the disapproving intimation that both have gone out of control, Cornwell with money and publicity, Scarpetta with increasingly cranky paranoia. Often, publicity details about Cornwell's personal life seem deliberately to invoke the most controversial aspects of the fictional Scarpetta: paranoid personal security systems, tightly controlled interviews, political friendships with the George Bush family, and tours of the local morgue for favorite journalists.[11]

In her interviews and in the material on her website, Cornwell remains fiercely private about her sexuality and much of her current personal life, simultaneously associating herself with high-level federal offices, conservative politics, and forensic science. In the fall of 2000, her website reported her enthusiasm for candidate George W. Bush and her support of a congressional bill to upgrade crime labs. The links on her website have included federal, international, and local law enforcement agencies, the Virginia Institute of Forensic Science and Medicine, and the Office of the Chief Medical Examiner of Virginia— all of this reminding fans about the earnest, nonfictional basis of Kay Scarpetta's forensics.

However, throughout the 1990s, Cornwell also gradually released more autobiographical information about her childhood and her past. So while the 2000–2001 website was secretive about her current private life, it featured a twenty-one-screen illustrated biography detailing her father's desertion of the family, her struggle in college with anorexia nervosa, her 1980–88 marriage, and her volunteer experience in morgues and with the police. "Her life has been incredibly productive and successful," the biography began, "yet she has experienced setbacks and failures that would have defeated a less talented, less determined person." The didactic tone continued with the website's earnest system of links to federal offices and to news stories about Cornwell's political alliances. The website also offered a variety of Cornwell merchandise—T-shirts and caps with her logo—so the overall effect was a package deal of seriousness and souvenirs.[12]

Proving herself as an investigator who should be taken seriously, in the fall of 2001 Cornwell instigated and personally financed an elaborate study of London's infamous Jack the Ripper case and came up with a hypothesis about his true identity as the artist Walter Sickert. The following year she published her findings as *Portrait of a Killer: Jack the Ripper, Case Closed*. Whether or not readers are convinced by her identification of Jack the Ripper, the book itself further cements the identification of Cornwell herself as a forensics investigator much like Kay Scarpetta. As of July 2003, the official Cornwell website looked like a sepia-toned documentary, with a scrolling video showing spooky, Victorian London and Cornwell herself at the graveside of a Ripper victim.

Dramatic nuances cling to Sue Grafton's public persona as well, but her celebrity reads more like a feature story in *Woman's Day* than a Gothic thriller. Certain biographical details of her early days as a writer conjure up Sylvia Plath: raising her three children as a single mother; writing Hollywood and television screenplays at night after the kids were asleep; directing her homicidal fantasies into her P.I. series so that she wouldn't actually kill her ex-husband, with whom she was engaged in a nasty custody settlement.[13] Grafton's issue isn't heterosexuality but its management, its demands and contradictions, its children and living rooms, the family burdens and legacies. Her website offers homey photos of her second husband, her personal chef, and beloved cats. A *People* magazine feature in 1995 revealed personal details about "the pain of her childhood," as the headline banner put it. The article went into detail about her background in Louisville, Kentucky, her strained memories of her alcoholic parents, her mother's death by an overdose of barbiturates, and her father's failed career as a mystery novelist.[14]

But this tragic-childhood/angry-divorcée profile is overwhelmed by its transformation into the American success story. The *People* article concludes with descriptions of the lap pool, antique pool table, and Williams-Sonoma accoutrements at the Louisville home that Grafton and her husband, Steven Humphrey, call their "playhouse." While Cornwell tends to shut and lock the door to her interior spaces, Grafton points cameras into her libraries, dens, and kitchens. In 2000 *Architectural Digest* did an eight-page spread on the estate Grafton and Humphrey purchased in Montecito, California, detailing the Edelman leather upholstery and the ceiling imported from a European palace. This is Sylvia Plath after rehab, a makeover, remarriage, and the accrual of a hefty stock portfolio.[15]

The Cornwell and Grafton celebrities include themes that could play as either feminist and/or fabulous, female power as both threatening and materially rewarding. The Cornwell website has included photos of the writer in her leather flak jacket but also in her high school prom dress. Grafton quips that she turned to writing rather than homicide to avoid shapeless prison gowns, but her photos suggest the grown-up cheerleader who never loses her cute figure and curls. Particularly telling was a 1998 interview that fine-tuned Grafton's previous jokes about her earlier homicidal revenge fantasies. Homicide was a fantasy "to funnel a lot of rage and a lot of frustration," she told a reporter for *Publishers Weekly*. But she added an explanation that brackets the female rage within an American success story: "At that point I didn't know how to fight. I thought it was enough to be a nice girl.

Now I know how to fight and now I have the money to fight if any-
body wants to take me on. In those days I was ill-equipped and so fantasy was the great equalizer."[16]

The meaning of "ill-equipped" slides between the gender limitations of being a "nice girl" and the limitations of money, so the feminist implications of the statement merge with a more traditional idea
about money as power and equality. Yet middle-class feminism has always been about equity, equal pay, and cracking the nice-girl facade. "I
am a feminist from way back," Grafton stated in a 1989 interview that
included her homicidal fantasy (Taylor, 11). But since then, Grafton
has backed away from gender politics in her interviews, declaring that
she detests gender-segregated groups of any kind and protesting that
women are neither victims nor in need of organized support.

A 1990 *Newsweek* article on Grafton and other new women mystery
writers entitled "Murder Most Foul and Fair" characterized the new
protagonists as "feminine feminists," evoking a kinder, gentler feminism, probably heterosexual, certainly not butch.[17] Notice the physical
detail in the description, the assurance that the body of this new heroine is familiar and appeasing: feminine. It's not an accurate description
of the heroines or the books, but it's marketing that makes them available at every airport bookstore.

My argument is that for both Grafton and Cornwell, the visual and
biographical prompts are tied to the "picturing" of the investigator-
heroine in these books. In numerous interviews, Grafton has made it
clear that Kinsey Millhone will never actually be pictured in a movie
or television series. But her Kinsey Millhone books have often been
described as "cinematic" in their details and style, an adjective with
particular resonance considering Grafton's background in film and
television writing. Grafton visualizes her scenes by carefully attaching
physical descriptions—what's being seen—to a character's point of
view, a technique basic to movies and television. The use of Grafton's
photo in the books' publicity further suggests who's doing the seeing,
in a constant play between photography and fantasy, hinting about
what Kinsey "really" looks like.

Cornwell's Kay Scarpetta series, like the Grafton series, uses Cornwell's celebrity image as stand-in for the heroine. In fact, the heroine
Scarpetta is herself a controversial celebrity in the later novels of the
series. But in addition, Scarpetta is doubled by her lovely lesbian niece,
clearly the alter ego of the heroine. The cinematic device that's most
evoked in this series is the body double, the substitution of one body
for another in order to create a more ideal or suitable body. In the
Cornwell series, the stakes for producing this ideal are especially high,

Fig. 3 Sue Grafton, author of the Kinsey Millhone series. Courtesy of Steven Humphrey.

given the specter of lesbianism both in the novels and in the publicity around Cornwell herself.

Our imaginations are preloaded with cinema's renditions of stories, so we're likely to imagine popular novels through the picturing devices we know very well. The popular images of Cornwell and Grafton are the most public nubs of the other imaginative visual devices in these books. Of course, these aren't *literally* cinematic devices. Our imaginations are more multimedia than that. From movies and televisions we know pictorial codes of storytelling, and from popular magazines and websites we know images of faces and settings for writers like Grafton and Cornwell. Given this merger of visual and print pop culture, two of the best-selling female investigation series offer rich examples of how we picture the woman detective.

GRAFTON: SHOT/REVERSE SHOT

Sue Grafton's relationship to Hollywood is refreshingly bratty: She may have started there and picked up some ideas, but she won't go back. Likewise, her Kinsey Millhone character was born of a cinematic imagination, but will never appear in front of a camera, no matter what her fans demand. Before Grafton started her mystery series, she worked as a writer in Hollywood for fifteen years. Her credits include a screenplay and a dozen television scripts, including a number of adaptations. Grafton has pointed out that this previous work trained her in writing plots: "There's nothing like a film script to teach you structure, which is what the mystery is about" (Bing, 41). Film scripts are also aimed toward a picturing process, a story easily conveyed through closeups, montage, camera movement, cuts between scenes. On the level of style, Grafton's alphabet series owes its vivid details of action and scene to an imagination trained to write for a camera.

Yet Grafton is emphatic about her dislike of Hollywood and about how the Kinsey series enabled her "escape" from that world. She vows that the series will never get adapted into film or television. "Kinsey Millhone was my tiny pickax where I got out of prison," she says in an interview, "And I would be a fool to sell her back to them" (Bing, 40). She has often voiced her specific dislike of Hollywood teamwork and production-by-committee, which spins the story and character out of the control of the writer. She's also commented on the sorry lesson gleaned from the Hollywood treatment of Sara Paretsky's character in *V.I. Warshawski*.

But the mystery is that the literary scene's most popular female detective is both graphically visual in style and visually evasive. The one "picture" that fails to emerge from the alphabet series is a good close up of Kinsey Millhone. Instead, the narrator's descriptions of herself are offhand and self-effacing. Looking in the mirror at the beginning of *F Is for Fugitive*, Kinsey reports first about her dark hair, which she herself trims with nail scissors: "Recently, someone told me it looked like a dog's rear end." She continues with the self-survey: "Hazel eyes, dark lashes. My nose blows real good and it's remarkably straight, considering it's been broken twice. Like a chimp, I bared my teeth, satisfied to see them (more or less) line up right."[18] This is about as detailed a description of Kinsey as we can find in the novels. The chimp face she makes at herself in the mirror is also made at readers attempting to figure out exactly what she looks like.

By delivering such minimal descriptions and forbidding her character to be identified with a specific film or television star, Grafton exerts control over how her heroine will be pictured. Like any prohibition, this control results in robust fantasies and imaginative play on the part of readers, as can be seen on Grafton's website forum. The forum has hosted several discussion threads about "who should play Kinsey" in the fantasy movie that will never be made. Between 2001 and 2003, the suggestions included Jamie Lee Curtis, Debra Winger, Jodie Foster, and Holly Hunter (all actresses who have already played investigators in movies, in *Blue Steel* [1990], *Black Widow* [1987], *Silence of the Lambs*, and *Copycat* [1995], respectively), Julia Roberts, Sharon Lawrence, Joyce DeWitt, and Sandra Bullock.[19]

In the fall of 2000, an argument broke out on this forum at the nomination of Ellen DeGeneres. One protest shows how thoroughly the imagined picture of Kinsey can obscure what's actually in the novels. "Please!! Ellen DeGeneres, never. Kinsey has dark hair and is quite feminine. She is tall and well sculpted and probably looks more like Jacqueline Smith when she was about 32." Kinsey often describes herself as five feet, six inches, which is medium tall, but feminine? Jacqueline Smith? This is a character who owns one dress and cuts her hair with nail scissors. In the same thread, a nastier protest objected to Kinsey being portrayed by "Ellen Degenerate," a remark that may register general homophobia or more specific anxiety about the possibility cited in the J.M. Redmann book jacket blurb, "Imagine Kinsey Millhone as a lesbian."

In interviews, when pressed about who would portray Kinsey if the never-to-be-made movie were made, Grafton has occasionally mentioned some of her favorite actresses. "I used to mention Sigourney Weaver as a possible Kinsey, though I was always quick to point out that Ms. Weaver was and is too tall. I also thought about Debra Winger. I'm sure Holly Hunter's name passed my lips as I've been a fan of hers since *Raising Arizona*."[20] Fantasizing a movie allows readers (and Grafton) to have it both ways: no real movie will disappoint us, but an ideal, imaginary movie remains part of the fan experience, tailored for the individual taste for Julia Roberts or Holly Hunter or Ellen DeGeneres.

The other fan strategy for visualizing Kinsey is even more obvious. Kinsey's "biography," *G Is for Grafton: The World of Kinsey Millhone*, addresses the picturing problem head-on. "What do most of us do in order to picture Kinsey's facial features, since Kinsey consistently resists telling us?" ask authors Natalie Hevener Kaufman and Carol McGinnis Kay. "Turn the novel over and look at the photo of Sue

Grafton on the back of the book, of course. Hmmmmm. Can't tell about the hazel eyes, but the thick, dark, unruly hair and the square white teeth are right there. . . . Better haircut, though."[21]

G Is for Grafton is written in the tradition of the numerous Sherlock Holmes handbooks, case files, archives, companions, and fanciful biographies of a character who's taken on a life of his own. With Grafton's help, Kaufman and Kay similarly pump up the details of Kinsey's world, the fictional Santa Teresa, by documenting its parallels in Grafton's world, Santa Barbara. Several pages of photographs show us Santa Barbara's courthouse and offices as the scenes of the series. In a whimsical detail, a 1970s VW bug with the license plate KINSEY M is parked in front of the police station. In addition to the chapters documenting the timelines and biographical details of Kinsey's story, the book includes maps, floor plans, and several charts of the books' villains.

This is a good-humored parody of serious biography, but it's also a good example of the power of fantasy. The elaborateness of the fantasy indicates a committed investment of readers in the reality of this world, the equivalent of the *X-Files* mantra: I WANT TO BELIEVE. *G Is for Grafton* places serious emphasis on visual proof to buoy up belief. Its preface opens with a description of Grafton herself as she pointed to the breakwater at the Santa Barbara marina. "And this is where Renata jumped," the mystery writer solemnly tells the book's authors, who in turn have us all look at the scene of the fictional crime, "the dark, pockmarked rocks directly below us, waves churning and foaming around them" (Kaufman and Kay, 3).

The real Santa Barbara, Grafton's home, in this way becomes evidence in the search for the real Kinsey Millhone, who is and is not Grafton. The title itself—*G Is for Grafton: The World of Kinsey Millhone*—conflates the character and the author. The cover shows the ghostlike impression of Grafton's face, giving the effect of a photographic negative. The image implies that the development of Grafton's negative will produce the photo of Kinsey, and the fictional biography is described forthright as a photograph. "From the thirteen novels," the first chapter tells us, "a vivid picture emerges—like a Polaroid taken at a family picnic—of the past Kinsey who shaped the present Kinsey we like so much" (Kaufman and Kay, 9).

The use of Grafton's image in assembling this fictional picture has become progressively more important as her popularity has increased. The first three books of the alphabet series used her photograph on the inside book jacket, but in 1987, *D Is for Deadbeat* offered a full-page photograph on the back cover. The Bantam paperbacks, which were issued from A to F, contain no photos, but when Fawcett picked up the paperbacks beginning with *G Is for Gumshoe* in 1990, each book cover featured a full-page color photo on the back. This corresponds to the marketing blitz that began in 1989 by sending Grafton on a twenty-six-city tour for *F Is for Fugitive*, the first of her books to be reviewed in the *New York Times Book Review*. Grafton was interviewed that year in *People* and *Armchair Detective*, and the following year in *Cosmopolitan*. The photo in a 1990 *Newsweek* article portrays a pensive film noir Sue Grafton who appears to be reaching for a handgun on a garden wall. But the subsequent author-photos are sunnier and more serene. These images continue to show the same pert smile and flecks of gray in shoulder-length, casually curled dark hair.

As Kaufman and Kay note, Grafton's hair is always better than Kinsey's awful self-inflicted cuts. And as Grafton continually points out in interviews, she both is and is not Kinsey—not as young, not as flexible. "She's the person I would have been had I not married young and had children. She'll always be thinner and younger and braver, the lucky so-and-so" (Taylor, 10). In *Q Is for Quarry*, the give-and-take between author and character takes a mischievous turn when Kinsey flips through a copy of *Architectural Digest* in a dentist's office—perhaps the very same issue in which Sue Grafton's Montecito house appears. Kinsey of course is cynical about the upscale rag and tries "to imagine a color spread on my studio apartment, all eight hundred and fifty feet of it."[22] As this little in-joke suggests, the relationship between Grafton and Kinsey is a picturing process that loops interminably—like a Möbius strip—between imagination and photography, between fantasy and fact. The back-cover photo of Grafton invites a fantasy, and the fantasy can be grounded in a photo we know is real.

In fact, a powerful element of the Kinsey Millhone series is that what the heroine looks like is relatively unimportant—unlike the traditional "woman's story" in which female beauty triggers the plotline. In both popular and highbrow literature of the past centuries, the woman has power or interest only insofar as she's attractive to men. Not that the woman-detective character is exempt from the beauty stereotype: when Robert B. Parker introduces Sunny Randall in *Family Honor*, her attractiveness is mentioned immediately by other characters in the first two chapters. Ken Follett's FBI agent Judy Maddox is introduced in *The Hammer of Eden* like a romantic heroine, her attractiveness noted first, and Judy's story actually mixes romance and business; she solves the crime but also marries the handsome principal witness.

The Parker and Follett novels might be brushed off as male fantasies. Yet Thomas Harris's complicated Clarice Starling in *The Silence of the Lambs* is as renowned for her beauty as for her brilliance. In the novel *Hannibal* (1999), Starling's beauty triggers the plotline in that she attracts the nasty Justice Department official who seeks revenge when she rejects him. The attractive detective heroine is a convention of women writers as well. Carol O'Connell's policewoman Kathleen Mallory is head-turningly gorgeous, but Mallory uses her formidable good looks to keep her distance from any romantic relationship. In the Patricia Cornwell series, male characters often tell Kay Scarpetta she's beautiful, an attribute that usually works against her by inciting jealousy and hostility from colleagues and villains alike.

Granted, this is a random sample, but it suggests the convention of the traditionally beautiful heroine is still an issue in the female investigation novel. So Grafton's refusal to play the game either way is worth noting. The early novels are simply opaque on the topic, but by *G Is for Gumshoe*, the refusal to comment on Kinsey's looks gets feisty: "If I were asked to rate my looks on a scale of one to ten, I wouldn't," the narrator states bluntly.[23] Kinsey may be attractive or not, but her power derives not from what she looks like, but from what she sees. The plots turn on her observations and deductions: "I've known P.I.s who conduct entire investigations on the phone, but I don't think it's smart," the narrator comments in *B Is for Burglar.* "Unless you're dealing with people face-to-face, there are too many ways to be deceived and too many things to miss" (*Burglar*, 16). In *I Is for Innocent*, Kinsey tracks down the poison because she remembers the toadstools growing in someone's garden; in *F Is for Fugitive*, she reads the faces and demeanors of a series of men to determine their sexual relationship with the town's *femmes fatales.*

But most detectives make these Sherlock Holmes kinds of observations, and the wide popularity of Grafton's series is more likely due to Kinsey's sharp *cultural* observations. Kinsey doesn't miss much in terms of social nuances, human foibles, and the idiosyncrasies of gender and class. The narrator's commentary comes from the wisecracking tradition of the hardboiled P.I. Kinsey's cynicism is funny and specifically female in its point of view, the perspective of the woman who reads *Ladies Home Journal* and *McCall's*, but only at the dentist's office and with a smart-ass smirk.

Kinsey is unfazed by haute couture people, places, or furnishings. Meeting a well-to-do woman, Kinsey observes that they both wear jeans, "though mine were cut without style, the kind worn to wash cars or clean hair clots from the bathroom stand pipe." The rich woman wears a jacket that "was wrinkled in the manner of expensive fabrics . . . linens and silks. . . . You know how it is with that shit."[24] Walking through a designer house full of silk screens and cloisonné vases, Kinsey notes drolly that "Many items seemed to come in pairs, one placed on either side of something grotesque."[25] Elsewhere, in a more middle-class neighborhood, she notices how quickly the neighborhood women appear with Jell-O and tuna casseroles after a death: "Christian ladies probably knew tricks with ice cubes that would render salads and desserts in record time for just such occasions. I pictured a section in the ladies' auxiliary church cookbook for Sudden Death Quick Snacks" (*Fugitive*, 85). Kinsey is also accurately funny about human motivation. "People always love it when you say their dogs are nice. Just shows you how out of touch they are," she notes in *C Is for Corpse*.[26]

This is a trustworthy and entertaining voice, exactly the kind of interior commentary impossible to render in a screenplay or film. By preventing Kinsey's adaptation into cinema or television, Grafton preserves this interior commentary. But first-person point of view always implies the presence of someone who's doing the looking and telling, the equivalent of a closeup of Kinsey's rolling eyes as she takes in the pretentious hostess or the chic ugliness of the manor house.

The picturing of this in movies is a familiar combination of shots: a closeup of someone doing the looking, followed by the shot of what is being seen. A "cinematic" style usually means vivid, graphic detail. But mainstream cinema is also relentlessly logical about these details, attaching views of a room or a scene to a specific character (so that a familiar cliché in the stalker films has become the tease of a moving camera whose "look" the spectator can't identify). Grafton's style is cinematic not only because we can see so clearly exactly what Kinsey sees, but because our attention is then refocused on Kinsey herself and her reactions. Film scholars have argued that this shot/reverse shot sequence powerfully engages the viewer, who's the pivot point between the seer and what is seen.

The opening scene of *C Is for Corpse* is a good example of this. The setting is a fitness club, a potentially sexy situation. Working out on the exercise machines as therapy for a broken arm, Kinsey is one of the few women in the place, exchanging glances with the men: "I tended to distract myself from the pain, sweat, and nausea by checking out men's bodies while they were checking out mine" (*Corpse*, 2). But the next sentence pinpoints one specific man, who is neither sexy nor attracted to Kinsey. This is Bobby Callahan, badly disabled by an automobile accident, who will become Kinsey's client and friend. A detailed description of his scarred and disfigured body concludes with a refocus on Kinsey and her reaction: "I watched him with interest, ashamed of my own interior complaints. Clearly, I could recover from my injuries while he could not" (*Corpse*, 2). Within the next few paragraphs, Bobby has hired Kinsey to find out who tried to kill him.

From a screenwriter's perspective, this is an economical scene with a good twist and a coercive visual dynamic. It establishes a provocative setting, the gym where people look and are looked at (California fitness!). Then the tease of flirtatious looking is quickly replaced by a more significant exchange of glances: Bobby's injured body and Kinsey's reaction to it, which shows maturity and compassion. Ironically, in a location where most people are trying to perfect their bodies, Kinsey is drawn to the man with the most imperfect body, and her reaction is to put her own injuries into perspective. Kinsey's body as shapely or attractive (her exchange of glances with the men at the machines) suddenly isn't important.

The visual rhythm of this scene is evidence of Grafton's experience as a scriptwriter, but her "escape" from scripts allows her to describe the interiority of Kinsey's character as well. In an often-quoted passage in *G Is for Gumshoe*, Kinsey is kept awake one night at a motel by the noisy lovemaking of drunken newlyweds in the next room. As the picture on her wall begins to rattle, she improvises earplugs for herself by stuffing socks in her bra and wrapping it around her head, "a cone over each ear like an alien." She lies there alone, "wondering at the peculiarities of human sex practices. I would have much to report when I returned to my planet" (*Gumshoe*, 68).

This commentary works as a funny spin on the *alienated* detective-as-loner, but the passage also delivers visual details: the picture bangs against the wall, and the reverse shot is Kinsey as the glum witness to this, her underwear glimpsed in a profoundly nonglamorous way. The image is witty in other ways, too. The bra as a traditional symbol of sex appeal instead symbolizes the lone detective in her bed, at odds with the sex next door, and more interested in pragmatic than romantic uses of lingerie. In fact, underwear in the Kinsey Millhone series is never glamorized and always treated with immense practicality. Kinsey keeps extras in her bag and in her car in case she's stuck somewhere overnight. Also, the image is a wonderful symbol of the "switching of bodies" in the woman detective genre. After all, the sock stuffed in a bra or in a crotch is a traditional accessory of drag queens or drag kings, male-to-female or female-to-male impersonators. With a bra wrapped around her ears, Kinsey shares drag's good-natured disrespect for the props of gender. The "alien" perspective is the ability to deromanticize and demystify human sex, parts, props, and desires.

When the action of *Gumshoe* takes us back to the motel the next morning, Kinsey spots the noisy newlyweds leaving their room and heading to their car on which the slogan JUST MERGED has been painted. "They were both in their fifties," she tells us, "a hundred pounds overweight, dressed in matching western-cut shirts and oversize blue jeans. . . . I watched them cross the parking lot, arms around each other's waists, or at least as far as they would go." The next sentence shifts to a contrasting closeup of Kinsey's own preoccupation at that moment: "While the car warmed up, I pulled my little .32 out of the briefcase where I'd tucked it the night before and transferred it to my handbag on the passenger seat" (*Gumshoe*, 71). These two brief "shots" are typical of Grafton's style: what Kinsey sees and then a closeup of Kinsey herself. The shot/reverse shot here moves from the couple to the handgun, suggesting Kinsey's wry relationship to romantic coupling.

This episode occurs in the alphabet novel that introduces P.I. Robert Dietz, who is Kinsey's most serious romantic and sexual partner in the series. But clues abound that this relationship is unlikely to be permanent or legal. On the day they meet, Kinsey and Dietz exchange information about their pasts. Kinsey explains that her first marriage was the result of a crisis in her life that also made her give up her job as a cop. "Six months later, I was married to a bum," she tells him. Without missing a beat, Dietz replies, "At least the story has a happy ending." In turn, he confesses he's had two children by a woman who refused to marry him. "She swore I'd leave her in the end and sure enough that's what I did" (*Gumshoe*, 95). Their cynicism about long-term commitment is reinforced later in the novel, when, tracking down records at the courthouse, they run into another set of newlyweds, a hugely pregnant bride and a cartoon husband who "smelled of Brylcreem and cigarettes, his blue jeans pleated up around his waist with a length of rope" (*Gumshoe*, 216). This time the reaction shot focuses on Dietz, who "was still staring off at the departing couple with a look of uneasiness" when he gets to the counter (*Gumshoe*, 217).

Screenwriters are under pressure to move stories quickly, delivering only information and images that contribute to the logic of the plot or the mood of the piece. The two newlywed couples briefly glimpsed in *Gumshoe* do both. On the one hand, they serve as comic relief and lend the effect of realism—yes, this is what you find at motels and at the county courthouse. On the other hand, they work for the bigger logic at stake here, the need to picture Kinsey as both available and forever single; attractive and attracted to certain men, but fated never to marry happily; divorced and wary but still open to a relationship when a man like Dietz appears on the scene. And this picture is developed through alternating images of the "alien" P.I. couple and other even odder couplings.[27]

Other cynical pictures of marriage occur throughout the series, with cases involving homicidal marriages and with ghoulish glimpses of Kinsey herself in relation to that institution. In the following book, *H Is for Homicide*, Dietz is (safely) away in Germany, and Kinsey frets about a wedding for which she's the maid of honor. The wedding is on Halloween, and for lack of time or interest, Kinsey wears her one, all-purpose black dress, despite the bride's protests that the effect would be that of a pallbearer. In *J Is for Judgment*, one of the characters is a bridal consultant, spurring Kinsey to reflect on her own lack of formal weddings, despite two marriages. Her only wedding gown, she remembers, was a Bride of Frankenstein costume she wore as a kid one Halloween, "probably the most beautiful dress I would ever own."[28] Little Kinsey as a monsterette and the association of weddings and Halloween reinforce the dark marital humor of this series—which started, after all, with Grafton's decision not to murder an ex-husband.

Grafton's Hollywood training lends visual punch and structural tightness to the entire alphabet series, but the Hollywood influence can also be seen in the occasional noir touch of plot and setting. Film noir is both a visual style—shadows, deep-focus photography, night scenes—and a narrative tradition about crime and moral compromise. Grafton's description of Kinsey's night driving in *Alibi*, for instance, recalls the lonely highways and stoic detectives of 1940s cinema: "Driving anywhere looks much the same to me," Kinsey reports in her hardboiled voice. "I stare at the concrete roadway. I watch the yellow line. I keep track of large trucks and passenger vehicles with little children asleep in the backseat and I keep my foot pressed flat to the floor until I reach my destination" (*Alibi*, 112). Likewise, the dramatic suicide/disappearance of Renata at the end of *J Is for Judgment* is a film noir moment on the breakwater wall at dusk: "I could see the ocean churning, a massive black presence disappearing into the blackness. All the flags were snapping. There were lights at intervals, but the effect was ornamental" (*Judgment*, 281). Renata dives and can't be saved, but she haunts Kinsey with the possibility that she remains out there somewhere, an eternal *femme fatale*, the black widow luring men to leave their families and pursue a shadowy life on the lam.

Film noir is noted for its stark categorizations of women as slithering *femme fatales*, dead bodies, or domestic (often victimized) mothers or wives. Highly touted versions of neo-noir in 1980–90s cinema replayed these traditional roles in films like *Blue Velvet* and *Red Rock West* (1992), or revealed only slight twists: the *femme* turns out to be not *fatale* in *L.A. Confidential* (1997), but the sweet wife/mother is purely victim in *Seven* (1995). Tellingly, women can survive and be more than stereotypes in this film tradition when female sexuality is defined in more radical ways, as with the pregnant deputy in *Fargo* or the lesbian outlaw couple in *Bound* (1996). But when the woman detective simply takes the male part, so to speak, she gets into deep trouble, as evidenced in *Blue Steel*.

The Kinsey Millhone book that pictures the woman detective in film noir is *K Is for Killer*, which evokes the 1944 Otto Preminger classic, *Laura*. Preminger's *Laura* complicates the stereotypes of film noir with a beguiling switch. The murdered Laura, supposedly an ambitious and scheming career woman, is investigated and condemned during the first half of the film. But the real Laura then appears from her cabin in the hills and reveals a series of misunderstandings: the body had been mistakenly identified, but more than that, the *femme fatale* profile of Laura turns out to be the venomous invention of several other characters. Meanwhile, the detective, who had fallen in love with Laura's portrait, is rewarded with romance and apprehension of the murderer of the other woman.

In *Killer*, Kinsey is commissioned to find the murderer of the beautiful, mysterious Lorna, found dead in her cabin in the hills. As in *Laura*, the case turns out to be a moral investigation of the murdered woman, but in the Grafton novel, Lorna's truly shady past involves pornography, prostitution, and attachments to powerful, brutal men. *Killer* also tests Kinsey's darkest instincts. When she figures out who murdered Lorna and realizes she can never prove it in court, she grimly reports her findings to Lorna's mobster fiancé, whose henchmen will dispense justice themselves. At the book's conclusion, Kinsey reflects on the serious implications of her decision: "Having strayed into the shadows, can I find my way back?"[29] More than any of the other books in the series, *Killer* leaves Kinsey seriously shaken about her ethics. The killer of the title refers to Lorna's murderer, but also to the others lurking in the shadows: the mobster who will get revenge, and Kinsey, who has dispatched him.

K Is for Killer is preoccupied with questions about the female body that—like the ambiguous title—eventually lead back to Kinsey herself. As in *Laura*, there's a question about the identification of Lorna's body, highly desired as a pricey commodity during her lifetime, but decayed beyond recognition when it's discovered after death. The book opens with Kinsey's misidentified body, in fact, when a client goes to Kinsey's office looking for the male detective, Mr. Millhone. Later, Kinsey is the one who's mistaken about bodies; she's wholly taken in by "Cherie," a voluptuous blonde who slowly takes off a wig and makeup to reveal Lorna's male porno costar.

The sex reversals continue as Kinsey is repeatedly positioned in the traditionally male role of voyeur. She pores over forensic photographs of the corpse and also views a porno video of Lorna, which at first seems to be a clue about the murder. "In some ways, it's hard to know which is more sordid," Kinsey notes, "the pornography of sex or the pornography of homicide" (*Killer*, 77). Unlike the heroine of the *Laura* movie, the "real" Lorna is never recuperated in this book. Instead, she's rendered only through cameras and a tape recorder, the (male) machineries of police, pornography, and surveillance.

Using these machineries and investigating this male-dominated milieu, Kinsey reverses sex and gender roles without radically changing its premises. At one point she pays a hooker the usual john's rate of $50/hour for an interview. Inevitably, the transgressive nature of Kinsey's own role takes on dismal parallels with that of the sex workers. She begins to work all night and sleep during the day, "drawn into the shadowy after-hours world Lorna Kepler had inhabited" (*Killer*, 185). When she phones Lorna's director, he mistakes her for a porno actress looking for a break. More than that, she befriends one of Lorna's hooker friends, the young Danielle, who taunts Kinsey about working a job that's as dangerous as turning tricks (both women have suffered broken noses, it turns out) but pays only half as much.

Danielle is doomed to a grim transformation herself. Beaten by Lorna's murderer, she's "nearly unrecognizable" (216) and dies later at the hospital. Devastated, Kinsey is told by the police that no evidence against the murderer would stand up in court. The Hollywood-handsome homicide cop is annoyed by her persistence and urges her to let it go. "I sat for a minute and stared at the photograph of Lorna and Danielle," Kinsey reports. "Was I the only one who really cared about them?" (277). Ironically, female friendship drives Kinsey to trade justice for blood revenge. In the more subversive world of the movie *Bound*, the lesbian outlaws succeed against the mob's bloody patriarchy. In contrast, the mob—or some male cabal just as scary—ends up as Kinsey's last resort in *Killer*.

At that point, Kinsey is neither doing her job nor upholding the law. And even though she's not prostituting herself, her moral position is no longer clearly distinct from the "shadowy after-hours world" of Lorna. This unsettling conclusion, with Kinsey nearly unrecognizable to herself, is true to the gloomy spirit of film noir, but very different from the conclusion of the *Laura* film, in which the detective succumbs to love rather than moral turpitude. Remember that *K Is for Killer* opens with the client looking for the male detective in Kinsey's office, hinting this might be the wrong body, the wrong gender for the job. The male noir detective, shady though he may be, at least has some entitlement among the street-wise male cops, all of whom share contempt for the women of the "after-hours world." Could it be a co-incidence that the book imitating the male tradition of film noir is the book in which Kinsey is most morally compromised in her work?

One other cinematic clue in this novel reframes the problem. The *mise-en-scène* of the crimes is the county water board. The chairman of the board is eventually found dead in his swimming pool, and the murderer—who also murdered Lorna and Danielle—is his son-in-law, who runs the water treatment plant. These details quickly invoke Roman Polanski's film *Chinatown*, the cruelest of film noirs, in which the detective is thoroughly helpless to bring charges against the evil patriarch or prevent the death of the victimized woman. By compari-son, Kinsey is more successful; motivated by female friendship and compassion, she avenges the deaths of two prostitutes. This may be the best the woman detective can do on the masculinized turf of noir.

Killer is the exception in the Kinsey Millhone series, in which Kin-sey occasionally bends the law but is never again quite so far outside of it. Maybe women love female-investigator novels as the equivalent of the "Take Back the Night" campaign to make public spaces safe for women after dark. We like to think that in the cold, shadowy world of crime, there are brave, vigilant women who are reclaiming the streets. *Killer* reminds us what they might have to do to stay out there.

PATRICIA CORNWELL AND THE BODY DOUBLE

Far more than Sue Grafton's books, Patricia Cornwell's crime novels are literally about bodies: finding them, examining them, taking them apart, and even boiling them down to the bones. Cornwell's heroine is Dr. Kay Scarpetta, a forensics medical examiner, and Scarpetta's pri-mary site of investigation is the body itself, as suggested by book titles like *Postmortem* (1990) and *Body of Evidence* (1991).[30]

In these novels, medical forensics guarantees the authority of the main character and the gritty realism of the details. Readers are offered meticulous accounts of autopsies, descriptions of police procedures with homicide victims, and the process of profiling criminals through physical evidence. These topics first came into American pop culture in 1988 through the *Silence of the Lambs* book and the 1991 film. Since then, a number of nonfiction books on both profiling and medical forensics have appeared, as well as a number of forensic novels.[31]

In Cornwell's first four crime novels, between 1990 and 1993, Kay Scarpetta's cases often involved the FBI, but beginning with *The Body*

Fig. 4 Patricia Cornwell, author of the Kay Scarpetta series. Courtesy of Corbis.

Farm in 1994, the heroine served as the consulting forensic pathologist for the FBI's Investigative Support Unit. Scarpetta's work overlaps with psychological and behavioral profiling in these novels, but she always begins with physical evidence, literally with questions of the body. In *Body Farm*, Scarpetta describes her work with "people who were not allowed to scream until they were wheeled into my morgue. For it was only there the body could speak freely."[32]

Yet what bodies have to say isn't always scientific in these novels. In *All That Remains*, for example, Kay Scarpetta solves the case only when she rereads one of the crimes—the murder of two women—as the murder of a romantic *couple*. And most often, Scarpetta resolves her cases because she intuitively reads her bodies more creatively than the facts and forensics allow. In *Point of Origin*, she makes this clear, admitting "there were times when I did not care as much about statutes or definitions. Justice was bigger than codes, especially when I believed that no one was listening to the facts." She uses this aside to tell us that "little more than intuition" leads her to make her next move.[33] Intuition is a big chunk of most detective work, and in most of these novels, Scarpetta's legal and forensic colleagues neglect "the facts" she believes are important. Only her personal passion and commitment press her to solve the case. Certainly a major attraction of Cornwell's series is Scarpetta's compassion, the profound moral obligation she feels toward the victims who appear in her morgue.[34]

But the focus on bodies in these novels points to other "facts" that come into question. Kay herself has an unscientific theory about her own body. "I was a woman who was not a woman. I was the body and sensibilities of a woman with the power and drive of a man," she tells us at an anguished moment in *The Body Farm* (341). This comment about the meanings of Scarpetta's body is a clue about a contradiction in these novels. In clinical logic, there are only two sexes or categories of bodies. Scarpetta's sentence, "I was a woman who was not a woman," makes sense only because the word "woman" has meaning in another context. There's the female biological body (the facts!) and the one weighted down with cultural, unscientific meanings—a woman shouldn't have "power and drive."

Remember, too, that this sentence about "a woman who was not a woman" could serve as one of the traditional definitions of the lesbian. So while Cornwell's series depends on clinical forensics, with the body as evidence of the truth, the most interesting conundrums about bodies in these books are not as easily resolved.[35] In fact, Scarpetta's problems are often about social expectations for women. She's hounded by sexist politics threatening her authority; the person she loves most, her lesbian niece Lucy, must always be on the defensive about her sexuality; and the most devious serial killer in this series slips among sex and gender identities.

Kay Scarpetta cuts an especially controversial figure within the establishments where she's a triple threat: doctor, lawyer, and Chief Medical Examiner of Virginia. But even as the Scarpetta character asserts her authority in these male-dominated professions, she has no political ambitions to change them. Unlike the paycheck-to-paycheck female P.I.s of Paretsky and Grafton, Scarpetta is the best-seller list's most upscale and, not surprisingly, most conservative female investigator. Her statement about having "the body and sensibilities of a woman with the power and drive of a man" shows traditional thinking about "power and drive" as natural for a man and unnatural for a woman.

These novels often remind us of Scarpetta's Catholic background, which reinforces traditional ideas about gender and bodies. Yet Catholicism also subtly undermines clinical forensics, because it cautions us against identifying the body as the person. Explaining her beliefs to an assistant in the morgue, Scarpetta says, "You look at their faces and you can tell. Their energy has departed. The spirit didn't die. Just the body did."[36]

Romance and physical attractions are mysteries in these novels, too. By 1998, as heroine Kay outlived wooden male suitors, and as Kay's niece Lucy grew more interesting in every book, reviewers began to get impatient with character development. In an article entitled "Come Out, Kay Scarpetta," a *Newsday* reviewer concluded that the heterosexuality of the series' heroine seemed no more than a safe convention for the best-seller list. A 1998 book review in *Entertainment Weekly* demanded outright, "Is Kay Scarpetta gay, or what?," pointing out the flimsiness of heterosexual romantic subplots and the "mild erotic humidity" obvious but never acknowledged between female characters.[37]

The title of the *Entertainment Weekly* review, "Body Double," alludes to Brian De Palma's 1984 film of the same name about voyeurism, obsession, and deceit. The headline implies that the surface appearances of the Cornwell novels are blinds for other agendas. Also, "body double" is a cinematic term for the substitute actor or actress used for the filming of nude scenes or physical feats. Sometimes a better, or more fit, or more athletic body is needed to produce an ideal effect. At other times, a body double is used if an actor or actress prefers not to do a nude scene. So the headline could refer to Cornwell's publicity images of herself as a stand-in for her character, and the coy lesbian themes of Cornwell's own celebrity.

The body double provides a useful way to think about the problem of bodies and identities in the Scarpetta series. Given the conflict between clinical and cultural ways of interpreting the body, Cornwell's crime novels are under particular pressure to produce identifiable bodies—especially the body of the heroine, but also the bodies of victim and villain. The conflicting expectations and conventions produce illusions similar to "body doubling," which always entails a cultural ideal and a substitution.

In movies, the technique of body doubling is used for both men and women, but its uses for actresses have attracted the most attention. When a double was used for Angie Dickinson's shower scene in De Palma's 1980 film *Dressed to Kill*, the resulting media stir prompted de Palma to make *Body Double*, released four years later. The dancer-double for Jennifer Beals in *Flashdance* (1983) was likewise exposed as an ironic twist to a movie about stardom and talent, given the racial identities of the two bodies involved.[38] While two bodies are used in body-double scenes, the audience sees only one, an illusion of edited shots: closeups of the known actress's face, closeups and medium shots of other parts of the other body or bodies.

The point is that two different bodies are necessary to produce the illusion of *one* perfect body. Also, the effect relies on a switch; at the place one body is expected, another *actually* appears. As a result, an impossible phenomenon—two bodies in the same place, two simultaneous materializations of the same person—becomes possible. In films, continuity editing works with the audience's ability to read a series of spliced shots as one continuous scene, and to see one continuous body.

Doubling and substitution are also devices used in fiction to develop or describe nuances of character. Doubling, of course, is an old standby in detective fiction, and Grafton's *K Is for Killer* is a perfect example of this. Most critics agree that the detective story thrives on its contradictions and subversions, including blurred boundaries of good, evil, crime, and justice. Considering the traditional link of detective and criminal, the professional female investigator is always doubly suspect as a woman in the man's place, female authority in a male legal/police world.

In *The Body Farm*, the doubling among characters is more complex. A number of suspicious or simply transgressive women reveal conspicuous overlaps and doublings, which in the long run also link them to Kay Scarpetta. Lucy has followed her aunt's career path in law enforcement and the FBI, but has been seduced on the job by the double-dealing Carrie Grethen. Carrie as *femme fatale* is in turn doubled by the book's villain, the murderous Denesa Steiner, who has deluded and seduced the vulnerable cop Pete Marino. Denesa as bad mother—a "murderous maternal creature with blood on her teeth" (*Body Farm*, 354)—is doubled by Kay's sister who is the neglectful mother of Lucy. The "respectable" traditional woman—the wife of Kay's lover—materializes only in a phone conversation, so the culturally legitimate female position is only a distant reference in this book.

The uncanny proximity of these various female bodies inhabiting *The Body Farm* provides no clear-cut way to locate and define Kay herself except as a series of substitutions and likenesses. Like many fictional female detectives, she was herself once someone's wife. Her most consistent commitment and relationship is to Lucy, but she often guiltily feels like a failed mother in her attempts to nurture her niece. And her role as adulteress inevitably connects her with this genre's dark lady. Furthermore, she overtly identifies herself with the troubled maverick Lucy. In Lucy, several threatening characteristics of the female investigator (rebel, lesbian, misfit, alcoholic) are deflected away from Kay, but Kay repeatedly mentions how much she and Lucy are alike.[39]

The Body Farm is part of a quartet of novels that include *Cruel and Unusual* (1993), *From Potter's Field* (1995), and *Point of Origin* (1998). These novels use strikingly similar strategies of illusion and doubling in their interlinked stories about the crime partners Temple Gault and Carrie Grethen. Gault and Grethen continually frustrate scientific efforts to track them down. In the first novel of the quartet, a young man known as Temple Gault is identified as the plot's serial murderer, and he's still at large at the end of the book. The next novel, *Body Farm*, introduces attractive Carrie Grethen, who is Lucy's colleague and lover at the FBI. We eventually learn that Carrie is connected to Gault, but both are on the loose when the novel closes. In *From Potter's Field*, Gault and Carrie resurface in Manhattan, where Gault is cornered and killed by Scarpetta herself. Finally, *Point of Origin* deals with Carrie, who escapes from jail for one last crime spree, intent on ruining both Scarpetta and her niece.

The Gault-Grethen story is significant as Kay Scarpetta's most personally menacing case, since it threatens her beloved Lucy. The criminal duo also undermines all the forensic and profiling techniques on which the Scarpetta novels rely. Gault "doesn't really fit any profile," we learn in *Cruel and Unusual* (352). Throughout this novel, he confuses the police by committing crimes that appear to be the work of an executed criminal. In fact, within the first few chapters, the definition of death itself comes into question during a state execution in which the time of death and status of the corpse/criminal become unclear. Then, because the villains have tampered with evidence, confusion ensues about *whose* body has been executed by the state. The technologies of identification not only fail, but contribute to the deceptions: because a fingerprint swap occurs in the Central Computerized Record Exchange, the fingerprints left at crime scenes are that of a dead man.

Gault's ability to produce conflicting or irrelevant forensic evidence enables him to evade the police through the first two novels of this quartet. The FBI profilers hypothesize that Gault "derived intense pleasure from leaving evidence that seemed to make no sense" (*Body Farm*, 195). His uncanny ability to penetrate security networks, underground tunnels, and even computer systems leads Scarpetta to think of him as a "virus," not just a computer virus, but a larger, more virulent, ever-changing threat: "He had somehow gotten into our bodies and our buildings and our technologies."[40]

Gault tests the limits of scientific criminology—fingerprints, psychological profiles, and visual evidence. So he also undermines the status of the body itself as evidence. His tactics are those of body-doubling: he's often not what he appears to be, and he relies on substitution and mistaken identity to avoid capture. The mistaken identities are consistently those of gender and sex. When Kay first glimpses him through a doorway in *Cruel and Unusual,* she sees only his eyes and mistakes him for a woman. In fact, she assumes he's a lesbian partner of the woman she's seeking, and she later learns he's involved in a sadomasochistic sex relationship with this woman. Photos finally reveal him to be "an exquisitely pretty blond young man" (*Cruel,* 349). Witnesses sometimes assume Gault is gay, but when he's sighted and reported as part of a gay male couple in *From Potter's Field,* we discover that he was in fact seen with a woman, who turns out to be his twin sister.

His doublings with Carrie Grethen, meanwhile, allow him to outwit the law. At the climax of the novel, as the police track Gault through the New York subways with elaborate computer and video technology, he and Carrie effectively substitute for each other to mislead them. "They're not sure if they have her or Gault. She and Gault are probably dressed alike again," Lucy reports grimly (*Potter's Field,* 403). This unreliability of visual evidence confounds the technology, so Gault is caught only when Scarpetta and Lucy leave the safety of the control room, crammed with monitors and computers, and track him on foot through the subway.

This dangerous underground pursuit occurs because the investigation has become a personal, passionate case for Scarpetta and her niece. An important subplot of the Gault-Grethen saga is Lucy's emergence both as another female investigator and also as a lesbian. In the previous novels, Lucy appeared occasionally as the disgruntled childgenius whose computer expertise helps solve her aunt's cases. But in *Body Farm,* Lucy has come of age. She's twenty-one, beautiful, and an intern at the FBI, and she's been seduced and entrapped by her colleague Carrie Grethen. Eventually, we learn that Lucy's attraction to Carrie was cruelly exploited by Carrie as a means to infiltrate the FBI and discredit Scarpetta.

The coupling of Lucy and Carrie is literally the coupling of the Gault plotline and the FBI-sabotage plotline. Gault's criminality is marked by deceptive bodily evidence that can't be read by the FBI's systems. But criminality is also located within the FBI itself, in the outlaw body of lesbianism, which is likewise unreadable as a bodily trait and thus undetectable by the tools of medical forensics. By the end of these four novels, which have introduced Lucy into professional law enforcement, Carrie has successfully inflicted long-term personal damage on both heroines. Lucy's sexual vulnerability becomes Scarpetta's professional vulnerability, the point of Carrie's disastrous entry into both their lives. So lesbianism is the subtext and scandal of "the woman who was not a woman," the female investigator.

Lucy's sexuality is clearly a threat to the male police in these novels, especially the macho cop Pete Marino. Kay's arguments to him about Lucy's lesbianism are careful and guarded, often sounding like a prim medical lecture. "There may be a genetic component to one's sexual orientation. Maybe there isn't. But what's important is that it doesn't matter," she tells him (*Potter's Field*, 194). Yet Lucy's lesbianism matters a great deal in the Gault subplot, since Lucy's seduction enables Gault's access to the FBI's systems. Given the long-standing tradition of the secret criminality of the detective, the homophobic stereotype of the lesbian as a criminal, and Kay's self-incrimination as a "woman who was not a woman," Lucy's lesbianism matters in terms of Kay's character, too.

Marino tells Scarpetta that some people assume she's gay herself (*Potter's Field*, 181), and in quarreling with him, she at one point openly threatens to give up men (*Body Farm*, 117). Kay's own mother offers a stumbling and humorous account of why Kay is *not* a lesbian: "Just because you're never with men and probably don't like sex doesn't mean you're a homo. It's the same thing with nuns. Though I've heard the rumors—" (*Body Farm*, 343). Yet this quartet of novels develops Cornwell's most desperately heterosexual subplot. Faced with the lesbianism of the young woman who is modeled after herself, Kay finds a male lover whose lovemaking is romantically described as healing the violence of men: "I felt his empathy, as if he wanted to heal those places he had seen so hated and harmed. He seemed sorrowed by everyone who had ever raped or battered or been unkind" (*Body Farm*, 341). If this sounds both suspicious and impossible, it is. Kay's lover is FBI profiler Benton Wesley, who's a married man. The hopelessness of the situation is also its safety. It allows Kay to remain impossibly heterosexual, which is perhaps what the female investigator on the current best-seller list must be.

Both Kay and Lucy exhibit the loneliness and borderline neurosis that are standard for the detective story. "I understood her secret shame born of abandonment and isolation," Kay says of her niece, "and wore her same suit of sorrow beneath my polished armor. When I tended to her wounds, I was tending to my own" (*Body Farm*, 45–46). Lucy is both more and less ideal than Kay as a heroine. *Body Farm* opens with Kay struggling to complete her morning run at Quantico, "in agony and aware of growing old" (4). When she goes to the women's shower, she's surrounded by younger and fitter "women in various stages of nudity" (7), including Lucy, who is obviously more fit for action and heroics. The novels further emphasize that the computer-savvy Lucy is more contemporary than Kay, more mentally flexible with virtual, hypertext, and electronic systems. Scarpetta is attached to technologies of the body (fingerprints, autopsies, biochemistry). But her lesbian cohort is attached to computer technologies that can imagine, connect, and create scenarios unfettered by traditional assumptions about what is "real."

Not surprisingly, Lucy is also the more dangerous, reckless, and self-destructive investigator. While both women are portrayed as intellectual and ambitious, Lucy's sexuality renders her more "guilty" of these gender transgressions. Both women are engaged in illicit affairs, for example, but Lucy's endangers the entire FBI criminal-apprehension system. Along the same lines, Kay Scarpetta's fondness for good food and drink is one of her warmer human qualities, but Lucy is an alcoholic, a familiar trait of the literary detective.

The doubling in detective stories usually links the detective and the villain, as in the coupling of Lucy and Carrie. So its occurrence between two *heroines*—Kay and Lucy—reveals the edginess of the Cornwell series, its management of Kay's dark side. The Kay-Lucy identification also illustrates the multiple meanings of the body in this series. Kay's identification with her niece isn't purely psychological, but is tied to family and physical resemblance. At times the resemblance itself is dangerous. In *Body Farm*, Kay's likeness to Lucy and their similar "deep, quiet voices" on the telephone nearly get Lucy killed (329–30). The resemblance also serves as a self-description for the first-person narrator: Lucy is the "frighteningly beautiful and brilliant woman with whom I shared snippets of genetic code," Kay tells us in *Body Farm* (170).

Yet this passage continues by describing Kay's *attraction* to Lucy. The description reveals not just two striking women who share "snippets of genetic code," but two women who are attracted to other women: "I realized that if I didn't know her and she walked past, I would turn to look again, and this wasn't solely due to her fine figure and face. One sensed the facility with which Lucy spoke, walked, and in the smallest ways guided her body and her eyes" (*Body Farm*, 170). In *Point of Origin*, Kay's assessment of her niece's beauty awakens a more explicit homoerotic response: "It was as if I had never really noticed her full lips and breasts and her arms and legs curved and strong like a hunter's bow. . . . I felt shamed and confused, when for an electric instant, I envisioned her as Carrie's supple, hungry lover" (*Origin*, 58). This is obviously desire—which explains the shame and confusion not only about the incestuous overtones, but about this new self-perception. My point here is the *importance* of Lucy's body in the Scarpetta series, a saga ostensibly about scientific bodily identification, but a saga profoundly infused with other accounts of the body's status, desires, and contexts.

This ambivalence of bodily evidence is illustrated by one of the doubling devices in the first two novels of the Gault-Grethen quartet. In *Cruel and Unusual*, Kay is incriminated and discredited when her own fingerprints show up at a crime scene—ironically, because she'd been fond of the murder victim and had given her a scarf. In *Body Farm*, fingerprints are also misleading evidence. Lucy is discredited by the FBI because Carrie was able to fake Lucy's fingerprint on a biometric lock system, a system supposedly foolproof about physical identity. But even though Carrie can fake a print, a more substantial imprinting has occurred between herself and Lucy. Although she knows Carrie betrayed her, Lucy admits she's still in love with Carrie at the end of the novel.

Point of Origin, the last novel of this quartet, concerns arson and pyrotechnics. These are crimes that leave the most inscrutable evidence: ashes, the traditional symbol of the body's final material form. The obliteration of identity likewise characterizes this novel's plot, for the murderer is a macabre collector who removes his victims' faces. This murderer has teamed up with the newly escaped Carrie Grethen. The title's "point of origin" refers to the start of a fire but is also a description of Carrie as a devastating, all-consuming force that likewise aims to destroy Lucy and Kay. In a highly effective smear campaign, Carrie releases to the national media an incriminating statement that she was the victim of a sexual conspiracy. She claims she was seduced by Lucy and then targeted by Kay, who was having an affair with Benton Wesley, the FBI profiler on the case. This tactic succeeds as raw sensationalism and also as a sly usage of sexual motivation, evidence that's not easily provable or disprovable. By the end of the novel, Carrie has reduced Lucy to the point of suicidal despair and has gotten revenge against Kay by arranging for the murder of Benton Wesley.

This novel terminates both relationships—Kay/Benton and Lucy/Carrie—that began this series. So the entire Gault-Grethen narrative is defined by sexual crises and, most emphatically, ends with images of bodily annihilation. In an aerial chase over the ocean, Lucy's helicopter successfully hits and blows up Carrie's. Little is left of Carrie except bits of debris washed up on the beach. The sea is also the final destination for the remains of Kay's lover Benton. The novel ends with the scattering of his ashes at sea, completing the novel's theme of personal obliteration—or at least, the obliteration of the troublesome lovers of Lucy and Kay. The latter pair are the couple that matter, this novel implies. The concluding image is of Kay offering Wesley's ashes to the water, as Lucy in her helicopter swoops to scatter them: "I opened the urn and looked up at my niece who was there to create the energy he had wanted when it was his time to move on" (*Origin*, 356).

This funeral invokes the larger cosmic question of personal identity, in one sense foreclosing the trickier questions about the body and identity raised in this quartet. The exchange also blatantly delivers Lucy as the replacement for Benton Wesley. She's Kay's true mate or cohort, her alter ego and smarter, younger self. Without the messiness of being Kay's actual lover, she can suggest what Kay's lover would be. The novel has already given us the "electric instant" when Kay was erotically moved by Lucy's "full lips and breasts and her arms and legs curved and strong like a hunter's bow" (*Origin*, 58). In this way, the outlaw lesbian identity of the female investigator flickers suggestively between the two characters. And this flickering suggests the mixed desires of the genre, the writer, and the fans about how to picture Kay Scarpetta.

In some ways, pop culture has already pictured Kay Scarpetta, indirectly but with plenty of innuendo. The television series *Profiler* debuted in 1996, just after the publication of *From Potter's Field. Profiler* featured the Cornwell look-alike Ally Walker as the main character, Dr. Sam Waters, so for Scarpetta fans anxious to *see* a blonde, vulnerable forensics heroine—with a "real" face, body, star—the series offered a substitution. As I detail in chapter 4, the show's many references to the Cornwell series suggest that the character Sam Waters can herself be understood as a body double for the more elusive literary character Kay Scarpetta. Scarpetta's popularity is also invoked in the women costars of the forensics series *CSI* and in the television series *Crossing Jordan*, since Jordan's occupation is also forensic investigator. The gruff, tomboy character of Jordan herself is more Kinsey Millhone than Kay Scarpetta, but the lesbian friendship episode of *Crossing Jordan* that I mentioned in chapter 1 is more Kay than Kinsey.

Meanwhile, the picturing of Kay Scarpetta in Hollywood continues as a rumor and a website topic. Reports of a movie deal for *From Potter's Field* surfaced periodically, and one website in 2001 offered a poll so fans could vote for the casting. Nominations included Sela Ward and Dana Delany as Kay Scarpetta, but for what it's worth, the top nominations for Lucy were the hotter actresses Cameron Diaz and Elisabeth Shue.[41]

3

JIGGLE, CAMP, AND COUPLES
1960s–80s Prime-Time Woman Investigators

THE BENEVOLENT TELEVISION GODMOTHER OF THE PRIME-TIME woman detective is without doubt Jessica Fletcher of the long-lived series *Murder, She Wrote* (1984–96). Clever, spry and apparently immortal as played by Angela Lansbury, Ms. Fletcher is the Americanized version of Agatha Christie's Miss Marple, so her literary credentials are impeccable. Her television credentials are impressive, too. The longest-running female sleuth in television history, she succeeded in a format that would seem deadly for prime-time ratings. The heroine of *Murder, She Wrote* was neither young nor sexy, the plotlines neither sleazy nor action-driven, and the format, more than a century old, was the classic whodunit, solved by the superior insight of a chess-playing woman in advanced middle-age.[1]

Jessica Fletcher had no license for investigations, and her occupations were safely feminine—retired teacher, then a mystery writer, and later in the series a part-time college instructor. She could out-think the ruthless thief or murderer, but she never used a gun or delivered karate chops or tore up cars in high-speed chases. The plots were complicated and the scripts were witty—clearly the triumphant picturing of an older, adventurous woman holding her own on network TV.

Generally, network prime time has offered more opportunities for women's roles and performances than movies have. So it's not surprising that television was quicker than cinema to picture the woman investigator. Television series, as ongoing weekly episodes, allow for contradiction, nuance, and character development. Viewers spent *years* getting to know the many sides of *The X-Files*'s Dana Scully. Also, mainstream movies typically feature a young female lead, positioned for the camera for maximum sex appeal: the soft-focus closeup, the significant exchange of glances with the leading man. The television camera can include these sexualizing shots, too, but the TV camera is also busier, more flexible, and more generous in its inclusions. As a result, prime time has provided space for actresses who would not likely be female movie leads, such as the middle-aged Lucille Ball, Bea Arthur, Carol Burnett, Penny Marshall, and Roseanne. For one thing, networks have always been interested in attracting female audiences. And television is inherently domestic, a home appliance, not as glamorous as the big screen.[2]

But television is also dominated by sexy marketing trends and attention-getting gimmicks. So its female investigators have often been pictured with cleavage and jiggle, typically on undercover assignments requiring swimsuits and heels. The direct predecessor of the woman investigator on television was not the amateur Miss Marple but Pussy Galore, James Bond's pilot, lover, and judo opponent in *Goldfinger* (1964). Honor Blackman played the role in the wildly popular Bond movie, and previous to that she had been the female costar of *The Avengers* on British television, which would be imported for American broadcast in 1966. In the meantime, when producers at ABC crafted a series for a sexy woman detective in 1965, they wanted Honor Blackman with her history as a fabulous action-*femme*.

This was at the height of the 1960s James Bond craze, which had infused the spy genre with wicked sexual wit. "Bond girls" showed up as deadly dolls or swimsuited allies like Ursula Andress in *Dr. No* (1962). The naughty new sirens clearly knew their places: the bad girls would get theirs, and the good girls would get theirs, too, in Bond's bed in the closing shot. This route from James Bond to Honey West is not exactly a liberated one, strewn as it is with bikinis, skin-tight jumpsuits, and Ursula Andress, but it illustrates how popular genres blend and borrow their best clothes and trends—in this case, a character-type from the spy story migrating into the detective tale.

In *Goldfinger*, Honor Blackman as Pussy was both Good Girl and Bad Girl, first an adversary and later an ally of Bond. Matching Bond flip for flip in judo, Pussy was the head of an all-girl squadron of other blonde, curvaceous pilots. When Bond first attempts to seduce her, she tells him she's "immune." With these clues, and clad throughout the film in tailored pantsuits, Pussy exemplified the not-so-subtle lesbian opponent, a nastier version of whom had already appeared in *From Russia with Love* (1963), played by decadence-flavored Lotte Lenya and wielding a lethal blade in the toe of her shoe. But with a big wink at the audience, Ms. Galore falls first for Bond's judo and then for his

kisses. By the end of the movie, her "immunity" is thoroughly reversed, and she's safely on the side of Bond, Fort Knox, and heterosexuality, redeemed by 007's sex and charm. Corny as this may be, Pussy's
profile, especially her flexible sexuality, is far more typical of future
picturings of the woman detective than is Jessica Fletcher's.

The television project for which ABC wanted Honor Blackman was
Honey West (1965–66), which was not only American television's first
female detective show, but the first long-running network drama to
feature a woman. *Honey West* was an early project of actor-turned-
scriptwriter-turned-producer Aaron Spelling, who would later develop *Charlie's Angels*. Spelling's genius had always been to spot a trend
and refashion it with an original twist. The woman P.I. character had
certainly not been imaginable in the macho hit detective series previous to this: *Peter Gunn* (1958–61), *Dragnet* (1951–59), *77 Sunset Strip*
(1958–64), and *Hawaiian Eye* (1959–63). These traditional crime stories continued in the 1960s with dramas such as *The FBI* (1965–74),
Mannix (1967–75), and a resurrected *Dragnet* (1967–70). In all these
series, women were sympathetic or imperiled girlfriends, loyal secretaries, evil mistresses to bad guys, or nightclub singers named Cricket.
It was Spelling who envisioned a character more aligned with Bond
girls than with Cricket or the girlfriends at Sunset Strip.

Honey West, a novelty heroine introduced by novelist G.G. Fickling in 1957, was solidly rooted in the male detective tradition. Pictured as a voluptuous blonde on the jacket covers, West was described
in the cover blurbs as "a fun-loving private investigator." Fickling (actually a husband-wife team), had produced a number of Honey West
books by 1965: *This Girl for Hire, A Gun for Honey, Girl on the Loose,
Honey in the Flesh, Girl on the Prowl, Kiss for a Killer, Dig a Dead Doll*.
Like traditional hardboiled detectives, Honey narrates each one in
staccato prose and violent detail. "He had my black sheath dress
yanked down to my waist and his dark eyes feasted hungrily. I bit his
cheek. Blood spurted from the wound."[3] In each, Honey punches out
creepy villains who inevitably threaten her with rape and sexual torture: "Honey, I'm going to kill you, but *first*. . . ." The sadomasochism
is no different from what's in Mickey Spillane, but Honey also offers
sexual vulnerability and tease. This is male fantasy that doesn't affect
or change the basics of the traditional story. In that sense, Fickling's
Honey West is the ultimate female dick, the woman as a man, the
phallic woman.

When Honor Blackman turned down ABC's offer, the network
turned to a Blackman look-alike, Anne Francis, who could similarly
wear sleek-fitting pantsuits and flip hefty men over her shoulder with

Fig. 5 Anne Francis as the private investigator heroine of *Honey West* (ABC, 1965–66). Courtesy of Photofest.

judo. In the Fickling novels, Honey relies on the traditional detective arsenal of guns, fists, and wits, but ABC's version of Honey was more electronically hip. The television season in which she debuted was saturated with international intrigue and gee-whiz spy gadgets. This was the era of *The Man From U.N.C.L.E.* (1964–68), *I Spy* (1965–68), *Get Smart* (1965–70), and a year later, *Mission Impossible* (1966–73). Even *The Wild Wild West* (1965–70) featured a federal agent whose horse and buggy hid a 007-style ejection seat.

Honey West was not a spy but accessorized like one, down to her radio-transmitter tube of lipstick. She also wore explosive-device earrings and a gas mask tucked in her garter, so she was as prepared for Cold War maneuvers as for the felony cases that came her way. The clever gadgetry and Honey's wardrobe—black leotards, a leather trench coat, clingy evening gowns for those undercover nights on the town—kept the mood light. For the television adaptation, Honey inherited her detective agency from her father, who also passed down a handsome business partner, Sam, so the tone was also somewhat romantic. To her credit, Honey rarely needed to be rescued by the guy, and she looked really good doing judo and karate. Her giant sunglasses (also containing a radio transmitter) linked her to Jackie Kennedy, but her leopard-skin coat and pet ocelot were reminders of her more feline connections to Pussy, though without a hint of Pussy Galore's lesbian associations.

Honey West should have been a hit, given her sexpot predecessor in the Fickling novels and her likeness to the Bond Girls, but ratings were poor and the series short-lived. The same fate awaited the spin-off *Girl from U.N.C.L.E* (1966–67), starring Stephanie Powers as April Dancer, the jazzy female agent poised against T.H.R.U.S.H. Critics dismissed both shows as silly, but were these series really *less* silly than the antics of Napoleon Solo (the man from U.N.C.L.E.) or James T. West and his ejector buggy? True, the Honey West episodes were fairly predictable in their plotlines and not especially well written. When Emma Peel arrived in a funnier and wittier British version of the female spy, she had a far happier life on prime time.

Emma Peel was played by Diana Rigg in the American version of *The Avengers* (1966–69), yet another James Bond fantasy of gadgets and diabolical plots to blow up Miami. *The Avengers* played it tongue-in-cheek as camp, the ironic posing that was being commercialized in the mid-1960s on television shows such as *Batman*. The triumph of Emma Peel over Honey and April may have also been due to a two-prong formula that would work well for future action-*femmes*.

First, the action heroine worked in a male-female duo. It defused the (lesbian) threat of the woman alone, it provided the opportunity for romance or at least the sexual innuendoes Emma traded with her partner Steed, and it reinforced traditional gender roles through the image of the couple. *Honey West* used this occasionally with Sam, but as the title of the series indicated, she was obviously the focus and star. Second, the action heroine was relegated to a stylized, make-believe world more playfully fictitious than the mean streets of *Dragnet* or even the Beverly Hills of *Columbo*. *The Avengers* relied on faux-pornographic scenarios of impossible physical feats, high boots, and black leather. Playing up the kinky parody, Emma in one episode is chased by a whip-cracking gamekeeper named Mellors, the character from *Lady Chatterley's Lover*.

In the long run, Emma Peel in her boots and leather was destined to be claimed as a lesbian icon. In the 1990s, the activist group The Lesbian Avengers embraced the campy Brit investigation series and used Diana Rigg as their first publicity figure. Emma Peel would also return in the movie version of *The Avengers* (1998), played by Uma Thurman, as part of the late 1990s–early 2000 trend of high-fantasy female action figures, which toyed with both lesbian chic and the techno-body made possible by computer animation effects. The title character of *Lara Croft: Tomb Raider* (2001) carries on the Emma Peel tradition of exotic costuming and aristocratic airs, and also the nuances of both straight and lesbian porn.

Considering Honey West's heritage of Pussy Galore and Fickling's S/M novels, she was only a heartbeat away from soft porn herself. Yet the TV version of Honey was also an early template of a woman with a fun, nontraditional career. Recently watching a sampling of *Honey West* episodes, I remembered my 1965 junior-high-school adulation of this series. I had only recently outgrown Nancy Drew, and it seemed obvious that Nancy had grown into Honey. Also, in this pre-*Avengers* era, Honey West was the only grown-up woman on television with an interesting life. The competition was Laura Petrie, Harriet Nelson, Donna Reed, nose-twitching Samantha, and a bevy of divorcées on *Peyton Place*. TV's teenage girls with whom I was supposed to identify were Gidget, Patty Duke, and Tammy, all of whom seemed likely to turn into Laura Petrie and Harriet.

But the other thing that struck me in watching old *Honey West* episodes was her alarming resemblance to more recent female investigators on television and in films. In a police lineup of women with glossy blonde hair, huge eyes, and perfect figures in tight pantsuits, she could easily be confused with Ally Walker of *Profiler*, Kathleen Turner in *V.I. Warshawski*, Karen Sillas of the ambitious, short-lived series *Under Suspicion*, and even Kathryn Morris in the series *Cold Case*, which premiered in 2003. The usage of Honey's body in the plotline was familiar, too. Like the heroines of *Police Woman, Get Christie Love*, and *Charlie's Angels* of the next decade, Honey most often was bait, lure, or undercover agent in situations requiring bikinis and flimsy evening gowns. The more recent *Miss Congeniality* reminds us that nearly forty years after Honey West, the basic requirements of the woman detective on screen— looking svelte in a swimsuit—remain the same.

This is all the more telling if we consider the bodies, shapes, and ages of television's male professional detectives and try to imagine their female equivalents: portly Frank Cannon, bald Telly Savalas as

Kojak, gnarled little Baretta, Ironside in his wheelchair, sixty-something Buddy Ebsen as Barnaby Jones. Consider, too, that television has generously allowed middle-aged women all sorts of other roles—comedy, drama, and even amateur sleuthing à la Jessica Fletcher. Yet with the exception of *Cagney & Lacey*, American television hasn't extended this prime-time generosity to the world of professional investigation, opening it up to multiple kinds of female bodies.

Because the detective hero has been naturalized as male (the dick), his body can take all shapes, ages, and forms—Kojak to Ironside to Columbo. But a female dick is inherently unnatural. Not surprisingly, with a few exceptions such as Cagney & Lacey, the female investigator has been obsessively pictured as the full-bodied calendar girl or blonde knockout, reassuring us of a "natural woman" who knows how to wear high heels—the traditional joke and test of cross-dressing men in films from *Some Like It Hot* (1959) to *Tootsie* (1982).

THE SEVENTIES: TITLE SEVEN AND T&A

After *Honey West*, it was more than fifteen years before another woman on television had her own detective business. Instead, the next women investigators pictured in prime time were undercover police detectives, players on mostly all-boy teams. Unlike the solo private investigator, the police detective—no matter how maverick—is part of the legal establishment. More important, these are *male* establishments, where a woman is unlikely to be in charge. For television, the woman on the police squad can bring a titillating sexual difference to the picture without changing the big picture in threatening ways.

Yet in the early 1970s, the picture of the policewoman *did* pose the threat of major changes within a staid, traditional organization, and it was a threat of the worst kind: it came from outside and it pushed outsiders in. Congress passed Title VII of the Civil Rights Act in 1972, prohibiting discrimination in public law enforcement hiring. The next year, it passed the Crime Control Act, which mandated equal-opportunity employment policies for law enforcement agencies getting federal aid.

Police departments and federal agencies were radically jolted by these laws, which literally demanded reimagining the *bodies* on the force. Most police departments had height and weight minimums of 5 feet, 7 inches, and 140 pounds—standards that would have eliminated 70 percent of American women. Also, for women to be promoted as the laws required, they had to get experience on all levels of the force. So in addition to changing the physical requirements, police forces also had to assign the women to the "men's" duties of patrol work, undercover, and backup. A *New York Times* story described the resentment of male cops assigned to female partners: "It was like a shotgun wedding for a lifelong bachelor."[4]

The uncomfortable coupling created immediate results, publicity, and drama. In 1971 there were only a dozen policewomen on patrol in the entire United States. By 1974 women comprised 6 percent of the police in Washington, D.C., while other major cities saw policewomen rise from nearly zero to 2–3 percent of the force. The public records, rumors, and perceptions were all drastically at odds. Most polls showed that residents preferred male cops and thought women were untrustworthy in the role. This contradicted the actual records, which found the policewomen were similar or equal to their male colleagues in terms of successful arrests and convictions, safety and driving records, and injuries sustained. And the problem most women cops complained about was not the hostility of the job but the hostility of their male colleagues. Meanwhile, in September 1974, headlines were made when a policewoman was shot and killed in the line of duty, the first such incident since the FBI began keeping records in 1960. But sexist rumors persisted, such as the circulating story of a woman cop who wouldn't get out of the car in the pouring rain to direct traffic around a blazing building because she'd just come from the hairdresser.[5]

By the mid-1970s, American television was in the midst of a law-and-order revival, prompted by the unsettling endings of both the Vietnam War and the Nixon presidency. In the late 1960s, there had been few police dramas on television. For that matter, the darkest and most scandalous televised police drama had been the live coverage of the Democratic National Convention in Chicago in 1968. Police violence against the protesters was part of the televised spectacle, and shocked audiences heard anchorman Dan Rather crying out in protest that the "thugs" were out of control. Throughout the later years of the Vietnam War, cops didn't fare well in public opinion. Most often they were caught by news cameras as the helmeted riot forces pitted against unarmed college kids and hymn-singing protesters.

But sympathy for the police is never entirely absent, and even during the days of the most turbulent antiwar and civil-rights demonstrations, NBC held onto the documentary-style police drama *Adam-12* (1968–75) as one of its most successful series. By 1974, a law-and-order revival had clearly occurred, and sympathetic cops infused the networks. *The Rookies* (1972–76), *The Streets of San Francisco* (1972–77), *Kojak* (1973–78), *Columbo* (1971–77), and *Police Story* (1973–77) were later joined by *S.W.A.T.* (1975–76), *Baretta* (1975–78), *Starsky and Hutch* (1975–79), and *CHiPS* (1977–83). The heroes of these series were tough guys, but they were also decent, fair, vulnerable human beings, obviously at odds with the counterculture's fascist-pig stereotypes of the previous era.

So when ABC and NBC launched shows about women cops in the fall of 1974, they were responding to these conflicting trends of conservative backlash (love your police authorities!) and liberal, even threatening change (women are now police authorities!). NBC's police drama *Amy Prentiss* lasted less than one season as part of the rotating stories on the *NBC Sunday Mystery Movie*, which more successfully launched *Columbo*, *McCloud*, and *McMillan and Wife*. The premise behind *Amy Prentiss* was that the police-detective chief of San Francisco dies unexpectedly, leaving the lovely widow Prentiss as next in line for the job. In the early 1990s, the PBS miniseries *Prime Suspect* would use a similar scenario of the lone woman in charge of a male squad, but for 1974, this may have been too bizarre. *Get Christie Love* with its black undercover cop also lasted only one season (1974–75), but *Police Woman* (1974–78) survived and thrived, offering a long-legged team-player in pinup-style, a way to allay the fears of having the woman in the job of the man.

Christie Love was the riskiest and most interesting character of these three, a hip, black L.A. undercover cop with advanced karate skills and a tough jive mouth: "You're under arrest, sugah!" Christie was actually modeled on a veteran black New York police detective, Olga Ford, who had been on the job long before the 1970s federal mandates about minorities in law enforcement. Ford served as an advisor for the series' premier episode, but the overall result was less gritty realism than comic-book Zap! Pow! and Whap! In that episode, Christie takes on six macho gang members, dispatching them easily with her bare hands and without streaking her mascara.

For her 1974 audience, Christie Love's physical prowess and African-American beauty would have been immediately recognizable as a version of Pam Grier, knockout star of the 1970s black action flicks I describe in chapter 5. Like the Pam Grier heroines, Christie Love was bad-ass and brash. Everyone was out to "get" this cop, not only the bad guys but also her police-force superiors, frustrated by her independent style and mouthiness. Christie, who wore unusually brief miniskirts as her undercover disguise, was played by Teresa Graves, the bikini-wearing comedian from *Laugh-In*, and in one of the final episodes of her police series, her costars from *Laugh-In* showed up in cameo appearances as witnesses, fellow officers, and perps.

Fig. 6 Teresa Graves as the undercover cop heroine of *Get Christie Love* (ABC, 1974–75). Courtesy of Photofest.

The series was not renewed, but as a jive-talking woman cop who was *not* a team player, Christie Love probably wouldn't have lasted long on a real police force, either. Yet in comparison to the similarly low-rated *Amy Prentiss*, *Christie*'s failure is more interesting. First, with so few black women on prime time in 1974, her very appearance, no matter how sexualized and one-dimensional, was remarkable. The show's executive producer, Paul Mason, had some high expectations or at least some idealistic marketing ideas: "I want to show a moral effect," he said in an interview about this character, "not only from the woman's point of view, but from the black point of view. How great it will be for young black women to see one of their sisters up there in Christie's position."[6] Neither the writing nor the production values for the show ever lived up to this ideal. Christie's character didn't develop beyond being cool and street-smart, and the poorly photographed chase scenes were nearly identical in every episode.

Yet the stereotype of the ultra-sexy woman cop was played out more successfully in its white, NBC version that year, *Police Woman*, starring Angie Dickinson. Dickinson portrayed Sergeant Pepper Anderson, who was, like Christie, an L.A. cop usually in undercover situations requiring cleavage, miniskirts, and stiletto heels. Pepper was far more feminine and vulnerable than Christie. In the premier episode, after she witnesses the death of a young male colleague ("And married with kids!") she goes back to her desk and weeps. Later, she uses her womanly touch to turn the case, getting a rape victim to confide in her and befriending some children who give her a Big, Important Clue. If Christie was familiar from Pam Grier scenarios, Pepper was familiar from more mainstream fantasies, from *Playboy* to the nurturing "angel of the house."

Critics panned both shows for bad writing, weak characters, and exploitation of the woman cop "gimmick." Many pointed out that the "liberated" premise of these series was contradicted by plots in which the women repeatedly have to be rescued by their male colleagues. "The girls [*sic*] are simply not credited with, say, Columbo's powers of ratiocination or Kojak's ability to get off a cynical wisecrack," *Time's* Richard Schickel complained. *Variety* placed its bets on Christie Love, though, as the character that was more fun than Barbie-doll Pepper, and concluded that with its hackneyed scripts, *Police Woman* was bound to "die of boredom."[7]

Instead, *Christie Love* was the one that faded away quickly, leaving behind only the echo of her trademark "You're under arrest, sugar," for pop culture trivia. (The phrase showed up in the movie *Reservoir Dogs* in 1992.) But *Police Woman* ranked among NBC's highest rated programs for the 1974–75 season and continued with respectable ratings for another three years, with Angie Dickinson regularly hailed as the "hottest ticket" on television. A good pal of Johnny Carson, Dickinson was a regular guest on the *Tonight Show* during those years, so her presence in pop culture extended well beyond the fictional police precinct.

The racial difference between Christie and Pepper was surely significant in the overall impact of each show. Since the female cop in the 1970s was *per se* a potentially threatening character, a sign of social and gender change, glamorization of this character would go only so far. Christie was sexually alluring, but she was also smart-mouthed, disrespectful of rules, and African-American, proudly flaunting her 'fro. She triumphantly summarized two 1960s liberation movements—women's and blacks'—as the powerful heroine who talks back. For

Fig. 7 Angie Dickinson as Sergeant Pepper Anderson in *Police Woman* (NBC, 1974–78). Courtesy of Photofest.

Pam Grier, this combination worked for films targeting an African-American market, but the formula didn't work for the white-dominated Nielsen audiences. Even the humor of *Get Christie Love* had to work against a triple threat: the *woman* doing the man's job, the *black* woman doing the man's job, the *smart-mouthed* black woman doing the man's job. In reviews of this series, the word that shows up constantly in describing Christie is "sassy," and this confrontational style for a black female character may have been the series' doom.

For *Police Woman*, the racial factor worked the opposite way. Angie Dickinson was one of the *blondest* women on television, a factor emphasized by the show's racially mixed cast. Unlike Christie, Pepper was an earnest team player, appropriately "womanly"—that is, nonconfrontational and polite, with a low, husky voice that said sex, not sass. In the premier episode, when Pepper shot her first perp, she handled it bravely but emotionally. Her colleagues reassured her that it's part of she job, and she nodded and sniffed, "Someday, sometime, I'll be able to accept that." Coincidentally or not, that first dead perp was a shotgun-wielding black woman, a representative of Pepper's prime-time competition.

Throughout the series, Pepper functioned in traditionally feminine ways, making comforting bedside visits to victims, listening sympathetically to sad stories, and acting as a gracious hostess for visitors to her brightly furnished apartment. These traditional values aren't exclusively white and middle-class, but when personified by a leggy blonde, they add up to Nice White Girl, a universe away from Christie Love's karate chops and jive. Even the character name "Pepper" suggested either a four-legged or *Penthouse* pet, neither of them very dangerous. Dickinson often claimed in interviews that she had made up the name herself because she "couldn't imagine a woman police officer named Lisa" (Cameron, 105). That's a clue that neither a real-life character nor real-life occupation was at stake.

Picturing the female cop as Angie Dickinson was a mainstream fantasy of gender change in the workplace making no change at all. As one PR piece put it, Dickinson was "a soft, sexy dish with a dash of Pepper," or "an all-American sex symbol. A grown-up glamour girl." The key words here—*soft, all-American, glamour*—could take the sting out of "female cop." In interviews, Dickinson further allayed fears about the show's concept. "Pepper does her job, but don't forget that a man is her boss," she told a reporter in 1975. "The idea is to work with a man, but not threaten him. Everything's okay as long as you don't get in the way of his virility."[8]

Actually, as Dickinson rose to stardom through this show, her talk-show interviews revealed a personality and sense of humor much sharper than this fluffy quotation would suggest. If anything, the dreadful scripts and clichés of *Police Woman* were saved by the Dickinson persona, warm and mature. The most progressive aspect of Pepper was in fact her age. Angie Dickinson was forty-three years old when *Police Woman* went on the air, with a movie career that had taken off in 1959 when she was discovered by director Howard Hawks for a small role in *Rio Bravo*. A 1976 feature article compared her to another Hawks discovery, "Lauren Bacall . . . very feminine but very much a man's woman, easy to kid around with, pal around with—and as good as a man with a gun or a deck of cards."[9] She was also an older woman with a past, which supposedly included liaisons with President John Kennedy, a rumor she heatedly denied but which undeniably heated up her star appeal.

Glamorizing the woman investigator and making her racially and culturally innocuous are fairly standard ways to picture this character. The most disturbing aspect of *Police Woman*, though, was its portrayal of the women surrounding Pepper Anderson, who were often sadistically treated victims or cold-hearted perps, like the woman Pepper blows away in the premier episode. That particular female villain was also shaded with lesbianism, since we see her sharing a motel room with a scantily dressed woman colleague from the evil bank-robbery gang. And just to layer the villainy of both these women, we find out later they were unblinking witnesses to a woman's rape by their male bank-robber buddies.

Rape victims abounded in this series. Pepper herself was constantly threatened with rape while teetering in the high heels that her undercover work required, but she was rescued each time by her male colleagues. Other women weren't as lucky. These minor characters were usually also attractive women, and creepy insinuations were made that they "were asking for it." Writing about this series, cultural critic Susan J. Douglas makes the point that at the very moment feminists were addressing issues of rape in the legal system, *Police Woman* "reinforced every negative stereotype about rape that perpetuated the system," including the portrayal of women "as being both responsible for male rage and violence and unable to escape from it."[10]

In a case of terrible poetic justice, this was exactly the fate of the character with whom Angie Dickinson was most famously identified after *Police Woman* ended: the chic victim in *Dressed to Kill*. In that film, the character is sexually humiliated when she picks up and sleeps with a stranger who has a venereal disease. Then she's stabbed to death by a tall blonde woman who is really Michael Caine in drag. *Dressed to Kill* was widely decried as a movie in which women's images and fashions were reviled and punished, providing a fitting coda for Dickinson's previous role in a supposedly liberated show that in reality punished women.

In 1995, at a Museum of Television and Radio event honoring the female-cop show *Under Suspicion*, clips from *Police Woman* were screened as funny reminders of the bad old days when a woman cop on television had to wear bikinis and serve coffee to the guys on the squad. The message of the screening was: well, we certainly won't go back *there*. Yet just a few years later, plans were being made in Hollywood to return to the 1970s for a campy but happier replay of investigators in bikinis. This of course was the 2000 movie version of *Charlie's Angels*, a series that ran from 1976 to 1981, overlapping with the last years of *Police Woman* and similarly providing a fantasy of women solving crimes and running very fast in high heels.

A generation after these series were aired, why is *Police Woman* a bad joke and *Charlie's Angels* a hip, campy one? For starters, the Angels never attempted the cardboard equality-in-law-enforcement pretense of the Dickinson vehicle. Because Pepper operated within the L.A.P.D., the show's supposed agenda was a look behind the scenes at the newly sex-integrated urban police force. *Angels* cheerfully dumped any affectation of realism and actual law-enforcement background. Each show's credit sequence reminded us that three gorgeous women were "rescued" from humdrum rookie police work and now worked for Charlie, a very private investigator thoroughly removed from accountability to taxpayers. Each episode took the heroines to an exotic locale—a race track, casino, dude ranch, beach, island, or ski resort—with maximum opportunities for wardrobe changes and cleavage.

If anything, the cleavage factor had escalated since the debut of *Police Woman* because prime-time television had developed the "jiggle

Fig. 8 Jaclyn Smith, Farrah Fawcett Majors, and Kate Jackson in the "Angels in Chains" episode of *Charlie's Angels* (ABC, 1976–81). Courtesy of Photofest.

genre"—ironically, in response to complaints about the excessive violence of 1970s police shows. By the end of the decade, network executives were eagerly reviewing what they called "T&A" scripts for shows
that substituted abundant female bodies for bullet-ridden ones.[11] This
was the era of Loni Anderson on *WKRP in Cincinnati* (1978–82) and
Suzanne Somers on *Three's Company* (1977–84) as well as less successful shows about sexy stewardesses (*Flying High*, 1978–79), sexy journalists (*The American Girls*, 1978), and a sexy lawyer (*The Feather and
Father Gang*, 1976–77). Aaron Spelling, who had previously bet on an
action-heroine in *Honey West*, returned to the female action formula
within the new jiggle milieu. His story idea, *Alley Cats*, was eventually
fine-tuned, given a less aggressive title, and added a twist to the en-
semble detective story (*77 Sunset Strip*) by having the trio of female
troubleshooters work *together* in each episode.

All three of the original *Charlie's Angels* cast—Kate Jackson, Jaclyn
Smith, and Farrah Fawcett—became overnight stars, and Fawcett immediately become an icon responsible for oversized hair in certain
subcultures for decades. The formula was tongue-in-cheek diversity:
the smart one! the strong one! the one with the big hair![12] The story
formula was predictable, too. In every show, the invisible but omni-
scient Charlie phones or tapes the problem to his "girls"; the Angels
dress up, get into danger, get wet if possible, and then use their combined wits and talent (flying a plane! race car driving! swimming!) to
break loose and capture the villains. Even the series' staunchest fans
admit that after the first season, the *Charlie's Angels* formula of undercover exoticism got stale and the dialogue and plotting got worse. Bad
plots, one-dimensional characters, artificial settings—none of it mat-
tered. For four years, the show was one of the highest-rated on television, faltering only in its final season.

The flimsiness of plots and costumes looked like scathing backlash
to "women's lib," as it was still called then. Even critics who weren't
feminists objected to the show's unabashed sensationalism. Yet women
formed a majority of the audiences that kept the ratings high.[13] Journalists guessed that the appeal for women was fashion and hairstyles,
but later critics pointed out that Aaron Spelling had hit on a brilliant
combination of feminism and antifeminism. On the one hand, the
show delivered a conservative picture of men in charge and women
obeying orders. Like God, Walter Cronkite, and powerful daddies
everywhere, Charlie was the male voiceover and ultimate authority.
The producers themselves had counted on this, as earnestly phrased by
an executive producer explaining how the show preserved traditional
values: "A series like *Charlie's Angels* performs a very important and

valuable public service. Not only does it show women how to look beautiful and lead very exciting lives, but they still take their orders from a man."[14]

On the other hand, the Angels worked without Charlie's direct help and without competing for his approval. They *looked* like traditional sex goddesses or heavenly creatures, but their jobs and scripts were anything but traditional. Not only were they the agents of adventure, but their stories would not end in romance. Even more radical for the 1970s was their teamwork. As Susan J. Douglas explains, "It was watching this—women working together to solve a problem and capture, and sometimes kill, really awful, sadistic men, while having great hairdos and clothes—that engaged our desire" (215).

Never before had television (or cinema for that matter) featured an equivalent of the male buddy formula, which was flourishing at the time in most of TV's police dramas—*Starsky and Hutch, Hawaii Five-O, Police Story*, and so forth. During the first season of *Charlie's Angels*, one of the producers was Barney Rosenzweig, who didn't last long with *Angels* but who later went on to produce *Cagney & Lacey*. Rosenzweig had heard about and later actually read the now-classic feminist film study Molly Haskell's 1974 book *From Reverence to Rape: The Treatment of Women in the Movies*. The women who handed him that book, self-described feminists Barbara Avedon and Barbara Corday, later became the writers of *Cagney & Lacey*.[15]

But in the 1970s, what intrigued all three of them was Haskell's claim that a cinematic "female buddy" tradition simply did not exist. Rosenzweig's plans for a film never materialized, and in fact, the female buddy adventure film didn't emerge until the likes of *Desperately Seeking Susan* (1985) and *Outrageous Fortune* (1987) in the next decade, as I describe in chapter 6. Significantly, the formula worked on television—the glamorous version with *Charlie's Angels*, the dramatic version with *Cagney & Lacey*—before it appeared at the movies, a good example of how the looser structures of television allow more flexibility for women characters.

Haskell's main point about the male buddy film was that, by the 1970s, it had replaced the "woman's film" and was a bad sign that women's concerns and presence were truly being displaced in Hollywood by male couples à la Newman and Redford. But in explaining why women audiences enjoyed the Newman-Redford plotlines, Haskell also put her finger on the future uses of the buddy story for women. In the Newman-Redford films, she points out, what's most appealing is their rapport and loyalty, "eroticism sublimated in action and banter . . . the willingness to die for someone," all of which were traditionally present in women's melodramas.[16] This emotional formula later worked successfully in *Cagney & Lacey*, and most notoriously in *Thelma & Louise* (1991).

As for that "eroticism sublimated in action and banter"—part of the later controversy of both *Cagney & Lacey* and *Thelma & Louise* was that they could be read with lesbian undertones, to the horror of some audiences and the joy of others. And by the time *Charlie's Angels* appeared as a movie in 2000, the prevalence of "lesbian chic" in 1990s pop culture and the heightened campiness of the movie itself had made such a reading not only probable but fashionable, even with flashy signs of heterosexuality all through the script and *mise-en-scène*. The *Saturday Night Live* spoof of the movie pictured the three leads in ecstatic erotic play with each other on a talk show, paying scant attention to the shocked and besotted male talk-show host.

In the original *Charlie's Angels* series, the lesbian possibilities occasionally surfaced as part of the general soft-porn scenario, most notably in the famous "Angels in Chains" episode from the first season, in which the Angels are undercover at a women's prison run by sadistic Maxine, who insists that the imprisoned Angels strip to be disinfected, a shot the camera cues us to imagine. At other times, the Angels' female adversaries emerge as lesbian stereotypes—butch or high-heeled killers—in ways that reassured us of the Angels' absolute difference from such nasty women. That didn't stop a lesbian cult following for Kate Jackson in particular, who played the "smart" Angel, attractive but not as dazzling as Jaclyn Smith and without the sex-goddess appeal of Fawcett and Fawcett's blonde replacement, Cheryl Ladd.

In a 2003 TV Land retrospective, "Inside TV Land: Charlie's Angels," the nostalgic praise for the series included Camille Paglia's nagging remark that "All of the feminist nags in the world are never going to make that particular show go away." Time travel might take us back to 1970s feminists clucking their disapproval of *Charlie's Angels*, but later feminists have been far more intrigued by this show's early versions of girl power and female buddies—Nancy Drew and her friends grown up and still blissfully unattached at the end of every adventure.

INVESTIGATING COUPLES: THE 1980S

Nineteen eighty-two was surely the Year of the Woman Detective. That was the year Sue Grafton and Sara Paretsky introduced their long-running female P.I. novel series and the year Marcia Muller published a second Sharon McCone mystery, so that the first female detective literary series were under way. And even though television was still

Fig. 9 Stephanie Zimbalist as private investigator Laura Holt in *Remington Steele* (NBC, 1982–87). Courtesy of Photofest.

dominated by male cops and investigators, 1982 saw the debut of both *Cagney & Lacey* (1982–88) and *Remington Steele* (1982–87), featuring strong, bright, nonglamorized women investigators. The tacky T&A trend of the 1970s had ebbed, so these heroines were spared the undercover-bikini assignments of their predecessors. Early readers of Sue Grafton may well have pictured Kinsey Millhone as Stephanie Zimbalist, who played the P.I. on *Remington Steele* with perky confidence and unstyled brown hair.

Also, the woman investigator was emerging as a character *aimed* at women readers and audiences, a character made possible by the women's movement of the previous decade. *Cagney & Lacey* writers Barbara Avedon and Barbara Corday spoke specifically about the show's political origins from the 1970s, claiming the series as "the greatest contribution to feminism in our day" and pointing out that the show's very premise—women as cops and best buddies—was a political statement.

Nevertheless, both 1982 television series had to make compromises about their heroines in order to get slots in prime time. While Grafton, Paretsky, and Muller could imagine detective heroines who were divorced and wary of romance, the visual version of such a character on *Cagney & Lacey* triggered a crisis about her "lack of femininity"—code phrase for the L word. Television's less controversial woman detective was the single-but-romantically-attached heroine of *Remington Steele*, a series that depended on the lighter touch of screwball comedy to guarantee the female investigator's femininity and heterosexuality. The screwball-investigation story was so popular that the formula was repeated three years later even more successfully on *Moonlighting* (1985–89).

For the "problem" of the woman detective, screwball is perfect for whipping sexual tensions into a light froth. A slapstick version of romantic comedy, screwball has hosted unruly women and board-game versions of the battle of the sexes since the 1930s. In screwball, the fiesty woman demands equality, kicks up a fuss, but ends in the arms of the guy who's all the better for having duked it out with her. So this comedy tradition permits the "madcap" (that is, unruly) heroine to rebel, but also requires her to settle down and usually to marry.[17] Screwball has its roots in Shakespearean romance, but its movie tradition began with Claudette Colbert and Clark Gable as bickering road companions in *It Happened One Night* (1934). The Colbert character is both batty and bratty, but as Gable yells when he admits he loves her, "I'm pretty screwy myself!"

Mutual craziness is part of the formula. Ditto the fierce independence of both parties, at odds with their abashed dependence on each other. So while screwballs often follow the courtship pattern of *It Happened One Night*, they also encompass the divorcing couple who reunite (*His Girl Friday*, 1940) and the married couple who fight to maintain the balance (*Adam's Rib*, 1949). The couples of the latter formula include sleuthing Nick and Nora Charles of *The Thin Man*, a series of films with William Powell and Myrna Loy from the 1930s–40s. Based on Dashiell Hammett's novel of the same name, the original film and its sequels featured the classy duo always in or at the brink of Happy Hour, their deductive capacities improving with each round of martinis. Nick has retired from the detective business following his wife's substantial inheritance. This ploy allows him to play charmingly but independently at investigations and allows Nora to dress in a succession of scrumptious evening gowns, each one, in her words, "a lulu."

The elegant Nora makes her entrance in the first movie when she trips over her dog and falls headfirst into a tray of drinks at a bar. Physical comedy is part of the screwball formula: pratfalls and torn clothes (*Bringing Up Baby*, 1938), staircase tumbles and scrambles into upper berths (*The Palm Beach Story*, 1942), disguises and wild car rides (*The Awful Truth*, 1937). Because of American movie censorship codes that were enforced until the 1960s, these physical antics replaced sex, which could only happen off screen, after the closing credits. But the more sustained sexual energy went into the couple's arguments and verbal banter. Above all, this was a formula in which women *talked back*: Katherine Hepburn scolding Spencer Tracy, Irene Dunne and Rosalind Russell quarreling with Cary Grant, Barbara Stanwyck arguing circles around Henry Fonda. Faced with Nick/William Powell's outrageous egotism, Nora/Myrna Loy coolly held her own and put him in his place. As Maria DiBattista lovingly describes them, these were the classic fast-talking dames, who insisted on a relationship based on equality and respect.[18] Molly Haskell was right to be nervous about the disappearance of these fun, bickering couples by the 1970s, although they returned to late 1980s cinema in a new wave of romantic comedy embodied by the American-beauties-next-door Meg Ryan and Julie Roberts.

But screwball had never left television, which featured wacky couples in sitcoms such as *I Love Lucy* (1951–57), *The Dick Van Dyke Show* (1961–66), and *Bewitched* (1964–72). Prime time had also adopted *The Thin Man* for the television series of the same name, which ran 1957–59, with Peter Lawford and Phyllis Kirk as the dashing Nick and Nora. The show maintained the spirit of the films if not the high-quality dialogue: the Upper East Side cocktail party occasionally crashed by low-life but not truly threatening con men and good-time girls. A dozen years later, Nick and Nora were reincarnated as *McMillan and Wife* (1971–77), with Rock Hudson and Susan St. James. McMillan was the police commissioner whose lovely wife kept stumbling into unsolved crimes, but who also helped McMillan figure them out. A few years after that series ended, the sleuth couple appeared again as millionaires in *Hart to Hart* (1979–84), starring Robert Wagner and Stefanie Powers as an updated Nick and Nora, sexy jet-setters who played at solving crimes. Jennifer Hart was a journalist, so that gave her access to crime scoops, and Stefanie Powers had already proven she could jump hedges and twirl away from bullets as *The Girl from U.N.C.L.E.* Generally, the couple never broke a sweat or ruined their evening clothes as they solved crimes in Monaco, the Cayman Islands, Lucerne—in fact, at many of the exotic crime scenes that used to summon Charlie's Angels.

One of the most intriguing partnerships along this line occurred not in the detective genre, but in the spy series *Scarecrow and Mrs. King* (1983–87), with the former Angel Kate Jackson as Amanda King, a bored Washington, D.C., divorcée who accidentally becomes an accomplice for "Scarecrow" (Bruce Boxleitner), who works for the American "Agency." As the series developed, Amanda King went through Agency training in order to become Scarecrow's official partner—after all, Jackson was the *smart* Angel—even though she also remained suburban mom for the family and neighbors, who had no idea she was a superspy. The dual roles of spy and suburban mom created comedy but also eerily evoked what would later be called the Supermom phenomenon, the fantasy of a woman managing the house, family, career, and in this case, the security of the United States, all the while looking like Kate Jackson.

Amanda King covered all fronts, *appearing* to be the traditional mom while she fought in the Cold War, but at least she had professional status and an equal role in each week's caper, unlike the women of *The Thin Man, McMillan and Wife,* and *Hart to Hart,* series which all cling more conservatively to the gender traditions of the detective story. In all three of the these shows, the wife was the beautiful screwball-style partner, adventurous and argumentative, but also limited to amateur sleuthing, her traditional status doubly guaranteed by her marriage. In the case of Jennifer Hart, she was the partner with slightly more serious credentials, but as a journalist rather than an investigator. And when *McMillan* dropped the wife from the title and the series, the story simply went on without her.[19]

Yet with a little adjustment, this formula of the capering couple was a logical frame for the emerging picture of the prime-time woman investigator. By 1982, the screwball-sleuth formula had already succeeded with *McMillan* and *Hart.* Also, the woman investigator was by then a proven network character, first as a sexy undercover policewoman or Angel, and then as amateur partner in a romantic couple. The Nick-and-Nora style of screwball could professionalize the woman but keep the tone and the character light. When *Remington Steele* adapted this formula, it used the twist of the woman as the serious investigator and the man as the more dubious detective of the two.

The title of *Remington Steele* humorously sums up the gender problem of the woman detective and also the show's witty solution. In the opening credits, Laura Holt explained in voiceover—typically, a device of the hardboiled male P.I.—that she had studied hard to learn the detective trade, but failed because no one would take business to a woman investigator. So she invented "a decidedly masculine superior," making up the name around the brand of her typewriter and her favorite football team. She even drew a sketch of her mythical boss, Remington Steele, for use in marketing. When a man calling himself Remington Steele actually showed up, looking strikingly similar to her illustration, Laura realized she had drawn the sketch from her memory of a handsome man in a police lineup. Remington's real identity was never revealed in the series, though we learn he was originally from Great Britain and had a questionable past as a con man. A baby-faced Pierce Brosnan played the role with the suave elegance he later brought to his embodiment of James Bond.

In this clever reversal of the Adam and Eve story, it's the man who's plucked from the imagination of the woman, and the woman who's then stuck with the results. Especially in the first season, the comedy revolved around Remington's ineptitude as an investigator and Laura's efforts to sustain the cover-up. In the episode "Tempered in Steele" Laura complains that Remington "knows as much about detective work as Bugs Bunny." The reference reminds us that, like Bugs, Remington started as a cartoon character, Laura's sketch that came to life. Because Remington was a quick study and could apply his previous experience in picking locks and dodging bullets, he eventually functioned as an equal partner in each episode's adventure. But the discrepancies continued as part of the comedy and conflict. Remington remained the better-known public face of the detective agency, while Laura was the one who knew how to do the legitimate investigation work, sometimes whispering directions to him about how to conduct an interrogation or sweep for fingerprints.

In its wittiest reversals, the show emphasized that Remington was the "pretty one," the head-turner, while Laura was the brains of the team. Stefanie Zimbalist portrayed Laura as an unpretentious cutie, her long dark hair usually pulled back like a schoolgirl's, her sleuth wardrobe centered on blazers and trousers. But Pierce Brosnan as Remington was stunningly Bond-to-be, usually clad in immaculate designer suits and obviously comfortable in a tuxedo. In "Steele Eligible," Remington was named as one of Los Angeles' top bachelors, a role that required him and his fellow bachelors to parade like beauty queens for a charity event and then submit to the "hot tub competition." In the course of the episode, Remington broke a leg and ended up, helpless, in a wheelchair with his leg in a cast—like Jimmy Stewart in *Rear Window* (1954). This is of course the nightmare exacted by the female dick: if the man and woman switch roles, the man might become feminized, helpless, an object of fun. But screwball comedy easily accommodates this role reversal and even the male embarrassment. In this case, Laura had to put herself in danger because he was the one in the wheelchair. But Remington nailed the bad guy by hurling himself, wheelchair and all, down the stairs, breaking the other leg in the process. The point is that the couple learns to cooperate under adverse circumstances, a lesson as old as *It Happened One Night*.

The role reversal was also handled through sophisticated comedy about role playing, acting, and fiction. As a "fictional" character within the fiction, Remington loved and talked about old detective movies. In his bachelor apartment, movie posters decorated the walls and a TV in the background often showed a scene from a *Thin Man* movie. We learn that when he met Laura, he was carrying five passports, all of them using various names of characters played by Humphrey Bogart. Remington was also well versed in the great literary detectives, frequently pointing out how Laura's cases resembled something from Agatha Christie or Sherlock Holmes. In fact, Remington knew more about movie and literary investigations than the "real" ones he was supposedly working on. But the "real" ones, too, are obviously fictional as well. So the *Rear Window* tribute of "Steele Eligible" typified the show's self-consciousness.

With his British accent, mysterious past, and implausible origins in Laura's imagination, Remington was presented as the less believable character of the two. But he was the more interesting one as well, as suggested by the title of the series. Was this a way to temper the focus on the female detective? Or did Laura, as the more "realistic" character, simply gain more credibility in comparison to her fanciful partner?

Actually, even as a more "realistic" character, Laura Holt was also part of this series' tongue-in-cheek play with detective games. One episode featured a mystery club in which members did impersonations of the famous detectives, so people dressed as Sherlock Holmes, Miss Marple, and Philip Marlowe interacted with Laura and Remington, cleverly playing up the latter's equally fictional nature. In the later seasons of the series, the opening credits showed Laura and Remington seating themselves at a theater where they see themselves on screen.

Stylized and nostalgic, the episodes relied on classic detective methods—fingerprints and deduction!—and rarely used violence. Laura and Remington sometimes pulled guns but most often hit people on the head with pipes or candlesticks, as in a game of Clue. Generally, the show was not a "realistic" crime drama in the tradition of mean streets and scary perps, where Laura Holt may have been a more risky character.

Laura Holt was also tempered by her position within the classic screwball courting couple, where women can enjoy both independence and tenuous attachment. She and Remington flirted and sparred, but opportunities for serious romance between them were inevitably interrupted by gunfire or the sounds of breaking glass. So their relationship was never consummated within the series. Instead, a year after the series ended, NBC kindly gave them two movie specials, allowing them to tumble into bed as a way to give their story closure. It's true that as the series progressed, Laura's character became more dependent upon Remington, more traditionally "feminine" in her gestures and behavior with him, prone to cuddling and nuzzling rather than standing on her own. Still (or Steele), Laura Holt proved that the game of the detective genre can be played with a ready-for-prime-time woman investigator who is smart, attractive, heterosexual—and not glamorized.

Laura Holt of *Remington Steele* may have been television's groundbreaking female detective character, but it was the later screwball sleuth series *Moonlighting* that captured cultural attention in the 1980s, out-sizzling *Remington* in several ways when it appeared in 1985. "Sexiest battle of the sexes ever!" exclaimed the reviews. *Moonlighting* didn't resort to bikinis, but it did play the glamour card with its usage of siren Cybill Shepherd and its high-fashion pretext. Investigator Maddie Hayes was a former clothes model who ends up owning a detective agency. She learned the business and became a professional P.I., but she also kept the supermodel wardrobe. This series marked the dramatic comeback of Shepherd, who had dazzled audiences in *The Last Picture Show* (1971), *Daisy Miller* (1974), and *Taxi Driver* (1976), made some bad movies, and gone into exile with a dubious reputation of has-been beauty-queen. Well into her thirties, Shepherd was now a formidable Grace Kelly type who was more or less playing herself, the former cover-girl grown up and wiser. And older. To soften the picture of this female detective, the cinematographer used a glass diffusion disk of the type that had been used for Joan Crawford.[20]

Cast opposite the sophisticated Shepherd persona was newcomer Bruce Willis, who inaugurated the insolent bad-boy role he would play for the next several decades. His character David Addison was plucked from the smirking old-boys school of television detectives, updated with doo-wop wisecracks and challenged with a female partner as smart and confident as himself. It was punk versus the prom queen, with "a

Fig. 10 Cybill Shepherd as former-model and private investigator Maddie Hayes in *Moonlighting* (ABC, 1985–89). Courtesy of Photofest.

sexual chemistry potent enough to curl plexiglass," as *Newsweek* put it. Each week, the ongoing verbal foreplay between these two was an Olympic event, in which Maddie and David were true equals in wit, sexual innuendo, and viciousness. The show's creators (one of whom had been a writer for *Remington Steele*) claimed they got their inspiration by watching hours and hours of classic screwballs such as *His Girl Friday*. The word "madcap" was used generously in news releases, reviews, and interviews, emphasizing the comedy tradition of fast-talking dames and their equally slippery paramours. While most one-hour television scripts run about 60 pages, the *Moonlighting* scripts usually came in between 90 and 100 pages, dense with the couple's quarrelsome, risqué dialogue.[21]

Moonlighting pushed its imaginative boundaries further than most television series of the time, with outlandish dream sequences, costume dramas, musical numbers, and self-referential patter. While *Remington Steele* played with the detective genre and the fictional nature of its mysterious hero, *Moonlighting* played with the medium of television itself. Its characters sometimes addressed the audience or chatted with each other about their Nielsen ratings and network time slots. The story concepts were often experimental, fancifully wandering far outside the narrative time and space of the Blue Moon Detective Agency in Los Angeles. The famous "Atomic Shakespeare" episode took place in Elizabethan England, and the "Womb with a View" episode took place in Maddie's uterus. This was postmodern television at its best and worst, sometimes too cute but often courageously original. Maddie and David occasionally appeared in the series as characters from other fictions, not only Kate and Petruchio from *Taming of the Shrew*, but Alice and Ralph from *The Honeymooners*, and split-screen lovers à la *Pillow Talk* (1959).

The issue of the heroine as a female investigator was buried beneath these other innovations and experiments. Usually, the episode's mystery and the Blue Moon Detective Agency were merely a backdrop for the romance and sexual battles between Maddie and David. "It's a placebo detective show," one of the writers said. "It tastes and smells like one, but it isn't. It's really a romantic comedy."[22] In the best episodes, the two plotlines converged, as in "To Heiress Human" from the 1987 season. Confronting a homicide case in which two lovers each took the blame for the other, the Blue Moon P.I.s confronted their own illusions and assumptions about love and romance. The episode took several clever twists not only through the murder, but through Maddie and David's relationship. "And people say we don't have good plots," David ruminated at the end.

Yet the larger investigation of the entire series was about equality and the question of how willful, fiercely individual men and women can work out a relationship—the old screwball tension, now in more sexually and politically explicit terms. David tried to get Maddie into bed for the show's first two seasons, and her resistance symbolized not virtue but hard-earned lessons from 1970s feminism: independence, self-protection, integrity. The word *feminism* was never used, but Maddie's coolness and lack of humor were shorthand for the dour feminist. David Addison, meanwhile, was the chauvinist American male who, by the mid-1980s, was enjoying a cocky backlash revival on prime-time television through characters like Sam Malone on *Cheers* (1982–93) and Sonny Crockett on *Miami Vice* (1984–89). In one *Moonlighting* episode, Ray Charles and a backup singing group appeared in David's living room on behalf of "all men who don't have to put the toilet seat down."

Screwball always involves a clash of ideologies, and here we see how the female investigator character is part of the larger issue of sexual politics. Maddie's character history of fashion model turned detective was a sly allegory of the impact of feminism: the woman *known* for what she looks like becomes the woman who *knows*. So even though the detective work was underplayed in the series, Maddie had gone from a traditional female position—the beautiful, silent object of the camera—to the traditional male position of knower and investigator. And she shared that space with the unreconstructed hardboiled dick—not the fantasy British gentleman from *Remington Steele*, but a swaggering punk who claims *he's* the one who knows *her*. The mystery plots were never as interesting as this more basic mystery, the 1980s version of Freud's puzzling question: what exactly does Maddie want? Is she deluding herself about loving or not loving David? How well does she really know him? Or know herself? Or does she know too well what all smart women know about the perils of relationships with macho men?

What David Addison claimed to know, of course, was the shameless cliché that the uppity woman just needs a good roll in the moonlight. But once that happened, at the end of the second season, the characters' problems grew far worse. Over the next three seasons, the romance spiraled into a number of break-ups and reunions that included a pregnancy and miscarriage (thus the "Womb" episode) and relationships with other people. Once the romance faltered, so did the ratings. In the series' final episode, a producer from ABC shows up to say the audience wants romance, not laughs, and to announce the show has been canceled. The mystery of that last episode is never solved, and neither is the ongoing human mystery about how strong men and women love each other and live together as equals.

Moonlighting's debut in 1985, during the popular run of *Remington Steele* and *Scarecrow and Mrs. King*, can be seen as television's attempt to handle questions of female professionalism and equality through romantic comedy. However, by 1985, questions of sex, gender, and the female investigator were being contested more seriously through that other female investigation drama, *Cagney & Lacey*, which had already survived two network cancellations and had made triumphant comebacks on the shoulders of overwhelming fan support. The rocky history of *Cagney & Lacey* had included the eviction of one star who had been stereotyped as "too lesbian," and an infamous *TV Guide* article quoting a network producer who had dismissed the characters as "too harshly women's lib," claiming the network "perceived them as dykes."[23] As a couple, Christine Cagney and Mary Beth Lacey evoked the very anxiety that screwball quells—the question of loyalty to men.

Fig. 11 Tyne Daly and Meg Foster as Mary Beth Lacey and Christine Cagney in the first season of *Cagney & Lacey* (CBS, 1982–88). Courtesy of Photofest.

These widely divergent pictures of women investigators claimed equally widespread attention in 1985. That year, both shows received splashy cover stories in *People* magazine: "*Moonlighting*'s Cybill Shepherd, TV's Sexiest Spitfire" and "*Cagney & Lacey*: TV's Best Actresses Turn Pop Culture into Painful Human Drama."[24] In one sense, Maddie Hayes in her silk pastel suits and Cagney and Lacey in the precinct locker room were in parallel universes, or at least parallel genres, screwball versus police drama, respectively. And it's true that in both series the crime investigation of each episode was often less urgent than the ongoing investigation of personal relationships. *Cagney & Lacey*'s most acclaimed episodes were the ones dealing with the "painful human drama" of Mary Beth Lacey's breast cancer. Often, the two plots of police drama and melodrama converged. In one episode they handled a series of burglaries occurring in the offices of sex and marriage therapists, for instance, at the same time Cagney was handling a question of equality and intimacy with her new lover. But as this episode plot suggests, both *Moonlighting* and *Cagney & Lacey* used the female investigator to anchor questions about gender, though in different idioms and tones.

Feminist concerns were coded in *Moonlighting* as "the battle of the sexes," or the portrayal of Maddie as the strong, independent woman, or the portrayal of David as a chauvinist, all in snappy screwball style. But *Cagney & Lacey* foregrounded women's issues in no uncertain terms: abortion, the rights of rape victims, battered spouses, sexual harassment. Political discussions abounded. The 1982 episode "Better Than Equal" focused on an antifeminist activist, a Phyllis Schafly type, who had been receiving death threats and needed police protection. The would-be victim was appalled that two women were assigned to protect her, and back at the precinct, the guys were intrigued by the antifeminist's crusade, challenging Cagney and Lacey to explain "this Gloria Steinem stuff."

One of the most controversial episodes was the 1985 show about the bombing of a clinic, which included Cagney and Lacey's locker-room debate on the topic of abortion. This episode triggered a far wider offscreen debate involving a protest by the National Right to Life Committee and support by Planned Parenthood. The network finally agreed to present a balanced view on the topic, by showing Cagney as a Catholic who was inclined to condemn abortion but who supported the ability of other women to choose for themselves. In that episode, Christine's father, the ex-cop, was the one who was most adamantly anti-abortion. And the maternal Lacey admitted she herself had an abortion in Puerto Rico when she was young, before Roe v. Wade.

In addition to these political topics, the police-drama format of *Cagney & Lacey* also included the serious crimes and violent cases avoided by the comedy milieu of *Moonlighting* and *Remington Steele*. The 1983 episode "A Cry for Help," about spousal abuse, located the Jekyll-and-Hyde wife beater as one of Cagney and Lacey's colleagues in the precinct, a guy who claimed it was private "family business." The women cops got the battered wife to a shelter and forced their colleague to turn himself in. Even in the "personal" episodes, the show never dismissed the seriousness and danger of these women's police work, so in the episode about Lacey's breast cancer surgery, Lacey got into a shootout with a drug dealer the night before she went to the hospital.

In her elegant and meticulous study of this series, Julie D'Acci points out how the episodes were usually constructed around two concurring stories, one of them the "straight cop story," plus a subplot and "runners," additional ongoing mini-narratives.[25] The "straight cop story" usually entailed a significant gender twist. Investigating a crooked judge, Cagney and Lacey discovered a deeply rooted old-boys network. In another episode, when a court overturned a rape conviction and ordered a retrial, they got themselves involved with the victim, who was horrified about taking the stand one more time. It's not simply that this show rigged crime plots to highlight gender. What *Cagney & Lacey* made clear is that *every* type of criminal case involves a gender issue because it involves women and men, through traditional crime dramas usually gloss over the impact of gender rather than calling attention to it.

This series was also a "women's" show in its emphasis on the committed friendship between Cagney and Lacey. They watched each other's backs not just on the job, but in their constant attention to the details of each other's lives—Mary Beth's children, pregnancy, cancer, and move to the suburbs; Christine's promotion, romances, and alcoholism. The buddy formula of *Charlie's Angels* had scripted women to work together as a team, but as one-dimensional characters within a stylized world of gorgeous people and places. *Cagney & Lacey* scripted the two women to develop as friends and complicated individuals, all within the milieu of Midtown's 14th Precinct, often not a pretty sight.

Serious politics, serious female friendship, and women as professional investigators—all three networks originally turned it down. Rosenzweig shopped a script by Corday and Avedon for five years, attempting to get it produced in any form—film, television movie, television series. At one point, he was told it would be viable if Ann-Margret and Raquel Welch took the parts of buddy cops who wore their badges on their bras.[26] In 1981 CBS relented and agreed to a do a pilot movie, which got a strong enough audience response to launch the series the following year.

The pilot starred Tyne Daly as Mary Beth Lacey, and Daly remained in this role throughout the series' history. Mary Beth was the working-class mother of two boys, married to an occasionally unemployed construction worker. When the thirty-eight-year-old Daly got pregnant in 1985, the pregnancy became part of the script, reinforcing the generous, earth mother dimension of Mary Beth Lacey as she nurtured her baby girl in the last years of the series. Characterized as a fierce proponent of marriage and family, Lacey was nevertheless in a nontraditional arrangement, since her husband took care of most household

Fig. 12 Tyne Daly with Sharon Gless, Meg Foster's replacement as Christine Cagney, in *Cagney & Lacey* (CBS, 1982–88). Courtesy of Photofest.

tasks. In their bedroom scenes, Mary Beth was often portrayed as the sexual aggressor, and she was likewise aggressive in her police work, quick to tackle a bad guy or engage in a chase. The series emphasized Mary Beth's grounding in her family and in her extraordinarily strong marriage, but her overall stability was revealed to have its limits in the first-season episode "Burnout," in which she suffered a minor break-down and took some time out to recover.

The more volatile character, however, was Christine Cagney, who most resembled the hardboiled male detective. Cagney was the tough, competitive loner, prone to impetuous sexual flings and hard drink-ing. Through the course of the series, she had a number of serious lovers and two marriage proposals, both of which she refused. She also confronted her alcoholism and was confronted with it by Mary Beth—and sobered up, going into AA and remaining in recovery.

Played by *M*A*S*H*'s Loretta Swit in the pilot, Cagney was introduced to the audience as hardboiled chick. The episode opened showing Cagney getting ready for work in the morning, leaving a guy who was obviously a one-night stand. "You were terrific," he says. She replies, with a David Addison smirk, "New York's finest." When he asks about seeing her again, she's noncommittal. Without a doubt, this was the woman cop taking the "man's part," not just with her job, but with her sexual confidence and control. And this was the start of the sex and gender jitters for the show's sponsors and producers.

The problem first surfaced as one of casting. When the series began in 1982, Swit wasn't free to take this role, which went to Meg Foster, an actress similar to Swit in conveying a no-nonsense attractiveness. Foster had played a lesbian real-estate agent in the 1978 film *A Different Story* and was quoted as saying it was her "favorite role." Now Foster was playing a working-class tough-gal role opposite another woman, and the press reviews harped on a "lesbian connection" on the show. Other reviews and interviews with network staff instead used the words *feminine* and *non-feminine* to describe the problem—which is surely the "problem" of the woman investigator. As D'Acci persuasively argues, *Cagney & Lacey* became a test case for what "femininity" might mean for mainstream television, especially since the stakes involved were feminism and lesbianism (D'Acci, 30–35). CBS gave the show a permanent slot only on the conditions that Meg Foster be replaced with someone more "feminine" and that her character become more upscale—the television class/beauty shorthand for "glamour," the female investigator's most bulletproof facade.

Sharon Gless, blonde and more conventionally attractive than Foster, was given the role of a more upper-class Cagney, whose cop father was divorced from a fairly well-to-do Westchester mother. The new girlie Cagney had softer, longer hair and wore makeup and better clothes. Yet even at the height of the show's popularity in 1985 (when both the series and Gless won Emmies), the Cagney character was considered "frightening" by some viewers, according to Gless, precisely because of behavior considered "male"—including her decision not to marry.

The writers wrestled with this problem, at first imagining the death of lovers or other dramatic scenarios that prevent her from saying yes. But eventually they agreed that the more realistic scenario, given Cagney's character, is that she didn't *want* marriage. "She doesn't need to be married," said writer Terry Louise Fisher in a *New York Times* article. "But that is a radical statement to be made in America today." Television audiences had certainly seen shows featuring single women by then—most obviously the hits *That Girl* (1966–71) and *The Mary Tyler Moore Show* (1970–77). But Fisher was referring to a more "radical" attitude about what women are "supposed" to want and do. Also, as the *Times* explained more bluntly, Cagney and Lacey "are unlikely figures in prime time, where most women are young, better looking and single. Cagney is single, but she is in her late 30s, late enough for her unmarried status to be an emotional issue for her, rather than a transitional stage."[27]

Cagney's "radical" singleness provided a sharp contrast to the detective heroines of *Remington Steele* and *Moonlighting*, whose characters are clearly in the "transitional stage" of romantic comedy and defined in relationship to one irresistible, if troubling, man. As the Meg Foster controversy suggested, Cagney's singleness could evoke lesbianism, for no matter how many boyfriends and fiancées she accumulated, her defining relationship was the one with Mary Beth Lacey. It could also evoke the pleasures of female friendship, a bonding that could be threatening to men not because it involves lesbianism, but because within it, men are simply less important. In the end, the series and especially Sharon Gless had a fervent and widespread lesbian following; the network's desperation to produce a more feminine Cagney ironically produced one that could easily be read as lesbian femme.

But the nuances around the Cagney character point to what made *Cagney & Lacey* most distinctive. While the Mary Beth Lacey character could be described as more traditionally "womanly"—married, a mother, pregnant for one entire season—the two characters together continually undercut any notion that there is a singular "female" response or attitude or way to be either a woman or a detective. They frequently differed about how to handle a case, how to think about marriage and children, and how to handle sexism. In one episode, Cagney heard that she and Mary Beth were promoted to detective only because an influential judge, a friend of Cagney's father, had intervened. Cagney was devastated. But the information didn't unsettle Mary Beth at all. She simply didn't believe it, calmly maintaining they were promoted because of their own hard work. The series also emphasized how their class differences influenced their responses. Brought up in an upper-middle-class home, Cagney was the one who could coolly handle upscale suspects and lawyerly types with whom the working-class Lacey was more awkward and gruff.

This portrayal of women's differences cuts to the very heart of the "female dick" as a body—in fact, a deviant body, female but equipped with the male power to probe. The 1970s policewomen and Angels had overcompensated with glamorized, pinup bodies, reinforcing a singular kind of female sexuality. In *Charlie's Angels*, the superficial differences among the three women belied the Barbie-doll mold of all three.

Cagney & Lacey instead suggested how sexual differences exist even within heterosexuality—differences due to marital status, health, and life choices. In the course of the series, Cagney faced date rape, pregnancy scares, and, conversely, the ticking biological clock as she contemplated commitment and marriage. As a married woman, Lacey's sexual issues were different; she struggled to balance attention to her husband and to her job, discussed the consequences of breast cancer in her sex life, and managed a successful late-life pregnancy.

Cagney and Lacey also *acted* like differing individuals within a long-term relationship, supportive and attentive, sometimes quarrelsome. When the Lacey family bought a house in Queens, Mary Beth and Christine temporarily drifted apart as Mary Beth becomes more invested in her family life. But when Mary Beth had breast-cancer surgery, the episode's most emotional moment was Christine's appearance at the hospital bed. In turn, Mary Beth sat up all night with her friend when Christine hit bottom with alcohol, and then went with her to her first AA meeting. Repeatedly in any given episode the two women catch each other's eyes with the concern and visual shorthand system of couples who have been together a long time.[28]

Cagney & Lacey eventually won both critical and audience support; the show itself, Gless, and Daly each won more than one Emmy. In its final seasons, more than 20 million viewers tuned in each week, two-thirds of them women, who obviously took pleasure in this series' female fantasy. Describing *Cagney & Lacey* as female fantasy, I don't mean to undermine its realistic depictions of crime or characters, but rather to describe its pleasures for women viewers, beginning with its casting of women not usually seen on prime time. Mary Beth Lacey may not have been a size 6, but she was surely an idealized figure, the woman who truly has it all—a loving marriage at home and a loving best friend at work. And Christine, no matter how she's interpreted, was a strong, no-longer-young woman on her own—a type that television most often plunks into comedies, not dramas. She was ambitious, she chose not to marry, and she too spent her days with her best friend. Within the precinct headquarters, they devised the women's locker room—"the Jane," as they called it—as their mini-conference room, the private space they'd carved out for themselves in a male world.

The breezy credit sequence summed up the thrill of this female fantasy. In the montage of shots, Christine and Mary Beth raced through subway cars pursuing a perp, ate junk food, window shopped, and hauled a bad guy into jail while dismissively waving away a flasher who opened his trench coat to them.

In the traditional understanding of the male flasher, the flasher reveals the part women supposedly want, but also the part that threatens them. So flashing is male power play, a gesture emphasizing that even exposure means invulnerability for men. But because the female dick raises threatening questions of what exactly is under *her* trench coat, the exposing gesture by a man doesn't carry the same threat. She's taken the part usually played by men and has proven it *is* just a part, a role, not a bodily appendage. Cagney and Lacey are wholly unimpressed by what's under his trench coat because it's *not* power, not invulnerability, not even a sexist statement worth addressing. It's just a dick.

4

UNDER SUSPICION
Women and Mystery in 1990s Television

FEMALE ENIGMAS

You can imagine her as Gillian Anderson, Helen Mirren, or Ally Walker, enfolded in a long tailored trench coat, poised in the darkness and, catlike, able to see what men miss. That's an image from film noir, of course, and the women investigators in the 1990s network TV series all shared noir's melancholy and shadowy paranoia: Jane Tennison in *Prime Suspect* (1991–96), Rose Phillips in *Under Suspicion* (1994–95), Dana Scully of *The X-Files* (1993–2002), and Sam Waters in *Profiler* (1996–2000). These prime-time heroines were tough, successful, and brilliant, but the somber tone of these series was 180 degrees from the sweet female fantasy of *Cagney & Lacey,* despite the fact that three of the four series were created by women. Sadistic violence, serial killers, and dysfunctional bureaucracies—that was the standard turf for 1990s crime stories, and television's new women investigators stoically marched in without a best girlfriend to meet back in the locker room at the end of the day.[1]

For one thing, despite multiple Emmies and critical prestige, *Cagney & Lacey* didn't begin a trend for police series similarly based on female bonding. A glossy, high-fashion version of the female sleuth duo was attempted in 1984 in *Partners in Crime*, starring Loni Anderson and Lynda Carter as ex-wives of a murdered detective. This series lasted just three months, maybe because its return to jiggle was out of sync with trends and audiences. The female-buddy action formula would eventually return to television in the fantasy form of *Xena: Warrior Princess* (1995–2001), and less successfully in a highly glamorized David Kelley version of female detectives, *Snoops* (1999). The more dominant trend was to put two women into larger coed teams of police or forensic investigators, as in *NYPD Blue* (1993–) and *CSI. Cagney & Lacey* creator Barbara Corday predicted this lack of imitation in 1985 when she described typical network response: "The attitude is, 'Hey, look at what they pulled off. They could *never* do it again.' "[2]

However, when Helen Mirren won an Emmy for her role on *Prime Suspect* in 1996, she cited *Cagney & Lacey* in her thank you speech, acknowledging the influence of this series in picturing women in the police. The other television drama that explored the sexual politics of police work was *Under Suspicion*, which was highly praised for its style and characterization but which received low ratings and lasted only one season. *Prime Suspect* and *Under Suspicion* were both created by women who were also writers for the show. Each featured a lonely, besieged female homicide investigator on an all-male police force. Both series emphasized the sexism of law enforcement and the bleakness of the woman detective's personal life. Both shows also relied on the visual style of film noir, suffusing most scenes with shadows and low-key lighting, and offering viewers rainy nights full of blood and crime.

The X-Files and *Profiler*, the other 1990s series featuring a female investigator, were also marked by dark, paranoid shot compositions and stories, but they were far less up-front about sexual politics. These series were instead influenced by the 1991 film adaptation of *The Silence of the Lambs*, adopting the gothic tone and horror-movie style of the Demme film, as well as the backdrop of the FBI. The setting of the FBI reflected recent fascination with a more upscale, prestigious, and corporate law enforcement group. While the real FBI suffers a notorious record regarding women and minorities, its pop-culture image got an upbeat makeover through *The Silence of the Lambs* and *Twin Peaks* (1990–91), both of which imagined the FBI as a place where the loner and even the quirky individualist could thrive. (*The X-Files*'s David Duchovny, after all, played Special Agent Dale Cooper's colleague, the transvestite agent Dennis/Denise, on *Twin Peaks*.)

Both *The X-Files* and *Profiler* drew on the paranormal and unexplained phenomena for themes and plots. *The X-Files* also drew substantially on fantasy and science fiction. All of these genres—sci-fi, horror, fantasy, and the occult—are usually acknowledged as "male" in their audiences, producers, and interests, but these are also the genres where radical gender role reversals are likely to take place. *Profiler* and *The X-Files* could draw outside the lines, imagining relationships and alliances not found in police procedurals and noir mysteries. Not surprisingly, then, as opposed to the solo women in the two police dramas, these FBI heroines had sympathetic male partners who treated them with equality and respect. As a result, sexism was rarely an issue in these series, and gender was explored in more unorthodox ways.

What all four of these series did have in common was the characterization of the female investigator as a mystery. The heroines of the two police series were literally "under suspicion" or "prime suspects" among the macho guys at the office. And the heroines of the two FBI series harbored mysteries within their own bodies: Samantha's psychic vision, and Dana Scully's illnesses, cures, and paranormal pregnancies. While these four characters weren't glamorized, they were given a mystique through plot quirks and anomalies that Columbo or Kojak would not have to endure. Why? Consider the legacy of the mysterious woman, the *femme fatale*, in this type of story. You can take the Bad Girl out of film noir, but you can't take the film noir out of the Girl who takes her place. These 1990s women detectives displaced those stealthy *femmes fatales* but wore a similar shadow and inscrutable aura, and sometimes the same slinky dressing gown.

The combination of dark scenes and dark sexual politics in *Prime Suspect* and *Under Suspicion* created unlikely offerings for prime time. In fact, *Prime Suspect* wasn't produced for American commercial television at all and so was free of commercial constraints for happy endings and attractive characters. Filmed in Great Britain, it was co-produced by Grenada Television and Boston's WGBH. Its creator, Lynda La Plante, was a powerful and well-known force in British television who eventually headed her own production company, so in Great Britain her signature was prominently used in *Prime Suspect*'s advertising and marketing. In the United States, the series was less known as a specifically female production and was instead associated with Helen Mirren's impressive performances. The show was broadcast in the United States on PBS, first as a three-part miniseries on *Mystery!* and later as a series on *Masterpiece Theater*.[3]

Because its first two episodes earned high ratings and rave reviews, CBS was interested in buying the *Prime Suspect* sequels. This deal failed, so CBS instead opted for *Under Suspicion*, which had originally been developed for Fox. Fox executives were nervous about a crime series with a female lead, claiming it wouldn't work for its network's "male demographic." But CBS also made a serious mistake about demographics, assigning *Under Suspicion* to the Friday night spot opposite Fox's *X-Files*, the only other weekly series featuring a woman investigator and a series that had picked up a wide audience by its second season. Reviewers first resisted the highly stylized look of *Under Suspicion*, but gradually came to admire its offbeat storytelling and its unsmiling heroine who didn't look like other prime-time women. But a strong audience base never materialized, and the show was canceled after one season.

Tellingly, until *Snoops* in 1999, American television's 1990s women investigators were part of police or federal agencies rather than private investigators like Maddie Hayes and Laura Holt. For that matter, the woman P.I. in cinema disappeared, too, after *V.I. Warshawski* in 1991; the other woman investigator flicks of the 1990s instead featured cops or FBI agents. This visual picture is sharply different from the literary one, since the 1990s was the boom period for the woman detective in the book industry. As *USA Today* commented in 1994, "Why, in a nation that fills bookshelves with the likes of Sue Grafton's Kinsey Millhone and Patricia Cornwell's Kay Scarpetta, can U.S. TV do no better with its female Sherlocks than aping Miss Marple with Jessica Fletcher?"[4]

Commenting on this trend, critic Sandra Tomc claims that the 1990s team-player female detective, affiliated with the police or FBI, is less threatening and also less politically exciting than her P.I. sister in pulp fiction. Looking at *Prime Suspect* and the film version of *The Silence of the Lambs*, Tomc argues that these stories deliver "the female detective not as a renegade but as an aspiring member of the very institution responsible for her victimization."[5] Tomc includes the 1990s popularity of Patricia Cornwell in this trend, since the Kay Scarpetta character works with local and federal agents and is most often teamed with the hopelessly sexist cop Marino. In fact, Tomc's 1995 comments about Cornwell are borne out by the 2000 Scarpetta novel, *The Last Precinct*, in which, frustrated by the corruption and homophobia of bureaucratic law enforcement, Scarpetta and her niece resign in order to join a "renegade" all-girl investigation unit in Manhattan.

Yet the political punch of the woman detective isn't necessarily tied to her position in the private or public sector. After all, *Snoops* gathered a female team of private investigators but drew them as fashion models. And condemning the cop or fed heroine, just because she's part of the legal establishment, casts too wide a net. Scooped up in that net would be Cagney and Lacey, who were likewise skilled professionals—and in Cagney's case, one with ambitions—within a traditionally sexist institution. Best-selling fiction is likewise inhabited by dozens of tough-minded women police characters: Lillian O'Donnell's Norah Mulcahaney, Leslie Glass's Chinese-American cop April Woo, both of Barbara D'Amato's series characters, Margaret Maron's Sigrid Harald, and Barbara Paul's Marian Larch, to name just a few. Many of the pulp-fiction lesbian detectives are also part of the police in series by Kate Allen, Laurie R. King, Katherine V. Forrest, Claire McNab, and others. The subversive thrill of these series, as in *Cagney & Lacey*, is that "routine" detective work takes on an electric charge with the female presence on the police force, as sex and gender issues become more visible.

In fact, Lynda La Plante was inspired to write *Prime Suspect* when she discovered that in the late 1980s, the London police detective force consisted of five hundred men and four women. One of the latter, Jackie Malton, volunteered to consult for the series.[6] Women audiences reported that the heroine's isolation in a male bureaucracy rang true outside of police work. Helen Mirren said of her *Prime Suspect* character: "All the women I've talked to say, 'I can't believe how accurate this is as a description of what I face in my professional life.'"[7] That's not good news about professional women. In the pilot episode, Jane Tennison was cruelly tested, taunted, and investigated by her subordinate officers when she assumed jurisdiction in a grisly case of serial murders. Newly promoted to Detective Chief Inspector in London, Tennison was also the object of curiosity from her male colleagues. One of them mumbled about her "skinny dyke ass" in this episode, and their interest in her sex life betrayed their suspicion she's a lesbian.

Tennison's specifically female vision often allowed her to see what her other colleagues missed. In the case of the serial murders, she realized that the police had misidentified a woman's body because she noticed expensive clothing labels that showed a lifestyle beyond what the presumed victim could have afforded. Eventually, Tennison's stubbornness, intelligence, and superior detective skills did win over "the lads" in her office, but she was repeatedly undermined and second-guessed by her superior officers. The series never allowed us to forget the grimness of her job, her life, and her choices. We frequently saw her alone in her flat, or cut off from colleagues, or without a friend to celebrate a triumph.

True to the traditions of film noir, *Prime Suspect* often depicted violent sex crimes against women. But the presence of Tennison emphasized the misogyny within the police itself, so this was noir with a daring difference. Television had rarely so shockingly exposed the police as an old-boys club, sexist and self-protective, into which a female presence was poisonous. The pilot episode opened with the scene of a cover-up, a silent decision to suppress evidence that would link a police officer to a murdered prostitute. In that episode, the violence directed against the prostitutes is paralleled with the hatred the cops direct against Jane Tennison.

Also true to noir was the profound ambiguity of Tennison's own motivations. As she succeeded in becoming "one of the lads," she could

Fig. 13 Helen Mirren as Detective Chief Inspector Jane Tennison in *Prime Suspect* (PBS, 1991–96). Courtesy of Photofest.

be as belligerent, driven, and insensitive as them at their nastiest. In one episode, she had a pleasurable one-night stand with a handsome black officer from another district. But when he was then assigned to one of her cases, she panicked and treated him badly, nervous about the repercussions if their sexual history had come to light. Later in the series, when it seemed as though Tennison had found and jailed the wrong man for a series of murders, her obsession to find the truth stemmed as much from egotism as from a sense of justice. And when she cajoled and deceived an old woman with Alzheimer's in order to get evidence for her case, the effect was chilling.

Helen Mirren described her character as "unlikable but sympathetic . . . a normal, sort of messed-up human being . . . who's flawed and selfish and egotistical, and also vulnerable." The vulnerability is specifically sexual, as Mirren pointed out in the same interview. "If a man has a fling with some junior fluff on the staff . . . it's accepted as jolly fun, nudge-nudge-wink-wink, then forgotten. But with a woman it becomes a weapon, a card to be used against her."[8]

As the lone woman among the lads, or the woman whose only female connections were prostitutes and victims, Jane Tennison had a profound sexual presence in every episode, like the *femme fatale* of traditional film noir. But her sexuality wasn't the *source* of her power, as was always the case for the *femme fatale*—think of Barbara Stanwyck in *Double Indemnity* (1944), Rita Hayworth in *Gilda* (1946), Mary Astor in *The Maltese Falcon*. The *femme fatale* used her sexuality to get attention and manipulate both villains and police. Instead, Tennison's sexuality was defined less narrowly. In fact, her embodiment as a woman in her forties was a gutsy move unlikely to be duplicated on commercial television. Unlike the soft-focus lenses that kept Cybill Shepherd in her earlier rather than later thirties on *Moonlighting*, the camera on Mirren was relentless. Throughout the series, she often appeared gaunt, her face hollowed and lined.

Yet the stories insisted on her sexuality, with all its desires and consequences. In "The Scent of Darkness" (1995), for instance, Tennison was involved with a psychotherapist, with whom we saw her relaxing in a bubble bath, but later in the story she turned on him in paranoid fury when she suspected him of meddling in her case. Her problem, he tells her frankly, is that she can't trust anyone at all. At the end, they've been reconciled and are even dressed in evening clothes for a police anniversary party. But when Tennison hears a group of male colleagues share a joke at her expense, she angrily tosses her drink at them, and this is how the episode ends. The "date" has turned into an explosive confrontation, and the possibility of a trusting relationship with any man looks grim.

The fourth *Prime Suspect* episode, "The Lost Child" (1994), began with a startling personal scene. Tennison was in the hospital having an abortion, about which she felt ambivalent. The script didn't explain the circumstances of the pregnancy, just as the series never revealed what happened with the psychotherapist boyfriend. Immediately after the abortion, Tennison was called to investigate the kidnapping case of a toddler, and her passionate pursuit of the crime indicated a personal, even physical identification with the loss. In two consecutive scenes, Tennison was connected by telephone first to her police supervisor, who refused to give her the staff support she needed, and then to the criminal world, personified in a male suspect. The parallels suggested she was equally distanced from both, alienated even within the law. Noir-style shot compositions emphasized her ambiguous positioning. When she returned to the crime scene, the nursery from which the child was kidnapped, her face and figure were entirely shrouded in shadow, so she seemed to embody the darkness of the crime in a space she'd personally disavowed: a child's room.

Yet this episode provided an interesting variation of film noir's sexual dynamics, in which the powerful woman—always the *femme fatale*—is sexually guilty. In "The Lost Child," the plot at first associated Tennison's abortion decision with a criminal act, and then carefully made important distinctions. We learn that the kidnapping was faked by the child's mother, who was overwhelmed with a sickly, all-consuming child and who unintentionally killed the child in trying to stop its crying. Tennison's gentle interrogation of the woman revealed not a stereotypical "unfit mother," but the unfitness of motherhood for certain women. In retrospect, Tennison's choice of an abortion reinforced her own fitness for another, arduous job as investigator in a culture where motherhood is a difficult decision either way. So although Tennison at first doubled for the woman criminal in this episode, criminality itself came into question as the story offered a compassionate rethinking of women's decisions and coercions about motherhood.

The muted conclusion of "The Lost Child" was typical of *Prime Suspect*'s uneasy mood. Once Tennison got the confession from the mother, she was able to end a horrific hostage situation begun by the man who had been the prime suspect of this case, a man now holding his own terrified little girl under a gun. But we didn't see Tennison accomplish this. We only saw that the hostage situation had been resolved, and the little girl was safe with her mother. The final scene began with an unnerving shot of Tennison's empty flat, which she entered sadly. She sat down tiredly as the credits began to roll. The episode ended with emptiness, not triumph, and with neither reward nor support system in sight for the exhausted woman investigator.

The bravery of this kind of move was widely lauded by critics, who likewise praised Mirren's accomplished, unflinching performances. The second and third episodes of *Prime Suspect* won Emmies—thus the interest of CBS in bringing this series to commercial prime time. *Under Suspicion*, the series CBS offered instead, had actually been conceived and its first episode written prior to the appearance of *Prime Suspect* in 1991, but it debuted in 1994 under the pressure of this history and with expectations that it could succeed not only as "television noir," as it was called, but also with a pensive, melancholy police heroine for whom there were no easy solutions.

The creator and executive producer of *Under Suspicion*, Jacqueline Zambrano, had become intrigued by the story of Los Angeles policewoman Kena Kramer, who had served as a "women's coordinator" in the L.A.P.D. to handle gender problems after the Title Seven infusion of women into the force in 1972. As La Plante had done with Jackie Malton, Zambrano hired Kramer as a consultant for the show. Zambrano likewise saw the series as being about more than police work: "Even though I have never been a police officer, I have on many occasions been the only woman on an all-male writing staff," she said in an interview. "And there's a certain universality of that kind of experience."9 So Zambrano was hoping for the professional female audiences who responded to Helen Mirren. In the first episode of *Under Suspicion*, when a colleague asked the heroine what it's like to work in an all-male office, she replied tersely, "The toilet seat is always up."

Detective Rose Phillips, who called herself Phil, was a good example of a female investigator pictured at the intersection of feminism—Zambrano and the influence of *Prime Suspect*—and the pressures of television-network style. *Under Suspicion* allowed Phil some companionship, an ongoing romance, and more likable colleagues than Tennison's, so life wasn't quite as bleak for the feminist heroine as it had been on PBS. But the office romance wasn't a happy one, and the companionship was haunted with loss. In the first episode, Phil's partner and mentor was killed, and Phil became a surrogate "father" for his troubled teenage daughter, Shane, who often stayed at Phil's apartment (which was also not as depressing as Jane Tennison's dark flat). Still, Phil's essential isolation in a male world was always emphasized. When she was assigned the position of police "women's coordinator," the real-life job Kramer had taken on the L.A.P.D., Phillips recognized the irony of this assignment in an office where female sympathy was scarce. One of her piggy colleagues openly taunted her with the traditional female-dick stereotype: "How come you don't have a boyfriend? Are you a dyke?" Phillips snapped back, "That depends. Are you the alternative?"

Phillips was played with icy presence by Karen Sillas, a Strasberg-trained actress from independent cinema, chosen by Zambrano after she rejected dozens of name-brand actresses who looked "anorexic," as she reported. Some reviewers admired the "physical and emotional heft" of Sillas, but others noted she was nevertheless a casting compromise, "a tall, killer-cheek boned Helen Mirren type, except she's more conventionally 'pretty.'" They also noted that for a woman trying to be taken seriously in a male office, her miniskirts and heels were disconcerting. And having been taught by *Prime Suspect* how *not* to glamorize a policewoman, a number of critics scolded the director for shots in the premier episode that gratuitously panned Sillas's body.10

The series dropped the panning shots but kept the miniskirted suits, supplemented by boxy pantsuits. "The character of Phil encompasses the very masculine and the very feminine," the show's costume

Fig. 14 Karen Sillas as police detective Rose "Phil" Phillips in *Under Suspicion* (CBS, 1994–95). Courtesy of Photofest.

designer explained. "Sometimes she shows a vulnerable side, sometimes she shows a powerful side. Like Marlene Dietrich, who you think of when you put a woman in a suit."[11] And Dietrich, with her ambiguous sexuality and inscrutable self-possession, could be a patron saint of pictured woman detectives. Phil indeed exemplified extremes of vulnerability and power. We saw her sobbing after the autopsy of a young girl who had been raped and murdered, but we also saw her playing a dangerous game of bait with a female serial killer, offering herself as a victim so the killer would show her hand. A female serial killer? Her colleagues mocked this idea, but as Phil pointed out, "We'll have to rewrite the rules."

Under Suspicion also rewrote the rules of pace and style for television police dramas, although precedents for the moody settings and music had been set with *Twin Peaks* and *Frank's Place* (1987–88). While *Prime Suspect*'s noir style had drawn on London's urban grubbiness, *Under Suspicion* (which took place in an unnamed city in the Northwest) relied heavily on art design and imaginative cinematography to produce a jittery world of alienation and distrust. Shots were sometimes diffused with blue light, or designed around shadows that cut faces into halves, or played with elaborate silhouettes. This kind of detailed shot is more likely to occur in movies, and in fact was seen in Kathryn Bigelow's female police drama *Blue Steel*.

The writers also admitted that they were far more interested in character than in plot, so episodes gave extensive time to reactions and interactions of Phil and her colleagues and to lengthy interrogation scenes.[12] Most radically, the series focused on Phil's self-interrogation, including sequences with her psychotherapist of the kind that would later appear on *The Sopranos* (1999–) for HBO. Phil's therapy scenes amplified the complexity of her character by posing questions about her job, her lover, and her motivations, and not allowing her to give pat answers.

These conversations with the woman therapist recall the ones in *Klute* (1971) and in Sondra Locke's woman investigator flick *Impulse* (1990), both of which pulled some reversals on the noir detective drama. In *Klute*, Jane Fonda played the articulate call girl Bree Daniels, whose therapy sessions lent an extraordinary female voice to the genre best known for the male detective's authoritative voiceover. And in *Impulse*, Theresa Russell played an undercover cop whose specialty was posing as a call girl. Like both these characters, Phil in her therapy sessions claimed a complexity beyond her sexual image. But in a more disturbing parallel, Phil was as much defined by her sexuality as the call girl and undercover call girl of *Klute* and *Impulse*. Phil's isolation always positioned her as different, *the* woman within the male police, even though her position gave her a legitimacy, authority, and agency impossible for the prostitutes of film noir.

When the series was close to being canceled, Zambrano wrote a dazzling season finale in which an accidental police shooting was retold several times from the perspectives of several witnesses, in the style of *Rashomon* (1950). This strategy summarizes the most basic problem of film noir: being able to trust what we see. Women in noir are traditionally part of this problem, representing deceit and the unreliability of appearances. Ironically, in the final moments of the episode, Phil became the victim of a man's bad vision. A revenge-seeking brother shot at the cop who had committed the accidental homicide, but the brother missed and hit Phil square in the chest. The episode closed on the image of Phil's collapsed body.

Was the wound fatal? Zambrano wrote the script not knowing, since she hadn't yet heard from the network about cancellation. A letter-writing campaign was started by Viewers for Quality Television, in the hope that Phil and *Under Suspicion* could, like the early *Cagney & Lacey*, be revived through viewer protest. But the "Please Don't Kill Phil" movement failed, and in the long run, Rose Phillips may have been the victim of an unfortunate time slot and an ambitious, artistic vision for which prime time was not quite ready. Despite the innovations of this experiment in television noir, Phil ultimately joined the female characters who have been noir's traditional victims, rendered as bodies (at the morgue or in bed) by the final scene.

But the Friday night competition for *Under Suspicion* featured, in contrast, television's most long-lived professional woman investigator, in a format as dark as film noir but without noir's cramped male-female strictures. This of course was Dana Scully of *The X-Files*, the part that made Gillian Anderson an international star as the gifted medical doctor handpicked by the FBI to become a very Special Agent. *The X-Files* wasn't focused on the female investigator and in fact was originally conceived around the character of maverick FBI agent Fox Mulder (David Duchovny), the hero attuned to the conspiracies of the government and the mysteries of the universe. Scully was at first his foil, the skeptical scientist who opposed Mulder's occult theories and methods. For the first several seasons, Scully was usually proven wrong by evidence that Mulder was allowed to see but which vanished or flew back into the sky before Scully entered the scene. But Scully's role increased with fan enthusiasm for the character, and eventually her skeptic's role changed, too, so that she didn't represent the point of view audiences were cued to reject.

The entire image of the character, in fact, shifted from the original expectations of both series creator Chris Carter and the Fox network. At the auditions, Gillian Anderson "came in looking a little disheveled, a little grungier than I'd imagined Scully," Carter remembers. The networks had hoped for a sexy costar. "They wanted somebody leggier," Anderson said in interviews, "somebody with more [sic] breasts, somebody drop-dead gorgeous." Once Carter realized how Anderson could embody a more subtle character, he fought network opposition. "What it came down to was that the network wasn't sure how Gillian would look in a bathing suit, they didn't really know what the show was," Carter explained.[13] The Fox network, remember, had rejected *Under Suspicion* because of "male demographics," and apparently saw *The X-Files* as an opportunity to combine sci-fi with some eye candy.

As it turned out, the picturing of the Scully character would actually become a major dimension of the show, but through a far more circuitous route, beginning with an early linking of Scully to Jodie Foster's Clarice Starling. In the first episodes of *The X-Files*, Anderson was dressed and coiffed as a virtual Foster/Starling look-alike, with identically styled hair, tiny pearl earrings, and loose, dark pantsuits. Pushing the association with the movie, the series used typed-in time and location scene identifications at the bottom of the screen, identical to that used in the Demme film. The first-season episode "Beyond the Sea" gave Scully a Lecter-like encounter with an imprisoned criminal and also a strong psychic connection to her own dead father, further paralleling *The Silence of the Lambs*.

The similarities also reinforced the enigma of Scully's sexuality. Paired with Mulder, Scully automatically took on a heterosexual slant not found in the Demme film, and the pilot even mentioned a possible romantic interest, "Ethan," who was quickly written out of the show. Yet for the first few seasons, not much in the script, the acting, and the costuming flagged Scully with the traditional signs of femininity or heterosexuality. Eager fans had to read sexuality into the smallest detail or gesture—a raised eyebrow, a silky bathrobe—as some fans had done with Demme's *Silence of the Lambs*. In the long run, *The X-Files* often attempted to transcend the usual either-or questions of sexuality (is she gay? is she straight?) by gradually untwining "sex" from its biological and cultural meanings and giving it some cosmic and metaphysical twists.

As for the picturing of Scully, the Foster/Starling haircut soon changed to the more chic bob that became Scully's trademark look, but her dowdy wardrobe and oversized trench coats continued in the second season when most of the episodes had to be shot around Gillian Anderson's pregnancy. By the end of that season, the series had gone from a kinky cult curiosity to a major hit. In the third season, when it was clear the Scully character was a hot commodity despite the frumpy clothing, Scully's fashion sense radically improved. The suits and pantsuits became more form-fitting and stylized. Anderson mentioned in interviews that the budget was bigger and allowed for Italian fabrics and better shoes. But Scully was never sexualized into an Angie, Angel, or miniskirted Rose Phillips, and reviewers were happy that this was "not yet another bimbo chasing after criminals in high heels."[14]

Possibly as a reaction against the tailored image of Scully on the series, the stardom of Gillian Anderson took on a life of its own as unabashed retro glamour. By the third season, Scully had amassed a fan following equal to or greater than Mulder's, and had accumulated an impossibly diverse and lush life on the Internet, in fan organizations, and in feature photos picturing Gillian Anderson as everything from Mata Hari and Marlene Dietrich to Fay Wray and feathered Vargas

Fig. 15 Gillian Anderson and David Duchovny as FBI agents Dana Scully and Fox Mulder in *The X-Files* (Fox, 1993–2002). Courtesy of Photofest.

girls. The publicity encouraged fantasies that the reined-in Special Agent had a secret life in strappy little sandals and teddies. Fans and the media often conflated the character and the actress, as in the title of the illustrated fan book, *Special Agent Scully: The Gillian Anderson Files*. The same was true for Duchovny/Mulder. When *Rolling Stone* featured a cover photo of a supposedly naked Anderson and Duchovny entwined in bed, the accompanying interview implied that it would be interpreted as Scully and Mulder.

Gillian Anderson made dozens of talk-show appearances in which she made it entirely clear that she was far more giggly and less educated than her knowledgeable Special Agent character. But she reported receiving fan mail admiring her as a role model for professional women, and British journalists dubbed her "the thinking man's crumpet." Her fans included the Gillian Anderson Testosterone Brigade but also the Gillian Anderson Neuro-Transmitter Association, which defended her intellectual and sexual integrity, claiming she was no "sexless brainiac."[15] The morphs in this paragraph already sound like an X-File, but the truth was out there—on the Net, on magazine stands: one of the decade's sexiest stars was embodied as a Special Agent, a female investigator.

As the flip side of Scully's serious persona, Anderson's calendar-girl stardom seemed to perpetuate the most clichéd strategy for picturing the female investigator: put her in a swimsuit to prove she's all-woman. But despite the star images outside the series, the character Scully within the series resisted most standard images of women—traditional, sexist, feminist, postfeminist, or alien—because she was so richly imagined.

On *The X-Files*, Scully inhabited mythic, fantasy, and science-fiction worlds in which bodies, genders, and categories aren't realistically held into place—a flexibility impossible for Clarice Starling or other more realistically drawn characters. Like Patricia Cornwell's Scarpetta character, Scully was a medical doctor and expert on the human body, but in a context that freed her from earthly biology. The first-season episode "Gender Bender," for instance, featured a serial killer who was an attractive man or woman, depending on the sex of the victim.

Scully's sex didn't change, but her body didn't follow biological rules, either. Scully's body became the site of mystery beginning with her alien abduction in Season Two. In a script using Anderson's real-life pregnancy in one of those episodes, "Ascension," Mulder had a vision of Scully on a laboratory table, her swollen stomach being threatened with extraterrestrial probing devices. Later, Scully realized a microchip had been implanted in her neck, and when she removed it, she was stricken with a rare, incurable cancer. After the cancer went into remission, it was unclear if that happened because of the power of prayer, the power of a counter-microchip discovered by Mulder, or the power of what Scully began to call her "destiny." Meanwhile, Scully's ovaries were used in an alien/government reproductive experiment which led to the birth of a daughter who died of mysterious causes. These experiments left Scully unable to have children, but she became inexplicably pregnant during the eighth season of the show, at the end of which—in an episode laden with New Testament imagery—she had a baby boy.

All this was possible because in both science fiction and mythology, male-female roles are infinitely pliable. Science fiction is often considered a male province, but it plays loose with gender, as demonstrated by the mother of sci-fi, Mary Shelley, who likewise imagined impossible kinds of reproduction and bodies. Also, Scully maintained an independence that belied her official capacity as a federal Special Agent. The character began as a toe-the-line government employee, assigned to investigate Mulder's dubious activities, but very soon she was Mulder's partner against evil government conspiracies. So she worked both inside and outside the FBI, officially employed as an agent but often acting in unofficial and sometimes even illegal ways. She also maintained her status as a medical expert, functioning as a liaison between conventional science and inexplicable belief systems.

In one sense, Scully was part of the bureaucracy (the government, the FBI, medical science) and was less threatening than the maverick, solo private investigator. But the series consistently showed her fierce loyalty only to her conscience. Early on, she was committed solely to scientific truth; her Ph.D. dissertation in physics, we learn, had been a new interpretation of Einstein. As the series developed, she learned to place faith in forces she couldn't explain, but finally her loyalty was foremost to Mulder, to the point that she willingly jeopardized her career at the FBI on his behalf.

The Scully-Mulder relationship was crucial to the series and to the picturing of Special Agent Scully. Their relationship was a startling innovation for television: an attractive male-female couple whose deep rapport was neither flirtation nor just-pals camaraderie. And the usual male-female team dynamic was revised. In a switch of traditional gender roles, Mulder was the "irrational" believer, Scully the rationalist. In competence and professionalism, they were equals.

Screwball it was not. With profound mutual respect, they gazed into each other's eyes and talked in hushed voices about autopsy results or species of mold found in sewers. They risked their lives for each other, outwitted government assassins, and peered into murky vials and alien body cavities together, but in the first several seasons, rarely registered emotions beyond grim determination and adrenalized courage. Unlike the aggressive comedy of *Moonlighting*, the dry humor and black comedy of *The X-Files* underplayed the sexual subtext—if that's what the subtext can be called. For years, creator Chris Carter promised in interviews that Scully and Mulder would never be romantically linked, and in fact "romance" wasn't quite the right word for their gradual coupling. During Season Four, one journalist called it "something more inexplicable than the knottiest X-File: TV's most successful progressive marriage."[16]

The odd progression of this marriage—the low-key exchanges and deadpan reactions—created a passion enacted, like Scully's sexuality, outside of the show itself, in titillating feature stories and photographs such as the *Rolling Stone* cover or the May 1997 cover photo of *Us* with a tight shot of Gillian Anderson hungrily licking Duchovny's face. But in a far more elaborate way, the relationship was amplified and scrutinized on thousands of conversations on the Internet. *The X-Files* came into being just as the world got online, and the show's followers quickly organized into discussion newsgroups and chatrooms. These online fans, or "X-Philes" as they called themselves, shared speculations about the series' plotlines and cast, reported on media coverage, fantasized about alternative stories, and also did in-depth analyses of individual episodes, scenes, and even shots. (David Duchovny reported that he once logged on and was "frightened" to find a discussion of why Scully doesn't adjust the car seat after the taller Mulder had been driving.) In the last year of the series, the newsgroup alt.tv.xfiles.analyses, dedicated to close readings of the episodes, listed more than 30,000 threads or topics.

The Internet conversations were well under way by the show's second season, when it became obvious that the Mulder-Scully relationship wasn't going to follow a standard romantic course, and many of these discussions became attuned to the characters' smallest interactions. In the "Paper Clip" episode from Season Three, Mulder and Scully exchanged a tense look, smiled, and entered an elevator together. End of scene. Internet newsgroups lit up with speculation. When Scully touched Mulder's hand at the end of the episode "Pusher" that same season, fans went wild. Generations of English professors have knocked themselves out getting students to do what *The X-Files* fans did obsessively—look for fine details and make an interpretation.

The Scully-Mulder duo made gender roles a preoccupation for Internet fans, with discussions keeping track of how often each agent rescued the other or how their respective masculinity/femininity was registered through gestures or clothing. (Mulder, rather than Scully, usually showed more skin, for instance.)[17] The X-Philes also revealed the extensive female audience for this show. Women joined *X-Files* discussions far more frequently than for other television series discussed online. Often, their discussions centered on Scully or on the Scully-Mulder relationship. So even though the context wasn't strictly realistic, Scully's role as investigator of government and cosmic mysteries was closely tied to real-life gender issues, as has been the case for other women investigators on television.

So what was the Scully-Mulder relationship about? At the end of Season Eight, the closing shot showed a happy mama Scully embraced by Mulder, with the implication he had fathered the impossible child.

In interviews over the next few weeks, Chris Carter confirmed Mulder's fatherhood, and this was further reinforced in the show's final season, which ended with Mulder, Scully, and son reunited in what looked like a nuclear, if not holy, family.

But as the Internet discussions overwhelmingly pointed out, this may or may not mean Scully and Mulder ever had sex! For that matter, "sex" on *The X-Files* rarely meant "sex" as on *Moonlighting*, even though Carter's series was densely erotic in its preoccupations, *mise-en-scène*, and innuendoes. The poster in Mulder's office, "I WANT TO BELIEVE," could mean a wish about sexuality as much as a wish about extraterrestrials. "I want to believe" is the mantra of the fetish, after all: "I know better, but. . . ."

Suspended belief kept viewers hooked on Mulder and Scully's carnality even though we didn't see explicit visual evidence. Or we were teased about what we saw. At the opening of "All Things," Season Seven, Scully prepared to go to the office, leaving Mulder asleep in bed. But at the end of the episode, we've learned she'd spent the night on his sofa. When we did see them coupled suggestively, the situation was usually refracted through fantasy or parody. They were undercover as a farcical suburban couple in "Arcadia" in Season Six, and in "Triangle" that same season they were in a time warp in which Mulder kissed a Scully lookalike on a British ship in the 1930s. Or they were played by other stars who in turn played amorous movie stars in "Hollywood A.D.," in Season Seven. The best joke in that one was that Scully was played by Téa Leone, David Duchovny's real-life wife.

The eroticism of the series' *mise-en-scène* was likewise sex seen through a glass, darkly. The episodes often took place in caverns, swampy pools, moist undergrounds, and labyrinths. These scenarios conveyed sexuality through cross-hatchings of the extraterrestrial, the biological, and the mythic.[18] So when we were cued to imagine Scully and Mulder acting on their desires, the fantasy scenario was a world in which "sex" had come untethered from its everyday meanings. The one occasion when Mulder had a sexual encounter verified in the plotline, it was with a vampire, played by Duchovny's then-girlfriend Perrey Reeves during the show's second season. The real-life girlfriend lent an earthly air to the occasion, but we could only fantasize what vampire sex entails, especially since it's notoriously associated with gay and queer sexuality. On other occasions, Mulder was seen with porno magazines or videos, but X-Philers pointed out there was no clear confirmation of what kind of porno or sex he was interested in.

Likewise, Scully enjoyed some bizarre erotic moments, such as her attraction to a psychic writer who extracted his own heart, in "Milagro" in Season Six. In "Never Again" in Season Four, she was drawn toward a murderer and his talking tattoo, allowing him to tattoo the image of a snake on her upper back. Given the Freudian meaning of snakes, this intimate act suggested sex, but sex enacted on the surface of the body instead of inside it. In neither episode did we see evidence of a consummated relationship in the usual sense of the term.

Though numerous Internet sites and conversations were devoted to imagining Scully's sex life, some X-Philes insisted Scully had never had heterosexual intercourse, despite her student romance with one of her professors, recalled in the episode "All Things" (written by Gillian Anderson). The student/teacher relationship as portrayed on that episode was *only* romantic, certain Philes argued. (This discussion thread from summer, 2001, was dubbed, in homage to Bill Clinton, "I Did Not Have Sex with That Man.") The nativity-like circumstances of the birth of Scully's child at the end of Season Eight—the unusual star in the sky, the hovel where Scully found shelter, the expectant crowd of strangers—pushed the Virgin Mary parallel, either as myth or parody.

But the aspect of Scully that wasn't disputable was her purity of motivation. Her integrity of character—much like Clarice Starling's—remained beyond reproach in the midst of political messes in the FBI and in complicated interplanetary conspiracies. Moreover, Scully as an investigator grew, in the course of the series, into an investigator of spiritual and cosmic mysteries. In more conventional ways, she reexamined her childhood Catholicism, particularly in the episodes when she was dealing with her cancer. And in less conventional ways, she explored ancient belief systems and genesis stories from several cultures.

Generally, *The X-Files* made Scully a character whose strengths were both conviction and *knowledge*. The series always pictured her as a top-notch scientist, well-versed in several kinds of medicine, ranging from forensics to genetics to biochemistry. And after a nine-year partnership, she still amazed Mulder with her encyclopedic command of botany, zoology, geology, and physics. ("You really *do* watch the Discovery Channel," Mulder deadpanned after one of her effortless factual citations.) The key to investigation fiction has always been knowledge, and the supposedly superior knowledge of the male detective has been part of his gendered entitlement. By the end of the eighth season, Scully also knew the specific female experience of bringing life into the world.

Perhaps only *The X-Files*'s blend of fantasy, science fiction, and myth could produce this prototype investigating woman. It's true that this same mode of storytelling mystified her as well, especially around questions of her body and sexuality. But as Bobbie Ann Mason has ruminated about the attractions of the detective genre, "Mysteries are a substitute for sex, since sex is the greatest mystery of all." Mason was referring to adolescents' interest in detective fiction, but *The X-Files* reminded us that sex never stops being a mystery. Not that this series didn't play to stereotypical male adolescent sci-fi fans, represented within the show by the nerdy group known as the Lone Gunmen, for whom Agent Scully was as astounding and scary as anything they'd sighted from other galaxies.

But viewers were also offered more thoughtful perspectives on the mysteries of Scully's body and sexuality, including the lens of Scully's own intelligence. Scully handled the mysteries of her own body by actively exploring all possible options: traditional medicine, experimental science, and prayer. So she never submitted to victimhood nor lost faith in her own ability to make choices. Also, women viewers had the satisfaction of seeing her relationship with Mulder treated as a series of questions rather than answers, as an imaginative speculation rather than a sexual or romantic cliché. The mechanics of Scully's pregnancy and Mulder's fatherhood are far less interesting than a nine-year male-female relationship of stunning equality, affection, and respect. The script and the camera averted our gaze from the activities we recognize as romance and instead cued us to imagine what an erotic, psychological, and spiritual bonding might entail.

In comparison to the major cultural impact of *The X-Files*, the series *Profiler*, the other long-running female investigator show of the 1990s, was more modest in its ambitions and effects. But it was similarly imaginative and unorthodox in its heroine and genre. The profiler around whom the show was created was Dr. Samantha Waters (Ally Walker), a forensics psychologist who had been in retirement since her husband was murdered by a pernicious serial killer, the spooky Jack of All Trades, who haunted Samantha throughout her time on the series. Sam was coaxed back to work by her friend Bailey Malone (Robert Davi), so that she could join the elite Violent Crimes Task Force (VCTF) of the FBI.

The gimmick of the series was that Sam had an uncanny (and truly unbelievable) ability to visualize crime scenes in graphic detail, a psychic gift of forensic intuition. So once again, a primary mystery of the series was embodied by the heroine herself, aligning *Profiler* with the occult slant and intriguing heroine of *The X-Files*. Sam's psychic power was also similar to that of the character Lance Henriksen on the Fox network's *Millennium*, which likewise featured the gruesome details of horrific crimes.[19]

Profiler also jumped into the intersection of fact and fiction about forensics and psychological profiling in the 1990s. *Profiler* debuted in

1996, a year after the publication of the best-selling nonfiction book *Mind Hunter: Inside the FBI's Elite Serial Crime Unit,* by John Douglas and Mark Olshaker, the former of whom was the model for Clarice Starling's FBI boss in *The Silence of the Lambs.*[20] *Mind Hunter,* while not exactly glamorizing the FBI's behavioral science unit, details the disturbing but fascinating work of the people who track the nation's most violent crimes. The fictional VCTF of *Profiler* was obviously based on Special Agent Douglas's unit, just as the female behavioral science expert Sam Waters seems based on Douglas's fictional student, Clarice Starling.

Also, as I pointed out in chapter 2, *Profiler* was developed just as Patricia Cornwell's novels were hitting the best-seller list. Coincidentally or not, the actress Ally Walker resembles the blonde Cornwell and the blonde Kay Scarpetta, often described in the novels as sensuous and beautiful. Some plots and episodes of *Profiler* very specifically echoed Cornwell's titles and stories. The episode "Cruel and Unusual" from the first season, for example, duplicated the plot of Cornwell's *Cruel and Unusual*: a man on death row seemed to be committing crimes on the outside. Also, serial killer Jack resembled Cornwell's recurring villain Temple Gault. Like Gault, Jack took on a female partner, a Jill, during the second season of the show. Jack didn't have Gault's sex/gender ambiguity, but he shared Gault's virus-like ability to permeate systems and to track Samantha while she was tracking him.

Whether or not Cornwell was being directly invoked, *Profiler* was one of the few series to focus on an investigating heroine who wasn't part of a couple, male or female, nor was a "bimbo chasing after criminals in high heels." Only *Prime Suspect* and *Under Suspicion* had done this, the first as noncommercial television and the second as a ratings failure. *Profiler* was never a hit, but it got a decent audience share until Walker left the show after the third season. Ratings showed that its primary audience was young women, despite its violent and unsettling topics each week.[21]

Why would women be attracted to this series? Created by a woman, Cynthia Saunders, *Profiler* gave its heroine far more female support characters than were allowed either Dana Scully or Rose Phillips. They were interesting and diverse women, too. Sam had a little daughter, Chloe, and together they lived with Sam's best friend Angel (Erica Gimpel), an African-American sculptor who worked at home and looked after Chloe while Sam was at work. So a profoundly nurturing and nontraditional female family lay at the heart of the stories. Sam's first romantic interest in the series, Nick Cooper (A. Martinez), fished around the traditional are-you-a-lesbian question when he found out about the living arrangements. Nick was doomed, but Angel survived.

At the FBI, meanwhile, Sam also had the support of the Latina forensics specialist Grace Alvarez (Roma Maffia), who did the autopsies and also occasionally had some key roles in the action. So even though Sam was the only woman on the VCTF, she didn't bear the onus of being the only woman in sight, unlike Phil in *Under Suspicion*. (However, both shows accented the gender twist by assigning male nicknames to their heroines.)

Like Scully, Sam Waters had an entirely dependable male ally on the job, her friend and boss Bailey Malone, who respected Sam's work and trusted her unorthodox psychic technique, unlike team member John Grant, who suspected and resisted it. In fact, Sam's psychic gift rather than her gender was the contentious issue on the show. Her capacity to think "in pictures" made her body the threshold of the investigation, a controversial instrument and methodology at odds with her scientific training.

Sam's psychic moments—the closeups of her huge blue eyes juxtaposed with her visions of violence—bordered on the hokey, but the emphasis and even obsession with *vision* on this series touched on key issues of picturing the woman investigator. Her ability to visualize the crime reversed traditional detective stories, where usually women got attention for what they looked like, especially how they looked to the dick *du jour*. The detective's extraordinary vision—the ability to see what others miss—has always been crucial to the genre. Blonde, svelte Sam Waters caused heads to turn when she went out to crime scenes, but in every episode, the turning points and moments of discovery depended on what *she* could see.

Predictably, Sam's nemesis, the villainous Jack of All Trades, was likewise an expert in seeing. He specialized in surveillance, so his ability to follow and "see" Sam through multiple technologies duplicated her own confounding visual powers. When he did cross paths with her, the face-offs were always about their dueling knowledges of each other, their abilities to visualize, see each other, picture the other. Even creepier, Jack implicated Samantha in his crime spree. She gradually figured out that all his victims had some connection to herself. Jack often spoke in riddles and left elaborate clues like any good serial killer, and Sam was inevitably herself a clue in the riddle she was attempting to solve. This was a far darker scenario than the mysteries of Agent Scully because it implicated the woman investigator herself in criminality.

Unfortunately, but true to detective tradition, evil Jack posed as the ultimate lover and soul mate of Sam, the only person who knew how easily she could "go over" to the dark side. His trademark was the red

Fig. 16 Ally Walker as FBI consultant Sam Waters in *Profiler* (NBC, 1996–2000). Courtesy of Photofest.

rose, which he left at crime scenes as his pledge of faithfulness to Samantha. At the end of their cat-and-mouse relationship (and the end of Ally Walker's time on the series), Jack kidnapped Sam and, in a brutally sadistic episode, attempted mind games to persuade her to become his partner. When that failed and she escaped, his last and worst ploy was to pose as little Chloe's psychologist, convincing Chloe that Samantha was responsible for the death of Chloe's father.

The ultimate encounter took all three of them to Chloe's father's grave, where Samantha was finally able to shoot Jack in the head. He fell on his red rose and on her husband's tomb, leaving a depressing pile-up of bodies of the men who loved her. Exhausted, Sam resigned from the VCTF and disappeared forever. A new nonpsychic female profiler took her place (Jamie Luner as Rachel Burke), but the show never regained momentum and was canceled at the end of the 1999–2000 season.

Profiler at its best was actually much better than the gothic graveyard conclusion, which reduced the story to a melodramatic love triangle and Sam to the black widow, a grim survivor of a murderous circle of lust. In previous seasons, when the FBI and the serial killer pitted their pithiest technologies against each other, *Profiler* was all about surveillance and watching, with Samantha Waters caught in the crosshairs but *also* in a unique, powerful position to *see*, scrutinize, and probe. And that's a sharp, bittersweet metaphor for the woman detective on television or at the movies, and the high stakes on what she can picture and who can picture her.

5

WOMEN DETECTIVES ON FILM
First Take

FBI GIRLS

The advertising slogan for the 1951 B-movie *FBI Girl* was "Woman on a Man-Hunt!" The ad poster showed Audrey Totter in a skin-tight sheath and spiky high heels, dressed for the only kind of man-hunting Hollywood and the FBI could imagine for a woman in the 1950s. As it turns out, the Totter character is an "FBI girl" because she's a secretary at the Bureau, reluctantly helping the husky G-men by getting information from her boyfriend.

FBI Girl would be no more than a funny footnote except that its quaint 1950s premise has an uncomfortably familiar ring. "Let me get this straight," says Shirley, the character played by Totter, to the poker-faced G-men, "you're going to use me to get information out of Carl!" Shirley rightly suspects the G-men don't give a fig about her or about her relationship to Carl or how much danger she might get into. They see her as the sexy soft spot, the place where the bad guys might loosen up and talk.

Liberated decades later, this is also the plot of the 1988 movie *Betrayed*, with Debra Winger as Special Federal Agent Cathy Weaver, who, albeit with more training, is set up like Shirley, with instructions to use a personal relationship to get information. The personal part of the relationship, the possibility she'll get emotionally involved, isn't of much interest to the G-men who—spookily enough—act a lot like the ones who bully Shirley. And if this all sounds *very* familiar, it's because, a few years later, in a far more high-profile movie, Jodie Foster as Clarice Starling is similarly sent by the FBI on "an interesting errand" to Hannibal Lecter, not realizing she's being used by the Bureau to get information about a different case. Like Cathy Weaver, Starling is sent in because she's attractive. And the lure works.

The Silence of the Lambs is a far more satisfying story of the Woman on a Manhunt, but in its sequel *Hannibal* (2001), the FBI Girl is abused and alienated by the Bureau, and actually treated even more badly than Cathy Weaver in *Betrayed.* The recurring themes are harassment and alienation—men behaving badly.

In the fifty years between *FBI Girl* and *Hannibal*, a little over a dozen first-run films were made that focused on a solo woman cop, detective, or federal agent. Most of these films were made after 1987, when the investigator heroine was "out there" in culture as a newly serious character and story on television (*Cagney & Lacey*) and the best-seller list. But in Hollywood, the new character was launched more nervously, with dick jokes, domestic props, unlikely romances, and corny maternal motivations.

The plots of these woman investigator films were also different from the novels and the television series. In the films, the women were more likely to be potential victims of the killer—usually a serial killer—and were likely to be sexually involved in a vulnerable way. Also, the unhappy endings of many of the films suggested that the heroine had wandered into the wrong role and script. It's true that the melancholy detective hero is part of the crime movie tradition, from the cynical Sam Spade to the bitter and frustrated Jake Gittes in *Chinatown*. But unlike these dour heroes, accepting their limitations in a limited world, the heroines are sometimes pushed out of that world entirely, as in *Betrayed, Blue Steel,* and *Impulse,* or are rehabilitated with heavy doses of domestic and family life, as in *V.I. Warshawski* and *A Stranger Among Us* (1992).

Tellingly, when Hollywood began to portray professional women investigators, the first three were African American, and the next two were Debra Winger. Both are "types" of women Hollywood rarely has in mind as leading ladies, a category that usually means white glamour. Winger was the first of several tomboy types—Holly Hunter, Jamie Lee Curtis, Jodie Foster—destined for this role, all of whom can look feminine or not, with the "not" ranging into the androgynous and the butch.

The black actresses in these early films were Tamara Dobson and Pam Grier, from the 1970s Blaxploitation era, and Whoopi Goldberg in the 1980s. Coincidentally (perhaps), both Grier and Goldberg had previously played roles as lesbians. Goldberg's compelling 1985 debut had been *The Color Purple*'s Celie, whose lesbianism, prevalent in the book, was played down for the screen version. In contrast, Grier had played over-the-top butch roles in two campy prison movies, *The Big Doll House* (1971) and *Women in Cages* (1971). But there are no traces of butch in the black women investigator flicks. Dobson, Grier, and Goldberg are each given a sympathetic boyfriend and one modest bedroom scene per flick, to prove their heterosexuality. The films make it clear that these women characters *like* men and only beat the crap out of the bad ones.

Considering that Hollywood's nonvillainous white women with guns at this time were mostly James Bond's girlfriends, Blaxploitation was two decades ahead of the game. It would take Hollywood that long to give pistols and aikado lessons to the likes of Geena Davis and Drew Barrymore on a regular basis. In the interim, action heroines were science fiction—literally, television's *Wonder Woman* (1976–79) and *Bionic Woman* (1976–78) and Princess Leia of *Star Wars* (1977). As a more realistic woman of action, Sigourney Weaver's Ellen Ripley would remain an anomaly; the role in *Alien* (1979) had been written so it could be played by either a woman or a man. But the action heroine hadn't yet come into her own as a cultural phenomenon in American gyms and movies. Instead, she appeared as the deadly but dolled-up *femme* in Blaxploitation.

As critics have pointed out, cinema's willingness to associate black women with violence suggests a nasty cultural undertow. "Blaxploitation" became a term in the 1970s, when white directors and producers began to cash in on films targeted for black audiences. Those films had always been macho in style and attitude—think *Shaft* (1971) and *Superfly* (1972)—but the Grier and Dobson characters strut some macho attitude, too. Like Charlie's Angels of the same era, these characters are both sexist cartoons and Amazon avengers, except more likely than Farrah Fawcett to slice off an enemy's penis, as Grier does in *Foxy Brown* (1974). Even though it's a white man's penis, the supposed masculinist appeal of this character for black audiences clearly needs some rethinking, just as critics now understand the audience identifications of slasher movies in more complicated ways.[1]

Sheba, Baby (1975) is part of the cycle of kick-ass Pam Grier films in which she single-handedly levels street gangs, drug cartels, and bumbling legions of white police. Sheba Shayne (yes, African queen and American cowboy) was technically the very first professional woman private investigator in the movies, but the story focuses on vengeance, not sleuthing, so the P.I. angle is minimal here. A Chicago P.I., Sheba is called back home to Louisville where some low-life thugs kill her father in a business scam, and she's immediately launched into high-revenge mode, similar to Grier's earlier movies. In *Coffy* (1973), she was avenging a sister killed by a drug ring, and in *Foxy Brown* she was avenging a brother and boyfriend who met the same fate. So in

Fig. 17 Pam Grier as private investigator Sheba Shayne in *Sheba, Baby* (1975). Courtesy of Photofest.

Sheba, Pam Grier gets even for the entire fictional family. Sheba uses oversize Magnum revolvers and kicks to the crotch, but she also satisfyingly puts a bad guy's head through a car wash and kills the biggest, meanest guy with a harpoon as she chases him in a speedboat. We're supposed to credit her agility and survival skills to being a P.I., but the truth is, we chalk them up to Pam Grier/Coffy/Foxy Brown, who in this movie looks like an ebony Sophia Loren–turned-action-heroine, full-bodied and trained to kill.

Sheba's status as a *woman* P.I. is never doubted or questioned. Instead, the tension of the movie is a racially inflected version of the savvy P.I. versus the dolt police, who fail to protect Sheba's father and fail to give her backup. The hoodlums who kill her father are black, but it turns out they work for wealthy white men who are behind the entire scam. The hapless cops are white, too. As a result, the big confrontation scenes are Grier/Sheba versus evil or incompetent white guys.

Sheba is a heady amalgam of superwoman and centerfold. The costuming and the framing usually emphasize Grier's statuesque body. In fact, the film's major budget expense may have been Sheba's stylish wardrobe of elephant bell-bottom pant suits, gargantuan hats, and full-skirted halter dresses. But for every exploitative camera shot (the loving closeups of Grier's rear end in a tight skirt), there's a shot of a formidable black woman towering above a pale, unfortunate white man in a leisure suit.

As a token of good black masculinity, Sheba's hometown boyfriend is loyal and helps her relax in bed, so the residue of Grier's lesbian roles is supposedly wiped away. Happily, though, the boyfriend is neither rescue device nor Sheba's closing destiny. He (and the cops) arrive too late to help Sheba in the climactic speedboat shoot-out, and in the final scene, she kisses him goodbye and heads for the airport. Aha! Here in 1974, in a low-budget subgenre, is the nascent female investigator just beginning to be imagined by P.D. James and Lillian O'Donnell on the literary front: her story is investigation, not romance and melodrama, and she's alone at the end, en route to the next case, savoring her independence.

Generally, though, the motor of *Sheba, Baby* runs on race rather than sex or detective work. The same is true of *Cleopatra Jones* (1973) and *Cleopatra Jones and the Casino of Gold* (1975), which feature Tamara Dobson as a federal agent—curiously, not specified as either FBI or CIA—assigned to wipe out drug lords who are preying on the black community. Her job title is vague because her actual role, as her name suggests, is mythical black goddess. Tall, willowy, and dressed in regal fur-lined capes, Cleopatra is an exotic empress of law enforcement, respected by the inept white cops, the cheesy local gangsters, and bevies of little street boys who gladly clean her Corvette while she's busy cleaning out dealers in the ghetto.

The Cleopatra movies are heavily brushed with James Bond gizmos like the arsenal of machine guns built into the Corvette's door. Also like Bond, Cleo is adept at both karate and judo, and she knows how to race that Corvette in hilarious chases with greasy villains. Cleo's physical agility gets highlighted in the bloody final confrontation of *Cleopatra Jones*, where she inexplicably loses her skirt and charmingly wears only a jacket and tights as she scrambles up and down ladders and cranes on a construction site.

Cleo roughs up an occasional black gangster, but she shoots and kills only white men. To make sure we know exactly where she stands racially and sexually in the first film, Cleo's nemesis and the story's center of evil power is a lesbian white woman, played with scary glee by Shelley Winters in blonde and red fright wigs. Winters's character is known only as Mommy, powerful leader of a scuzzy white drug ring. Mommy is a clue that despite the film's adoration of Cleo, there's a nervousness about powerful women in this movie, deflected entirely away from the super-glamorous Cleopatra and landed like a big house on Shelley Winters.

Cleopatra Jones also uses some of the same male-appeasing strategies seen in later films like *Betrayed, A Stranger Among Us,* and *Blue Steel.* Cleo never competes directly with a black man considered her equal; instead, her boyfriend is conveniently down with a bullet wound and unavailable to help her through most of the movie. Also, she's pictured as a rescuer of weaker women, in this case a delicate young black singer who does all the screaming and writhing. Finally, she's given quasi-maternal opportunities to be cute with little black boys who sigh and imagine lustful adulthoods with her.[2]

Despite these make-nice tactics for Sheba and Cleopatra, these characters had no mainstream Hollywood counterparts for more than a decade. The testosterone-heavy 1970s American box office was no place for the woman investigator—not even a white, fluffy one like Angie Dickinson's policewoman. On the big screen, this was the era of *Dirty Harry* (1971) and *Magnum Force* (1973), with Clint Eastwood setting the pace for the "Make My Day" type of outlaw-lawman. True, Donald Sutherland's Klute offered a gentler alternative, but the influential movie detectives were Gene Hackman's gritty Popeye Doyle in *The French Connection* (1971) and Jack Nicholson's cynical Jake Giddes in *Chinatown.* The investigative-cop story had gained respectability, too, with *Serpico* (1973). Through the first part of the 1980s, both cops and detectives in the movies were hunky stars à la Nick Nolte and Harrison Ford or super-cool Eddie Murphy in films like *48 Hrs.* (1982), *Deadly Force* (1983), *Beverly Hills Cop* (1984), *Tightrope* (1984), *Witness* (1985), *Manhunter* (1986), and *Someone to Watch Over Me* (1987). The end of that decade was dominated by the *Die Hard*–style action thriller and the buddy-cop movie *Lethal Weapon* (1987) and their sequels and imitators.

In such a masculine hardboiled realm, the action-style woman investigator or cop would be a novelty item at best, and certainly a box-office risk. Hilary Henkin's original screenplay for *Fatal Beauty* offered that risk: a sexy woman cop driven to solve the crime cases the city had forgotten, a woman who "spent her Friday nights at home with the radio on carving dumdum bullets," as Henkin described the character in an interview. But for the 1980s, Henkin's hardboiled heroine was out of the question for Hollywood. Instead, *Fatal Beauty* was rewritten as comedy, with a sentimental "back story" explaining the woman cop's obsession with crime.[3] It didn't matter that by the mid-1980s, bookshops were filling with tough women P.I. novels by Sara Paretsky and Marcia Muller. The evolution of *Fatal Beauty* (1987) from story idea to screenplay to production powerfully illustrates the difference between what can be imagined in a novel and what can be backed with Hollywood cash.

When the part of narcotics cop Rita Rizzoli in *Fatal Beauty* was rewritten in comic mode for a black actress, Tina Turner was the first choice. In an interview, Whoopi Goldberg said the part was "written with a beautiful woman in mind. When they couldn't find one, they had to pay an ugly woman's price—$1.5 million." Whoopi Goldberg was a safe bet for that kind of money. *The Color Purple* had made her an overnight star, but she would always be cast in roles slightly off-center from traditional (that is, white/young/pretty) Hollywood female images. As critic Yvonne Tasker puts it, given this narrow and racist imagination, Hollywood can't quite picture Goldberg as a woman.[4] In *Jumpin' Jack Flash* (1986), she had proven herself as a comic, which is a typical fate for nonglamorous women in Hollywood. And as a black actress, she could get away with the strut and tough talk of a Sheba or Cleopatra, all in the smooth repartee of rap. Rattling off castration jokes, colorful insults, and streams of foul-mouthed invectives, she's a fast-talking dame of the type never seen in screwball comedy. Faced with a naked white guy at his swimming pool in *Fatal Beauty*, she looks down and asks, "Does that come in adult size?"

Unlike *Sheba, Baby*, which simply used a woman detective character for a vengeance movie, *Fatal Beauty* was actually made in the mold of the Dirty Harry and buddy-cop crime films. So it is the first time we see how the gender switch works: in the first five minutes of the movie, Rita is beaten up and called "nigger" (four times) and "bitch" (twice). She shoots her attacker dead and then tells him, "Don't call me bitch." It's a signal that we're supposed to pay more attention to her sex than to her race, but it's impossible to watch this movie without seeing how she's doubly marginalized within the police force. Through most of it, she's harassed and besieged far more often and more venomously than the Nick Nolte and Clint Eastwood mavericks. Rita is derided for being a woman, a black, and a cop, and *everybody* harangues her—the perps, the cops, the witnesses, the street informants—so it's a good thing she has such a fluent dirty mouth for smartass retorts.

Also obvious is the difference gender makes in how Rita works as a cop. Her prostitute friend gives her good street information, but is also really a friend, in a way that would be impossible for a male cop. And the danger Rita gets into is different, too. A punk she'd previously arrested threatens her with rape, and it's a tense scene until Rita uses her fast mouth and wit to turn the punk into a limp joke. Fortunately, Whoopi/Rita doesn't have to parade as eye candy, as Grier had done in *Sheba*. If anything, her undercover whore clothes—oversize sunglasses, glittery jacket, and miniskirt with a zipper from hem to crotch—are more comedy than come-on.

Whoopi's "ugly woman" casting works for the big emotional scene in *Fatal Beauty*, in which Rita the street-savvy narc breaks down, sobbing, confessing her own past in the drug business. As a teenager, she explains, she'd gotten into heavy drugs as a way to pretend she was pretty, a way to fit into the crowd. The cruel irony is that "fatal beauty" doesn't refer to the heroine of this movie, but to the designer drug she's trying to stop as it kills street kids in Los Angeles. The breakdown and confession about addiction and popularity is one of the film's best moments, but it's followed by one of the worst. As an addicted single mother, she further confesses, she had been responsible for the death of her child. This explains her career as a narc, trying to save the kids on the street from a similar bad end.

Up to that point, Rita Rizzoli seems happy enough as a hip, single cop with a cat and a pink Mustang, so the tacked-on lost child is an unneeded reassurance to the audience: why would a woman be a tough street narc? Well, it's just the maternal instinct. Needless to say, as cops, narcs, and dicks, the Nolte or Hackman or Ford characters of this era don't have to be motivated by fatherhood. The weepy scene with Rita is also the first of many career explanations the female detective has to recite in these early movies. In *Betrayed, Blue Steel,* and *A Stranger Among Us*, the women investigators all have to pause and give some plausible reason for their jobs, as opposed to the more "natural" male detectives who apparently are born with genital justifications.[5]

Fortunately, the rest of *Fatal Beauty* gives Rita the opportunity to show off her street smarts, fast-footed police work, and cool use of at least four kinds of guns, including a snub-nosed little revolver she keeps under a billowy skirt. A slime-ball suspect tries to feel her up, and this is how he discovers she's a female dick. He's promptly hung on a meat hook where Rizzoli threatens his own equipment, so the castrating terror of "the female dick" gets both foregrounded and—cannily—laughed off.

Rita is also given a romance—in fact, the best romantic partner of any of the woman-detective movies until *Out of Sight* eleven years later. Rita's love interest is studly Sam Elliott as Marshak, a suspicious

Fig. 18 Whoopi Goldberg as undercover cop Rita Rizzoli in *Fatal Beauty* (1987). Courtesy of Photofest.

security guard for a drug lord. He's suspicious because until very late in the film, we're not certain of his motivations. With charming panache, he provides loyal backup for Rita and enjoyable suspense: he's immensely likable, but can she trust him? Shooting up the bad guys together, they do the interracial cop-buddy dance seen that same year in *Lethal Weapon*, although at least Rita and Marshak don't have to sublimate *their* erotic tension.

Marshak is respectful of Rita and clearly not threatened by "our dusky little dick," as one of her white cop colleagues calls her. But the Rita-Marshak relationship also pulls into focus the film's hesitation about picturing Rita as an African American, as a woman, and as an African-American woman. When she meets Marshak and introduces herself as Rita Rizzoli, he waxes poetic about his "weakness for Italian ladies" and their endearing brown eyes—which we glimpse in flashes beneath Rita's shades. If this is a good joke about the instabilities of racial identity in America, it's a joke without context, follow-up, or explanation in this movie. Likewise, even though she and Marshak are coupled as gun-buddies, their sexual coupling is handled coyly and off screen. We see only a tousled empty bed, which is reliable enough Hollywood shorthand, but the film doesn't actually picture them in physical contact except for the closing shot's tender kiss as Marshak is about to be hauled away in an ambulance. This may have been the limits of interracial sex in 1987, but it's also a nervous tic about the "dusky little dick" and exactly how to picture her—as black, as sexual, as maternal, as romantic heroine.

The two Debra Winger investigator movies made at this time similarly stall around issues of romance in picturing this new character. Like Whoopi Goldberg, Winger is not easily categorized for Hollywood. At this very moment when the woman-investigator story became feasible onscreen, she was cast in the part three times within a four-year period, 1984–88. This is a curious fate for an actress who had made her reputation in romance and melodrama, first opposite John Travolta in *Urban Cowboy* (1980), then as the swept-off-her-feet working-class woman in *An Officer and a Gentleman* (1982), and as the melodramatic victim of infidelity, cancer, and Shirley MacLaine in *Terms of Endearment* (1983).

But Winger's success in those traditional roles relied on a gutsy casting-against-the-grain. With her deep, froggy voice and small stature, Winger was a lower-voltage Jodie Foster in the 1980s, minus the lesbian reputation, but with similar tomboy spunk. Winger was brought up in a working-class home in Cleveland, Ohio, and her off-screen claim to fame is her brief teen years' service in the Israeli army, though her working-class aura conveys an ethnicity that's less specific than Jewishness. Teen fans later knew her as an action heroine on television, Wonder Woman's kid sister Drusilla, the Wonder Girl. Winger can be cute and feminine on screen, but she can play it the other way, too. She was a stalwart defense lawyer in *Legal Eagles* (1986) opposite Robert Redford; and as a cameo joke, she appeared in drag in her then-husband Timothy Hutton's *Made in Heaven* (1987). Her androgynous potential was later mined in *The Sheltering Sky* (1990), in which she plays a woman ambiguously named Kit, who becomes a "boy" prisoner of a desert sheik.

Froggy voice, Israeli army, appearance in drag—there's some butch potential here that explains the thread of movies in which Winger takes the traditionally male part of investigator. The films portray successively more professional sleuths. In *Mike's Murder* (1984), she's a quiet bank teller who turns amateur detective when her boyfriend is murdered. For *Black Widow*, she's a feisty Justice Department desk worker who convinces her boss she should single-handedly go undercover to solve a series of murders. And in *Betrayed* (1988), she's an anxiety-ridden FBI agent who's infiltrated a right-wing American terrorist group.

In both *Black Widow* and *Betrayed*, the heroine becomes emotionally and sexually involved with the person she's investigating, thus following the pattern of male crime noir stories. And though the Winger character nails the perp in both films, she herself faces an unhappy ending, alone and with nowhere to go. The male investigator, no matter how grimly compromised, at least knows where he belongs, even if it's his darkly unsettled niche just at the edge of the law. Neither *Black Widow* nor *Betrayed* can guarantee that place for the heroine. And considering the high sexual stakes of the woman investigator as a new kind of movie character, it's not unexpected that both films focus on her sexual choices.

Black Widow is actually the more original of the two films, as the only Hollywood movie that matches a woman sleuth with a woman criminal. So it fully rises to the challenge of what a "female dick" might mean: is this a lesbian? Is it a woman who imagines herself as a man? Or is it a woman who wants power—in fact, the traditionally male power to be a killer of men?[6]

While the early female investigator movies often use the plot of the serial killer, *Black Widow* gives us the female serial killer—statistically almost nonexistent, but mythically alive and well, a version of the *femme fatale* who in this case is the treacherous female spider who kills after she mates. Theresa Russell plays the fetching widow, taking up different identities and names as she weds and murders a series of millionaires.

Sweetly and ironically, all the men in the film (including the feds) are duped by the widow, and only another woman can see her for what she is. That woman is the Winger character, Alex Barnes, who insists that the millionaires' accidental deaths are no accident and that the widow in each case is the same person. Frumpy and not especially feminine, Alex is portrayed as one of the boys in the office, a good sport at card games, resistant to romance, restless on the job. Why exactly do the widows get her attention?

In one of the most imaginative scenes in this entire category of films, Alex projects on the wall a series of photos of these beautiful women, trying to match their faces. But she herself steps to the wall and places herself against the images, caressing them but also stepping

Fig. 19 Debra Winger as Justice Department investigator Alex Barnes and Theresa Russell as the serial killer Reni in *Black Widow* (1987). Courtesy of Photofest.

into them, obviously captivated by the killer-widow and willing to identify with her.[7] As the film goes on, Alex becomes more obsessed, giving up her desk job and taking on a new identity in order to follow and investigate the woman currently known as Reni. Posing as a bored tourist, Alex pretends to befriend Reni and have Gidget-style fun with her, borrowing clothes and hairdresser and makeup. In fact, the whole story teeters at the edge of the makeover movie, as Alex gets a better haircut, learns to use eyeliner, and shapes her body into expensive clothes.

Obviously, Alex wants to catch Reni but also wants to *be* Reni— powerful, alluring, seductive. This is all old territory for the detective story—the attraction to the criminal's power, the identification with the dark side, the willingness to think like the criminal to catch him. But the *homoerotic* attraction between criminal and detective is explored less often (subtly, in the 1989 *Sea of Love*, for instance) while in *Black Widow*, these erotic nuances are strongly suggested. Once Alex has come into Reni's life at a beach resort, they end up practicing mouth-to-mouth resuscitation in a diving class and share underwater breaths when their little diving adventure gets dangerous. Working on her next victim, Reni marries a real estate tycoon, but the wedding-day kiss we see on screen is between Reni and Alex, an aggressive kiss initi-ated by Reni as both a warning and an acknowledgment: she *knows* that Alex knows, and knows the erotic attraction involved as well.

Lesbian audiences and critics have been entranced and irritated with *Black Widow*, since it titillates with its lesbian implications but doesn't develop them.[8] In fact, once Alex learns to dress and coif like Reni, she gets bedded by Reni's fiancé, so it's possible to see Alex's transformation as sexist platitude: she goes from asexual Justice De-partment frump to properly sexy heterosexual woman, with a lesbian "phase" in between.

Or does she? At the end of the film, Alex departs from the en-trapped Reni, who tells her passionately, "Of all the relationships I'll look back on in fifty years' times, I'll always remember this one." With Alex forlornly leaving Reni behind bars, we're led to believe that for Alex, too, this has been the most important relationship of her life. In this way, *Black Widow* shares the refreshing indifference to male-female romance that we find in 1980s woman-detective literature. No matter what Alex's feelings toward Reni might entail, Alex's quest on a basic level is for herself—finding out what she wants and who she really is. She knows from the start that a man is not the answer to this quest and not the key to her identity. And *that's* liberated for 1987 Hollywood.

But for a full embrace, so to speak, of the probing woman sleuth and the *femme fatale,* we have to go outside Hollywood and fast for-ward to the 2000 Australian movie by Samantha Lang, *The Monkey's Mask.* Here the lesbian eroticism teased by *Black Widow* comes out of the closet. Jill Fitzpatrick (Susie Porter) plays a lesbian private investi-gator hired to solve the murder of a young female poet. In traditional hardboiled style, Jill tells us in clipped voice-over how she falls for the victim's sexy professor Diana Maitland, played with breathtaking cru-elty and plucked eyebrows by Kelly McGillis. For some McGillis fans, the poetry-professor role is poetic justice, given the rumors about an on-the-set romance between McGillis and Jodie Foster during the filming of *The Accused* (1988).

The tagline for this movie was "No evidence, just the smell of sex and violence." Both smells are indicated or discussed more than once, and after the two women get involved, it's hard to understand why Jill isn't getting a whiff of something very suspicious about the older, mar-ried, intellectual Diana. But that's the number-one rule of the hard-boiled tradition: the *femme fatale* leaves the detective utterly senseless. Even when Diana tries erotic asphyxiation on Jill, creepily acting out the death of the poetry student, Jill claims she "can't remember" what it was like. Pressing on the detective story's deepest nerve, *The Monkey's Mask* makes the sobering point that in the detective–*femme fatale* relationship, sexual knowledge *is* knowledge of the crime. Jill wakes up to the truth and gets a confession literally as she's being seduced by Diana's husband, an act that she's secretly recorded. When the police play the tape, the sound of the murder confession is punctuated by Jill's sexual grunts—an effect as shocking as anything in the last ten minutes of *Angel Heart* (1987).

Handing over the tape to the police, Jill has handed over her lover, too, as coolly as Sam Spade in *The Maltese Falcon*. Her voice-over at the film's close tells us, "Forget the bitch. Case closed." Most reviewers tallied up all these echoes and parallels as clichés of the detective genre, missing the film's more subtle take on them. In *The Monkey's Mask*, both sex and poetry are codes for mixed desires and anxieties that aren't easily paraphrased—after all, what does sexual pleasure *mean*? Likewise, both Jill and Diana are characterized as expert readers or interpreters, eventually rivals in understanding both the victim and her art. Jill cracks the case when she's willing to read the part of Diana she most wants to gloss over, which is Diana's marriage and its sexuality. And brutally, Jill has to take this on as sexual knowledge, literally lapsing into heterosexuality to realize how the murder took place. The film was adapted from a verse-novel by Dorothy Porter and aims—not always successfully—for poetic nuance as well as film noir wretchedness.

In sexually matching the female investigator and *femme fatale*, *The Monkey's Mask* takes *Black Widow* where mainstream Hollywood certainly couldn't go in the twentieth century. But at least *Black Widow* explored female identity by imagining how women imagine other women. There's no such interesting agenda for women in the Constantin Costa-Gavras movie *Betrayed*, the other Debra Winger investigator film of the 1980s. In this film, the FBI faces off against some homegrown terrorists, farmers from the heartland who believe they're the "real" Americans, destined to reclaim this country from Jews, blacks, and gays. Winger plays Cathy Weaver, the FBI agent assigned to infiltrate the group by posing as a migrant farm worker and sexually attracting the group's leader, the handsome widower Gary Simmons, played by Tom Berenger.

The punch of this film is its appalling revelation of the hatred, anti-Semitism, and violence tucked away into Norman Rockwell America. Gary's charm-your-socks-off little girl Rachel recites her credo about "killing niggers and Jews" like a nursery rhyme. The local sport is "coon hunting," with a young black man set loose in the swamp against a half dozen white guys with shotguns. "Going camp-

Fig. 20 Debra Winger as FBI agent Cathy Weaver in *Betrayed* (1988). Courtesy of Photofest.

ing" means a night at a cross-burning festival in the woods. Special Agent Weaver is appalled, too. She'd gone undercover not believing Gary and his farmer friends could possibly be part of this group. And by then it's too late: she's fallen in love with Gary, has become a mother-figure for Rachel, and then must betray a community that's welcomed her.

But the "betrayed" character of the title is Cathy herself, who is set up by the FBI as sexual and emotional bait, with no concern for what it might do to her head—and body. Cold and inflexible, the FBI in *Betrayed* is just a shade more sympathetic than the bigoted terrorists. In fact, since one of the callous G-men is black, the film suggests the FBI is more than willing to use sexism to combat racism.

The problem is the film's unconsciousness about its *own* sexism in its condescending treatment of Cathy Weaver. Her FBI boss is her ex-boyfriend who sadistically enjoys seeing her emotional upheaval, especially when he learns she's sleeping with the enemy. So Winger's role is less intrepid-Special-Agent than the stereotypical woman-caught-between-two-men. She's also set up as flighty, sentimental, and not especially savvy. Slithering through the woods to spy on the terrorists, she cracks too many twigs and is spotted. And in the primitive days before cell phones, she uses the family phone on the farm to call the feds once too often. One of the terrorist farmers immediately suspects her of being a ringer. (He's played by adenoid-voiced Ted Levine, who later plays the serial killer in *Silence of the Lambs*, as if he'd been typecast as a menacing force against women FBI agents in this genre.)

Leftist director Costa-Gavras has done political irony more deftly than this, in *Missing* (1982), and of course in the powerful *Z* (1969). But in *Betrayed*, the focus on a female character diverts the film into every possible stock melodramatic ploy—Cathy's tormented intimacy with the bad guy, her maternal connection to little Rachel, and finally her decision to shoot the man she loves. Ouch!

In the end, Cathy succeeds in her assignment. She identifies the terrorists, and the Bureau is pleased with her work. But Cathy herself doesn't psychically survive the emotional schizophrenia. Disgusted with the feds, she resigns. In the last sequence of the film, we see her drifting across the country, at one point dirty and unkempt, part of a homeless group camped around a fire. In the final scene, she's returned to visit the farm community she'd infiltrated so she can say goodbye to little Rachel, while the bigoted farmers glare at her from afar.

Snow blankets the ground and Rachel in her knit tassel cap puckers her tiny face into tearful confusion. The scene is Currier & Ives via D.W. Griffith. Cathy's hope, apparently, is that she'd gotten through to Rachel earlier, when she tried to teach her to think of the daddies of Jews and black people—that is, to humanize the people Rachel is being taught to hate. As a slim thread of sentiment, it's not quite enough on which to hang the movie: racist terrorism thrives in the American heartland, the FBI is cruel in its usage of women, but perhaps one little girl will remember the humane whisper of the woman who shot her daddy.

Similar problems surface later with *V.I. Warshawski* and *A Stranger Among Us*. In the first wave of female investigator movies, it was tempting to use the props of adorable children and ready-made families in order to ease the strain of this novelty character. When two women filmmakers went to work on this topic at the end of the 1980s, they ditched the domestic props and took up the malicious scene of the police procedural, with women cops stranded in mean streets, men's plots, and dangerous fantasies.

WOMEN FILMMAKERS: *IMPULSE* AND *BLUE STEEL*

It can't be a coincidence that the two most ambiguous and self-conscious female investigator movies of this era were projects of women directors. No coincidence either are the insider jabs and campy mockery of these movies—over-the-top role-playing and rub-your-nose-in-it cop film aphorisms. Directors Sondra Locke and Kathryn Bigelow are Hollywood insiders via the powerful men with whom they've been associated (Clint Eastwood and James Cameron, respectively). As Christina Lane has pointed out, collaborations among men in Hollywood often go unremarked, while women's associations with men usually come with sexist assumptions. More rarely are these associations examined for thematic overlaps and common concerns.[9] Bigelow was briefly married to Cameron, who had directed *Aliens* (1986) and *The Abyss* (1989), films with substantial female action roles. Locke had been married to Eastwood who, in addition to playing make-my-day heroes, had also directed a series of offbeat films, such as *Pale Rider* (1985), that reworked the material of box-office formulas.

Locke's *Impulse* and Bigelow's *Blue Steel* likewise take familiar material into offbeat directions, beginning with the casting. In *Impulse*, Theresa Russell (who played the *femme fatale* in *Black Widow*) switches sides and becomes the cop, while female guilt and treachery remain the themes. In *Blue Steel*, Jamie Lee Curtis, survivor of teen serial-killer horrors, joins the police, who are famously ineffectual in the horror film. Russell is super-glamorous and Curtis gets progressively more butch. Most critics couldn't steer past the clichés, but both movies are worth the drive.

These films focus on how these women cops are *pictured* and the fantasies those pictures induce. In Locke's *Impulse*, we first see Theresa Russell as Lottie Mason walking the streets as part of her undercover job. In the next scene, it's evident that her boss, a corrupt police lieutenant, also sees her as body-to-be-had for the right price. Lottie herself, it turns out, is fascinated by her own "vice" roles, so *Impulse* revolves around role-playing and images. *Blue Steel* likewise explores the fantasy of the licensed woman with the gun: the image of the woman cop blowing away the perp makes one man crazy and ultimately ends the woman cop's career. That is, what they *look like* is crucial for both heroines in a way it's never crucial for the *Lethal Weapon* guys. No matter how cute Mel Gibson appears on the job, it's not what turns the plot around.

In both films, too, the women begin as investigators and end up being investigated, both of them accused of murder. But in *Impulse*, the woman cop really is guilty of a crime—not homicide but grand larceny. Talking about her undercover work on the police force, Lottie Mason makes it clear that she's in it for the money. That's standard hardboiled detective talk. Look at *The Maltese Falcon* again and count up how much money Sam Spade takes and keeps along the way. Cops and P.I.s are blue-collar workers, always looking for some extra cash.

But Lottie's work, posing as a "working girl," conjures snide stereotypes about the "dirtiness" of working-class women.[10] Already an outsider, the woman out of place on a police force, Lottie is doubly suspicious because her expertise is her ability to use her body and sexiness on the job, to turn it off and on, as work. The film poses sly questions about these assumptions. Aren't women "naturally" good at sexual deception? Is this really work if role-playing is what women always do? Twice during *Impulse* we see Lottie's dressing room, which looks like the dressing room of an actress, filled with wigs, pots of makeup, and brushes. But these undercover disguises—makeup, heels, miniskirts—are versions of what women are *encouraged* to wear in order to look attractive. Several times in the film, it's unclear to Lottie's colleagues if she's "on the job" at a given moment or just made up for a date. Women are always suspicious, *Impulse* hints, because they're always able to fake a sexual attraction or sexual pleasure.

Even more intriguingly, Lottie Mason likes role-playing. She confesses to the department shrink that she gets off on playing prostitutes. She likes the power, she says. The two scenes with the therapist bring to mind the therapy scenes in *Klute*, in which the articulate prostitute Bree (Jane Fonda) similarly admits her attraction to difficult or impossible men, her affinity to role-playing, and her impatience with "nice" guys. In *Klute*, Bree is the would-be victim of a serial murderer, and her life is saved by the "nice" detective Klute whom she both loves and resists. But in *Impulse*, Lottie shoots the perps herself. In fact, she's been assigned to therapy because she shoots to kill. The nice guy in her life is the assistant D.A. played by Jeff Fahey, who is, if anything, even prettier than Russell. Always the clever cop, Lottie deliberately role plays with the therapist, too. As a result, we really *can't* tell her motivations by what we see or even by what we hear in a supposedly therapeutic situation. In the twenty years between *Klute* and *Impulse*, the woman has been licensed to kill and the therapy scene has become suspect as one more place where roles can be played.

One night, after an undercover setup that nearly gets her killed, Lottie gives in to an impulse. She goes to a bar *not* on a job, but on her own, and plays her own game of pickup with a rich guy. But her pickup is a criminal who is murdered while Lottie is in his house. And Lottie—on an impulse—steals a briefcase full of drug money, enough to allow her to escape her job and her life if she chooses. It's a clever variation on the hooker exchange of body and cash.

At first, the cops only know there was a female witness, the hooker seen at the bar. When a police artist does a sketch of the woman, the all-male investigation team is too thick to realize she's right there in

Fig. 21 Theresa Russell as undercover vice cop Lottie Mason in *Impulse* (1990). Courtesy of Photofest.

the room with them. Only the corrupt lieutenant guesses correctly because he, too, thinks like a criminal.

Unfortunately, all these witty reversals and teases of the male cop film go limp at this point. The problem—predictably—is romance. Lottie had been resisting her feelings for that cute D.A., but the more trouble she gets into, the harder she falls for him. Eventually, after she's quit her job and is about to take off with the money, he's the one who comes to her physical and moral rescue. The big fight scene occurs, significantly, in the airport *men's* room, exactly where Lottie doesn't belong.

The schmaltzy closing love scene is embarrassing, but even more alarming is the fate of this female investigator, who is now jobless and apparently back in the role of "natural" woman: mate, lover, sweetie, girl without a gun. Often, male cops or detectives in movies like *Lethal Weapon* are given a love interest to soften them up, make them vulnerable and human. But they don't have to resign or retire or quit the police force at the end as well.

Lottie is the most hardboiled of this first generation of women cops and detectives, and she's the most sexualized, costumed in strappy, backless, tight, low-cut whore clothes for nearly half the movie. So she's more threatening than Dirty Harry, whose "natural" macho violence is culturally acceptable. To recuperate this character, Lottie is not just coupled but disarmed at the end of *Impulse*, with all that sexual energy redirected safely toward love rather than toward work on the streets.

Kathryn Bigelow's *Blue Steel* also has some disappointing plot turns and—more so than *Impulse*—some downright awful dialogue. The movie works if you remember the awfulness is camp, especially in the guns-are-penises sequences. Heroine New York City cop Megan Turner (Jamie Lee Curtis) tracks down her ex-boyfriend serial killer, obsessed that they both "have one" and can shoot it out as equals. When she finds him floundering for his weapon at one point, she offers him her extra gun. "It's okay," she tells him, "I've got one. Grab for it."[11] It's easy to miss the parody. Most of us like our camp served up flambé, Danny Kaye prancing through *White Christmas*, rather than an ambiguous Jamie Lee Curtis in regulation-blue drag.

At its best, *Blue Steel* both mimics and honors the Hollywood tough-cop movie, often with dazzling visual style. Bigelow is a rarity in Hollywood, not just a woman director but one with formal training in both film theory and art. The artsy look of this film is a classy tribute to film noir. The scenes at the police station, for instance, are washed in chiaroscuro shadows and shades of blue. The wit of the film is often visual, too. At police-academy graduation, when the cops are posing for photos with their girlfriends and wives, Megan poses with her best friend Tracy, a clue that this cop movie will *picture* things differently and will present disquieting questions about bodies and sexualities.

The credit sequence is an enthralling visual coup that eroticizes Megan's Smith & Wesson revolver, a theme that's taken up by the plot in more problematic ways. But we first see this gun abstracted into textures and designs as the camera lovingly moves over its surface and then focuses on the bullets being slowly inserted into the speed loader. When the loader is full and spinning, it turns into a reel of film—a clear announcement that this film *knows* what it's doing with cameras, guns, and the woman in the man's place.

The gun-loading sequence is part of Megan's preparations on graduation day from the academy. In crisp closeup shots of body parts, we see the female body taking on traditionally masculine props and attire: a blue regulation shirt buttoned over a lace bra; men's dress shoes being laced up with military precision; a necktie knotted; hair tucked into cap—giving Megan's body a different presence, power, and meaning.

The difference is also Jamie Lee Curtis. Long and lean, Curtis as a cop is a fetishist's dream come true. Every time I teach this film, at least a few students offer details about Jamie Lee Curtis's unusual genetics, apparently taught in college biology classes these days. Sexed female, she nevertheless has two male chromosomes. So there's an offscreen story in circulation about Curtis's female masculinity, reinforced by the handsome closeup of Megan Turner proudly straightening her cap. When Megan saunters down the street in her sleek new uniform, two young women respond with flirtatious smiles, and it's not clear if they're smiling because they think it's a man or know it's a woman.

Megan's body and gender are strikingly malleable in *Blue Steel*. At one point, in a dress and seen by candlelight, Megan looks soft and feminine. But through the course of the film, she looks more butch as she grows more driven. Toward the end, in bed with her lover, played by tow-headed Clancy Brown, Megan is pointedly masculinized, and Brown has much better hair.

Like other woman investigators in the movies, Megan is quizzed about why she's a cop, and she gives lame-joke replies that make men nervous: "Ever since I was a kid, I wanted to shoot people." But we quickly learn that Megan became a cop to arrest men like her wife-beating father. "I got a goddamned cop for a daughter," her outraged father complains. For a moment, this looks like a way to even the score with men who hurt women. However, Megan learns that even with a gun and a badge, she is up against the larger gender dynamics of the working-class cop scene. In her very first night on the beat, Megan kills a suspect in self-defense, but the suspect's gun doesn't show up, so Megan instantly becomes a suspect herself. Worse still, the gun has been stolen by a witness, wealthy Wall Street trader Eugene Holt (Ron Silver). With his contraband gun and obsessed by the sexy image of Megan shooting the perp, Eugene turns serial killer.

So the visual image of Megan with the gun jump-starts the series of murders and calamities in this movie. It also kindles sexual desire, because Eugene turns into Megan's suitor, and Megan responds with passion. By the time she's finally on to him, she's already been discredited

Fig. 22 Jamie Lee Curtis as officer Megan Turner in *Blue Steel* (1990). Courtesy of Photofest.

by the police, who in turn are reluctant to touch a prestigious businessman who lives on Manhattan's Upper West Side. Eugene is a lunatic, but his killer instincts are respectable on Wall Street. It's not just that Megan doesn't have a chance. *Blue Steel* coldly lays out the whole stacked system of no-chances.

And her only tool for revenge is the gun, of course. More than any of the other films, *Blue Steel* poses female violence as the main issue in picturing the "female dick," with the gun as the appended body part. In one sense, this reduces the gender switch to the level of biology. When Megan is being interrogated at the police station, a detective interrupts to tell a coarse story that summarizes her predicament. The story is about a prostitute who accidentally bit off her client's dick and tried to sew it back on again, but sewed it on backward. It's a guy joke, told by a handsome cop unfortunately named Nick Mann. The story puts Megan in her place as outsider, reminds the male cops about the treachery of women, and handily delivers a vulgar image of the woman who wants to carry a gun—a sewn-on dick, so to speak.

Blue Steel often suggests masculinity is just a disposable prop. After all, the image of gun-as-dick reduces masculinity itself from a natural, biological force to a piece that can be packed or not. In that case, the woman with a gun isn't imitating a man but is accessing a tool that men access, too. "Grab for it," as Megan says.[12]

Unfortunately, *Blue Steel* never follows through on this suggestion and instead goes the direction of the vengeance movie, with Megan turned vigilante and criminal. Eugene torments her with the classic cop-criminal mirror: "We're two halves of one person," he tells her, even as she's snapping him into handcuffs. "I know you better than you know yourself." He's right. When he slips through the system, trashes her credibility, kills her best friend, wounds her lover, and attempts to rape her, Megan no longer wants his arrest or even his death sentence. She wants to kill him herself. She finally executes him in cold blood, exactly as he'd killed his own victims. Megan can't get away with murder, so the film ends sadly, the bloody, wounded heroine being lifted into the arms of the law.

Blue Steel explodes the illusion that a woman in the man's place will change the crime scene or the power structure. For the last bullet-ridden chase, Megan slugs a male cop and steals his uniform, so she enacts her vigilante pursuit in drag, doubly illegitimate in the stolen uniform. Considering her ill treatment at the hands of the police, Eugene's insight about her secret criminality takes a new spin. Angry at the system and all its abusive men, she shows that her capacity for violence is as volatile as his. Little wonder this movie appeals to women, with its satisfying enactment of female rage at the old-boys network, jokes, bad daddies, and smug Wall Street lunatics.

Blue Steel is also conscious of itself as a new story that's still in rehearsal, noir with a kink, the female blues story as a woman in blue. The self-consciousness shows up in the opening sequence, which is actually a training test at the police academy, though the film viewer doesn't know this. Instead, the scene looks like domestic violence, with a woman screaming, a man yelling back at her, and the cop—Megan—breaking in to investigate. Megan makes a mistake, a gendered mistake. Focusing on the abusive man at the scene, she doesn't notice that the woman picks up the gun and aims it at Megan, the intrusive cop.

It's a bittersweet metaphor of the woman detective in film. Surprise! Beware the new script! Women aren't taking their old roles and positions! And Megan fails the test. This new story and heroine are still raw, unproven at this point. The police-training sequence is actually a thread that can be traced through other movies of this genre. It appears again in *Silence of the Lambs*, in a short scene made especially for the movie version, in which Clarice Starling practices an arrest at FBI school and similarly fails. But by its third appearance, in *Copycat*, women have become more successful: the woman detective is in charge of the training.

Neither *Impulse* nor *Blue Steel* were critical hits. Most critics scorned *Impulse*'s glamour and missed its more subtle critiques of women's role-playing. Likewise, journalists blasted *Blue Steel*'s over-the-top "Dirty Harriet" stance, missing its self-conscious criticism of the male crime story.[13] In this earlier stage of the female investigator in Hollywood, the films themselves stumble at key moments, still haunted by those old scripts and roles.

FIRST WAVE FIZZLES: *V.I. WARSHAWSKI* AND *A STRANGER AMONG US*

The Locke and Bigelow films posed ambitious questions about the woman investigator, even if the films failed to satisfy those questions or fully explore them. But the two more mainstream films of this era, *V.I. Warshawski* and *A Stranger Among Us*, launched with bigger stars and budgets, pulled back from those questions (violence, bodies, sexuality, class) altogether. In fact, we can see the drag marks, the exact places where the conventions lug the female investigator back into safe, FBI Girl predictability. Most strikingly, neither *V.I. Warshawski* nor *A Stranger Among Us* want to give up the *romantic* heroine, no matter how many guns she packs. They also want to recapture her into a ready-made family, saving her from the lonely life of P.I. or cop, hoping she'll find her way around a kitchen. Desperate to picture a domestic woman detective, these films are badly hatched hybrids of mystery and makeover, with the woman investigator in each case emerging with some trite lessons about "true womanhood."

A Stranger Among Us uses a plot device that worked better in Peter Weir's film *Witness*. Harrison Ford was the tough big-city detective forced to hide out in an Amish community, where he gets romantically involved and where he learns to respect a culture he barely understands. In *Stranger*, the premise is that NYPD detective Emily Eden (Melanie Griffith) must live inside the Hasidic community in Brooklyn in order to solve the murder of one of its members.

The casting of Melanie Griffith and her Betty Boop voice would cramp the best of detective movies. "Get a court order, 'kay?" she chirps to her cop colleague. But *Stranger* is also handicapped by the sheer flimsiness of its supposed mystery, which, as most of the reviewers pointed out, anyone past Nancy Drew could solve. When a young Jewish merchant disappears from his shop for two days, does *no one* notice the blood stains on the ceiling tiles until Emily comes on the scene? Those of us who read mystery novels also know that after two days, murder victims tend to reveal their presence via a give-away *eau-de-corpse*. In *Stranger*, the murderer-among-them also emits alarming clues that Emily doesn't follow until it's almost too late. The main smell of this movie is amateurism.

Unlike *Witness*, which was strung on the tension of big-city corruption versus the sheltered Amish, *Stranger* is hung up on its forbidden-romance story, the chic *shiksa* tempting the untouchable rabbinical student destined to be the next *rebbe*. The big moments aren't the crime scenes but the would-be seductions, laden with stock dialogue: "But I'm the next *rebbe!*" "But is it what you *want?*" *Fiddler on the Roof* meets daytime soaps.

Chain smoking and prone to a loveless sex life, Emily is aghast that the Hasidic women want to be wives and mothers. "Is that it?" she asks in disbelief. Meanwhile, the film intersperses warmly lit, soft-focus scenes of Hasidic life with Emily's cold, empty one: a clueless father, a so-so lover, a bleak apartment. We see her gradually charmed by the community, participating in its rituals, helping with the baking, learning to stuff chicken breasts and keep separate kosher refrigerators.

The effect is very different from Harrison Ford learning to build a barn in *Witness*, though both films are sincere enough about respecting traditional subcultures. But Harrison Ford films can as easily hand him hammers as Magnums. For men, either kind of tool is "natural." For the female character that has only had a dozen years in the squad room, picturing her back in the kitchen—her "natural" place—makes her job as cop all the more "unnatural," à la the female dick.

In the greater nimbleness of the literary imagination, Patricia Cornwell's authoritative heroine can move easily from autopsies to gourmet cooking. But Melanie Griffith's authority only barely registers, so the culinary coziness further undermines her as a serious investigator. At least the movie remembers to pull her out of the romance plot and solve the mystery. Emily gives up the forbidden love and returns to her job, supposedly a better woman, wearing less outrageous lipstick and dreaming of her true destiny with the right man—a wish that, incredibly, is her last line in the movie.

V.I. Warshawski is the more troubling film—or the more interesting failure—since its source is as elegant as the movie is clumsy. In a series of first-rate mystery novels, Sara Paretsky had developed her female private investigator into literary respectability and best-seller stature. She introduced Vic (Victoria) Warshawski in 1982 and had published six V.I. novels by the time the Jeff Kanew film came out in 1991. Unlike Grafton's fun-read series, Paretsky's is weighted down with complex characters and an intricate inner-city sociology of welfare hotels, abortion clinics, and seedy neighborhoods near Wrigley Field.

On the surface, the novels seem patterned after traditional macho hardboiled yarns. Vic is a former public defender, now a private investigator with insider connections to Chicago's cops, politics, and underworld. She drinks, eats, and has sex like a guy—freely, without qualms.

She's divorced, like most literary female detectives, and her relationship to the opposite sex is cautious. When a culpable ex-lover shoots himself in the head, her memories aren't poignant: "I hadn't known Peter well enough to be eating my heart out for him. His bones and brains on the desk top flashed into my mind. Horrifying, yes. But not my personal burden."[14]

But the hardboiled talk and action are wired to fiercely woman-centered politics. Vic is no female dick along the lines of Honey West, a male fantasy in a male tradition. We find out in *Killing Orders* (1985) that Warshawski was a feminist activist during her days at the University of Chicago. Her ally throughout the series is her friend Dr. Lotty Herschel, a Holocaust survivor who runs a clinic for the poor. True, Vic knows the Chicago old-boys network, but her own network is mostly women: the staff at Lotty's clinic, the waitresses, diner owners, and barkeeps Vic can depend on for information and support. It goes without saying that her relationship with the police bristles with anger about their sexism. In *Burn Marks* (1990), when a policeman father-figure tries to set her up romantically with a young turk cop, the violent result is Vic's kidnapping and attempted murder by the would-be beau.

The novels also depart from the conservative detective tradition in which clues lead to a criminal whose arrest brings all the plotlines to a wrap. Instead, Vic usually confronts inbred political and institutional corruption—junk bonds, insurance fraud, police corruption, industrial pollution, and even a scheming archbishop in the Catholic Church. Individual scumbags get fingered, but there's no illusion the bigger problem has been solved. The victims she helps are often the elderly, the addicted, the impoverished, none of whom magically bound back to health and prosperity.[15]

How could this gritty, politically tense scenario be sold to Disney-owned Hollywood Pictures? Tri-Star Pictures optioned the character because the topic was timely and it was a perfect lure for a female audience. Paretsky for her part was able to use the money to become a full-time writer (and she has discreetly kept silent about the results of the film). *V.I. Warshawski* is loosely based on the first two novels in the series, *Indemnity Only* (1982) and *Deadlock* (1984), but the movie version is crammed with sexist details and sappy stereotypes likely to turn off the very fans Tri-Star hoped to bring in.

Fans knew they were in trouble during the film's opening scene, in which Vic worriedly steps on the scale and then decides to go jogging. In the novels, Vic is careful to keep her weight *up* because she needs the bulk and heft to go against the bad guys. *V.I. Warshawski* goes lightweight in other ways as well. Intricate politics and women's networks disappear. The spectacular climax of *Deadlock*—the explosion of a grain freighter—is replaced with a low-budget shootout on a tugboat. The pensive, intricately knotted character of Vic is flattened to a smart-mouth chick prone to castration jokes. And the richly textured Chicago landscape is replaced by views of Kathleen Turner's body—closeups of her legs and red stiletto heels, shots of Vic in the bathtub, teasing glimpses of Vic changing clothes in the back of a taxi.

The advertisement for the film brazenly suggested retro campiness: "Killer eyes. Killer legs. Killer instincts." In the poster image, Kathleen Turner poses in high heels and short skirt, her legs far apart, reminiscent of Angie Dickinson's days as Pepper Anderson. And much of the dialogue and Kathleen Turner's performance is (I hope) intended to be campy, a comic capacity she later developed in full for *Serial Mom* (1994). In *V.I. Warshawski*, her drop-dead bass voice is perfect for delivery of funny lines that threaten a man with a nutcracker and pose that in-your-face question I quoted in chapter 1: "Whatsa matter, haven't you ever seen a female dick?" Swaggering and foul mouthed, she plays the detective like a mean Mae West, a character not imaginable in the Paretsky novels, but one that could have carried the film if the camp agenda had been carried through, too.

Fig. 23 Kathleen Turner as the private investigator heroine of *V.I. Warshawski* (1991). Courtesy of Photofest.

But her camp performance is screechingly at odds with the film's mushy sentimentality. *V.I. Warshawski* haltingly aims for warm fuzziness that may be intended to appeal to women, no matter how gagging it was for readers of Paretsky. In the movie, domestic disaster though she may be, Vic finds herself becoming a mother figure when she takes care of Kat, a little girl whose father she'd picked up at a bar. Kat's father is murdered, and the villain is Kat's treacherous, manipulative mother, who has to be blown away—a bullet directly between the eyes!—by Vic herself. So even though Vic is roughed up by some bad guys, she loses those battles so that she can triumph over her true enemy, another woman. Vic and her steady boyfriend become surrogate parents as the movie ends.

It's hard to keep track of so many clichés at once, but a scorecard would look something like this. V.I. talks and dresses like a hooker or the *femme fatale* from the crime movie, but she's secretly maternal at heart (prostitute with heart of gold). She's threatening to men, but she's a man's woman after all (just one of the boys). When the line is drawn, the protective Vic defeats the truly awful mother (good mother versus bad mother). She's a tough detective, but is easily drawn into a makeshift family (a woman's place is in the home.) And it almost got worse. Because Tri-Star had rights to the character, they originally planned to do a second film showing Vic in midlife crisis, deciding to settle down and have a child of her own. Fortunately, *V.I. Warshawski* was such a total box-office bomb that the world is safe from sequels.

Some critics claimed the movie was pure backlash against the emerging feminist action heroine, who would show up that year in *Thelma & Louise* and *Terminator 2: Judgment Day* (1991). Other reviewers chalked the failure up to Hollywood's retreat, or "How to Create a Strong Female Character without Offending Anyone," as the *New York Times* put it. And feminist film critics were both aghast and intrigued that male sexual anxiety could be so transparently acted out with nervous penis jokes and the sexually powerful woman who is tamed and pushed into domesticity.[16]

In retrospect, *V.I. Warshawski* may explain why it took so long for cinema to picture the woman investigator. Its banalities—the whorish red heels, the dick jokes, leg shots, retreats into romance—are a compendium of generic Hollywood picturings of powerful women. They're the clichés that 1991's classier killer women bite off and spit out: Susan Sarandon as Louise confidently driving her convertible, Linda Hamilton priming her muscles, Jodie Foster blowing Ted Levine as Buffalo Bill into eternity.

6

ACTION BODIES
Women Detective Movies, 1995–2000

THE ACTION HEROINE

You could tell the female investigator was doing better in late 1990s Hollywood because she was no longer Debra Winger. Nor was she Kathleen Turner cracking dick jokes or Melanie Griffith learning to stuff chickens. By the end of the decade, Jennifer Lopez in *Out of Sight* (1998) played a federal marshal with a snappy wardrobe and no apologies. It was possible because a new kind of character was emerging in Hollywood, the action heroine, first cousin of the woman detective and popular enough to draw a market and an audience. In *Out of Sight,* Lopez doesn't need to explode through giant plate-glass windows or somersault out of burning cars. But when she's threatened by some mouthy testosterone, she whips a blackjack out of her designer handbag and makes the guy very, very sorry.

The female action body had become naturalized on screen by 1998, sporting glossy lipstick and serious skills in sharpshooting and martial arts. Because she was a fantasy figure, she crisscrossed genders, desires, and politics, imaginable as supermodel, Wonder Woman, and reverie from the *Sports Illustrated* swimsuit issue, cooler and more self-confident than her predecessors in *Impulse, Black Widow,* and *Blue Steel.*

Granted, the *best* of the 1990s woman-detective films featured women who were far less glamorous—Jodie Foster in *The Silence of the Lambs* and Frances McDormand in *Fargo,* both of which were among the most honored film performances of the decade.[1] The two award-winning roles for these actresses proved beyond doubt that this new character, the female investigator, could yield box-office gold against stereotype odds. Here was a powerful woman character wholly outside romance, neurosis, or melodrama—the traditional "good" box-office roles for women. And she could be pictured as a mainstream draw such as Lopez.

To put it bluntly, not a single one of the first-wave female investigation movies, the ones discussed in chapter 5, was a hit. And the box-office record had delivered some mixed messages for Hollywood producers. On one hand, over-the-top glamorization in *V.I. Warshawski*, even associated with a stylish best-selling book series, had flopped. On the other hand, the huge success and prestigious awards of *The Silence of the Lambs* in 1991 had set an impossibly high standard for a female investigator who was at least as interesting as Sam Spade or Jake Gittes. In the long run, Clarice Starling's legacy would develop not in cinema but on television, through complicated characters such as *The X-Files's* Dana Scully, *Profiler's* Sam Waters, *Crossing Jordan's* Jordan Cavanaugh, and *Alias's* Sydney Bristow.

Certainly *The Silence of the Lambs* was a turning point because it made the female investigator character respectable and visible. In fact, given the mainstream attention focused on *The Silence of the Lambs* and *Hannibal*, both book and movie versions, Clarice gets the final chapter of this book all to herself. But *The Silence of the Lambs* was also part of a larger moment of unsmiling, gun-toting heroines. Clarice Starling was one among the remarkable spate of these heroines who appeared in 1991. That was the year of *La Femme Nikita*, *Eve of Destruction*, *Mortal Thoughts*, *Thelma & Louise*, and Linda Hamilton flashing enviable biceps in *Terminator 2* (known as *T2*). These avenging heroines and politically charged plots made for a heady redefinition of "the woman's film." The traditional Hollywood idea of "strong" women's roles had been Meryl Streep in a child-custody argument or Joan Crawford in shoulder pads. It's true that Bette Davis had smoldering eyes that could kill. But the women in these newer films *did* kill, either with professional training or homegrown determination. Louise admits to Thelma that she learned to shoot by watching TV.

Shocked critics were aghast at these heroines' use of violence, speculating about "Women Who Kill Too Much" and "Killer Bimbos," but some of us were thrilled to see high-profile films featuring women in nondomestic, nonromantic roles.[2] Hollywood money was immediately interested enough to remake the French *La Femme Nikita* as *Point of No Return* (1993), with Bridget Fonda playing the trained assassin. Sharon Stone strutted as a gunslinger in *The Quick and the Dead* (1995), and Meg Ryan took a respite from cute comedies to fight the Gulf War in *Courage under Fire* (1996). Even Meryl Streep got an action role as the suburban mother facing murderous criminals on a raft in *The River Wild* (1994). A-list films in Hollywood were finally getting women out of the house.

As Hollywood insiders pointed out, this moment occurred only because equality politics met the bottom line. Action films make more money than melodramas. As opposed to her nuanced "talk" films, Meryl Streep on white-water rapids sells to overseas markets. And actresses like Streep and Stone wanted the action-movie salaries of Bruce Willis and Sylvester Stallone. For their part, producers needed to keep the wham-bam action-adventure market fresh by providing something new, like a gender bend. Hong Kong martial arts movies had already gone this route, and some of their action actresses, such as Michelle Yeoh, would eventually be imported by Hollywood. By the late 1980s, American experiments along this line had produced the China O'Brien movies (1990 and 1991), which were bad even by low-budget standards. *Fatal Beauty* was better, but not a box-office hit. The turnaround didn't come until the idea found money, mainstream directors, and stars. *T2* got $100 million, James Cameron as director, and Schwarzenegger as the name draw, and that's why the Linda Hamilton character could pump those biceps in the asylum, waiting for her day. That day had come.

More to the point, the day had come when it was possible to imagine a woman's body as an *action body*. Through the 1980s, high-profile women athletes such as Jackie Joyner had given women's sports some chic celebrities. Also, women in that decade were the first to have grown up with Title IX of the Education Amendments of 1972, requiring equal opportunities for girls' sports in public schools. And as body-building for women gained popularity in the late 1980s, women's physical fitness evolved from a health to a fashion issue. Kathleen Turner wearing long sleeves throughout *V.I. Warshawski* was virtually a health-club advertisement about a girl's unhappy options without upper-arm definition.

The more serious female action bodies of the decade were trained and toned—Jamie Lee Curtis in *True Lies* (1994), Sigourney Weaver in *Alien: Resurrection* (1997), Michelle Yeoh as James Bond's astonishing, equalizing partner in *Tomorrow Never Dies* (1997). Television through the 1990s also featured fantasy action heroines in the top-rated series *Buffy the Vampire Slayer* (1997–2003) and *Xena: Warrior Princess* (1995–2001) followed by *Witchblade* (2001–2) and *Dark Angel* (2000–2) at the turn of the century. Surreal creatures though some of these may be, they made possible the screenings of other female adventurers.

The films got slicker and the heroines sexier. The "action" of these heroines was just a flick away from the soft porn of *Hard Evidence*

(1995) and *Femme Fontaine: Killer Babe for the CIA* (1994). As the Blaxploitation films had proven decades earlier, the curvaceous woman loaded down with Uzis and ammo belts is more thrill than threat. At the end of the decade, Lara Croft easily stepped out of video games and onto the screen as full-lipped Angelina Jolie in *Lara Croft: Tomb Raider*, proving that soft porn can be boring. While the high-class 1991 avenger films had tended toward political inquiry, the later films lost this critical edge. Soon Geena Davis battled pirates (*Cutthroat Island*, 1995) and Demi Moore grunted through basic training (*G.I. Jane*, 1997) with neither controversy nor much originality.

So this new action heroine, pumped up and conditioned, could put on her badge and pack her .38 with mixed effects. When Jamie Lee Curtis pulls her hair into her cap and ties the laces on her boots in *Blue Steel*, the drag-king overtones are brazen. When Angelina Jolie does it in *The Bone Collector* (1999), it's dishy. The later film is far less haunting, but its heroine is also far less harassed.

SERIAL KILLERS AND COPYCATS

The heroine of *The Silence of the Lambs* may have been unique for Hollywood film, but the story of the serial killer versus the woman investigator was prime material for spinoff. The serial-killer plot was already familiar and even overused in Hollywood by the 1990s. Like pop culture itself, as critics have pointed out, serial killing is all about sequel, suspense, and repetition. For both tabloid and mainstream journalism, as for books and movies, it's a catchy story—the killer at large, the repeated bloody details, the female victim and anonymous male murderer.[3] The Jack the Ripper story is the prototype, its killer still on the loose in the cultural imagination more than a century later.

The serial killer had long been a cinematic favorite, beginning with Fritz Lang's *M* (1931), but routed most often into the horror movie tradition from which *The Silence of the Lambs* dips heavily for its labyrinth basement and Gothic chills. *Psycho* (1960) is the much-imitated modern granddaddy of this story, stocked with the immortal male killer, female victims, wicked knives, a terrible basement, and a plucky female survivor that Carol Clover has named The Final Girl, usually named Sidney or Stretch or Laurie or Marti. In *Men, Women, and Chainsaws*, Clover spells out these elements as the repeated formula of the slasher and splatter films that dominated horror movies following the wild success of *Halloween* (1978), *Friday the 13th* (1980) and their sequels.

As Clover argues, even though these movies were supposedly aimed at a male teenage audience, the films themselves encouraged identification with the heroic Final Girl, who screams nonstop as she discovers the bodies, but who escapes the knife or chainsaw and usually turns it against the superhuman Jason or Leatherface or Michael Myers.[4] The Final Girl's survival is linked to her tomboyish resistance to sex. From *Psycho* to *Scream* (1996), the victims are all women caught in the act or at least guilty of sleeping around, while the virginal and resourceful sister or babysitter witnesses the carnage and lives to recall the horror.

Throughout the slasher genre, the police are pudgy, middle-aged guys who show up too late or are easily disarmed by the killer. But here's the brilliant loop in the genre, made possible with the action heroine as investigator: the Final Girl herself becomes the police, smarter but also more vulnerable. She's Clarice Starling, of course, as well as prime-time television's androgynously named Dana, Sam, and Jordan, all versions of Marti, Sydney, and Stretch with college degrees in criminology and forensics.

Having a woman investigator interrupt the violent male cycle of killings is a satisfying female fantasy, long overdue, as Clarice Starling realizes in the Harris novel: "All of Buffalo Bill's victims were women, his obsession was women, he lived to hunt women. Not one woman was hunting him full time. Not one woman investigator had looked at every one of his crimes." This insight galvanizes Clarice into outrage and action. " '*Fuck* this,' Starling said aloud" (*Silence*, 268).

This remark comes at the end of the 1980s, a decade when women writers had had similar cranky reactions to the boys-only stories of violence and crime, in which women were victims but never the ones to hunt the killers. *Blue Steel* participates in this comeuppance fantasy, but for the big screen, Clarice was the first wholly successful Final Girl turned investigator. Unlike slasher film monsters that keep rising from the dead, Buffalo Bill was dead forever, thank you, earning Clarice her badge and creating the new score, 1–0, between the woman investigator and the murderer of women.

The new formula was popular enough to be slicked into a low-budget, quick-bucks product, the straight-to-video *Serial Killer* (1995). As the title suggests, this was a generic, dumbed-down *Silence of the Lambs*, so it's a cultural index of the factors that make Clarice, and in a bigger sense, the woman investigator, both frightening and important.

The heroine of *Serial Killer* is an FBI profiler, Selby Younger, with a Final Girl's androgynous name but played by statuesque Kim Delaney, who would be cast that same year as a tight-sweater cop on *NYPD Blue*. Selby survives some brutal encounters with the serial killer, who has targeted her because she's accurately tracked and profiled him.

Unlike the solo Clarice, Selby is pictured throughout as part of a romantic couple. In fact, her on-and-off relationship with her *GQ*-looking FBI boyfriend (Gary Hudson) is part of the so-called suspense. The movie begins and ends showing them as a couple, not at the office, but at home where Selby's nontraditional job isn't apparent at all. So *Serial Killer* "corrects" the edgier issues around Clarice, making her domesticated and above all, giving her a boyfriend.

Like Clarice, Selby has a childhood history that the plot will exploit. But unlike Clarice's complicated class positioning as the Appalachian girl in the FBI, Selby's past is canned Catholicism, the kind that can be easily opened and spread on the surface—guilt-inducing nuns, a bad conscience about sex, a rosary to pull out when the killer comes close. For the movies, Catholicism is all about sexual repression, and sex is easier to deal with than class, the latter of which perplexes American assumptions about equality and access to power.

The serial killer, played by Tobin Bell, is a B version of Hannibal Lecter, with the tastes of a studious sophomore—Shakespeare, poetry, psychology, taxidermy. The script even has him do a Lecter-like escape from a hospital gurney on an elevator. His appearances are heralded by the whoosh sounds lifted from *Halloween*, and he leaves imaginative clues, including an inadvertently hilarious carton of decorated eggs. The egg theme gets worse. The killer wants to impregnate Selby in order to assure his own immortality. Once Selby figures this out, she fakes her own suicide, sets herself up as bait, and then—wince!—has the boyfriend come to her rescue and shoot the killer dead.

As the title of the film suggests, *Serial Killer* is attuned to popular support for Hannibal Lecter, in the same way that the slasher films of the 1980s were always more interested in Jason or Michael Myers than in the endless teens they pursued. As a revision of *Silence of the Lambs*, this movie eerily prefigures the Thomas Harris sequel, which likewise switches focus to the mass murderer Hannibal.

For the developing detective heroine, though, the legitimate heir of *The Silence of the Lambs* was *Copycat*, also released in 1995, a thriller that even raised the stakes on *Silence*'s premises and characters. The female investigator is again paired with a brilliant, imprisoned psychologist in order to track the killer. But the imprisoned psychologist is a woman, and her prison is psychological. Together, the women get the killer—who is devious enough, but in the end not as cunning as the working-class cop and elegant intellectual played respectively by Holly Hunter and Sigourney Weaver.

The odd-couple pairing is faithful to the tradition of the action-buddy formula, which often mismatches race or ethnicity (*Rush Hour*,

Fig. 24 Sigourney Weaver as Dr. Helen Hudson and Holly Hunter as Detective MJ Monahan in *Copycat* (1995). Courtesy of Photofest.

1998) or doubles racial difference with age difference (*Lethal Weapon, Seven*), or cultural difference (*48 Hrs.,* 1982; *Enemy of the State,* 1998; *Men in Black,* 1997). The antagonism between the two heroes and two sets of values gets resolved as they solve the crime.[5] A rough-house American optimism pervades these movies, as if enough exploding plate-glass windows and high-speed chases proves that all *male* Americans, at least, are buddies beneath the skin.

There's no such cultural optimism in *Copycat,* where the pairing produces a more dissident female front, more like the butch-femme duo of *Bound* than the white-black pairings in cop films. The comparison to *Bound* explains why *Copycat* is the *only* female investigation movie that comes close to the buddy formula, a staple of the cop or detective movie since the early 1980s. It's one thing to put women together in sepia-colored friendship films (*Beaches,* 1988) or zany comedies (*Outrageous Fortune,* 1987); it's quite another to pair them up and give them Smith & Wessons (*Thelma & Louise*). In male action-buddy films, the homoerotics get naturalized because we see guys doing guy stuff—shoot-outs, car chases, fistfights—the usual proofs of masculinity. At the end of *Lethal Weapon,* Mel Gibson and Danny Glover melt into each other's arms and then emerge with an explosion as one of them pulls a gun on a break-away villain. Some of us giggled, some of us didn't. But women in pairs who take on masculine roles, as in *Thelma & Louise*, take on the risk or thrill of lesbianism, which is already the risk or thrill of the woman detective.

Copycat's shrewd exploration of differences among women doesn't actually deliver erotic tension so much as intricate gender play. Sigourney Weaver appears as Dr. Helen Hudson, "Helen" being the classical beauty of Greek mythology. A brilliant psychological expert on serial killers, Helen Hudson is confident and authoritative in her lecture scene that opens the film. Clearly, she's Ripley with a Ph.D. and a smart red Givenchy suit. Making a point about the average-Joe profiles of serial killers, she has the men in the audience stand up for scrutiny, coolly turning them into visual objects for a scrutinizing female gaze. But when Dr. Hudson is attacked by an escaped serial killer who had attended her lecture, she's traumatized into acute agoraphobia. Suddenly, she can't leave her upscale apartment, where her mental illness transforms her into a traditionally feminine victim—dependent, emotional, cowering, slightly hysterical, addicted to pills and booze.

Holly Hunter plays Detective M.J. Monahan, "MJ" being resistance to a girlie name like Mary Jo or Mary Jane. Diminutive and wearing short bangs and long hair, Monahan looks butch only in contrast to Weaver's Helen Hudson (who in turn takes to Victoria's Secret-style lingerie once she's agoraphobic.) "The wee inspector," Helen calls her satirically. As they join forces for the manhunt, MJ embodies the hardboiled dick, unblinking as she gazes at mutilated corpses, quick with smartass retorts to her superiors. Complementing this, Helen works like the classic armchair detective, sealed into her privileged ivory tower with only her computer and her gay male (thus safe) assistant connecting her to the outside world. Wearing disheveled lounging pajamas, she phones in her impassioned interpretation of the serial murders to the homicide squad, looking and sounding like the stereotypical hysterical woman. The difference is that she's dead right. Eventually, MJ stubbornly believes in Helen's analyses even after the police chief has ordered MJ to stay away from her.

The traces of male-female coupling around these two women originate in the film project itself. The first script had Helen romantically involved with a male homicide cop. Director Jon Amiel rejected the project, but then rethought it as a vehicle for two women and had the cop role written specifically for Holly Hunter. Hunter doing the "guy's" role brought to the film her history of take-charge, no-nonsense women from *Raising Arizona* (1987), *Broadcast News* (1987), and *The Positively True Adventures of the Alleged Texas Cheerleader-Murdering*

Mom (1993). Hunter was also associated with some specifically feminist projects. She played the woman whose abortion case went to the Supreme Court in *Roe vs. Wade* (1989) and more notably, won an Academy Award for her role as the mute heroine of Jane Campion's *The Piano* (1993). So Hunter belongs to the school of offbeat/quirky actresses cast as women investigators when the script call for "nonglamorous" (non-Hollywood) women. In this case, the contrast with Sigourney Weaver's femmed-up Helen creates tension around questions of female roles, postures, and styles. But in one wonderful sequence, alternating shots of Helen and MJ show them intensely studying photographs of female victims, and their differences dissolve into the greater difference of women instead of men looking at women's bodies in order to solve a crime.

Copycat is bookended by two horrific scenes that take place in a women's room, of all things. Marilyn French's 1977 novel *The Women's Room* was a bible for feminists from Sigourney Weaver's generation who would remember the book's cover design, with "Ladies Room" crossed out. "Ladies" meant politeness and niceness-to-men. "Women," in contrast, were the authentic, back-talking real thing—at least for 1970s feminism. Ironically, the women's room is also traditionally a safe space. We teach our daughters to duck into the women's restroom if they feel uneasy about their surroundings at a bus station or airport. Likewise, in *Copycat*, the security guard assigned to Helen in the opening sequence assumes she's alright once he checks the room and sees only a pair of shaved, high-heeled legs in a stall.

But the serial killer stalking Helen knows that "women," like "ladies," is only a sign on the door. In the postmodern world, there's no "real thing," only bodies and clothes—or in this case, shaved legs and high heels. Besides, the serial killer in drag is the founding trick of slasher movie history, made infamous in *Psycho* and *Dressed to Kill*.

So the women's room attack not only suggests the "copycat" scheme of this movie, but also suggests how much or how little clothing has to do with female identification. The climactic scene at the end of the movie takes place in the same women's room with Helen forced to wear the same red suit. A different serial killer, intent on copycatting the unsuccessful first attack on her, disguises himself as a security guard and nearly kills both Helen and MJ, who have walked into his trap. But MJ is wearing special clothes, too—a bulletproof vest that saves her life. It's not what "ladies" or women traditionally wear. Earlier, she commented wryly that it ruins the effect of her Wonderbra. The Wonderbra of course gives the illusion of real bosom. But the bulletproof vest stops a real bullet. For woman-cop fashion, there's no contest: a girl would die without it.

And thrillingly, the two women prove to be a real team, each of them drawing on her professional expertise for the finale. Trapped on a rooftop with the killer and traumatized by her agoraphobia, Helen is still able to muster up her authority; in fact, her contempt for the murderer, who—from a suddenly absurd, near-death perspective—is no more than a specimen, something she studies for a living. In her opening lecture, she had argued that we should *study* serial killers, not kill them. Faced with his seemingly triumphant checkmate, she laughs in his face. It's enough to keep him distracted from MJ, who has crept up behind him and uses her perfect marksmanship to shoot him dead. The laughter is that of the Medusa, as feminists know all too well, the female laughter that refuses to take machismo seriously.

But the last laugh here is MJ's, who had also earlier talked about capturing criminals rather than killing them. In her first scene, MJ is teaching a male rookie that he should shoot to incapacitate, not to kill. It's the third "training sequence" in 1990s female dick flicks. *Blue Steel* opens with Megan in a practice intervention, and *The Silence of the Lambs* inserts a training scene in the film version. In both films, the rookie women make a mistake, emphasizing their newness and vulnerability. However, in *Copycat*, MJ is doing the training, and the trainee is cute Reuben Goetz (Dermot Mulroney), who flirts with both MJ and Helen, which is *his* mistake in a movie about two women investigators.

As it turns out, MJ's follow-the-rules habit of not shooting to kill is what gets Reuben killed. This happens in a bizarre subplot in which Reuben is held hostage and MJ successfully frees him by shooting his captor in the shoulder—exactly as she'd taught Reuben to do. But the wounded perp manages to shoot Reuben fatally. MJ's sad lesson is underestimating a killer. And Reuben, who hadn't served much purpose except as prop for the women's heterosexuality, is gone for good, leaving Helen and MJ on their own.

The copycat serial killer in this film is imitating famous previous serial killers—Son of Sam, the Hillside Strangler, Ted Bundy—in hope of achieving his own celebrity. But his pattern is even more nefarious than this, because the order of killings follows the order in which Helen had discussed them in her last public lecture, the opening scene. It's a cold-blooded tactic to make *her* responsible, a version of the old women-are-asking-for-it ploy. And even though Helen and MJ kill him off, he'll be imitated by the next celebrity-seeking psycho, as the creepy last shot of the movie makes clear.

Yet *Copycat* disrupts the pattern, the sheer seriality of this gruesome old story, in subversive ways. Most important, the two women throw off the plans of the serial killer and powerfully confound him in the later scene in the women's room, in which Helen risks her life to save MJ. It's a stunning scene, and one that obviously shocks the killer, who has to scramble to rethink his evil little scenario. What he hadn't counted on was the willingness of one woman to die for another.

In a larger sense, *Copycat* also breaks new ground by pairing two very different women and giving them equally important roles—the *Cagney & Lacey* formula—which diverts from the Hollywood path of either the singular heroine or the singular female victim. And finally, it's the killer, not the women, who's the copycat, lacking originality, repeating someone else's story. In contrast, Helen and MJ enact the cop-buddy story without repeating it. They don't become pals, and in fact are rarely placed in the same shot together. But neither are they rivals, sisters, or sentimental friends in the way that Hollywood usually imagines women costars.

The final 1990s serial-killer movie featuring a female cop was *The Bone Collector*, with an investigator-duo mix recalling both *The Silence of the Lambs* and *Copycat*. Denzel Washington plays Lincoln Rhyme, a brilliant forensics expert who barely survived an accident on a job a few years previously. A quadriplegic, he's bound to his bed and computer system much like Helen in *Copycat*. The MJ role is played by Angelina Jolie as Amelia, the policewoman who carries out the tasks Rhyme can no longer undertake, crawling through tunnels and diving into the Manhattan harbor to pluck out corpses, fingerprints, and body parts.

Amelia is a veteran patrol cop, but she's not a forensics expert, so she works as Lincoln's apprentice, tutored by him in a dynamic familiar from *The Silence of the Lambs*. In fact, through key scenes of the movie, Lincoln's voice is hooked into Amelia's ear through a wireless transmitter, hauntingly recalling the famous warning from Clarice Starling's superior: "Don't let Hannibal Lecter into your head." Lincoln Rhyme is no Hannibal Lecter, of course. Played by Denzel Washington, he's not even as crabby as the Rhyme in Jeffery Deaver's 1997 novel on which the movie is based. Rhyme is merely cantankerous in the movie version, which grants him some lively spars with Amelia but tones down his sarcasm and coldness. In short, it's the Denzel Washington persona, generically noble and able to play racially generic, too, in films like *Much Ado about Nothing* (1993), or *Philadelphia* (1993), or *Pelican Brief* (1993), where his romantic pairing with a white woman is unremarkable.

In the Deaver novel, there are no hints that Rhyme is a black man, nor is race referenced in the movie. The film suggests that it's not supposed to matter; he belongs not to black culture but to the culture of health care and disability. Yet it adds one more dimension of difference to this unusual hero and the unusual romance with Amelia. Paralyzed except for one index finger that runs the computers, Lincoln Rhyme's body has been wholly immobilized and mechanized—connected to gadgetry, screens, and monitors. But in the most classic detective tradition, what he can do is *think* and *see*. His formidable forensic and historical knowledge is emphasized in the movie by repeated closeups of his eyes. And what he most likes to see is Amelia, the gorgeous patrol cop with a gift for criminology.

In both the novel and the film, we learn that Amelia had given up a career as a child model in order to follow her father's line of work as a cop (even more shades of *Silence of the Lambs*). So Angelina Jolie's attractiveness in this role isn't an incidental detail of casting, but is rooted in the storyline. In a very traditional dynamic, Lincoln is all eyes and brains, and Amelia is all body, even all mouth in their requisite spunky-argument scenes. In fact, she's *his* surrogate body, agile and courageous as she faces each horrendous crime scene (rats! severed fingers!), following his instructions in her ear. Even with minimal makeup and workday cop clothes—dark jackets, plain white shirts, loose-fitting trousers—it's difficult to ignore Jolie's exquisite presence.

But the conservative elements here—the male intellectual who does the looking, the female body that's the object of attention—are turned inside out. She's the action body, speeding in cars and handling the guns. Lincoln, paralyzed and black, is hardly the typical Hollywood hero, though he does have affinities to the temporarily crippled Jimmy Stewart character in *Rear Window*. Playing up this connection, the movie changes the sex of Lincoln's nurse from the Deaver novel and names her Thelma, after Thelma Ritter, who played the housekeeper in *Rear Window*. In the Hitchcock film, the courageous girlfriend (Grace Kelly) was as dazzling as Jolie. But the Grace Kelly character was in the fashion business in that movie, while Amelia in *Bone Collector* has rejected fashion modeling in order to join the police. An expert shot, she's the one who comes to Lincoln's rescue and kills the serial killer in a fairly predictable climax.

The sexual/romantic tension between Lincoln and Amelia is far more interesting than the hackneyed serial-killer antics. In one startling scene, Amelia watches Lincoln while he's sleeping and delicately touches the tracheotomy scar on his neck, then caresses his index finger. The film doesn't go as far as the book, in which Amelia sleeps with him in his hospital bed one night. But they're romantically linked at the end of the film, when we see them hosting a Christmas party as a couple.

PG-rated fantasies can interpret it as platonic, but a more adult imagination can give them more credit for a sex life.

In the Deaver novel, Amelia is recovering from a lost love, but has a loner reputation. "A face and body like that, you'da thought some good-lookin' hunk woulda snagged her by now. But she doesn't even date," one character says of her. "Lipstick lesbos's what the rumor is."[6] That kind of rumor doesn't make it on screen, of course. The movie version introduces her by showing her waking up and breaking up with a boyfriend; macho-style, she's the one saying she can't make a commitment. But the film ends with her being introduced to Lincoln Rhyme's sister and looking fairly settled into couplehood. For Hollywood heroines, it's a well-worn groove—moving out of a relationship with one man and into the arms (well, hospital bed) of another.

The Bone Collector includes these compromises as a package deal. We get a smart, brave heroine who's apprenticing with a man who respects her but who is not Hannibal Lecter. This appealing formula also steers clear of the *Fatal Attraction* version of the woman investigator, which lines her up with exactly the wrong man.

THE WOMAN DETECTIVE AND FATAL/NON-FATAL ATTRACTIONS

In the world of detective fiction, dangerous coupling is a pleasurable occupational hazard. The *femme fatale* appeals to the secret criminality of the traditional male detective. Ditto the female detective and *homme fatale*—the dangerous man. It was the plot of Sue Grafton's *A Is for Alibi*, initiating her long-running series by having Kinsey both bed the guy and shoot him dead as the occasion demanded. On television, the mythologized version appeared as the ongoing theme of *Profiler*. As the female investigator character developed in films in the 1990s, the theme showed up in both toxic and playful versions respectively in *Bodily Harm* (1995) and *Out of Sight* (1998).

As sexual allure in the woman-detective story, the fatal man is a trickier character than the male detective's fatal woman. Both are seductive and both can kill. But the fatal man is also capable of rape, an ugly element in the mix. For the fictional woman investigator, whose body is already a high-stakes element in the game, rape represents her ultimate vulnerability as a heroine. And since detective fiction *is* a formula or game, rape is usually outside the rules. Male detectives can be unfaithful cads but not rapists; women detectives can get beaten up but not raped.[7]

So there's a significant difference in the sexual threats that fictional detectives face as men or women. The *femme fatale* may be castrating as a symbol or as a threat of sexual power, but she's usually not associated with real castration. In *Blue Velvet*, Isabella Rossellini wields a huge butcher knife near the quaking Kyle MacLaughlin, but she doesn't actually use it. Except for highly publicized flukes, female castrators are rare in real life. Male rapists are not.

For this reason, the woman investigator's involvement with a dangerous man is always a thorny sexual issue. He needs to be a reckless affair but a safe screw, to put it frankly. *Bodily Harm* and *Out of Sight* put different spins on this, with the earlier movie deluding the woman into the illusion of safety and the later movie overwhelmingly ensuring it. What they have in common is female desire as the driving engine of the plot. In both films, we see the women fantasizing about the sex before it happens, although these films give very different accounts of what can happen when the woman investigator follows her dangerous desires.

Out of Sight, the lighter version of the *Fatal Attraction* theme, is more fun because it focuses on women *not* getting hurt. In fact, it specifies that the detective's criminal lover is, above all, not a rapist. When sexy federal marshal Karen Sisco (Jennifer Lopez) meets irresistible bank robber Jack Foley (George Clooney), she's immediately kidnapped and placed in a car trunk with him as he's spirited away from a prison break. One of the first things he tells her, as they're curled together in the dark, is that he's never forced himself on a woman and—despite a long recent celibacy in prison—won't do so now. Again at the end of the film, when Foley has a chance to make a clean getaway with the loot, he stops and returns to the ongoing robbery because, he says, his less scrupulous comrades-in-arms will otherwise rape the household maid. His chivalrous gesture gets him caught—actually, shot by his lover Karen and sent back to prison.

Out of Sight, based on the quirky novel by Elmore Leonard, alternates between the drenching shadows of traditional film noir—including bluesy, snowy Detroit—and the sunny Cuban streets of Miami. Intriguingly, Karen Sisco is introduced in dark bars and night scenes, while Jack Foley emerges in the Florida sunshine. This is exactly right for Foley's character, the gallant criminal from a sunny Hollywood tradition. Cary Grant had perfected the role in *To Catch a Thief* (1955) and *Charade* (1963), and equally sophisticated versions were played by Steve McQueen and Pierce Brosnan, respectively, in the two versions of *The Thomas Crown Affair* (1968, 1999). The tradition's golden boy for the 1990s was Brad Pitt's polite bank robber in *Thelma & Louise*, which likewise required a dangerous man who was a woman's sexual fantasy rather than sexual threat.

Fig. 25 Jennifer Lopez as federal marshal Karen Sisco in *Out of Sight* (1998). Courtesy of Photofest.

The first erotic scene in *Out of Sight* is Karen's fantasy about female pursuit and mutual seduction. We see her hunting for Foley in a hotel suite, her gun ready, but when she finds him in the bathtub, she kisses him and crawls in, clothes and all. Fade to Karen waking up. Only then does the audience realize she's been dreaming this encounter. Later, when there really is a jazzy love scene with Foley, its editing and out-of-sync soundtrack at first blurs how much is in her head, how much is really in the plotline.

I'm emphasizing female fantasy because *Out of Sight* is organized more around the sweet illogic of wish fulfillment than around the usual plot logic of romantic comedy, crime film, or cop film. *Out of Sight* intersects all three genres; in 2002 *Entertainment Weekly* named it one of the top twenty-five movie romances in contemporary cinema. The crazy premise is that Karen, the self-confident law-enforcement agent prone to affairs with married or questionable men, falls for the charming outlaw whom she must eventually turn in. But instead of traumatizing her with a choice—her lover or the law!—the movie generously allows her to succeed with the case and have the outlaw lover, too.

We get the first big wink when Karen and Foley, folded into the car trunk, talk about movies. She brings up *Bonnie & Clyde* (1967), insinuating her own outlaw proclivities, and this gets him going on other Faye Dunaway movies, including *Three Days of the Condor* (1975). About the latter, they agree it's unrealistic that the romantic leads "got together so quickly," as they themselves are doing in an even more unlikely situation. Notice they don't mention Dunaway's less happy detective movie, *Chinatown*. That's because *Out of Sight* isn't Polanski and genuine noir; it's Elmore Leonard and his oddball Miami.

So the female-detective clichés get dunked in the Florida surf. There's a cop daddy, but at least he's not dead and saintly, and Karen cheerfully ignores all his advice. There are sexist colleagues in the FBI and on the police force, but Karen knows in advance how to get around them and do as she pleases. In fact, even though the Clooney character gets more screen time, Karen is the only character who gets exactly what she wants. She cracks the case, shoots (and kills) the perps, gets dreamy Foley to bed but also, later, to jail, *and* ensures he has a way to escape so she can keep pursuing him. It's hard to be critical of a movie so thoroughly devoted to female pleasure.

Even the big bad issue of the phallic gun gets undermined. The first time we see Karen, a suave older man is offering her a small gift-wrapped box, so the setup looks like sugar daddy and the babe. But we learn it's her father giving her a Zig Sauer 380 for her birthday ("Thanks for the gun, Daddy!"). When she's kidnapped by Foley and his friends, he steals this little Sauer and returns it to her much later in the story, after their night together, leaving it on his pillow in the morning. The daddy-to-lover transfer would be a classic Freudian move, but instead it's an ironic one. Foley returns the gun because, we find out, he himself doesn't shoot people—unlike Karen, who apparently has a reputation for kneecapping guys she's dated. Moreover, the first time she pulls the gun out, during her kidnapping, she doesn't use it to stop Foley. The FBI agent who questions her about this later is puzzled, not realizing Karen is devising her own private rules of pursuit.

Eventually, Karen kneecaps Foley, too, so he can't escape after the big heist at the end of the tale, when the backup cops are already en route. "I can't shoot you," she says consolingly as he writhes on the floor. "You did! You shot me!" he protests, gasping. "You know what I mean," she sighs as she handcuffs him. It's a double code. The private one between lovers guarantees they won't *really* hurt each other, while the legal one requires her to shoot him. Usually, women investigators don't fare very well when there's a doubled, private/public code involved. In *Blue Steel, Impulse, Black Widow*, and *Betrayed*, private codes and relationships doom the women into bad decisions and impasses. But Karen Sisco works both codes at once.

As a result, she manages to be inside and outside the law at the same time, just as she hovers but never quite lands inside her father's zone of protective love. "My little girl!" he exclaims proudly in a closing voice-over when he learns about her capture of Foley. However, cop-daddy's little girl unites Foley with an experienced prison-escape artist in the final scene. She beams, her lipstick gleaming, as she overhears their conversation hinting at another escape. It's her escape, too, from daddies and rules, the laws she's hired to enforce. And for audiences it's an escape as well, into a romantic fantasy rarely glimpsed in the world of crime and police. It's not surprising that of all the female detective movies, this is the one picked up by television for a prime-time series, *Karen Sisco* (2003–), that bets on the long-playing appeal of daddy's tough little girl, kinky romance, and crime-scenic Miami.

An intrinsic fantasy appeal of the film version was Jennifer Lopez, the first woman of color to play a woman investigator since *Fatal Beauty*. *Out of Sight* never directly references Karen Sisco's ethnicity, which functions more as exotic sexuality—part of the colorful Miami backdrop—than as specific identity, as is often the case with Latina actresses in Hollywood films. Ethnic female stars are often overidentified both as fantasies (of escape, sexuality, authenticity) or as bodies—servile, maternal, sexual, or excessive. Lopez functions both ways, as site of an impossibly glamorous sexuality and a fetishized rear end, which has gotten more attention than her acting ability and almost as much attention as her love life.[8]

Out of Sight provides the requisite rear-end shot of Lopez early in the film and dresses her in snug, miniskirted suits even in the Detroit snow. But Steven Soderbergh's imaginative editing, the quick-witted script, and Leonard's offbeat story construct a woman of action, not a woman posing for the camera. So while Lopez's embodiment of the woman investigator is particularly lush, what's more remarkable is the number of men in the film who are physically afraid of her and the number she overcomes, including the ex-con who screams, "You're really mean!" as she pins him down. Note, though, the class and racial identities of the men she bullies and "tussles," to use the term one of them threatens her with: an African-American thug, a Latino ex-con, and a brainless criminal characterized as white trash. She verbally humiliates some WASP-ish businessmen who try to pick her up in a bar, but her coupling with Foley/Clooney establishes a class-racial hierarchy in her interactions with men, one that both erases and emphasizes the Latina identity that Lopez brings to the role.

Out of Sight nevertheless provides every possible safety net for the woman investigator's tussle with the Wrong Man. *Bodily Harm* is the flip side of the fantasy, the erotic attraction to the man who is not just dangerous but deadly. A well-acted but so-so film noir from 1995, *Bodily Harm* is the gender-switch version of *Basic Instinct*, the detective erotically obsessed with the serial killer. In the earlier film, the homicide detective played by Michael Douglas is doomed to be the next victim of the exquisite killer, played by Sharon Stone. The famous last shot shows the murder-weapon knife waiting under the bed as the detective enjoys his final amorous fling in the sheets. In traditional film noirs, the *femme fatale* dies at the end, but in some neo-noirs of the 1990s, this fascinating female character was reborn into a luckier cycle of plot twists.[9]

Linda Fiorentino had in fact played the clever, victorious *fatale* in *The Last Seduction* (1994), so her casting in a central role in *Bodily Harm* ties it all up, so to speak, as the woman investigator erotically led astray. Raven-haired Fiorentino plays Rita Cates, a Las Vegas homicide detective who had been scandalously involved with bad-boy cop Sam McKeon, played with burly charm by Daniel Baldwin. We learn in flashback that Rita's husband, also a cop, had walked in on their lovemaking and had shot himself on the spot. Shortly thereafter, Sam left Rita and the police force. Sam turned investor and retired to a life of leisure usually enjoyed by the *femmes fatales* in this tradition. His poolside idleness looks a lot like Faye Dunaway's in *Chinatown*, and his home decor is as upscale as Stone's in *Basic Instinct*. Sam is a big hunk of macho sexiness, but his decadence places him in the black-widow school of sinuous entrapment.

Despite their twisted past, Rita insists on being assigned as key investigator when Sam becomes a homicide suspect. Two women who had been associated with Sam are murdered—"sliced open like a melon," as the coroner puts it—and a witness even places Sam at one of the scenes. But Sam is an expert at mind games, with women and with the police. Given so much evidence pointed his way, he convinces everyone (including most viewers, I would guess) that it could *only* be a setup.

Meanwhile, Rita's scalding sexual memories apparently outweigh the guilt about her husband's suicide. Rita is a cool professional, entirely poised at the office, chic in her linen pantsuits. But when it comes to Sam—as her male partner, JD, puts it—if she were a man, she'd be "thinking with her dick." The air-conditioning in Rita's apartment is broken, so that may be why she's awake and writhing alone in the sheets, but the better explanation is the flashback to a sweaty moment in those sheets with Sam. Hollywood movies hardly ever portray women like this, physically tormented by lust, though *The Piano* comes to mind as a refreshing example of unabashed female horniness. *Bodily Harm* is not nearly as romantic. Like other smitten noir movie detectives, Rita follows the sex instead of the clues, and all her professional judgment gets shot to hell. Even when all evidence points to Sam, she finds an alternative suspect, a mentally deranged stripper with multiple names and a serious grudge against Sam's previous detective work.

At one point, Sam books a room at one of the big Vegas hotels and instructs Rita to walk through the casino in order to meet him. The suspenseful music cues us, not for an ambush in the casino, but for the sexual gamble and ambush Rita is willingly walking into. Unfortunately, *Bodily Harm* situates this dangerous fantasy within the old banality of the good girl versus the bad girl. Sam's two victims are a (bad) Vegas showgirl and a (good) woman therapist. A police shrink describes Sam as someone attracted to shady women, like the showgirl, but also to "pure" women like the therapist. That puts Rita somewhere in between. Like the therapist, Rita is a "good girl," a legitimate professional, licensed by the law and the justice system. Her "badness" might be her sexual obsession with Sam, but it might also be the badness of being the woman cop, suspicious for violating a "natural" law about who should be doing the grisly work of criminal investigation.

In that sense, *Bodily Harm* is a somber critique of women's choices in a man's world of work. If she uses her body, she's the dirty girl who gets punished; but if she uses her mind for analysis, she can get punished too. The woman detective can't win here. She needs to do "masculine" analysis, but she does dirty work as well, snooping in back alleys and strip joints, and collecting seamy evidence. This "dirtiness" surfaces in a scene of Rita and Sam in bed, teasing each other about his status as a suspect and about a court order to get a fluid sample. "Did you bring a receptacle?" he leers, insinuating not only that sex is part of her work, but that she won't be able to separate herself from the evidence.[10]

The surprise ending of *Bodily Harm* repeats the surprise ending of *Basic Instinct*. Sam is free, all charges against him are dropped, but the last shot reveals the murder weapon in the glove compartment of his car. Rita has said goodbye to him, supposedly putting him out of her life again, but the logic of the murders indicates that she's next on his list. A low point for woman detective flicks in the 1990s, it's a movie where all the noir formulations gang up on the female investigator, as if to prove it's a genre where she won't do well. Fortunately, neither Hollywood nor the indies lingered there for her. And just a year later, the indie *Fargo* showed that this character fares best when the film noir conventions are tossed to the wind—in fact, to the cold north winds of Minnesota.

FARGO: "HECK, NORM, WE'RE DOING PRETTY GOOD"

The heroines of the most original and prestigious female-detective films of the 1990s, *The Silence of the Lambs* and *Fargo*, spoke in regional dialects and brought down scary villains with precise sharp shooting. But while *The Silence of the Lambs* looked and felt like a Big Hollywood thriller, *Fargo* looked and felt like Ingmar Bergman—snowy, hushed, not easily summarized. When Foster accepted her Academy Award, she claimed it for feminist heroism. Frances McDormand made no such claim for her sturdy, pregnant police chief character Marge Gunderson, whose heroism is less easy to align with a politics or a genre or, well, anything.

Instead, *Fargo* delivers a deceivingly simple premise—that a decent, sympathetic, small-town female cop can outwit the evil, urban, unlucky villains. In this sense, it's a shockingly old-fashioned story, secured by the first and last shots we get of Marge, large and ungainly in bed with her large, ungainly husband. When they're awakened by a predawn phone call alerting Marge about a triple homicide, Norm insists on cooking a warm breakfast for her before she heads to work. As she lumbers past the camera, we see that her girth and awkward movement are due to her being in one of her final months of pregnancy, though the tenderness of his fussing looks more habitual than that. He'll stay home and paint wildlife scenes while she examines murder victims on a snowy highway. You could call this postfeminism, but Marge and Norm wouldn't. It's just life at home.

In the form of two goony villains, violence has blundered into Marge and Norm's Minnesota town of Brainerd, home of Paul Bun-

Fig. 26 Frances McDormand as Police Chief Marge Gunderson in *Fargo* (1996). Courtesy of Photofest.

yan, whose oversized statue guards the city's limits like a huge joke god. In the black comedy of this film by brothers Ethan and Joel Coen, the joke is on the murderers and conspirators, who all come to bad ends while Marge and Norm are allowed to snuggle back to bed at the end of the tale. The movie begins in (and never returns to) the no-man's-land of Fargo, North Dakota, where nervous Jerry Lundegaard (William H. Macy) hires two career criminals to kidnap his own wife back in Minneapolis. He knows his wealthy father-in-law will pay the million-dollar ransom, which Lundegaard himself will then split with the criminals.

The criminal duo is a Mutt 'n' Jeff combination described by other characters as a tall, silent "Marlboro Man" and a small "funny-looking" one who talks too much. They can't even drive to their assigned crime scene without stupidly attracting police attention near Brainerd, about halfway to Minneapolis. The police stop ends with the bloodbath Marge is assigned to investigate. Nor can these villains execute a competent kidnapping once they find their victim at her home, finally pursuing the hysterical wife into the shower, where she wraps herself in the shower curtain while attempting to escape.

Since *Psycho*, of course, the shower has been movie shorthand for terror and, even more specifically, female vulnerability. So when Mrs.

Lundegaard hides in the shower and then flees with the curtain wrapped around her like a shroud, jumping and flinging herself down the stairs, the mixture of comedy and terror is wicked. We know the kidnappers don't want to hurt her, but we also know violence is near at hand. The most chilling murder of the film in fact is Mrs. Lundegaard's, near the end of the story, because we don't see it and get no explanation except that she "started shrieking," according to Grimsrud, the morose "Marlboro Man" who had quickly and indiscriminately murdered three people on the Brainerd highway.

In the film's most famous, surreal, and comic-absurd scene, police-chief Marge—pregnant, alone, and isolated by acres of snow—confronts this hulking murderer as he feeds his partner's body parts into a wood chipper at the lake outside of Brainerd. Unlike woman-investigator flicks in which the heroine is caught alone in a dank basement or shadowy apartment or dark alley, *Fargo* sets its heart-stopping confrontation scene in a snowy woodland. The snow is Swedish modernism, the butchery is Hollywood horror, but the goofy details are Midwestern farce. Marge pulls her gun and shouts at Grimsrud repeatedly, but he can't hear her over the wood chipper. She finally gets his attention, mouthing the word "Police" and pointing to the insignia on her Deputy-Dog flap-eared cap. Because she's "carrying a load," as she says on two earlier occasions, she can't chase him as he runs off. However, this satiric film still respects Marge's cool head and precise trigger finger. Her second shot gets him neatly in the leg, and he's down.

Fargo asks us to accept the bloody wood chipper, Marge's extraordinary bravery, and her confident marksmanship as part of this movie's eerie mix of horror and homey heartland ethics. We can only imagine the ensuing scene of the mortified villain dragged to the prowler under the gun of a stern, seven-months-pregnant policewoman. Instead, we cut to a shot of him glum and surrendered, already caged in the backseat, while Marge in tight closeup delivers her earnest, puzzled summary of the entire bloody mess: "There's more to life than a little money, ya know. Don't cha know that? And here ya are. And it's a beautiful day. Well. I just don't understand it." The "beautiful day" in Brainerd looks as forbiddingly frigid as the ones in Paul Bunyan tales where the cow's frozen milk comes out as ice cream. And in the middle of Marge's schoolmarmy speech, the police prowler zooms past the giant statue of Bunyan himself.

Bunyan and the original Marlboro Man (as opposed to his sullen counterpart, now Marge's captive)—step right out of hearty American folklore. Framed in a rugged terrain—the Northwest and West, respectively—these larger-than-life figures do the manly American work of cutting down forests and selling cigarettes. The tall tales of Bunyan eating forty bowls of porridge a day and using giant mosquitoes to drill the trees are as unlikely as the tall tales of cigarettes imbuing us with rugged independence. Surely Marge, whose appetite at the all-you-can-eat buffet nearly equals Bunyan's, is more believable than either of these characters. She doesn't have to ride a horse or snap trees in half, and her largeness and appetite—far from being tall tales—are natural and healthy. Her gun is neither phallic toy nor symbol of exchanged roles. It's simply the tool that equalizes her with a violent criminal and enables her to cripple him and bring him in. Unlike the fantasy figures of Paul Bunyan and the Marlboro Man, her power isn't hyped or exaggerated.

Instead, Marge *naturalizes* the role of woman investigator, which becomes unremarkable in this film, like her pregnancy. Some critics claimed that Marge's successful police work and the film's casual acceptance of her role suggests that gender doesn't matter in *Fargo*.[11] After all, Marge's single-handed capture of this monster shows competence that doesn't call attention either to her pregnancy or her sex. That may be true, but it's not what we *see*, which is Marge's fertile hugeness, juxtaposed first with the hulking murderer and then with the gargantuan Paul Bunyan on the highway. The gender signs are everywhere—they're just not where we expect them to be: large, pregnant femaleness versus grotesque masculinity.

In Hollywood cinema, pregnancy is usually a melodramatic crisis, occasionally a comic one, and often—in the horror genre—a monstrous one, spawning Rosemary's baby or the dragon fetus of *Alien*. This tradition is spoofed in *Fargo* when we find the "Marlboro Man" murderer waiting at the lake hideout, watching a soap opera on TV, seriously engrossed as the woman on screen announces dramatically, "I'm pregnant!" No such melodrama attends Marge's pregnancy. At one point, examining the highway murder victims, she pauses for morning sickness. "You alright there, Margie?" her deputy asks anxiously. "Oh, I just think I'm gonna barf," she replies, and shortly adds, "Well, that passed. Now I'm hungry again." The joke is on Hollywood, the only place on earth where pregnancy is weirdly unnatural—as unnatural as a female detective.

Wholesome Marge really doesn't understand why someone would kill for a million dollars. There's no dusky flirtation with criminality here—no dark side, no secret past—just Midwestern politeness. With her less-than-brilliant deputy, who doesn't recognize a dealer license plate, she's gentle but firm: "I'm not sure I agree with you a hundred percent on your police work, there, Lou," she tells him when he reports his search for a license beginning DLR. With the squirming, evasive Jerry Lundegaard, Marge is courteous even when she's righteously angry. "You have no call to get snippy with me. I'm just trying to do my job here," she says sternly. It's enough to frighten Lundegaard into bolting.

But is this, too, a tall tale—homespun, pregnant Marge triumphing over terrifying villains? Marge, Brainerd, and the regional culture hover at the edge of caricature. Even critics who loved the movie and the heroine worried that it was a satire of the Midwest. Jerry's teenage son has a poster of the Accordion King on his bedroom door, and a swinging night-on-the-town in Minneapolis is a Jose Feliciano performance at a hotel lounge. In re-creating the Minnesota of their childhood, the Coen brothers also re-created the quaint speech patterns of this region, where a Norwegian-inflected accent ("yah" for "yes") joins 1950s Americana: "You're darned tootin'!" "You betcha!" "What the heck you mean?" Marge's strongest comment, seeing a corpse with blown-out brains, is "Aw, geeze." And she interviews two eager, cooperative teenage hookers to a hilarious chorus of "Yah . . . oh yah . . . yah," as the girls cheerfully describe the killers they had sex with.

Thrillers have sunken their teeth into American subcultures before, as in Carl Franklin's rural Arkansas in *One False Move* (1992). But the flat conversations and corny details in *Fargo* often slide into parody. In the final scene, when Marge and Norm have settled in for a more peaceful winter's nap, Norm announces that "it was on TV tonight," and we think he means Marge's incredible capture of the villain and resolution of the sensational murder case. But no, he means the announcement that his wildlife design will appear on a three-cent postal stamp. "Heck, Norm, we're doing pretty good," she sighs as she snuggles against him.

Yet the film respects Marge's intelligence and courage even when the cheesy dialect makes us smile. More troubling than the corny Midwest, in fact, is the corny placement of women in this movie. Besides Marge, the only women on screen are the hookers hired by the criminal duo and Lundegaard's doomed, daffy homemaker wife, taking us back to the oldest clichés of women as sex workers or domestic workers. So Marge is the exceptional woman in this caricatured landscape, in which macho stereotypes are comically deflated but minor female stereotypes remain in place. But it's easy to forgive this in *Fargo*, mainly because Marge's heroism isn't fussed over or fetishized. The movie asks us to accept it as all in a day's work for Brainerd's woman police chief. And that's a comforting thought about the woman investigator at the box office at the end of the twentieth century, scarce as she was. Heck, Marge, maybe we're doing pretty good.

DETECTIVE LITE: *CHARLIE'S ANGELS* AND *MISS CONGENIALITY*

In the last month of the century, December 2000, four of Hollywood's hottest women stars appeared in glossy, bubbly comedy-adventures about women investigators. Picturing the *body* of the female investigator has always been the crux of this character's problem, and glamorization has always been its easiest answer—the FBI Girl with a gun and a push-up bra. But *Charlie's Angels* and *Miss Congeniality* returned to the license-with-lipstick images with irony and humor, and with some decidedly female perspective. These movies also plugged the woman detective into familiar formulas (the action film, the romantic comedy) and topics that were hip in the late 1990s (the 1970s as retro camp; the makeover).

This fantasy of the woman investigator as sexy fun was happening while publicists were hyping a far darker female investigation movie, the upcoming *Hannibal,* which was released two months later. But the latter wasn't being hyped as anything remotely female. Despite the publicity buzz about Julianne Moore as the new Clarice, *Hannibal*'s posters and trailers focused on its sequel appeal—"Break the Silence!"—and its villainous hero: "Never forget who he is"; "How long can a man stay silent before he returns to the thing he does best?" Clearly, the studio was hedging its bets on the success of Julianne Moore and pushing the macabre aura of Hopkins as everybody's favorite cannibal.

So the century ended with the female detective pictured everywhere and nowhere—the serious new Clarice not yet revealed, but lots of swimsuit revelation in comic versions of professional women with guns. The most popular of the films in the latter category, *Charlie's Angels,* featured Cameron Diaz, Lucy Liu, and Drew Barrymore in a camped-up version of the 1970s prime-time hit. *Miss Congeniality* starred Sandra Bullock as an FBI agent forced into a beauty pageant (eventually a swimsuit pageant) to thwart a mad bomber. But wait a minute—isn't the forced-to-wear-a-swimsuit ruse straight out of the old *Charlie's Angels* TV series? It doesn't take much detective work to deduce that both movies simultaneously mocked and embraced 1970s-television versions of the shapely woman with a badge. This is the ploy of current James Bond movies that stop and point to their own sexism, shrug, and then get on with it. We *know* better now, so it's

OK to put women investigators back into bikinis and halter tops. The 2000 *Charlie's Angels* wasn't coy about its sexual come-on. The taglines for the posters and ads were "Get some action!" and "Action doesn't get any hotter than this!" In the publicity stills, the stars take threatening martial arts poses, but they're wearing heels and leather body suits, so their threat is luscious soft-porn.

What *was* different was the conscious targeting of this film to female audiences who brought a vastly different perspective to the high-heeled woman of action. The dazzling kickboxing in the 2000 *Charlie's Angels* was hardly new; women were accustomed to seeing it on TV's *Buffy the Vampire Slayer*. And their daughters and little sisters may have been watching similar antics on *The Powerpuff Girls* (1998–) on the Cartoon Network. The muscular female presence wasn't limited to movie and television screens. By the 1990s, women were pumping iron, populating tai chi studios and black belt leagues, getting fit at coed boxing gyms, running marathons, and becoming basketball and soccer stars. Health and fashion industries combined to convince women of the *pleasures* of fitness, sports, and martial arts.

Not surprisingly, then, in *Charlie's Angels* the ticket is fun, not suspense, as cued in the opening sequence where travelers are watching an in-flight film called "T.J. Hooker: The Movie." The script of *Angels* was haphazardly sewn together by seventeen different writers, including a comedy team from *Seinfeld*, so even the fight scenes are comic-campy. In her final martial-arts face-off with the devious female villain, Natalie (Cameron Diaz) tries to keep her new boyfriend on hold on her cell phone, and when the cell phone gets smashed, Natalie goes ballistic on her doomed opponent: "Do you know how hard it is to find a quality man in Los Angeles?" The balance of ballistics and boyfriend is from *Buffy*, of course, with a good dose of *Girls Romance* comic books, the ones Roy Lichtenstein camped up: "Oh Jeff . . . I Love You, Too . . . But . . ."

The film's colors are bright and flat, the car chases and fight scenes are choreographed with Indiana Jones exuberance, and the crime scenes unfold in oceanfront mansions or fortresses. In playful homage to the TV series, the Angels don undercover disguises as geishas, race car drivers, cocktail waitresses, and Bavarian singers, one costume more garish than the next. They also satirize 1970s Farrah Fawcett hair effects, with each Angel able to toss her hair in glorious slow motion, smiting any male in her path. The "diversity" of the Angels is also a joke reference to the fake differences between the original Angels, Jaclyn Smith, Kate Jackson, and Farrah. This time the Angels are played by women who are stars in their own right, and the characters are take-

Fig. 27 Drew Barrymore, Cameron Diaz, and Lucy Liu as the updated Angels in *Charlie's Angels* (2000), paying tribute to the "Chains" episode from the television series. Courtesy of Photofest.

offs on their star personas. Cameron Diaz is the dizzy blonde, Drew Barrymore the bad-girl redhead, and Lucy Liu the exotic dragon-lady. When a minor character asks an Angel (doesn't matter which one), "Hey, aren't you supposed to be a detective?" his surprise speaks for all of us.

Each Angel gets a harmless boyfriend who, thankfully, doesn't have to rescue her. Nor are they rescued by Charlie's deputy Bosley (Bill Murray), as often happened on the TV series. In fact, just the opposite occurs, with both Bosley and, later, Charlie himself saved by the Angels from comic-book-terrible fates. By then, the ineffective boyfriends have been long forgotten by this script, which gives the Angels a triumphant all-girl finale, as they jump from an exploding helicopter down to the California surf. True to the television series formula, they appear in a cutesy postscript on the beach with Bosley, Charlie hovering attentively in the background, the Angels heading for the water for one last splashy wet-suit effect.

Frothy as it may be, this fairy tale isn't so bad as an end-of-decade bedtime story for girls, at least as far as Hollywood movies go. Once upon a time, Charlie rescued these women from humdrum police work, the opening voice-over tells us—a repetition of the opening of the TV show. But as we've seen, television has been much better than movies at rescuing women from humdrum plot lines. In the beach postscript, the Angels are having fun together and are ready for the next adventure, not for the true love and marriage that will cap their stories. Compare this to the ending of the fairy tale movie for young female audiences at the beginning of the 1990s—*Pretty Woman* (1990). In the closing scene, Julia Roberts and Richard Gere tweet at each other about how he had rescued her and how she "rescued him right back." *Pretty Woman* couldn't imagine a rescue except as the transition from woman-alone to woman-coupled. Charlie's Angels are still Pretty Women, and the depressing part of the message for young girls is still "you must be gorgeous"—but at least they commandeer a helicopter and save the world. As female fantasy, it's more ambitious than a reformed prostitute "rescuing" Richard Gere from bachelorhood.

As suggested by the *Saturday Night Live* skit in which the *Charlie's Angels* stars can barely keep their hands off each other, the sexual reversibility of the Angels fantasy confirms buddy-movie homoerotics, a subtext made even campier with the gee-whiz dialogue and nifty teamwork. *Miss Congeniality* acknowledges lipstick lesbian glamour more directly, in a small but priceless moment in the film when Miss New York dramatically and exuberantly comes out during the televised Miss USA pageant, shouting her love to "Tina" in the audience and proclaiming to the world that all lesbians "out there" have a shot at getting to the Miss USA Top Ten as she did. *Miss Congeniality* does best when the pageantry's pretenses get blown up—literally—in the last part of the film. True, it's easy to satirize pageantry's witless chatter ("Miss New Jersey's hobbies include figure skating, water ballet, and taking long, luxurious bubble baths") and baton-twirling frippery. But this movie also plays it both ways, mocking the ideal female body and feminine behavior and then retreating from the mockery with breathless praise for the "liberating" experience of a beauty pageant—which is actually part of the dialogue.

But what's most fascinating here is the insertion of the woman detective, that most controversial of bodies, into the double feminine fictions of the beauty pageant and the makeover. The makeover is a multimedia myth and visual trick (before and after) that's at least a century old, as can be seen in women's magazine ads from the 1890s. Makeovers promise miraculous transformation through expert instruction and the use of specific cosmetics. By the 1990s, it was a staple of both beauty advertisements and talk-show segments. As the basis of a story, it boasts film precedents as classical as *Now, Voyager* (1942) and *Pygmalion* (1938) and maintains a high profile through pop vehicles like *Pretty Woman* and *She's All That* (1999).[12] The makeover is a potent cocktail of mixed messages, ranging from Cinderella magic to cynical consumerism. At its most unruly, it suggests that beauty is no more than a bag of tricks. But at its most optimistic, it promises that every woman can be beautiful. The movie versions usually play out the shallow maxim that life, love, and inner self will all change once you look better—more feminine, more glamorous, more like the ads in the magazines.

In *Miss Congeniality*, the awkward FBI agent Gracie Hart needs a makeover to "pass" as a girlie girl for the pageant. As a one-of-the-boys investigator who owns neither a dress nor a hairbrush, Gracie is even more uncomely than Debra Winger at the beginning of *Black Widow*. Gracie's makeover is humorously rendered as an industrial production inside an airplane hangar, where her assigned (gay) pageant consultant Victor Melling (Michael Caine) supervises her assembly. Gracie needs not just a physical makeover, but a gender makeover as well, since she eats, talks, and moves like John Goodman. "I haven't seen a walk like that since *Jurassic Park*," Victor laments. True to the makeover's Magic Moment tradition, Gracie emerges ravishing and coiffed, fabulously outfitted in a skin-tight sheath and gingerly maneuvering in dangerous high heels. That is, the makeover gets ridiculed as a factory production, but the end result is serious Hollywood babe.

In line with the 1970s/2000 message of *Charlie's Angels*, the new Gracie is both super-beautiful and super-tough FBI gal. Her "talent" for the Miss USA pageant is a self-defense demonstration, using her FBI cohort and new romantic interest Eric (Benjamin Bratt) as the unfortunate would-be attacker. "She's kicking his ass!" the television producer exclaims with delight. (And the television producer herself later gives pointed empathy to Miss New York.) In perfectly predictable style, Gracie and Eric foil the plans of the mad bomber after the FBI has officially turned its back on the case. More gratifying is that the terrorist is the uptight former Miss USA Kathy Morningside (Candice Bergen). With the pageant nearing its crowning moment, the line between Miss USA and ruthless terrorism runs thinner and thinner, as fistfights break out onstage and the orchestra bravely plays the Miss USA hymn in the background.

Yet *Miss Congeniality* is careful not to explode *all* of the Cinderella/Eliza Doolittle/Miss USA fairy tale material. Gracie begins as the skeptical outsider whom Kathy Morningside immediately nails as the enemy, one of the "feminists, intellectuals, and ugly women," she says, who make fun of beauty contests—which are really "scholarship contests," according to Morningside. But as Gracie befriends the earnest

Fig. 28 Sandra Bullock as FBI agent Gracie Hart after a makeover into Miss New Jersey, in *Miss Congeniality* (2000). Courtesy of Photofest.

contestants, even the one whose talent is baton twirling, she grows sympathetic toward them. At her pageant personality interview, she admits she was one who of the "feminists" who used to dis the pageant, but now she understands what a "liberating experience" the whole thing is. Since the movie has relentlessly satirized just about all the Miss USA trappings—the dieting, the innocuous interviews, the canned niceness, the falsies tucked into swimsuit tops—it's tough to figure out what these young women have been "liberated" from, except feminism, intellectualism, and ugliness.

If we believe the sentimentalized script, Gracie isn't just "passing"—like Miss New York was passing for straight—but has moved permanently into both gorgeousness and the girlie behavior she used to mock. She even places in the pageant. Her colleagues vote her Miss Congeniality, which assures us that she fits in as the all-American trophy girl. The final scene shows her accepting her award, weeping and blushing and fluttering her hands exactly like the contestants she'd earlier laughed at. From rough-edged FBI agent, Gracie is transformed into the standard Hollywood romantic heroine, as cute as Meg Ryan, as gangly-charming as Julia Roberts. Even Debra Winger, who got a chance to clean up and wear good clothes in *Black Widow*, didn't have to become a fluttering sweetie in order to nail the case. This final package—femininity, boyfriend, good looks, plus powerful kick-ass competence—is the same fantasy package of *Buffy* and *Charlie's Angels*. *Miss Congeniality* shrinkwraps it into pratfall comedy rather than sci-fi, fantasy, or *Crouching Tiger, Hidden Dragon* (2000) sky ballet.

And is it nervous comedy? You bet. Consider the huge gap between the made-over Gracie and her predecessors on the best-seller fiction list. If anything, the investigating heroines of Sue Grafton, Patricia Cornwell, Sara Paretsky, and Marcia Muller thrive on their gutsy *resistance* to traditional femininity. The grooming habits of Grafton's Kinsey Millhone character—self-inflicted haircuts with manicure scissors—are a lot like Gracie's before the makeover.

For female images, you can't get much more traditional than angels and pageantry queens. But these are angels and pageantry queens who kickbox, shoot straight, and outsmart terrorists. There's a measure of antifeminist anxiety in these comedies, but an equal measure of post-feminist spunk, which embraces the glamour as camp or—more deliriously—rereads it as "liberating." For me, the more convincing explanation is that these comic versions of female investigators are signs of a big-screen character and storyline still in the early stages of mainstream acceptance. Comedy is a way to make the character affable, familiar, part of the bigger picture of heroines at the cineplex. If audiences can relax and laugh, maybe they can think she's not so bad.

Proof of this is the subsequent picturing of Sandra Bullock in a far more serious investigating role in the 2002 movie *Murder by Numbers*. Critics mostly panned it, but even the ones who disliked it often pointed out the bravery of casting Bullock as a not-especially-likable character. Bullock plays Cassie Mayweather, a police detective investigating senseless murders perpetrated by two teenaged Leopold and Loeb wanna-bes. Cassie's nickname among the police is Hyena because the female of the species has "a small mock penis," which Cassie archly says she hides with loose-fitting clothes. Cassie has neither charm nor manners, not even in bed, from which she tosses the guy she seduces, who happens to be her new detective partner. "It's not just about sex. I really respect you as a person," she deadpans.

At first, the hardboiled poses seem trite, but the film's most compelling dynamic is Cassie's deep suspicion and distrust of men. Cassie is the survivor of a particularly horrific sexual assault, a memory that makes her obsessive about the case at hand, the torture and murder of a young woman. It also makes her automatically wary of smooth-talking guys like Richard (Ryan Gosling), one of the teenagers who plants forensic evidence that will implicate the school's drug-dealing janitor. Long after the police have arrested the janitor and closed the case, Cassie dogs Richard and his partner in crime, putting herself in more and more danger as she figures out the murder.

It's not the most suspenseful or original crime film ("You're getting way too involved in this!" the police chief barks), and the Leopold-Loeb theme has been done before, in *Rope* (1948), *Compulsion* (1959), and *Swoon* (1992). But none of these films imagined a female victim and a misogynist bond between the gay murderers. What Cassie immediately recognizes is the hatred of women that drives the crime and the killers, a hatred much stronger than their occasional heterosexual inclinations.

Cassie also understands the traces of this misogyny in so-called normal men, like the ones who call her Hyena at the police station. And this is the quality of the woman investigator—her deep skepticism about men's relationships with women—that has made her so valuable in print, so scary on film. How can a sympathetic female *movie* character be this cynical about the sexes? *Murder by Numbers* doesn't spare us the male thinking about this cynicism. "She pees standing up," one of Cassie's male colleagues says dismissively. That is, only an "unnatural" woman—or a lesbian—could be so distrusting, at least in the movies.

Murder by Numbers doesn't reconstruct Cassie into a romantic heroine or smiley face of congeniality. Sandra Bullock was the executive producer of this movie. I like to imagine her purchasing the risk of this uneasy character through credit she'd built on the previous comedy. Remember that at the end of the twentieth century, the female detective in pop culture was only one generation old and had had even a shorter time than that in movies. Some of her pictures are bound to be braver than others. And not all the pictures can be as complicated as that of star FBI Girl Clarice Starling, who is never comic, always heart-stopping, and whose two film incarnations are the bookends of the 1990s and the ending of this book.

7

CLARICE AND HER FANS
The Silence of the Lambs and *Hannibal*

LIKE SCULLY & MULDER OR CAGNEY & LACEY, Clarice Starling comes as part of a pair, and in reality her cohort Hannibal Lecter is even more popular than she. The Academy Awards ceremony of 1992 began with host Billy Crystal being wheeled on stage in the infamous Lecter-in-bonds apparatus and hockey mask, a stunt confirming Lecter's popular status as kinky cannibal. People who have never seen or read *The Silence of the Lambs* or *Hannibal* know Lecter's eerily enunciated greeting, "Hello, Clarice," which has shown up in ads for Blockbuster and in *Dr. Doolittle 2* (2001). Lecter's line about his gourmet cannibalism—a census taker's liver served with fava beans and a nice chianti—has made the mere mention of "fava beans" a cue for wicked laughter. Bryant Gumbel once paralyzed a *Today* show cooking sequence by asking if these were the beans Hannibal Lecter had made famous.

Although both Jodie Foster and Anthony Hopkins won Academy Awards for Demme's *The Silence of the Lambs*, Foster's portrayal of Clarice Starling didn't generate the imitations, quotations, jokes, and images that Hopkins's did. In a sense, this follows the more conservative ways the Demme film pictured her: disciplined, serious, well-scrubbed, clothed in drab colors, and framed so that her body faded into the background scenery. Starling's lesser visibility also suggests the wider cultural problem of picturing the female investigator as opposed to picturing the killer. As I pointed out in the previous chapter, serial killers and mass murderers boast a long list of film credits, from

M through *American Psycho* (2000). Lecter's excesses and eccentricities, no matter how distinctive, fall into line with the campy terrors of Norman Bates, Jason, and Michael Myers.

Clarice's fate is tied to Lecter's in the fiction plots as well as in the hype. In *The Silence of the Lambs*, Starling's quest for the serial murderer Jame Gumb is accomplished only through the imprisoned Lecter's help. Starling tracks down and kills Gumb, but Hannibal escapes. In the 1999 novel *Hannibal* and its 2001 movie version, Hannibal is lured out of hiding by Starling, and they pursue each other, but Hannibal is also hunted and then captured by a far more evil villain, one of his own former victims. Starling goes to his rescue, but when she's wounded, he becomes her rescuer, spiriting her away to private quarters where he nurses her back to health.

Many of Clarice's fans were disappointed by the second novel, in which Clarice is no longer the primary character and which ends with her as Lecter's partner or paramour, sharing his luxurious exile in a banana republic. The film version of *Hannibal* stopped far short of this, but generally both the book and film sequels confirmed the mutual attraction of Clarice and Hannibal subtly implied by the conclusion of *The Silence of the Lambs*, when the two had coiled into the cagey dynamic of hunter and hunted.

The differences between the novel *Hannibal* and its movie version indicate some limits on how romantically this scandalous attraction could be pictured for mainstream cinema. But Clarice's Beauty-and-the-Beast connection to the cannibal gourmet is central to both *The Silence of the Lambs* and *Hannibal*, the novels and adaptations. So what exactly is the appeal of this tale about a beautiful FBI agent and a flesh-eating mass murderer?

The campiness of this question is voiced through the recurring tabloid chorus in the three Lecter novels. Lecter first appeared in Harris's 1981 *Red Dragon*, where he's already behind bars as the trophy catch of that novel's hero, a forensics investigator who needs Lecter's expertise for the next case. This story in the *National Tattler*, "Insane Fiend Consulted in Mass Murders," shares space with stories on "Elvis at Secret Love Retreat" and "Filth in Your Bread!"[1] Both *Red Dragon* and *The Silence of the Lambs* emphasize Lecter's widespread celebrity in supermarket weeklies. In the second novel, the rookie Starling joins him in these headlines once the story leaks about her visit to his prison cell: " 'BRIDE OF FRANKENSTEIN!!' screamed the *National Tattler* from its supermarket racks" (*Silence*, 59). And at the end of the novel, after Hannibal's escape, even the respectable FBI section chief Crawford describes Lecter's notoriety in campy terms, as a pop culture hit:

"'Lecter's gone platinum—he's at the top of everybody's Most Wanted List,' he said" (327).

The point of camp, after all, is *bad* taste—the embarrassed but gleeful revelation that our Most Wanted characters, movies, and entertainments are excessive indulgences, from Mae West and gladiator movies to Batman and Robin. And Hannibal Lecter. Seizing on the spectacularly *unnatural,* camp batters assumptions about what the "natural" might be. Camp humor is mainstream enough for Old Navy television commercials, but it was once the province of gay subculture, and the aesthete Hannibal Lecter, especially in the Demme film, has been interpreted as gay. This category may be too simple, though, for a character who transgresses all categories—culture/nature, crime/order, human/animal, rationality/madness.[2]

Camp is all about the trespassing of categories, the ability of Lecter, Carmen Miranda, *Dynasty,* and Peggy Lee wigs to go either way, to raise either a giggle or a shudder. As movies like *Young Frankenstein* (1974), *The Rocky Horror Picture Show* (1975), and all the *Evil Dead* flicks (1981, 1987, 1993) illustrate, camp is naturally wedded to horror, which likewise can provoke either laughter or screams. Those movies also illustrate horror's preoccupation with sex and bodies—monstrous bodies, seductive bodies, bodies caught in violence and violation. Little wonder that Clarice Starling shows up there, too, not a campy figure herself but able to be pictured that way, as a tabloid Bride of Frankenstein—the camp version of that unnatural body, the female investigator.

PICTURING *THE SILENCE OF THE LAMBS*

The genius of Thomas Harris is his ability to write a thriller that touches on a cultural horror *du jour.* His first novel, *Black Sunday* (1975), had taken up the psychological aftermath of the Vietnam War; his second novel, *Red Dragon,* focused on the dysfunctional family. In *The Silence of the Lambs,* he combined the topics of the woman investigator, sexual identity, and the serial killer, delivering Title VII as the nightmare female initiation story.

The initiation story comes through in the openings of both his novel and the film version, but Demme's movie also makes a clever nod toward film history.[3] The opening scene shows Clarice running an obstacle course at FBI training headquarters, a course marked with the signs "Hurt," "Agony," "Pain," and "Love It." These are qualities of the more traditional "woman's film," the weepie or melodrama, in which women suffer divorce, disease, heartbreak, and loss: the classics are *Stella Dallas* (1937), *Mildred Pierce* (1945), *Johnny Belinda* (1948), and *Imitation of Life* (1934, 1959). The hits from the previous decade included *Terms of Endearment* and *Steel Magnolias* (1989). Those women's films take place in homes, kitchens, and hospitals, in families and romances. But when those "signs" of pain show up on an athletic field, female suffering has been reframed as self-empowerment: the discipline of weight-training gyms, aerobics classes, and athletic regimens to which women had been attracted by the late 1980s.

Yet it's difficult not to detect a dose of masochism here, too, on the training grounds of the FBI, an institution promising pain and agony to all its recruits, but which has already targeted attractive Clarice Starling for one very special errand with an imprisoned cannibal. Running an obstacle course with signs instructing her to love the pain, Clarice in this scene sums up the predicament of the female investigator. Sweating and sincere in the opening sequence, she obediently reports for her assignment to cannibalism and flesh-stripping murder.[4]

You can see the appeal of the classic American success story in the next scene, the office of the FBI section chief, where Clarice responds to questions politely and diligently in her unmistakable Appalachian accent. Here's the working-class outsider succeeding against the odds, struggling from West Virginia hill country "all the way to the F.B.I.," as Lecter later puts it. But she also has special meaning as the *female* outsider determined to rescue the woman poised as Buffalo Bill's next victim. Women reviewers often praised *The Silence of the Lambs* as a feminist film, pointing out its triumphant storyline of a woman rescuing another woman. Many scholars later disputed this, but this interpretation was reinforced when Foster accepted her Academy Award for this role, expressing her happiness with playing "such an incredibly strong and beautiful feminist hero."[5]

Meanwhile, even more special meanings were attached to Jodie Foster's portrayal of this strong female outsider. Lesbian fans of Foster were thrilled with her casting as an FBI heroine, especially when Foster in an interview described Clarice as "savior of women in peril." As Larry Gross has pointed out, despite Foster's reputation in the gay community, she "followed the rules" when she returned to Hollywood after college, remaining silent about her private life and refusing to respond to her lesbian devotees.[6] These admirers had been established long before *The Silence of the Lambs*. Foster's tough onscreen persona and her non-feminine offscreen images had made her a cult favorite—a talented, Yale-educated actress who resisted Hollywood stereotypes. Foster's best roles had been her punky characters in *Taxi Driver* and

Fig. 29 Jodie Foster as Clarice Starling in *The Silence of the Lambs* (1991). Courtesy of Photofest.

The Accused, the latter of which earned her an Academy Award for her portrayal of the working-class rape victim who fights back and wins. *The Accused* had also provoked torrid Hollywood gossip about a romance between Foster and her costar Kelly McGillis. Lesbian fans celebrated the moments of screen intensity between the two female stars in that film and in *Hotel New Hampshire* (1984), when Foster shared some special scenes with Nastassja Kinski.

The popular press has always used broad strokes of innuendo about Foster's sexuality. Biographical sketches often emphasize her childhood "masculine" role in her fatherless family, when her work as a child star was the family's means of support. For her featured 1987 story in *Interview*, the cover photograph reinforced a non-feminine persona: Foster in a black turtleneck and jeans, sitting with her arms around her knees, sternly returning the camera's gaze. But it's also true that Foster's own persona in interviews reinforces the different-drummer mystique. When she was honored with a *Time* magazine cover story for her directorial debut in *Little Man Tate* (1991), just a few months after the release of *The Silence of the Lambs*, her interview again referenced the tomboy childhood and implied that some of its traits are ongoing: "I never had the gift of looking cute. I hate dresses and jewelry, and the only doll I played with was a G.I Joe."[7] We're talking gender roles here, not sexual orientation, but this is obviously rich material for a gay following.

The reputation and the innuendoes had specific repercussions with *The Silence of the Lambs.* While the film was still in post-production in 1990, it was virulently attacked by gay activists for its portrayal of the serial killer as yet another of Hollywood's gay psycho killers. Harris's novel had made clear that Jame Gumb (a.k.a. Buffalo Bill) was not homosexual, but the film doesn't make this distinction while picturing Gumb as a lisping tailor who adores his little white poodle. Coming at the height of AIDS activism, the controversy threatened to overwhelm publicity about the film, to the extent that director Demme addressed the issue in interviews and attempted to make the difficult case that Gumb only *looked* like the fruity stereotype.[8]

But the activists' sharpest weapon was the casting of Jodie Foster in a film that featured such a homophobic image. In a campaign waged mostly by gay men, Foster was vociferously "outed" during the first half of 1991 by columns in *Outweek* and *The Advocate* and by the anonymous publication *Outpost,* which at that time was devoted to identifying gay celebrities through the circulation of ABSOLUTELY QUEER posters. *The Village Voice* crackled with arguments about whether or not Foster's prestige was being used to justify the film's nasty representation of gay men. The politics of Foster's casting got even more complicated. Lesbian critics were more interested in Foster's portrayal of a woman who rescues another woman. And on another front, some straight women fans of the film complained about having a strong female character or actress labeled a lesbian. The interpretation of Clarice Starling as gay had already occurred in some prominent early reviews of *The Silence of the Lambs,* such as the one by Stuart Klawans in *The Nation.*[9]

Over the years since the film's release, the issue of its homophobia was eventually separated from its usage of Foster, and *The Silence of the Lambs* is more likely now to be seen as her star vehicle rather than a site of controversy about her sexual orientation. Foster's offscreen and onscreen images softened quite a bit after this film. She appeared on magazine covers from *Redbook* to *Ladies Home Journal* in soft makeup and delicate earrings; she also took more traditional film roles in *Sommersby* (1993) and *Maverick* (1994), both of which gave her male romantic interests, and in *Anna and the King* (1999), which placed her in safely sweet unrequited love.

Throughout the 1990s, Foster continued to top lists of the most popular and most powerful women in Hollywood, at the same time that journalists strung along the sexual insinuations. The birth of Foster's sons in 1998 and 2001 only further obscured the sexuality issue, since Foster refused to name the father(s) and gave warm fuzzy interviews, laced with spunky quirkiness, about motherhood. "Mine is not a traditional household, and my mom's wasn't either," she said in a 2000 *Ladies Home Journal* interview. "Everybody is brought into this world with a different set of events." In his 1995 biography *Jodie*, biographer Louis Chunovic asks that, out of respect for all varieties of sexuality, we simply not label Foster at all.[10]

But the fantasies that propel popular stardom are bound up with sexualities and identities, and part of Foster's fascination is her ability to occupy several at once. Even the *Ladies Home Journal* cover photo can be interpreted as heterosexual glamour or lesbian *femme*, depending on where those fantasies land. One critic, describing Foster's widely varied appeals, reminds us that the most notorious Foster fantasy was that of John Hinckley, who in 1981 attempted the assassination of President Ronald Reagan in order to get her attention. Hinckley fantasized Foster first as virginal and then as treacherous, having betrayed his love with her refusal to respond.[11]

To the contrary, lesbian fans have been good sports about Foster's refusal to respond. In fact, Foster's silence about the lesbian rumors actually ensures their endless continuation. As numerous gay-lesbian websites make clear, her silence is no longer relevant to how her films are welcomed and interpreted among lesbian audiences. Those audiences don't generally interpret the character Clarice Starling as a lesbian, but they're interested in how carefully *The Silence of the Lambs* avoids making her heterosexual. Or as critic Clare Whatling puts it, Starling may not be gay, but she's "never comfortably recuperable" as straight.[12] So Demme's film version pictures not only a slippery character for Hollywood—a serious, nonglamorous female investigator— but also a slippery actress, Jodie Foster, in an ambiguous role.

The ambiguity stems from a screenplay that curiously erases the heterosexuality of Clarice's character found in Thomas Harris's novel. The film doesn't fill in the gap with lesbianism, either. It simply leaves her sexual orientation unclear. In the Harris novel, Clarice and her roommate Ardelia discuss men as dates and possible love interests. One of these dates is the Smithsonian entomologist Noble Pilcher, consulted by Clarice for the case, and this is the man in whose bed we find Clarice in the final pages of the novel. The bed is in a "big old house" on the Chesapeake shore, in a room lit by a fireplace. A careful reading of Harris's last paragraph shows an interesting reluctance to place Pilcher in the bed with her: "On a large bed there are many quilts and on the quilts and under them are several large dogs. Additional mounds beneath the covers may or may not be Noble Pilcher, it is impossible to determine in the ambient light." But Clarice is certainly there for a weekend date, and "she sleeps deeply, sweetly, in the silence of the lambs" (338).

This peaceful ending is far different from that of the film version, which takes place not in a cozy private room, but at a public event, Clarice's FBI graduation, where her moment of triumph is undercut by a phone call from Lecter. Lecter is the suitor who is far more important to Clarice than the young entomologist, but his unnerving call leaves her alarmed and helpless—and, of course, sets up the sequel. The film does retain Noble Pilcher, but for comic rather than romantic reasons, allowing him no further than the graduation party. There he is last seen fumbling with his camera to get a shot of his entomologist buddy posing with Ardelia. This is certainly not the picture he wants—a "couple" shot with Clarice—an option that's not in the picture.

Adaptations are intriguing because they expose a decision-making process, something kept or rejected for a film's effect. The decision to erase Clarice's love life seems aligned with other decisions about picturing her without the usual sexual trappings of the leading lady. Almost all the shots of her are medium shots that deemphasize her body; the exceptions are the startling shot in the elevator that I discussed in chapter 1 and the shot of her initial confrontation with Jame Gumb. In that shot, she's small and vulnerable at his kitchen door, unaware that it's the threshold to hell. Generally, director Demme seems to be trying hard to avoid the sexual clichés—straight or gay—of films like *Impulse* and *Black Widow*. Yet the very absence of a love interest, male or female, for the beautiful young Clarice creates its own oddness.

At one point, Hannibal quizzes her about a lecherous connection to Crawford, her boss at the FBI, asking if Crawford fantasizes about her. "That sort of thing doesn't interest me, Doctor," she replies, and we have no way of knowing if she means sex with Crawford, sex with men, or sex in general. Clarice has been instructed not to let Hannibal Lecter into her head, so her stonewalling is understandable. But the film also stonewalls us about Clarice, with no information about what indeed interests this intense, lovely woman beside her keen ambitions as an investigator.

Despite the nondescript clothing and lack of makeup, Starling is richly sexualized in this film in other ways. At Quantico and at the

West Virginia funeral home, she's depicted as the lone woman among groups of men. We see lustful gazes fixed on her by the tacky Dr. Chilton, the Smithsonian entomologists, and her male colleagues at Quantico. But the most startling sexualization is the crude act that makes the entire story possible. On her first visit to the imprisoned Dr. Lecter, she's contemptuously dismissed by him and retreats down a grimy, underground corridor lined with the cells of the other insane prisoners. Suddenly she's splattered with semen from an inmate, an act of psychological violence that outrages Lecter, who instantly calls her back and—as compensation for this outrage—gives her the first clue that will lead her to Gumb. This scenario is identical in the novel and the film. Both plots turn on Clarice's sexual humiliation, a symbolic rape, that enables her investigation and launches her initiation into both horror and success in the FBI.

This may be an all-American story about upward mobility, but for women, it leaves a mean sting. Clarice burns to be accepted into a male organization with a nasty history regarding women and minorities. For this first interview with Lecter, she doesn't realize she's being used by the FBI as bait to lure his interest in the Buffalo Bill case. Eventually, this investigation lands her in another grimy underground, the labyrinthine horror chambers of Gumb, where corpses rot in bathtubs and human skins hang on fashion mannequins. Gumb's perverted use of women's bodies and the FBI's cold "use" of Clarice are parallel in their indifference toward women—although this doesn't become evident until the sequel, *Hannibal*, which cruelly reveals the true nature of the club in which Clarice so badly wants membership.

Even more disturbing, *The Silence of the Lambs* associates Clarice's initiation story with two images shared by Buffalo Bill. One is a nightmare image of the transvestite Jame Gumb's project of "making himself a girl suit out of real girls," as Hannibal puts its (*Silence*, 149). Clarice's transformation from rookie to full-fledged FBI unfortunately rhymes with the transformation attempted by Gumb, both of which involve reversals.[13] In the psychotic version, Gumb is Frankenstein, creating a new self out of body parts. Posing in the mirror with his penis tucked away, he wants a female body to appear where the male body would be. In the Title VII version, Clarice is the woman who takes the man's traditional role. In the investigation story, a heroine appears where the hero would be. The Harris novel goes into detail about Gumb as a "failed transsexual," a metaphor that unfortunately echoes the mean metaphor of the woman detective: the female dick.

The other image shared by Starling and Gumb is the death's-head moth, the specific symbol of Gumb's wish to change his sex. Moths

and butterflies flutter through his horror chamber as he stitches together his girl suit. "Worm into butterfly, or moth. Billy thinks he
wants to change," Hannibal says (*Silence*, 149), and Hannibal is also
the one who charts Clarice's changes, from West Virginia rube to
fledgling investigator to agent for the FBI. The best-known poster and
ad for *The Silence of the Lambs* depicts this association with its closeup
of the face of Foster/Clarice, the death's-head moth in the place of
her mouth. Because Gumb had placed moth cocoons into the mouths
of two of his victims, the ad image also suggests a victimization of
Clarice. Like the dead women, she appears to be silenced, and because
the moth appears to be "stitched" onto her face, she becomes a hybrid,
a face pieced together in a monstrous way.[14]

A closeup of the skull-face on this moth reveals yet another image.
The skull is actually composed of nude female bodies, a detail from
Philippe Halsman and Salvador Dalí's surrealist 1951 photograph *In
Voluptate Mors*. In the photograph, Dali in tuxedo and top hat is posed
before this startling dream image. The "teeth" of the skull are actually
the feet of three women, two of them holding a third on their shoulders. Four other nude bodies frame them and make up the skull's other
bones. In short, this is a male vision of death as female sexuality, invit-
ing and deadly, contemplated or imagined by the gentleman-artist.

This fantasy of voluptuous death mirrors Jame Gumb's "girl suit" in
its eerie transformation of women's bodies into a male design and
dream. But its usage, fixed over Clarice's lips, is alarming, too. Her
mouth is the focus of a secret little erotic scene available only to those
curious enough to find it with a good magnifying glass. For a while, a
website simply called "Lesbian sex scene in *Silence of the Lambs*" provided this closeup, and its homoeroticism might be a comment on
Clarice's sexuality as embodied by Jodie Foster. But its ghastly design
has little to do with female desire and far more to do with men's fears
and anxieties about female sexuality. Traditionally, Hollywood film has
used precisely such images—fetishizations, turning women's bodies into
elaborate designs—to allay those fears.

This promotional image for the film version, later used for the cover
of the paperback novel as well, is a clue about the changes in Clarice's
representation between the novel and the film. Again, some specific
choices made in the adaptation suggest a diminishment of character
from novel to film, or at least a compliance with some Hollywood
clichés about women investigators, including ambivalence about their
skills and power. For one thing, in Harris's novel, Clarice's superior
status as a trainee at Quantico is never in doubt. In a classroom test of
hand strength, the instructor uses her as an example of how well the

class should be doing (32). She also has a reputation as a sharpshooter, chosen to represent the Bureau in a match against the DEA and Customs (253). The novel further emphasizes Clarice's considerable forensics skills with fingerprints, handling of evidence, and lab techniques. Because of these skills, Crawford asks her to accompany him to West Virginia to assist with the preliminary autopsy examination of one of Gumb's newly discovered victims.

Instead of this emphasis on her skillfulness at Quantico, the film version shows a training sequence in which Clarice fails. In a scene that doesn't appear in the novel, Clarice practices making an arrest and slips up, forgetting to check her "danger zone" and enabling her instructor to "shoot her" from behind. "You're dead, Starling," he says. The test takes place on a stage in front of a classroom-audience, suggesting Clarice's status not just as a student but as a role-player, someone taking a part. As I pointed out in chapter 5, this scene is similar to the opening sequence of *Blue Steel*, which likewise shows the female investigator making a mistake in a training exercise. These self-conscious moments act out a larger cultural uncertainty about this character in 1991 Hollywood.

The West Virginia autopsy sequence also makes significant changes from the novel. The film emphasizes Clarice's reluctance to look at the flayed body and assigns her the job of assisting the FBI forensics specialist, while in the Harris novel she performs all the forensic work herself. More important, Harris's novel emphasizes the *emotional* connections Clarice makes at the autopsy. After this experience, her first direct witnessing of Buffalo Bill's work, Clarice feels personally connected to the victims. Kimberly, the West Virginia victim, symbolizes not only the horror of the serial killings, but also Clarice's direct relationship to them: "It was Kimberly that haunted her now. Fat dead Kimberly who had her ears pierced trying to look pretty and saved to have her legs waxed. Kimberly with her hair gone. Kimberly her sister" (267).

The film version is faithful to the novel in emphasizing the maleness of the investigation, particularly with the cluster of awkward male state troopers who gawk at Clarice at the West Virginia funeral home. Crawford decides to do a male-bonding trick with them, as in the novel, excluding Clarice by announcing that this kind of "sex crime" is better discussed without her. Both film and novel give Clarice a brave moment with Crawford in which she later tells him exactly what's wrong with that kind of old-boys gesture: "Those cops know who you are. They look at you to see how to act," she tells him in the Harris novel (87). In the film she adds with quiet dignity, "It matters, sir."

When I screen this movie in my classes, this line gets my women students' applause.

But the film also uses the West Virginia autopsy sequence to sentimentalize Clarice's relationship to her dead father. The funeral home and the humiliating remark from Crawford cue a flashback to her father's funeral, just as her initial interview with Lecter—and the humiliating episode with Miggs—had cued a flashback to her adoration of her sheriff-daddy. The timing of these flashbacks might answer the question of why a woman would put up with these hassles in the male world of investigation: A woman would do this if she was inspired by a lost, good-cop daddy whose love she can secure forever by taking his place.

As sentimental pop-psychology, this is standard Hollywood sop. But it deliberately replaces the specifically *female* emotional support described in the novel, in which memories of Clarice's mother, not her father, are her repeated inspirations. During the autopsy scene, casting about for a "prototype of courage," she summons the image of her mother dealing with her father's death (74). Later she recalls it: "In the Potter Funeral Home, standing at the sink, she had found strength from a source that surprised and pleased her—the memory of her mother" (112). While Lecter coaxes from her the memory of her father's death, her own reminiscences throughout the novel return instead to maternal strength and endurance. In contrast, the Demme film insists on multiple daddies: the adored sheriff father, FBI section chief Crawford, and of course Lecter, so that all Clarice's teachers and inspirations are male.

Why the switch? Given the scarcity of Hollywood female investigators, it's safer to give Clarice a paternal rather than a maternal connection because she's part of, rather than opposed to, a male tradition. It's also a stereotype—daddy's girl, the soundbite for a complex character whose motivations need to be explained in a two-hour movie. And finally, the warm, supportive father is also an effective contrast for the coldness of Crawford and the kinkiness of Lecter.[15]

The impact of Lecter in the film version is crucial in the picturing of Clarice. On one hand, his film image as cool, inscrutable insider to the world's evil makes the innocent, transparently worried Clarice all the more sympathetic. When she peers into his darkened prison cell from which he suddenly ejects the message tray, *everyone* in the audience jumps. On the other hand, Lecter is clearly Clarice's superior in education, intellect, and imagination. As a psychiatrist, he's already an expert in profiling, the field Clarice hopes to learn. And what is psychiatry but detective work, the uncovering of secrets, the investigation into darkness, the revelation of what has been suppressed?

In the famous Lecter-in-the-cage scene in Memphis, contrasting shots make him luminous and godlike, as the camera brings successive shots closer and closer to his unnaturally backlit face. He remains perfectly still during this interview, while Clarice paces like the proverbial caged animal. Eventually, the closeups of Hannibal move through the bars and eliminate them, so Clarice is the one who appears to be caged.

Demme's *The Silence of the Lam*bs invites the audience to share Clarice Starling's anxieties and point of view, but Hannibal gets all the best lines and all the laughs, including the film's outrageous closing remark, as he eyes the insufferable Dr. Chilton from afar: "I'm having a friend for dinner," he tells Clarice casually. In the novel, Lecter gets the wittiest lines, too, but readers are hooked to Clarice through her running internal commentary, while Hannibal is poised as a superior but alien being. Once he's actually been embodied by Anthony Hopkins, though, the film can show what the novel cannot—Lecter's performance, his self-conscious role-playing and posing. Readers might miss the campy inflections of the novel, but it's hard to miss the camp in Anthony Hopkins's tone of voice and insinuating overtones. Hearing Clarice approach his cage in Memphis, he smoothly quotes a Broadway song: "People will say we're in love."

In love indeed. Though paired together as transgressive detectives in the Harris novel, the film pushes this coupling slightly further. When Lecter hands her the Buffalo Bill case file in the Memphis cage scene, we get an isolated closeup of his finger running down hers, and we might remember this is the first time we've seen a man touch her. In the film version, his closing phone call to her is more tantalizing than the letter he writes in the novel, because of its immediacy. By phone, they're intimately connected, and Clarice is urgently spurred to attention, while the novel allows her sleep and peace. The marketing around the book and film eventually changed to emphasize this Lecter-Clarice connection. Later paperback copies of *The Silence of the Lambs* replaced the face of Clarice with the half-faces of Clarice and Lecter, a chain of death's-head moths linking them together.

The attraction between investigator and criminal is a traditional fold in this genre, but as we've seen with *Impulse*, and *Bodily Harm*, the dynamic can more seriously undermine the woman detective, whose legitimacy and sexuality is suspect from the start. Harris's *The Silence of the Lambs* both proposes and mocks this coupling by imagining it as tabloid headlines characterizing Clarice as BRIDE OF FRANKENSTEIN and then *Bride of Dracula*. The headlines cast Lecter as our culture's two most popular monsters, with Clarice as his mate. After Clarice has killed Jame Gumb, the *National Tattler* "implied that Starling had made frank sexual revelations to Lecter in exchange for information, spurring an offer to Starling from *Velvet Talks: The Journal of Telephone Sex*" (332). In one sense, the mockery prevents us from thinking seriously about connecting Clarice and Lecter as either "monstrous" or coupled. But jokes are often nervous twitches, calling attention to something not directly addressed. In this case, the tabloid joke reminds us that the "sex scene" in *The Silence of the Lambs* is the powerful behind-the-bars interview in which Lecter penetrates Clarice's mind and memory, and makes her touch herself in her most vulnerable place, with the recollection of her childhood story. It's neither straight sex nor Velvet Talks, but there's nothing straightforward or conventional about what Lecter and Clarice need in each other, as the sequels make clear.

MOVIE TO BOOK: HARRIS'S *HANNIBAL*

At the end of *The Silence of the Lambs*, both the film and the movie, Hannibal Lecter makes a promise: "I have no plans to call on you, Clarice, the world being more interesting with you in it" (337). A "call" from Hannibal is deadly, but the language is courtly and even quaint—the mass murderer as gentleman caller. The promise is broken in the sequel, through most of which it's unclear if Lecter wants Clarice as a date or as dinner.

Eagerly awaited by fans of the first book and movie, Thomas Harris's *Hannibal* appeared in 1999, its appeal cutting across pop and high-brow tastes.[16] It was featured on the covers of both *The New York Times Book Review* and *Entertainment Weekly*. "He's Back!" proclaimed the latter, with a photo of Anthony Hopkins from the 1991 film. The expectation was obviously that Hopkins would be back for a film version of the new novel, too. The *Hannibal* novel arrived in pop culture suspended between the buzz of two movies: the reputation of one and the anticipation for the next one that ideally would feature both the stars from *The Silence of the Lambs*.

Was it *possible* to read the new novel without picturing Jodie Foster and Anthony Hopkins in their previous roles? For the past few decades, the novelization of a popular film—a book version that appears in the wake of the movie—has become a common device that extends the shelf-life of the movie. Harris's *Hannibal* presented a twist on this. Technically, *Hannibal* was a sequel to the earlier novel. But in terms of readers' expectations and preconceptions, Demme's *The Silence of the Lambs* film was more important in how the new book was being sold and read—and how it was already being thought about as a film. In a headline with consciously camp affect, "The Hunger," *Entertainment Weekly* announced that with the novel's publication, "everyone in Hollywood is gearing up for a feeding frenzy."[17]

Both Anthony Hopkins and Jodie Foster were, in effect, written into Harris's *Hannibal*. But Jodie Foster had a greater impact. The changes in the Clarice character from Harris's earlier novel would be otherwise inexplicable. In plain terms, at the end of Harris's *The Silence of the Lambs*, Clarice is on a date with a man. In *Hannibal*, seven years later, she's still living with Ardelia, she doesn't date men, and we learn she's rebuffed the attractive FBI agent she had a crush on during the time of the previous novel. Also, in the plot of *Hannibal*, Starling is plagued by questions of celebrity, visibility, and media exposure, the themes associated with Jodie Foster. And since stardom and celebrity in our culture are so tightly wrapped in issues of sex and sexiness, the "coupling" of Clarice and Hannibal involves questions of what sex would mean for these two, the female detective and the campy cannibal. Neither the Harris novel nor the film version tell us this directly, though they tease us with how much we want to know.

The sexy question bonding Lecter and Starling to each other and to us, the hungry consumers and audiences, is how dangerous our tastes might be. For more than two decades, popular culture has both sought and resisted the character of the female investigator. Here she is, transgressive and desirable, entwined with an even more transgressive villain who apparently suits our tastes. Lecter's cannibalism marks him as the perfect postmodern commodity—consumer and consumed.

To go back to Lecter's expertise on this—we desire what we see every day. Harris's *Hannibal* is all about mass-media images. The novel begins with Hannibal successfully living in disguise, with a face that doesn't match the public faces in the FBI's Most Wanted ads. Clarice, on the other hand, becomes in this novel an overexposed and infamous media image. Her appearance in the tabloid press gets the attention of the exiled Hannibal, and soon they're in heated pursuit of each other. Eventually, Clarice is transformed, by Hannibal, into something unrecognizable by any public medium. Together they fade into sweet criminal anonymity at the novel's closure.

This ending is a radical switch from the ending of *The Silence of the Lambs*, in which Clarice graduates from the FBI academy as a celebrated heroine, the slayer of the monster-murderer Buffalo Bill. In the film version, Starling proudly accepts her badge as multiple cameras flash to capture the moment of triumph. In *Hannibal*, we learn that Starling is a respected legend among women agents at the FBI. "All the girls—the women know about you, I mean everybody does, but you're kind of . . . kind of special to us," a female colleague tells her.[18] But we also learn that her high-profile excellence has marked her for the FBI's worst sexism and petty politics. Her record as the FBI's pistol champion had won her the moniker, among the men, of "Poison Oakley" (*Hannibal*, 7). Far from being promoted and trusted seven years after her encounter with Buffalo Bill, Clarice Starling is stalled in her career and relegated to dreaded assignments like drug-busting.

In the novel's bloody opening sequence, Starling survives a badly planned bust by shooting five people in self-defense, including a woman who was shielding herself with an infant. The headlines of the *National Tattler* proclaim her "DEATH ANGEL: CLARICE STARLING, THE FBI'S KILLING MACHINE" (*Hannibal*, 19). The accumulation of horrifying photo images from the shootout creates a publicity nightmare for the Justice Department, which then targets Starling as scapegoat.

The FBI betrays Starling because it can't *imagine* her outside stereotypes and one-dimensional images: man-hating lesbian, denizen of "some goddamned dyke den" (*Hannibal*, 339), or simply woman out of place. The FBI's Assistant Director is caught musing that "there was an emotional element in women that often didn't fit in with the Bureau" (*Hannibal*, 360). She also suffers classic sexual harassment at the Justice Department, of all places. She had previously refused the advances of Paul Krendler, the Deputy Assistant Inspector General, a married man, who is now happy to humiliate her and end her career. He calls her "cornpone country pussy" (*Hannibal*, 265), earning himself one of the most lurid death scenes in pop culture history.

On a more public level, Starling's torrid new stardom in the tabloids prompts Hannibal Lecter, on the lam in Italy, to get in touch with her for the first time since his escape. Lecter sends her a private letter—tellingly, a letter about finding and believing an image. He instructs her to disregard the portrayals of herself by the FBI and the public media, and instead to look at herself reflected in a "black iron skillet" (*Hannibal*, 30) of the kind she would have known from her West Virginia home. The private image, he says, is more reliable than the public one. This contact quickly reactivates the FBI's pursuit of Lecter, but the letter is also curiously a fan letter, with Lecter rooting for the celebrity whose image has been tarnished by the press.

Clarice certainly suffers bad press. Eventually, the local television station runs embarrassing footage of her getting a speeding ticket as she flees the scene of her Justice Department hearing. Eventually, too, the novel suggests that only Hannibal Lecter has the imagination to *picture* Clarice Starling sympathetically. As an artist, his sketches are impressionistic rather than realist. In *The Silence of the Lambs*, he had drawn her as a Christian madonna and shepherdess; in *Hannibal*, he sketches her as a version of the little sister he had lost during the Second World War.

Lecter's obsession with the lost sister is offered as a primary motivation for his murders and also for his attraction to Starling. His pursuit of Starling hovers between courtship and a mad dream of re-creating the past. When the pursuit and rescue plotlines have ended, *Hannibal* takes a turn toward the poetic and the surreal. Lecter begins studying astrophysics in order to reverse time and make broken teacups fly together again. And the novel's gruesome revenge scene is a bizarre Mad Hatter's gourmet dinner/tea party.

So while the novel begins as straightforward action thriller (the opening shootout sequence in a grimy D.C. neighborhood), it ends in a far more dreamy style and *mise-en-scène*. Its conclusion in Buenos Aires resembles South American magical realism, with Starling as chrysalis-turned-butterfly, freed from the nasty misogyny of the FBI and suddenly located far from the realist conventions of crime fiction. Transformed, Clarice Starling is no longer the besieged "Poison Oakley," the woman out of place in the guys' game. In the final pages of the novel, Lecter positions Starling in front of an antique mirror that is "slightly smoky and crazed," so that even though we get details of what she's wearing, her actual image eludes us, except that Lecter proclaims, ominously, that she's "a delicious vision" (*Hannibal*, 466).

What exactly should we be seeing here? How should we imagine this new, transformed Clarice? Harris's *Hannibal* provides smoky impressions rather than answers. This includes impressions of her sexuality, which in this novel is not as straightforward (or straight) as the heterosexual characterization Harris had given her in *The Silence of the Lambs*. *Hannibal* implies that in the previous seven years, only one other man was seriously interested in Starling. This was the FBI shooting instructor John Brigham, who had first appeared in *The Silence of the Lambs* novel as a man considered attractive by both Clarice and her roommate Ardelia. But in *Hannibal*, we get the news that Clarice had turned him down. "A long time ago John Brigham had asked her something and she said no. And then he asked her if they could be friends, and meant it, and she said yes, and meant it" (*Hannibal*, 27).

The opacity of this description—and the novel never gives us more detail—is capped by Brigham's death. He's one of the fatalities in the opening shootout, so this possibly romantic subplot closes before the main action gets under way. The next time the novel references their relationship, when Starling visits his grave, the tactic is repeated nearly word for word: "She felt a bond with Brigham that was no less strong because they were never lovers. . . . He asked her something gently and she said no, and then he asked her if they could be friends, and meant it, and she said yes, and meant it" (*Hannibal*, 246). More than two hundred pages later, we haven't gained any more information about the question between them, its context, or what exactly it implied.

If the "something" Brigham had asked was commitment, romance, or sex, then FBI-agent Starling stands among the fictional female investigators who are poised forever in an impossible heterosexuality, always having lost or about to lose a desirable man (Cornwell's Scarpetta, Grafton's Millhone, *Profiler*'s Sam, etc.). On the other hand, the "something" Brigham asked might be more basic: whether or not she dates men. Strikingly, the butch lesbian character in this novel, the villainous Mason Verger's sister Margot, is placed in an identical situation. When a sympathetic male character makes a sexual move and is rebuffed, Margot asks if they could be friends (*Hannibal*, 320). *Hannibal*'s Starling isn't characterized this directly, but—until her seduction by Hannibal at the end of the novel—she isn't directly characterized as straight, either. In this way, she resembles the Clarice of the Demme movie far more than Harris's own previous Clarice. That is, she resembles the star image of Jodie Foster.

The Starling of *Hannibal* has clearly had a tough seven years isolated from most relationships and certainly from heterosexual ones. Even though she's not a lesbian in this novel, the innuendoes spell out stereotypes of same-sex romantic love. In shades of the nineteenth-century Boston marriage, Starling shares a duplex with her close friend Ardelia. And at the end of the novel, she sends Ardelia a ring engraved with both their initials, a gesture that can easily be interpreted as more than friendship.[19] If Jodie Foster is in a sense *written into* this novel, then the mysterious "something" posed in Brigham's question is less mystifying and more positive. As in the case with Foster, we simply don't know—or rather, what we know is slanted and indirect.

Stardom also figures in *Hannibal* as an ironic part of the action. The scandal at the FBI has made Clarice Starling a celebrity—in fact, a comeback, since she'd been keeping a low profile since the Buffalo Bill episode seven years before. After her sudden rise in the media, she's pursued by her single most ardent fan, Hannibal Lecter. Lecter begins by sending her mail, and then small gifts. He starts to follow her and spy on her while she's jogging. He breaks into her car to breathe the air she has breathed and touch his tongue to the steering wheel. This is no less than the possessive fan who becomes the stalker.

In the final pages of *Hannibal*, Lecter's various therapies with Starling seek her ultimate secret, the "something" that would explain the most private level of her being. Yet what Lecter extracts is also what he most needs for himself, accomplishing a fan's most ardent desire—that the fantasies of the star and the fan perfectly coincide. He finds in Starling "the incestual taboo," an attraction only to "good" men like her father, and thus her inability to have a sexual relationship with them. Lecter's own most important fantasies are likewise incestual, focused on the lost sister whom he increasingly identifies with Starling. He succeeds with Starling through classical transference. Because he himself has been a father figure toward her, he can release her from the incest taboo by becoming her object of desire.

Hannibal remains oblique about what sex actually means for this couple: "Their relationship has a great deal to do with the penetration of Clarice Starling, which she avidly welcomes and encourages. It has much to do with the envelopment of Hannibal Lecter, far beyond the bounds of his experience. It is possible that Clarice Starling could frighten him. Sex is a splendid structure they add to every day" (*Hannibal*, 483). Suggestively, this description moves the couple into the poetic and the mythical, a relationship we can't picture clearly or in great detail. Likewise Clarice's final transformation, the promise of the chrysalis from *The Silence of the Lambs*, renders her an elegant figure glimpsed from afar—in fact, glimpsed at an opera in Buenos Aires, in an evening gown, at Lecter's side. The closing vignettes in the novel show us Starling and Lecter dancing or dining, speaking in one of several languages, but always described from a distance, as if picked up by a surveillance camera and a microphone that can't quite make out the words.

The shock of this novel's ending—for me, more shocking than the cannibalistic dinner-party scene that alarmed many critics—is Clarice Starling's virtual disappearance into elegance, myth, and romance. In her new status as outlaw, her face doesn't match the one currently being sought by the FBI. We can picture her as versions of Jodie Foster; later readers could picture her as Julianne Moore. But picturing her will always be the problem itself.

This move may be poetic and surreal, but it's also a suspiciously smug, pseudoliberal response to Title VII. It seems to say that the FBI is so misogynist that Clarice has to be rescued from its clutches—by a brilliant cannibal outlaw. Left behind are those women colleagues at the FBI for whom Clarice was "kind of special." Left behind also are disappointed readers like me, to whom Clarice was also "kind of special," the courageous rescuer of another woman and once embodied by Jodie Foster. Her new incarnation as outlaw certainly has its pleasures—at least for this obsessed fan—but I remain suspicious of Hannibal Lecter's paternal desires, which the novel instructs us are now Starling's desires as well. If we desire "what we see every day," Clarice's disappearance from literature leaves the world a little less interesting. And it raised the stakes on the picturing of Clarice in the next Hollywood production.

"THAT'S MY GIRL": RIDLEY SCOTT'S *HANNIBAL*

The fictional *National Tattler* couldn't have done better in producing sensationalistic headlines about the movie version of *Hannibal*. The cover of *Entertainment Weekly* characterized Julianne Moore as "Hannibal's Next Dish," and the cover of *Premiere* magazine teased, "Hungry for Moore?" The casting of Clarice for Ridley Scott's *Hannibal* involved an enigmatic refusal by Jodie Foster and high expectations from fans. "C'mon, did anyone really want to see a different Scarlett O'Hara?" asked Ted Tally, the Oscar-winning screenwriter from *The Silence of the Lambs*.[20]

The film rights to Harris's *Hannibal* were snatched up just a few months after the novel's debut, with Dino De Laurentiis shelling out a record nine million dollars to produce the film with Universal. The good news after that was Anthony Hopkins's willingness to return as Lecter, but Jonathan Demme and Ted Tally both turned down offers to direct and write, respectively. Far more disastrously, Jodie Foster refused to play the new Clarice. Her representatives claimed it was bad timing. Foster was planning a movie with ingenue Claire Danes and wouldn't be available for a year. But other sources claimed she was offended by the violence of the Harris novel or by Clarice's characterization. Eventually, she was quoted as saying about Clarice, "I would never betray a person to whom I owed so much," a startling suggestion that the character had a life of its own outside anything the sequels might do.[21]

De Laurentiis's studio, Universal, made some loud clanking noises about the project being canceled without Foster, although De Laurentiis himself was confident a good replacement could be made. At the same time, polls, websites, and feature journalists began to guess who the next Clarice would be. The names that came up were from the very top of the A-list in Hollywood: Ashley Judd, Angelina Jolie, Rene Russo, Gillian Anderson, Michelle Pfeiffer (who had originally been a top choice for *The Silence of the Lambs*.) But after director Ridley Scott chose Julianne Moore, there was a journalistic sigh of consensus—yes, of course, Moore would be perfect as the next Clarice.

By then, Moore was thirty-nine years old and—like Jodie Foster—a nontraditional star. Most striking, after more than a decade in Hollywood, Moore had avoided being typecast in any way. Each of her performances was solid, original, and unlike the others. She was the isolated housewife in *Safe* (1995) and one of the artist's lovers in *Surviving Picasso* (1996). Twice she was nominated for Academy Awards, for performances as a porno star in *Boogie Nights* (1997) and as the spiritually awakened adulteress in *The End of the Affair* (1999). Moore can appear slinky sexy or absolutely plain. And her only offscreen reputation is for hard work and devotion to her young son.

Gone was the volatile edge of Jodie Foster's Clarice—the fan expectations of toughness and sexual enigma. But Julianne Moore brought to the role a sharp intelligence and intensity, and—maybe more important—no distracting baggage of kink (Jolie), sexpot heat (Russo) or little-girl vulnerability (Pfeiffer). Taller and more substantially built than Jodie Foster, Moore has the body and steady gait of a young

Fig. 30 Julianne Moore as Clarice Starling in *Hannibal* (2001). Courtesy of Photofest.

Sigourney Weaver. It would be easy to imagine Moore as Ripley, suited up to face the aliens.

As Clarice, Moore suits up to face the monsters at the Justice Department. Gone is the anxious rigidity of Foster's younger rookie Clarice. Gone too is the Title VII innocence of the Appalachian scholarship girl, hopeful about her big break in the FBI. Moore is older in the part, and the part is older, too, more cynical, and terrifyingly lonesome. The *Hannibal* film takes away the character Ardelia and gives Clarice not a single female colleague—in fact, not even another female speaking part during her scenes in the film.

In this chilly version of the FBI, there are no other women, no mentors, and no sympathetic colleagues. Harris's novel at least provided Clarice the quiet bevy of female fans and even her old supporter Crawford. Instead, the film gives Clarice good reason to leave police work altogether. The opening drug-bust sequence, which in the novel is simply a bad plan, is instead the specific sabotage of a sexist Baltimore cop who resents Clarice's "smart mouth" authority. The FBI's subsequent treatment of Clarice is blatantly unfair and without a hint of the political complications that would make the unfairness plausible.

The screenplay also eliminates Margot, Mason Verger's lesbian sister, so the only other significant female character is Allegra, the sultry wife of the Florence police detective who (fatally) thinks he can outwit the notorious cannibal. Allegra's voluptuousness is all Mediterranean glamour; through a doorway, we catch her at her dressing table, clad in a delicate teddy, slipping into strappy high-heeled shoes.

Allegra's traditional, European femininity makes Clarice look Yankee-style androgynous in comparison. Until the final sequence, Clarice usually wears plain T-shirts and loose-fitting trousers, her long straight hair sternly pulled back from her face. Ridley Scott frames her as Demme had done, mostly with medium shots from the waist up, her body, in drab-colored jackets and suits, rarely emphasized. Instead, her sexualization is cleverly accomplished through the eyes of others. While she talks with an Italian policeman on the phone, we see that he's sketching a suggestive nude. With his letter, Lecter includes a sketch of her bare-breasted; when Clarice includes it in her office gallery of Lecter evidence, she modestly covers the breasts with a Post-It note. The evil Paul Krendler is the one who lecherously lifts the note to peer beneath, and it's also through his perspective we see Clarice's crossed legs and thighs, on the one occasion that she wears a skirt.

Yet the film invites us to watch her through Lecter's eyes, too, and we're never sure exactly how to feel about this, because he's pictured as both tender courtier and ruthless monster. At one point, Clarice runs a video of his unprovoked attack on a tending nurse, and we see blood run from his mouth as he turns from the torn face. In a long sequence of mutual pursuit, Lecter lures her to D.C.'s Union Station and torments her through their phone connection, in which he whispers both intimate advice and elusive clues about how to find him. When he can't resist touching her hair—so lightly she doesn't know—he inadvertently points himself out to his kidnappers and enemy. So Lecter's intentions toward Clarice, until the very final shot, are never entirely clear. Mason Verger puts it crudely, as he does in the book version: "Does he want to fuck her or kill her, or eat her, or what?" (*Hannibal*, 276).

Or what. Ridley Scott's *Hannibal* opts for the last—romance laced with creepy obsession. In Italy, Lecter has carefully handpicked the extravagant fragrance that lingers on his letter to her. Traveling to the States, he breaks into her home and then, like a protective lover, watches her sleep. The film associates Hannibal Lecter with the warm duskiness of Florence, opera music, perfumes, candles, flowers, art, Dante's sonnets. Like a Caravaggio painting, his obsession is pictured in the deep rooms of a palace, where he plays the piano while meditating on Clarice's photo in the newspaper.

Clarice is obsessed, too, but in stark American Puritan tones. Instead of listening to music, she listens to tapes of her interviews with Lecter. Her clothing, home, and private life are austere and coldly colored. The one piece of furniture in the front hallway of her house is a wooden bench, as if to announce, "No comfort here." Her office is illuminated by the wall-size board on which she's posted Lecter's police files, crime photos, and papers. In fact, the brilliance of the film is its alternations of their interlaced obsessions with each other, the moves between romantic imagery and surveillance photography, the interplay of police work and poetry, the manhunt and the romantic quest.

The film's portrayal of Clarice's sensuously impoverished life, on the one hand, and Lecter's sumptuous, romantic one on the other, actually sets us up for the conclusion of Harris's novel. Betrayed and abandoned by the FBI, the institution for which she's sacrificed any personal life, Clarice achingly deserves Florence, the opera, fine wines, perfumed letters—at least a fun weekend at the bayside house commandeered by Lecter. Even the film's opening shot of Clarice points us toward that conclusion. The opening is a tight closeup showing her peacefully asleep, dreaming in the silence of the lambs, Sleeping Beauty waiting to be awakened by the cannibal prince.

But the scandalous conclusion of Harris's novel was apparently too much for mainstream cinema. Instead, when Clarice awakens from Lecter's surgery and medical care in the final sequence of the film, she's dressed like Sleeping Beauty but still packs the instincts of J. Edgar Hoover and Elliot Ness. Lecter has clothed her in a stunning black evening gown, a backless halter affair cut low between her breasts. The impracticality of her exquisite Gucci heels is straight out of *FBI Girl*. Drugged and off-balance, she looks for weapons and calls 911 for backup.

Screenplay writers David Mamet and Steven Zaillian had scripted at least three different endings for this film, all of them veering dramatically away from the ending of Harris's novel. In all these versions, Clarice heroically attempts to capture Lecter, and Lecter eludes her, giving her one passionate kiss goodbye before a mysterious disappearance. For the final version used in the film, they're briefly handcuffed together, twin prisoners in the tradition of past screen lovers: Cary Grant handcuffed to Rosalind Russell in *His Girl Friday*, Humphrey Bogart and Katherine Hepburn with nooses around their necks at the end of *African Queen* (1951). These are romantic comedies, and *Hannibal*, for all its gore and tensions, savors those comic twists. "This will hurt," Hannibal promises wickedly, brandishing his cleaver. But pain is a cherished element in the courtly love tradition Hannibal knows all too well. Earlier in the film, he'd quoted one of Dante's love sonnets to the fair Allegra, who is only a stand-in for Clarice. Hannibal would rather chop off his own hand than hurt his beloved.

So it's a love story after all, in fact, the classic unrequited love story we know through Dante, featuring bittersweet departure, eternal separation, the lover left only with perfume on the billet-doux and traces of fireworks in the air. It's also a love story that preserves an essentially heroic Clarice, loyal to the FBI and the law despite the shabby treatment she's received. The last we see of Clarice Starling, she's at the boat dock in her evening gown watching his distant signal—fireworks, the traditional film code for sex—from another shore.

With the squad cars piling up behind her, she's had to raise her hands high to signal she's unarmed. "I'm Clarice Starling, FBI," she calls out, affirming loudly that despite her horrendous treatment by the Bureau, she's going back. But it's difficult not to see the raised arms as surrender, too. Lecter has escaped the FBI. She hasn't been as lucky. Unlike the book version of this character, Ridley Scott's Clarice is never seriously tempted to go over, to turn outlaw, no matter how cruelly she's been betrayed by the law. With Lecter bent close to her face in their last scene together, she tells him that not even for love could she stop her pursuit of him. "That's my girl," he breathes contentedly. In one of Mamet's visual jokes, Lecter has locked her long hair into the refrigerator door, tethering her to the kitchen and domesticity—from which, of course, she escapes.

In the end, Clarice has retained her integrity, her courage, and her gritty determination. Lecter flies back to Europe, and Clarice remains on the Puritan shore, untouchable despite that incredible gown from which her breasts always seem about to swing loose. So why is this a sad ending for her fans?

In the film version of *The Silence of the Lambs*, we could savor Clarice's moments of triumph even though Lecter leaves her hanging in the final scene. But in the *Hannibal* film, Clarice is often a victim, first of the sexist cops who sabotage the drug bust, then of the FBI. The first scene of the film shows off her sharpshooting skills and cool head. But the second scene opens with Clarice in tears, watching her colleague's funeral on television. She's manipulated by Krendler's betrayal and by Mason Verger's evil plans, and manipulated less malevolently by Lecter. In the dizzying Union Station scene, he's the lovingly sadistic puppeteer, pulling her strings. When he leans forward to brush her hair with his fingertips, we recall with a shiver that Buffalo Bill had done the same thing in the darkened basement labyrinth.

The truth is, there's no comfortable outcome for Clarice Starling in these sequels, in which her choices are Hannibal Lecter and a woman-hating FBI. Ridley Scott pictured his heroines at a similar point at the end of *Thelma & Louise*, when there was nowhere to go and no reason to trust the law. I'm glad Clarice doesn't put stones into her halter top and dive into the Chesapeake, but the film cues us to imagine a sad, hard life for this heroine, no matter how fabulous the gown and Gucci heels.

That's all right. These investigating women are almost always at odds with the job title, the traditional ending, and the usual romantic suspects. Their best pictures are cagey, not comforting. Karen Sisco shoots her lover, Scully aims her giant flashlight, Jane Tennison paces in her office, and Marge Gunderson pulls her gun and plunges through the snow.

NOTES

Chapter 1: Watching the Women Detectives

1. Thomas Harris, *The Silence of the Lambs* (New York: St. Martin's, 1988), 209; hereafter cited in text as *Silence*.

2. The most thorough summary and history of the fictional woman detective is the one given by Kathleen Gregory Klein in *The Woman Detective: Gender and Genre* (Urbana: University of Illinois Press, 1988; reprint, 1995). Also see Patricia Craig and Mary Cadogan, *The Lady Investigates: Women Detectives & Spies in Fiction* (New York: St. Martin's, 1981), and Maureen T. Reddy, *Sisters in Crime: Feminism and the Crime Novel* (New York: Continuum, 1988).

3. In her essay on the short-lived cable series *Veronica Clare*, Susan White comments on the importance of fashion and décor details in the woman detective story. For White, the postmodern surplus of feminine details works in tension with the codes of the hardboiled narrative and style. See "Veronica Clare and the New *Film Noir* Heroine," *Camera Obscura* 33–34 (1995): 77–100.

4. B. Ruby Rich comments on Foster as "the repository of audience fantasies," and discusses Foster's position as political target in the controversy about homophobia in *The Silence of the Lambs*. See "Nobody's Handmaid," *Sight and Sound* (December 1991): 7–10. For more on the mixed reception of this film and the various interpretations of Clarice, see chapter 7 in this book.

5. Steffen Hantke discusses this visual dynamic—Clarice's lack of private space and her constant surveillance by others—as part of his argument about cultural fascination with the serial killer's privacy. See " 'The Kingdom of the Unimaginable': The Construction of Social Space and the Fantasy of Privacy in Serial Killer Narratives," *Literature/Film Quarterly* 26, no. 3 (1998): 178–95.

6. Rhonda Wilcox and J.P. Williams discuss the plotting of Scully's visual failures in " 'What Do You Think?' The X-Files, Liminality, and Gender Pleasure," in *"Deny All Knowledge": Reading the X-Files*, eds. David Lavery et al. (Syracuse: Syracuse University Press, 1996), 99–120.

7. In discussions of fantasy and film spectatorship, film scholars often rely on the vicissitudes of identification described by Sigmund Freud in " 'A Child Is Being Beaten': A Contribution to the Origin of Sexual Perversions," in *Sexuality and the Psychology of Love* (1919; reprint, New York: Collier, 1972), 107. The other psychoanalytic source often cited is the essay by Jean Laplanche and Jean-Bertrand Pontalis, "Fantasy and

the Origins of Sexuality," in *Formations of Fantasy*, eds. Victor Burgin et al. (1964; reprint, London: Methuen, 1986), 5–34. The discussions of fantasy in feminist film theory are best summed up by Judith Mayne in *Cinema and Spectatorship* (New York and London: Routledge, 1993), 86–91.

8. Priscilla L. Walton and Manina Jones comment that the story structure itself "makes possible the convergence of different readerships." They also note that this mainstreaming of the lesbian detective has not occurred in film and television, citing the occasion when Cybill Shepherd optioned Sandra Scoppettone's series and was turned down by all the networks. See *Detective Agency: Women Rewriting the Hardboiled Tradition* (Berkeley: University of California Press, 1999), 107 and 281; hereafter cited in the text. Also see Yvonne Tasker's discussion of the role of fantasy in sexually ambiguous female characters in "Pussy Galore: Lesbian Images and Lesbian Desire in the Popular Cinema," in *The Good, the Bad, and the Gorgeous: Popular Culture's Romance with Lesbianism*, eds. Diane Hamer and Belinda Budge (London: Pandora, 1994), 172–83. Regarding the appeal of such characters as those played by Linda Hamilton in *Terminator 2* and Sigourney Weaver in the *Alien* films, Tasker writes, "These fantasy representations mobilize a range of readings, and the pleasures are many. They are pleasures which can't be easily assessed in terms of the desire for a gay version of heterosexual suburban family life. Neither can we find in such images the reflection of an imagined, stable sexual identity," 175.

9. The article on the women in television crime shows is by Diane Anderson-Minshall, "Take That! TV's Top 10 'Lesbian' Crime-Fighter Shows," *Curve* (June 2003): 26+. The topic of fans as active consumers and creators of meaning has received considerable attention in cultural studies. See, for example, Cheryl Harris and Alison Alexander, eds., *Theorizing Fandom: Fans, Subculture, and Identity* (Cresskill, N.J.: Hampton Press, 1998). For an overview of fan scholarship, see Henry Jenkins, "Reception Theory and Audience Research: The Mystery of the Vampire's Kiss," in *Reinventing Film Studies*, eds. Christine Gledhill and Linda Williams (London: Oxford University Press, 2000), 165–82. An excellent example of fan interpretation and community is Steven Cohan's essay, "Judy on the Net: Judy Garland Fandom and 'The Gay Thing' Revisited," in *Keyframes: Popular Cinema and Cultural Studies*, eds. Matthew Tinkcom and Amy Villarejo (Routledge: London and New York, 2001), 119–36. For in-depth analysis of how women fans have thought about and idolized female stars, see Jackie Stacey, *Star Gazing: Hollywood Cinema and Female Spectatorship* (London and New York: Routledge, 1994).

10. See Doty's introductory chapter, "There's Something Queer Here," in *Making Things Perfectly Queer: Interpreting Mass Culture* (Minneapolis: University of Minnesota Press, 1993), 1–16. Also see Judith Mayne's chapter "The Paradoxes of Spectatorship," 77–102, in *Cinema and Spectatorship*. In an often-cited passage explaining the appeal of cinema to straight and gay audiences, Mayne points out that "one of the distinct pleasures of the cinema may well be a 'safe zone' in which homosexual as well as heterosexual desires can be fantasized and acted out," 97.

11. Hemingway starred as the lesbian Olympic tennis competitor in *Personal Best* (1982) and as the wife-turned-lesbian in *The Sex Monster* (2000). In *Chutney Popcorn* (2000), Jill Hennessy played the lover of an Indian woman involved in a surrogate pregnancy plan.

12. See Art Linson, "The $75 Million Difference," *New York Times Magazine* (16 November 1997): 88–89.

13. Dana A. Heller points out that the pairing of the lesbian and the Latino gives the film a superficially liberal veneer. See "Almost Blue: Policing Lesbian Desire in *Internal Affairs*," in *The Lesbian Postmodern*, ed. Laura Doan (New York: Columbia University Press, 1994), 173–88.

14. In *Fatal Women: Lesbian Sexuality and the Mark of Aggression* (Princeton: Princeton University Press, 1994), Lynda Hart claims that the fields of criminal anthropology,

sexology, and psychoanalysis together assembled a homophobic profile of the woman criminal as lesbian, a trend she reads from Victorian novels to *Thelma & Louise*. See especially 28. From another perspective, Priscilla L. Walton and Manina Jones interpret the "outlaw" status of the woman investigator as the genre's trademark, claiming this character is a "generic outlaw" who appropriates a masculine genre "to subvert some of its most powerful traditions" and "make a kind of feminist 'outlaw agency' possible." See Walton and Jones, *Detective Agency*, 195.

15. Klein uses Monique Wittig's famous description of the lesbian as Not-Woman; the category of Woman exists only in relationship to Man—a heterosexual, patriarchal relationship. Refusing this relationship, the lesbian is the third term in the binary pattern—or rather, her resistance to the binary categories makes her Not-Woman. Klein points out that because lesbians are interpreted as "not really female," then women who are "not really female" for whatever reason can be interpreted as lesbians. In the traditional male-female roles of the detective genre, role-switching has sexual consequences: "If female, then not detective; if detective, then not really female." See "*Habeas Corpus*: Feminism and Detective Fiction," in *Feminism in Women's Detective Fiction*, ed. Glenwood Irons (Toronto: University of Toronto Press, 1995), 174.

16. Janet Evanovich, *One for the Money* (New York: Scribner, 1994), 3.

17. *D Is for Deadbeat* (New York: Henry Holt, 1987), 20; hereafter cited in text as *Deadbeat*, and *B Is for Burglar* (New York: Henry Holt, 1985), 64; hereafter cited in text as *Burglar*.

18. Ann Wilson (in "The Female Dick and the Crisis of Heterosexuality," in *Feminism in Women's Detective Fiction*, ed. Irons, 148–56), describes the "crisis of heterosexuality" in the detective heroines of Sue Grafton, Marcia Muller, and Sara Paretsky. She argues that each of their failed heterosexual romances is structured as a "a matter of personal incompatibility rather than a symptom of larger social issues of gender and sexuality," 155. But I find the "crisis of heterosexuality" itself a transgressive element of these heroines, and would argue that the decentralization and demystification of romance in these stories are themselves the larger social issues of sexuality and gender.

19. Sandra Scoppettone, *My Sweet Untraceable You* (Boston: Little, Brown, 1994), 125.

20. Robert B. Parker, *Family Honor* (New York: Putnam, 1999), 8.

21. J.M. Redmann, *Death by the Riverside* (Norwich, Vt.: New Victoria, 1990), 2; Marc Vernet, "*Film Noir* on the Edge of Doom," in *Shades of Noir*, ed. Joan Copjec (London: Verso, 1993), 17.

22. Though most mainstream film and television versions of this character strain for some traditional feminine, heterosexual identity traits, the occasional indifference to these traditional categories suggests Judith Halberstam's widely cited concept of female masculinity. See *Female Masculinity* (London: Duke University Press, 1998).

23. In a widely anthologized essay, Robin Wood provides a useful list of the values of American capitalist ideology that are most often found in popular genres: private enterprise, the work ethic, marriage, agrarianism, progress, and so on. See "Ideology, Genre, Auteur," *Film Comment* 13, no. 1 (1977). For an analysis of the social work and contracts of popular genre and genre as an economic enterprise, see Walton and Jones, 44–77. Also see Ernest Mandel, *Delightful Murder: A Social History of the Crime Story* (London: Pluto, 1984).

24. See Barry Keith Grant's introduction to the anthology he edited, *The Dread of Difference: Gender and the Horror Film* (Austin: University of Texas Press, 1996), 1–12.

25. See Linda Williams's essay on the social implications of "body genres" in "Film Bodies: Gender, Genre, and Excess," *Film Quarterly* 44, no. 4 (1991): 2–13. The best-known work on popular genres includes Tania Modleski's *Loving with a Vengeance: Mass-Produced Fantasies for Women* (1982; reprint, New York: Methuen, 1984); Janice A. Radway's *Reading the Romance: Women, Patriarchy, and Popular Literature* (Chapel Hill: University of North Carolina Press, 1984); and Carol J. Clover, *Men, Women, and Chainsaws: Gender in the Modern Horror Film* (Princeton: Princeton University Press, 1992).

26.   Cornwell is quoted as protesting that "the mystery genre doesn't apply to what I do. . . . My books are crime novels and about the people who work crime—and not mysteries, which I've never read in my life anyway." See Mary Cantwell, "How to Make a Corpse Talk," *New York Times Magazine* (14 July 1996), 15–17. In focusing on the character instead of a category, I am following those critics who have moved away from thinking of popular genres only as categories or classifications and instead are asking other kinds of questions about the cultural work being done by these entertainments in publishing history, in film history, in nationalist agendas, or in shifting racial and gender relationships. See, for example, Linda Williams, "Melodrama Revised," in *Refiguring American Film Genres* (Berkeley: University of California Press, 1989), 42–88. Along the same lines, Rick Altman argues for thinking about genre less as a classification than as a discourse, a recognizable way of imagining and representing certain stories, characters, settings, or problems. See Rick Altman, *Film/Genre* (London: British Film Institute, 1999), 83–99. Though his main focus is film genre, he outlines the history of genre criticism in literature as well, 1–13.

27.   In this book, I examine this character's appearance in all her formulas—the mystery, the crime story, the police procedural, the thriller. I draw the line at spy stories, which don't have the same sexual dynamics. Women have a long history in espionage, especially in wartime, with Mata Hari—Margaretha Geertruida Zelle—as the poster-girl from World War I. It's not exactly a flattering fit, since the woman spy doesn't contradict popular notions of women as two-faced, deceptive, and manipulative. At any rate, the woman spy doesn't embody the same contradictions and tensions as the woman detective, who is stepping into a job usually done by a man.

28.   On the comparison of Dana Scully to Clarice Starling, see Wilcox and Williams, 102–3.

29.   This is reported by Michele Malach in " 'I Want to Believe . . . in the FBI': The Special Agent and *The X-Files*," in *"Deny All Knowledge*," 70. In her British Film Institute series book on *The Silence of the Lambs*, Yvonne Tasker discusses that film in relation to Cornwell's novels and to *The X-Files*, noting that the popular focus on women and corpses could be a "perverse manifestation of the caring professions with which female characters have so long been associated." See Tasker, *The Silence of the Lambs* (London: British Film Institute, 2002), 45. Tasker's analysis of this film is one of the few that considers it as an adaptation and contextualizes it across other media treatments of serial killers and forensics.

30.   Several excellent histories of the detective genre are available for fuller descriptions. See Howard Haycraft, *Murder for Pleasure: The Life and Times of the Detective Story* (1941; reprint, New York: Carroll and Graf, 1984) and Julian Symons's critical history *Bloody Murder: From the Detective Story to the Crime Novel*, 3rd rev. ed. (1972; reprint, New York: Mysterious Press, 1992).

31.   For early discussions of the detective as Oedipus, see Jan R. Van Meter, "Sophocles and the Rest of the Boys in the Pulps: Myth and the Detective Novel," in *Dimensions of Detective Fiction*, eds. Larry Landrum et al. (Bowling Green, Ohio: Popular Press, 1976), 12–21, and Tzvetan Todorov, "The Typology of Detective Fiction," in *The Poetics of Prose*, trans. Richard Howard (Ithaca, N.Y.: Cornell University Press, 1977). Critical discussion of the detective genre abounds. In addition to Haycraft, Symons, and the Landrum anthology, see Robin W. Winks, ed., *Detective Fiction: A Collection of Critical Essays* (Englewood Cliffs, N.J.: Prentice-Hall, 1980). For contemporary cultural studies, John Cawelti's *Adventure, Mystery, and Romance: Formula Stories as Art and Popular Culture* (Chicago: University of Chicago Press, 1976) is especially useful in its study of narrative structure and formula. The gendered implications of the hardboiled detective are the focus of Frank Krutnik's *In a Lonely Street: Film Noir, Genre, Masculinity* (London and New York: Routledge, 1991). Summing up the masculine dynamics of the genre, Krutnik cites Todorov and describes the hardboiled detective story as a narrative

"structured around principles of masculine testing where the hero defines himself through the conflict with various sets of adversaries (criminals, women)," 40.

32. As Frank P. Tomasulo points out in his psychoanalytic reading, the falcon in this film "is both a phallus *and* a fetish, a real symbol and a fake," 83. See "The Maltese Phallcon: The Oedipal Trajectory of Classical Hollywood Cinema," in *Authority and Transgression in Literature and Film,* eds. Bonnie Braendlin and Hans Braendlin (Gainesville: University of Florida Press, 1996), 78–88.

33. For the racial implications of these journeys to "dark" neighborhoods, see Eric Lott, "The Whiteness of *Film Noir*," in *National Imaginaries, American Identities: The Cultural Work of American Iconography,* eds. Larry J. Reynolds and Gordon Hutner (Princeton: Princeton University Press, 2000), 159–81.

34. These statistics come from Kevin McManus, *The G-Women* (Washington, D.C.: Department of the Treasury, 1989) and "Census of State and Local Law Enforcement" (Washington, D.C., 1996).

35. Bobbie Ann Mason, *The Girl Sleuth: On the Trail of Nancy Drew, Judy Bolton, and Cherry Ames* (1975; reprint, Athens: University of Georgia Press, 1995), 63.

36. B. Ruby Rich was among the first critics to realize this, pointing out in a 1989 essay that the woman detective novel "weds the subversive potential of an established form to the political and subjective desires of a community." See "The Lady Dicks: Genre Benders Take the Case," *Village Voice Literary Supplement* (June 1989), 24–26.

37. For an excellent analysis of the Grafton, Muller, and Paretsky series and their impact, see Walton and Jones, 10–38. Also see Gary Warren Niebuhr's assessment of the private investigator novel and its dramatic changes in the fiction market since 1982 in *A Reader's Guide to the Private Eye Novel* (New York: G.K. Hall, 1993), xi–xii.

38. Sue Grafton, *A Is for Alibi* (New York: Holt, Rinehart and Winston, 1982), 274; hereafter cited in the text as *Alibi.*

39. Walton and Jones report this statistic, 28.

40. Lucinda Dyer, "It's Not Whodunit, But How-Do-You-Do-It?" *Publishers Weekly* (25 October 1999), 34–43, and Heather Vogel Frederick, "Revisiting the Scene of the Crime," *Publishers Weekly* (24 April 2000), 38–51.

Chapter 2: Picturing the Best-Seller List

1. Detective novels were not the only genre circulated in this format, but histories of pulp fiction acknowledge its identification with 1930s and postwar "hardboiled" popular literature. See Geoffrey O'Brien, *Hardboiled America: The Lurid Years of Paperbacks* (New York: Van Nostrand Reinhold, 1981).

2. In the past century, this has played out most dramatically with widely publicized writers like Ernest Hemingway and Sylvia Plath. Multimedia connections of fans have fueled the cult followings of authors ranging from J.D. Salinger to Stephen King. The reading experience in such cases may begin not with the book at all, but with exposure to the writer, who serves as real-life clue to the fiction. The kinkiness of Anne Rice's world, for instance, has been established by marketing that blurs the distinctions between the world of the novels and the world that Rice herself inhabits and publicizes: her house in New Orleans, her nineteenth-century costumes, her penchants for jazz funerals and the color purple. No matter how convincingly literary theories discount authorship as the source of a book's meaning, it's not surprising that generations of schoolchildren still learn that the "correct" reading of a book is what the author intended.

3. Melanie Rehak, "What Are Cops Afraid Of? Questions for Patricia Cornwell," *New York Times Magazine* (21 February 1999), 17; Christina Ferro, "How to Be Your Own Private Detective," *McCalls* (August 1991), 50+.

4. Priscilla L. Walton and Manina Jones have argued that the author images associated with women detectives are special cases of authorial identification. While author im-

ages are often glamorized and thus distanced, they say, the association of the female author with the hardboiled investigator instead invites the woman reader to identify with this image. The author's photograph and autobiographical commentary in interviews serve to focus a liberating fantasy—independence, cleverness, confidence, authority—around someone in the real world. See Walton and Jones, *Detective Agency*, 184–86.

5. Two different readings of Grafton's *F Is for Fugitive,* for example, focus on how Kinsey assesses the men in a small town who have all taken advantage of the town's bad girls. For the positive reading of this book, see Maureen T. Reddy, "The Feminist Counter-Tradition in Crime: Cross, Grafton, Paretsky, and Wilson," in *The Cunning Craft: Original Essays on Detective Fiction and Contemporary Literary Theory*, eds. Ronald G. Walker and June M. Frazer (Macomb: Western Illinois University Press, 1990), 174–87. The less optimistic critical interpretation is by Timothy Shuker-Haines and Martha M. Umphrey in "Gender (De)Mystified: Resistance and Recuperaton in Hard-Boiled Female Detective Fiction," in *The Detective in American Fiction, Film, and Television*, eds. Jerome H. Delameter and Ruth Prigozy (Westport, Conn.: Greenwood, 1998), 71–82. Other feminist interpretations of Grafton's series are that of Scott Christianson, "Talkin' Trash and Kickin' Butt: Sue Grafton's Hard-boiled Feminism," in *Feminism in Women's Detective Fiction*, ed. Glenwood Irons (Toronto: University of Toronto Press, 1995), 127–47, and that of Sabine Vanacker, "V.I. Warshawski, Kinsey Millhone and Kay Scarpetta: Creating a Feminist Detective Hero," in *Criminal Proceedings: The Contemporary American Crime Novel*, ed. Peter Messent (London: Pluto, 1997), 62–86. Peter Rabinowicz gives a brilliant split reading of Grafton in " 'Reader, I blew him away': Convention and Transgression in Sue Grafton," in *Famous Last Words: Changes in Gender and Narrative Closure*, ed. Alison Booth (Charlottesville: University Press of Virginia, 1993), 326–46. The best discussion of the feminist value of Sue Grafton's Kinsey Millhone series is Priscilla L. Walton's essay, " 'E' is for Engendered Readings" in *Women Times Three: Writers, Detectives, Readers*, ed. Kathleen Gregory Klein (Bowling Green, Ohio: Popular Press, 1995), 101–16.

6. For discussion of the political implications of lesbian detective fiction, see Paulina Palmer, "The Lesbian Thriller: Transgressive Investigation," in *Criminal Proceedings,* ed. Messant, 87–110; Gillian Whitlock, " 'Cop it sweet': Lesbian Crime Fiction," in *The Good, the Bad, and the Gorgeous*, 96–118; Liahna Babener, "Uncloseted Ideology in the Novels of Barbara Wilson," in Klein, *Women Times Three*, 143–61; and Jo Ann Pavletich, "Muscling the Mainstream: Lesbian Murder Mysteries and Fantasies of Justice," *Discourse* 15, no. 1 (1992): 94–111.

7. For a description of this history, see Verta Taylor and Leila Rupp, "Women's Culture and Lesbian Feminist Activism: A Reconsideration of Cultural Feminism," *Signs: Journal of Women in Culture & Society* 19, no. 1 (1993): 32–62.

8. See Rebecca A. Pope, " 'Friends is a Weak Word for It': Female Friendship and the Spectre of Lesbianism in Sara Paretsky," in *Women's Detective Fiction*, ed. Irons, 157–70.

9. See Mary Cantwell, "How to Make a Corpse Talk," 15–17, and Judy Bachrach, "Death Becomes Her," *Vanity Fair* (May 1997), 147.

10. For sample coverage of the scandal in popular media, see Alex Tresniowski et al., "Stranger than Fiction: Novelist Patricia Cornwell Gets Caught Up in a Real-Life Crime," *People* (22 July 1996), 44–46. Also see Jeanette Walls, "Jodie, Jodie, Jodie," *Esquire* (January 1997), 14.

11. See Patricia Cornwell, *Scarpetta's Winter Table* (Charleston, S.C.: Wyrick, 1998). For biographical details typically cited in articles and interviews, see, for example, Mark Miller, "A League of Her Own: Patricia Cornwell Mines Her Dark Side," *Newsweek* (22 July 1996), and Don O'Briant, "Pistol-packing Author's Dreams Are Just as Grisly as Her Thrillers," *Atlanta Journal and Constitution* (2 August 1998).

12. As of July 2003, the official website was http://www.patriciacornwell.com.

13. Grafton first offered this motivation for her writing in a 1988 interview for *Newsweek.* See Katrine Ames, "Sue Grafton's Alphabetic Mystery Tour," *Newsweek* (18 July

1988), 55. She repeated it in an interview the following year, See Bruce Taylor, "G Is for (Sue) Grafton: An Interview with the Creator of the Kinsey Millhone Private Eye Series Who Delights Mystery Fans as She Writes Her Way through the Alphabet," *Armchair Detective* 22, no. 1 (1989): 11; hereafter cited in text as Taylor.

14. Jane Nicholls and Bonnie Bell, "Banishing Old Ghosts: In Louisville, Novelist Sue Grafton Tries to Bury the Pain of Her Childhood," *People* (30 October 1995), 116. The official Sue Grafton website as of July 2003 was http://www.suegrafton.com.

15. Irene Borger, " 'M' is for Montecito," *Architectural Digest* (May 2000), 258.

16. Jonathan Bing, "Sue Grafton: Death and the Maiden," *Publishers Weekly* (20 April 1998), 41, hereafter cited in text as Bing.

17. Katrine Ames, "Murder Most Foul and Fair," *Newsweek* (14 May 1990), 66–67.

18. Sue Grafton, *F Is for Fugitive*; hereafter cited in text as *Fugitive*.

19. As of July 2003, the address of the official Grafton website containing this forum was http://www.suegrafton.com.

20. Correspondence from Sue Grafton, 4 Jan. 2001.

21. Natalie Hevener Kaufman and Carol McGinnis Kay, *G Is for Grafton: The World of Kinsey Millhone* (New York: Henry Holt, 1997), 63; hereafter cited in text as Kaufman and Kay.

22. Sue Grafton, *Q Is for Quarry* (New York: Putnam, 2002), 199.

23. Sue Grafton, *G Is for Gumshoe* (New York: Henry Holt, 1990), 2; hereafter cited in text as *Gumshoe*.

24. Sue Grafton, *O Is for Outlaw* (New York: Henry Holt, 1999), 52.

25. Sue Grafton, *I Is for Innocent* (New York: Henry Holt, 1992), 66.

26. Sue Grafton, *C Is for Corpse* (New York: Henry Holt, 1986), 140; hereafter cited in text as *Corpse*.

27. The other clue that Dietz and Kinsey won't be a settled married couple is the haunting of the gothic family romance in *G Is for Gumshoe*. The investigation centers on a twisted family who named their daughters after the Bröntes, with macabre fates similar to Brönte characters.

28. Sue Grafton, *J Is for Judgment* (New York: Henry Holt, 1993), 71; hereafter cited in text as *Judgment*.

29. Sue Grafton, *K Is for Killer* (New York: Henry Holt, 1994), 285; hereafter cited in text as *Killer*.

30. A version of this section of the chapter appeared in my essay "Bodies of Evidence: Patricia Cornwell and the Body Double," *South Central Review* 18, nos. 3–4 (2001): 6–20.

31. See John Douglas's *Mind Hunter: Inside the FBI's Elite Serial Crime Unit* (New York: Scribner, 1995) and *Journey into Darkness* (New York: Scribner, 1997). See also William R. Maples, *Dead Men Do Tell Tales: The Strange and Fascinating Cases of a Forensic Anthropologist* (New York: Doubleday, 1994). Best-selling fictional forensics novels, in the style of Cornwell, include those of Kathy Reichs and Jeffery Deaver. For an excellent commentary on this trend, see Ronald R. Thomas, *Detective Fiction and the Rise of Forensic Science* (Cambridge and New York: Cambridge University Press, 1999).

32. Patricia Cornwell, *The Body Farm* (New York: Scribner's, 1994), 196; hereafter cited in text as *Body Farm*.

33. Patricia Cornwell, *Point of Origin* (New York: Putnam, 1998), 186; hereafter cited as *Origin*.

34. Critic Sue Turnbull reads this compassion as a rejection of Cartesian duality: "Scarpetta sees the body as the person, and the violence directed at that body as violence directed at the individual concerned. Cornwell therefore insists on the coherence of individual identity expressed through the materiality of the body." To the contrary, this insistence on coherent identity strikes me as a fascinating problem in Cornwell

rather than a viable materialism. See Turnbull, "Bodies of Knowledge: Pleasure and Anxiety in the Detective Fiction of Patricia D. Cornwell," *Australian Journal of Law and Society* 9 (1993): 30.

35. As Walton and Jones point out about this popular subgenre, a major appeal of the female "private I/eye" is the very scandal of her embodiment and "an awareness that the body in question is a gendered body." See *Detective Agency*, 187.

36. Patricia Cornwell, *Cruel and Unusual* (New York: Scribner's, 1993), 161; hereafter cited as *Cruel*.

37. Peg Tyre, "Come Out, Kay Scarpetta," *Newsday* (20 July 1997), G14; Mark Harris, "Body Double," *Entertainment Weekly* (17 July 1998), 75–76.

38. Though this film focused on Beals' bodily performance, it was later revealed that most of the dancing was done by Marine Jahan, an African-American dancer who was the uncredited stand-in for Beals.

39. On one level, this only confirms theories that literary characters in the classic realist tradition are produced through contrasts with other characters. See, for example, Catherine Belsey's summary of the construction of classic realism in *Critical Practice* (London: Methuen, 1980), 73–84. However, the cinematic body double, as a model for rethinking this device, foregrounds the issues of bodily coherence and reader/spectator desire that have particular implications for this genre and for the medical forensics of Cornwell. The reader of the crime novel, like the viewer in cinema, expects and desires characters who are consistently and identifiably embodied; the desire may have more specific investments in the case of the female investigator character.

40. Patricia Cornwell, *From Potter's Field* (New York: Scribner's, 1995), 156; hereafter cited as *Potter's Field*.

41. The website offering a casting poll was http://www.freevote.com/booth/pccasting. The article citing a television series is O'Briant, "Pistol-packing Author's Dreams."

Chapter 3: Jiggle, Camp, and Couples

1. Patricia Mellencamp provides a delightful analysis of this series in *High Anxiety: Catastrophe, Scandal, Age, and Comedy* (Bloomington: University of Indiana Press, 1992), 302–9. As Mellencamp points out, women in movies are usually allowed to be young or old, but television has always represented women in their middle years as well.

2. These generalizations come from feminist television scholarship. For an overview of these issues, see Mary Ellen Brown, ed., *Television and Women's Culture: The Politics of the Popular*, ed. Mary Ellen Brown (London: Sage, 1990). Brown's introduction, "Feminist Cultural Television Criticism: Culture, Theory, and Practice," 11–22, explains television's capacity to embrace contradiction and multiple agendas within a single series. Caren J. Deming's essay in that volume, "For Television-Centered Television Criticism: Lessons from Feminism," 37–60, elaborates on the "open" nature of the ongoing series. Also see Kathleen Rowe's analysis of television's female audiences and rebellious female characters in *The Unruly Woman: Gender and the Genres of Laughter* (Austin: University of Texas Press, 1995), 78–81.

3. G.G. Fickling, *Dig a Dead Doll* (New York: Pyramid, 1960), 6.

4. Ted Morgan, "Women Make Good Cops," *New York Times Magazine* (3 November 1974), 18+.

5. See "Arresting Preconceptions," *Time* (27 May 1974), 8, and "No Longer Men or Women—Just Police Officers," *U.S. News and World Report* (19 August 1974), 45–46.

6. Sue Cameron, "Police Drama: Women Are on the Case," *Ms.* (October 1974), 104; hereafter cited in the text as Cameron.

7. Richard Schickel, "Viewpoints," *Time* (21 October 1974), 126–27; review of *Charlie's Angels*, *Variety* (September 18, 1974).

8. See Helen Van Slyke, "Calling on a Lady Cop," *Saturday Evening Post* (1 December 1975), 50–51.

9. "TV's Super Women," *Time* (22 November 1976), 67–71.

10. Susan J. Douglas, *Where the Girls Are: Growing Up Female with the Mass Media* (New York: Random House, 1994), 211; hereafter cited in the text as Douglas.

11. See Todd Gitlin's account of this in *Inside Prime Time* (New York: Pantheon, 1983; reprint, 1985), 71–73.

12. Molly Haskell later commented that "the show offers only the choice between Beautiful and Strong (Smith), Beautiful and Smart (Jackson) and Just Beautiful (Fawcett)." See "Can 'Charlie's Angels' Still Fly in a 'G.I. Jane' World?" *New York Times* (10 September 2000), 70+. Haskell's point was that "Beautiful" was the primary message for young women at the time who were seeing their first female action heroines.

13. This was based on the estimate that women made up 60 percent of the audience tuned into that time slot. In its first year, *Charlie's Angels* regularly got up to 59 percent of its audience share, a number "usually achieved only by special events like the World Series." "TV's Super Women," 67.

14. Quoted by Gitlin, *Inside Prime Time*, 73. Both Gitlin and Douglas agree that the feminism/antifeminism balance was important to the show's formula. See Douglas, 213. A similar case was made years later by Emily Nussbaum, on the advent of the 2003 *Charlie's Angels* film, in "Misogyny Plus Girl Power: Original-Recipe Angels," *New York Times* (29 June 2003), sec. 2, 26. Also see Ric Meyers's account of this show's popularity and history in *Murder on the Air: Television's Great Mystery Series* (New York: Mysterious Press, 1989), 156–67.

15. The story of Haskell's influence on Avedon, Corday, and Rosenzweig is reported in Gitlin, *Inside Prime Time*, 73. It is also described in Julie D'Acci's *Defining Women: Television and the Case of Cagney & Lacey* (Chapel Hill: University of North Carolina Press, 1994), 16–17.

16. Molly Haskell, *From Reverence to Rape: The Treatment of Women in the Movies* (1974; reprint, Chicago: University of Chicago Press, 1987), 187–88.

17. Because the stakes involve female independence, these comedies on one level undercut conventional gender roles for the woman, even though her place in romance and marriage is inevitable in the end. Wes D. Gehring explains the split conservative-liberating position of the heroine in this genre in *Screwball Comedy: A Genre of Madcap Romance* (New York: Greenwood, 1986), 155. Also see Kathleen Rowe, "Comedy, Melodrama and Gender: Theorizing the Genres of Laughter," in *Classical Hollywood Comedy*, eds. Kristine Brunovska Karnick and Henry Jenkins (New York and London: Routledge, 1995), 39–59. Rowe points out that "the stronger the presence of women, the more a romantic comedy is likely to undercut or problematize the heterosexual couple," 51. Rowe also discusses screwball heroines and gender ideology in *The Unruly Woman*, especially chapter 4.

18. See Maria DiBattista, *Fast-Talking Dames* (New Haven: Yale University Press, 2001), especially the introductory discussion of the important power of female speech in these films, 5–35.

19. During this time, yet another couple-style police drama aired briefly on ABC in a more serious mode. This was *MacGruder and Loud*, featuring a secretly married police couple who, because of department regulations, had to hide their passionate attachment as they undertook dangerous assignments. The series lasted from January to September 1985.

20. This catty detail is reported in Joy Horowitz's essay, "The Madcap behind Moonlighting," *New York Times Magazine* (30 March 1986), 24+.

21. See Harry F. Waters and Nikki Finke Greenberg, "Sly and Sexy: TV's Fun Couple," *Newsweek* (8 September 1986), 46–52.

22. Quoted in David Handelman, "The Dark Side of the Moon," *Rolling Stone* (26 March 1987), 52+.

23. Frank Swertlow, "CBS Alters 'Cagney,' Calling It 'Too Women's Lib,'" *TV Guide* (12–18 June 1982), A-1.
24. *People* magazine covers (4 November 1985 and 11 February 11, 1985).
25. Eventually, D'Acci points out in *Defining Women*, the series was "transformed from a police drama to a combination police genre/melodrama/soap opera/comedy," with changes to each segment. See her chapter 3, especially 121–25.
26. Rosenzweig described this at the Museum of Television Broadcasting's Fifth Annual Television festival, March 25, 1988.
27. Karen Stabiner, "The Pregnant Detective," *New York Times Magazine* (22 September 1985), 82+.
28. This subverts the usual position of women as objects for the (male) camera. Danae Clark describes how this series subverts traditional treatment of women by the camera in other ways as well, by emphasizing voice over looks, for instance, and by refusing to show sensationalistic scenes. See Clark, "*Cagney & Lacey*: Feminist Strategies of Detection," in *Television and Women's Culture*, ed. Mary Ellen Brown, 117–33. Also see Lorraine Gamman, "Watching the Detectives: The Enigma of the Female Gaze," in *The Female Gaze: Women as Viewers of Popular Culture*, eds. Lorraine Gamman and Margaret Marshment (Seattle: Real Comet, 1989), 8–26. Gamman connects the women's exchange of glances to the show's overall philosophy that "doesn't presume there is one 'feminine' way of looking at the world," 23.

Chapter 4: Under Suspicion

1. This chapter focuses on the series that ran on the major networks. The profile of the enigmatic, noir detective heroine also fits the main character of *Veronica Clare*, a series that ran nine episodes on the Lifetime Network in 1991. See White, "Veronica Clare."
2. Quoted in Stabiner, "The Pregnant Detective," 103.
3. See Walton and Jones's discussion of this series and its origins in *Detective Agency*, 261–68.
4. Matt Roush, "'Anna Lee': Mystery with Unorthodox Energy," *USA Today* (4 October 1994), 3D. Roush's review discusses the 1994 American broadcast of a British three-part PBS miniseries *Anna Lee*, based on writer Liza Cody's P.I. series. *Anna Lee* was lighter in tone than *Prime Suspect*, but also less popular.
5. Sandra Tomc, "Questing Women: The Feminist Mystery after Feminism," in *Women's Detective Fiction*, ed. Glenwood Irons, 46–63.
6. Reported by John J. O'Connor, "Feminism on the Force in a Three-Part 'Mystery' Tale," *New York Times* (23 January 1992), 15C.
7. Quoted in William Grimes, "Detective Tennison Returns to PBS," *New York Times* (2 February 1993), B1–2.
8. Quoted in James Wolcott, "Columbo in Furs," *New Yorker* (25 January 1993), 102. The ambiguities of the Tennison character are discussed in Tomc, "Questing Women," and also in a superb discussion of this series by Walton and Jones in *Detective Agency*, 249–61.
9. Quoted by Daniel Cerone, "Making Waves in a Man's World," *Los Angeles Times* (8 September 1994), 1F.
10. Joe Rhodes, "Profile: Karen Sillas," *Los Angeles Times* (15 January 1995), 78; John J. O'Connor, "A Woman among Men: Just Call Her Phil," *New York Times* (13 October 1994), C20; Joyce Millman, "Latest Cop Series Commits Serious Dramatic Felonies," *Vancouver Sun* (20 September 1994), C10; Howard Rosenberg, "Promising Series Still 'Under Suspicion,'" *Los Angeles Times* (16 September 1994), F24.
11. Andy Meisler, "The Arbiters of TV Style: How to Fashion a Character," *New York Times* (4 September 1994), sec. 4, p. 5.

12. Visual style and scripting are among the topics discussed by the actors, writers, and creator of this series on the video of the *12th Annual Museum of Television and Radio Festival*, 10 March 1995, Museum of Television and Radio, New York.

13. These details are reported by Bret Watson, "A Gillian to One," *Entertainment Weekly* (9 February 1996), 20+; Deborah Starr Seibel, "Gillian & Dave's Excellent Adventure," *TV Guide* (11 March 1995), 8+, and Malcolm Butt, *Special Agent Scully: The Gillian Anderson Files* (London: Plexus, 1997), 26.

14. Anderson discusses the new wardrobe in Benjamin Svetkey, "Xplanations," *Entertainment Weekly* (10 July 1998), 24+. The remark about bimbos in high heels comes from Bret Watson, "A Gillian to One."

15. These varieties of fans are discussed in Rich Sands, "The Fans Are Out There," *TV Guide* (6 July 1996), 10. The various images and photographs are discussed and displayed in Stephanie Mansfield, "Gillian Looks Like a Million," *TV Guide* (6 July 1996), 6+. The titillating cover of *Rolling Stone* is touted in David Wild's article, "*The X Files* Undercover," *Rolling Stone* (16 May 1996), 39+. In the interview with Chris Carter, Wild follows up a question about Scully and Mulder's celibacy with a question about how Carter feels about the cover photo. Carter is the one who makes the distinction: "That's David and Gillian in bed, *not* Mulder and Scully," 42.

16. Ken Tucker, "Spooky Kind of Love," *Entertainment Weekly* (29 November 1996), 34.

17. Susan J. Clerc gives an in-depth report of these issues and others on the Internet discussions of this series in "DDEB, GATB, MPPB, and Ratboy: *The X-Files'* Media Fandom, Online and Off," in *"Deny All Knowledge,"* ed. Lavery et al., 36–51. Duchovny's remark about reading the online X-Philes comes from Mark Nollinger, "Twenty Things You Need to Know About *The X-Files*," *TV Guide* (6 April 1996), 18+.

18. See Linda Badley's excellent discussion of this complicated erotic milieu in "The Rebirth of the Clinic: The Body as Alien in *The X-Files*," in *"Deny All Knowledge,"* ed. Lavery et al., 148–67.

19. Critics at first rated *Millennium* (created by *X-Files* producer/creator Chris Carter) the better show, but gradually gave *Profiler* higher marks, noting it was unbelievable but nevertheless compelling, mostly because of Walker's performance. Reviewers often noted the unusual situation of a forensics thriller created by a woman, Cynthia Saunders, and starring a woman. See, for example, John J. O'Connor, "In a Season of Grays, One Show That's Noir," *New York Times* (7 November 1996), 26C, and Kinney Littlefield, "In 'Profiler,' Ally Walker Boasts Intriguing Persona," *Seattle Times* (4 May 1997), 59.

20. See chapter 2, note 31, above.

21. At the end of its first season, it was the year's highest-rated drama among women ages 18–49. See "Her Big Little Drama: 'Profiler' Gave Walker More Than She Expected, *USA Today* (8 May 1997), 3D.

Chapter 5: Women Detectives on Film

1. In "Chic and Beyond," *Sight and Sound* (August 1996): 25–27, Mike Phillips remembers how black audiences loved the scene in which Foxy puts the genitals into a jar and takes it to the man's girlfriend, who screams out his name in recognition. Phillips' larger point is that Blaxploitation films provided black expression of anger and assertion but also provided white culture with convenient caricatures to reinforce stereotypes and biases. Commenting on the stereotypes of African-American women, Kimberly Springer points out the assumption that "African Americans are thought to be always already violent due to their 'savage' ancestry," 174. See "Waiting to Set It Off: African American Women and the Sapphire Fixation," in *Reel Knockouts: Violent Women in the Movies*, eds. Martha McCaughey and Neal King (Austin: University of Texas Press, 2001), 172–99.

2. Carol M. Dole discusses these strategies of "first generation" women cop/detective movies in "The Gun and the Badge: Hollywood and the Female Lawman," in *Reel Knockouts*, eds. McCaughey and King, 78–105.

3. Hilary Henkin's description of her script for *Fatal Beauty* can be found in Lizzie Francke, *Script Girls: Women Screenwriters in Hollywood* (London: British Film Institute, 1994), 120–21.

4. Yvonne Tasker, *Working Girls: Gender and Sexuality in Popular Cinema* (London and New York: Routledge, 1998), 172–73. Tasker also reports the interview with Goldberg about "an ugly woman's price," 172. Also see Tasker's excellent chapter, "Investigating Women: Work, Criminality and Sexuality," 89–114, on *Fatal Beauty* and most of the other 1980s–90s woman cop/detective films. For more on Whoopi Goldberg's star images, see Chris Holmlund, *Impossible Bodies: Femininity and Masculinity at the Movies* (London and New York: Routledge, 2002), 127–40. Also see Andrea Stuart's essay on Goldberg, "Making Whoopi," *Sight and Sound* (February 1993): 12–13. Stuart argues that Goldberg is often portrayed neither as female nor as black.

5. Carol Dole points out this pattern of self-rationalization in these films in "The Gun and the Badge," 85.

6. Valerie Straub argues that these questions are actually cultural questions concerning what a lesbian might be: a woman who wants to be a man, a woman who wants to be the other woman, a woman who is outsider or outlaw. See Straub, "The Ambiguities of 'Lesbian' Viewing Pleasure: The (Dis)articulations of Black Widow," in *Out in Culture: Gay, Lesbian, and Queer Essays on Popular Culture*, eds. Corey K. Creekmur and Alexander Doty (London: Cassell, 1995), 115–36.

7. See Judith Mayne's analysis of the projection scene in *The Woman at the Keyhole: Feminism and Women's Cinema* (Bloomington: Indiana University Press, 1990), 46–48.

8. In addition to the Straub essay, see Yvonne Tasker, "Pussy Galore."

9. Lane comments on Kathryn Bigelow's status in relationship to Cameron and points out the "need to critically circumvent the long history of the ideology of 'sexual favors' ('sleeping one's way to the top,' 'casting couch,' etc.) through which women's hard work and professional authority are undermined by sexual innuendo." See Lane, *Feminist Hollywood: From 'Born in Flames' to 'Point Break'* (Detroit: Wayne State University Press, 2000), 102.

10. As Yvonne Tasker points out in *Working Girls*, women investigators are associated with prostitutes in these movies as objects of suspicion and contempt, 94. Tasker also offers an excellent analysis of this film's sexual politics and its clever usage of role-playing and therapy, 100–102.

11. A version of this section of the chapter originally appeared in my essay, "Picturing the Female Dick: *Blue Steel* and *The Silence of the Lambs*," *Journal of Film and Video* 45, nos. 2–3 (1993): 6–23.

12. Cora Kaplan explores the significance of this film for feminist theory and for the meanings of phallic femininity in "Dirty Harriet/*Blue Steel*: Feminist Theory Goes to Hollywood," *Discourse* 16, no. 1 (Fall 1993): 50–70. Also see Christina Lane's reading of this film and its centralization of Megan's perspective in *Feminist Hollywood*, 113–17.

13. David Denby called *Blue Steel* "bloody and absurd—a visual exercise in the eroticism of gun barrels." Caryn James of the *New York Times* thought both films were "caught in sexist clichés you'd think they would have been shrewd enough to avoid." See Denby, "Dirty Harriett," *New York* (26 March 1990), 76–77, and James, "Women Cops Can Be a Cliché in Blue," *New York Times* (15 April 1990), sec. 2, p. 17+.

14. Sara Paretsky, *Bitter Medicine* (New York: William Morrow, 1987), 221.

15. For a more detailed analysis of Paretsky's feminist revision of the hardboiled detective genre, see Margaret Kinsman, "A Question of Visibility: Paretsky and Chicago,"

in *Women Times Three*, ed. Klein, 15–28. Also see Pope, " 'Friends Is a Weak Word for It,' " *Women's Detective Fiction*, ed. Irons, 157–70.

16. See Kathleen Gregory Klein, "Watching Warshawski," in *It's a Print! Detective Fiction from Page to Screen*, eds. William Reynolds and Elizabeth Trembley (Bowling Green, Ohio: Popular Press, 1994), 145–57. Also see Walton and Jones's discussion of this film in *Detective Agency*, 234–43.

Chapter 6: Action Bodies

1. McDormand was named Best Actress in the Independent Spirit Awards, the National Board of Review Awards, Screen Actors Guild Awards, and Broadcast Film Critics Awards. Foster won Best Actress in the British Academy Awards, Golden Globe Awards, and New York Film Critics Awards. Both also won Academy Awards.

2. See Richard Grenier, "Killer Bimbos," *Commentary* (September 1991), 50–52; Laura Shapiro, "Women Who Kill Too Much," *Newsweek* (17 June 1991), 63; Charles Fleming, "That's Why the Lady Is a Champ: Women in Action Roles," *Newsweek* (7 June 1993), 66; and Mandy Johnson, "Women as Action Heroes: Is Violence a Positive Direction for Females?" *Glamour* (March 1994), 153.

3. Mark Seltzer writes compellingly about the obsession with seriality and its fit into other cultural obsessions. See Seltzer, *Serial Killers: Death and Life in America's Wound Culture* (New York and London: Routledge, 1998). Also see Richard Dyer's discussion of *Copycat* and other serial-killer films in "Kill and Kill Again," *Sight and Sound* (September 1997): 14–17.

4. Clover argues that the gender switches in the slasher film, especially the heroism of the Final Girl, are symptomatic of an "adjustment" in gender roles in popular culture. See Clover, *Men, Women, and Chainsaws*, 21–64. Also see Linda Williams's essay "Film Bodies" on how this gender shift works in conjunction with fantasy.

5. Jeffrey A. Brown makes this argument about the resolution of cultural differences in "Bullets, Buddies, and Bad Guys: The 'Action-Cop' Genre, " *Journal of Popular Film and Television* 21, no. 2 (1993): 79–87. What Brown doesn't point out is the specific maleness of the "American culture" at stake in these movies.

6. Jeffery Deaver, *The Bone Collector* (New York: Viking, 1997), 219.

7. Kathleen Klein discusses rape and its implications for the woman detective in "Habeas Corpus," 180. In the film *Blue Steel*, serial killer Eugene attempts to rape Megan after he's broken into her apartment and shot her lover toward the end of the film. Some critics have read the scene as an actual rape, others as an attempted rape. Either way, it's an ugly scene that contributes to Megan's rage and sets up the vengeance mode for the final sequence.

8. Chris Holmlund includes Lopez in Hollywood's "impossible bodies" that serve as symbols, ideals, or boundaries of what is normal or respectable. She discusses the "outrageous" bodies of stars such as Lopez, Dolly Parton, or Rosie Perez who become identified with a specific body part. See *Impossible Bodies*, 117–21. Diane Negra includes the fantasy of escape in her discussion of fantasies around ethnic female stardom in *Off-White Hollywood: American Culture and Ethnic Female Stardom* (London and New York: Routledge, 2001), 136–63.

9. In *Basic Instinct, The Last Seduction* (1994), and *Bound*, the *femme fatale* is criminally triumphant in the final reel. Chris Straayer sums up the history of the *femme fatale* in cinema in "*Femme Fatale* or Lesbian Femme: *Bound* in Sexual Difference," in *Women in Film Noir*, ed. E. Ann Kaplan (London: British Film Institute, 1998), 151–62.

10. Yvonne Tasker, writing about this movie, uses this scene to emphasize how often Hollywood associates the woman investigator with the prostitute, as women doing disreputable work. See *Working Girls*, 103–5.

11. See Carol M. Dole's argument about this in "The Gun and the Badge," 92.
12. I am indebted to Angela Dancey and her dissertation in progress, "The Makeover Film," Ohio State University, for her insights about the makeover film, its conventions, and its cultural implications.

Chapter 7: Clarice and Her Fans

1. Thomas Harris, *Red Dragon* (New York: Putnam, 1981), 94.
2. Critics have referred casually to Hannibal Lecter as a "campy gay aesthete" or to his "pronounced swish." See Bruce Robbins, "Murder and Mentorship: Advancement in *The Silence of the Lambs*," *UTS Review* 1, no. 1 (1995): 30–49. Also see Julie Tharp, "The Transvestite as Monster: Gender Horror in *The Silence of the Lambs* and *Psycho*," *Journal of Popular Film and Television* 19, no. 3 (1991): 106–13. Diana Fuss argues more extensively for "the specter of a perverse and monstrous homosexuality" connoted by his image as "an insatiable oral sadist" (195). See Fuss, "Monsters of Perversion: Jeffrey Dahmer and *The Silence of the Lambs*," in *Media Spectacles*, eds. Marjorie Garber et al. (New York and London: Routledge, 1993), 181–205. For an extended analysis of Lecter's transgressive disruption of categories, see Cary Wolfe and Jonathan Elmer, "Subject to Sacrifice: Ideology, Psychoanalysis, and the Discourse of Species in Jonathan Demme's *Silence of the Lambs*," *boundary* 2 (Fall 1995): 141–70.
3. A version of this discussion of Demme's *The Silence of the Lambs* appeared in my essay, "Picturing the Female Dick."
4. See Yvonne Tasker's reading of this film as a "woman's film" and also as a form of the gothic, another distinctly female narrative, in *The Silence of the Lambs*, 22–24 and 58–70.
5. For reviews applauding this film's feminism, see Amy Taubin, "Demme's Mode," *Village Voice* (19 February 1991), 64; and Julie Salamon, "Weirdo Killer Shrink Meets the G-Girl," *Wall Street Journal* (14 February 1991), A12.
6. Larry Gross, *Contested Closets: The Politics and Ethics of Outing* (Minneapolis: University of Minnesota Press, 1993), 77.
7. Richard Corliss, "A Screen Gem Turns Director," *Time* (14 October 1991), 68–72.
8. See Gross's account of this in *Contested Closets*, 75–77.
9. Janet Staiger gives a full account of the many ranges of interpretation of this film in newspaper and magazine reviews in "Taboos and Totems: Cultural Meanings of *The Silence of the Lambs*," in *Film Theory Goes to the Movies*, eds. Jim Collins et al. (New York and London: Routledge, 1993), 142–54. The Stuart Klawans review appeared in the column "Films," *The Nation* (25 February 1991), 246–47. For a summary of the outing issue in relation to *The Silence of the Lambs*, see Lisa Kennedy, "Writers on the Lamb: Sorting Out the Sexual Politics of a Controversial Film," *Village Voice* (5 March 1991), 49+. Also see Yvonne Tasker's summary of the controversy on this film in her book *The Silence of the Lambs*, 36–40. Tasker usefully sorts out the gender issues concerning Jame Gumb—his misogyny—as opposed to the sexual issues around this character.
10. The quote about motherhood comes from Melina Gerosa, "Fascinating Mom," *Ladies Home Journal* (January 2000), 88+. Louis Chunovic makes the comment about not labeling Foster in *Jodie: A Biography* (Chicago: Contemporary Books, 1995), xxiii.
11. Terry Brown describes Foster as the object of contradictory fantasies in "The Butch Femme Fatale," in *The Lesbian Postmodern*, ed. Laura Doan (New York: Columbia University Press, 1994), 229–43. Brown gives an excellent analysis of the Hinckley case as an example of Foster's mixed messages and appeals.
12. See Clare Whatling, "Fostering the Illusion: Stepping Out with Jodie," in Hamer and Bridge, *The Good, the Bad, and the Gorgeous*, 184–95. The quote about Clarice ap-

pears on p. 193. Also see Clare Whatling's *Screen Dreams: Fantasizing Lesbians in Film* (Manchester: Manchester University Press, 1997), and her chapter on Foster, 134–59. Gay and lesbian film sites that keep watch of Foster's roles and public appearances include Planetout.com, GLWeb.com, Queery.com, gaylesissues.about.com, gay.com, lesbianlife.about.com, and i-out.com.

13. See Elizabeth Young's extended analysis of this identification in "*The Silence of the Lambs* and the Flaying of Feminist Theory," *Camera Obscura* 27 (1991): 5–35.

14. See Janet Staiger, "Taboos and Totems," 148–51.

15. In her book on *The Silence of the Lambs*, Yvonne Tasker attributes the switch from maternal to paternal inspiration as the unhappy influence of psychoanalysis and its emphasis on paternal power, 74–75.

16. A version of this discussion of Harris's novel *Hannibal* appears in my essay "Stardom and Serial Fantasies: Thomas Harris's *Hannibal*," in *Keyframes: Popular Cinema and Cultural Studies*, eds. Matthew Tinkcom and Amy Villarejo (London and New York: Routledge, 2001), 159–70.

17. Chris Nashawaty, "The Hunger," *Entertainment Weekly* (7 May 1999), 24+. This was the issue of *EW* with Hopkins on the cover. The *Hannibal* cover of *The New York Times Book Review* was 13 June 1999. Also see Janet Maslin's comments on the book *Hannibal* as a "spinoff" of the Demme film in "Cultural Cross-Pollination: A Thousand Markets Bloom," *New York Times* (26 August 1999), B1+.

18. Thomas Harris, *Hannibal* (New York: Delacorte, 1999), 312; hereafter cited in text as *Hannibal*.

19. My thanks to Judith Mayne, who pointed out this parallel with nineteenth-century romantic friendship.

20. "Hannibal's Next Dish," *Entertainment Weekly* (17 March 2000); "Hungry for Moore?" *Premiere* (February 2001). The statement by Ted Tally appeared in Daniel Fierman, "Killer Instinct," *Entertainment Weekly* (17 March 2000), 25+.

21. *Empire* (February 2000), 44, quoted in Tasker, *The Silence of the Lambs*, 29.

BIBLIOGRAPHY

Altman, Rick. *Film/Genre*. London: British Film Institute, 1999.

Ames, Katrine. "Murder Most Foul and Fair." *Newsweek*, 14 May 1990, 66–67.

———. "Sue Grafton's Alphabetic Mystery Tour." *Newsweek*, 18 July 1988, 55.

Anderson-Minshall, Diane. "Take That! TV's Top 10 'Lesbian' Crime-Fighter Shows." *Curve*, June 2003, 26+.

"Arresting Preconceptions." *Time*, 27 May 1974, 8.

Babener, Liahna. "Uncloseted Ideology in the Novels of Barbara Wilson." In *Women Times Three*, edited by Kathleen Gregory Klein, 143–61.

Bachrach, Judy. "Death Becomes Her." *Vanity Fair*, May 1997, 147.

Badley, Linda. "The Rebirth of the Clinic: The Body as Alien in *The X-Files*." In *"Deny All Knowledge,"* edited by David Lavery et al., 148–67.

Belsey, Catherine. *Critical Practice*. London: Methuen, 1980.

Bing, Jonathan. "Sue Grafton: Death and the Maiden." *Publishers Weekly*, 20 April 1998, 40–41.

Borger, Irene. "'M' is for Montecito." *Architectural Digest*, May 2000, 258.

Brown, Jeffrey A. "Bullets, Buddies, and Bad Guys: The 'Action-Cop' Genre." *Journal of Popular Film and Television* 21, no. 2 (1993): 79–87.

Brown, Mary Ellen, ed. *Television and Women's Culture: The Politics of the Popular*. London: Sage, 1990.

Brown, Terry. "The Butch Femme Fatale." In *The Lesbian Postmodern*, edited by Laura Doan, 229–43. New York: Columbia University Press, 1994.

Butt, Malcolm. *Special Agent Scully: The Gillian Anderson Files*. London: Plexus, 1997.

Cameron, Sue. "Police Drama: Women Are on the Case." *Ms.*, October 1974, 104.

Cantwell, Mary. "How to Make a Corpse Talk." *New York Times Magazine*, 14 July 1996, 15–17.

Cawelti, John. *Adventure, Mystery, and Romance: Formula Stories as Art and Popular Culture*. Chicago: University of Chicago Press, 1976.

Cerone, Daniel. "Making Waves in a Man's World." *Los Angeles Times*, 8 September 1994, 1F.

Christianson, Scott. "Talkin' Trash and Kickin' Butt: Sue Grafton's Hard-boiled Feminism." In *Feminism in Women's Detective Fiction*, edited by Glenwood Irons, 127–47.

Chunovic, Louis. *Jodie: A Biography*. Chicago: Contemporary Books, 1995.

Clark, Danae. "*Cagney & Lacey*: Feminist Strategies of Detection." In *Television and Women's Culture*, edited by Mary Ellen Brown, 117–133.

Clerc, Susan J. "DDEB, GATB, MPPB, and Ratboy: *The X-Files*' Media Fandom, Online and Off." In *"Deny All Knowledge,"* edited by David Lavery et al., 36–51.

Clover, Carol J. *Men, Women, and Chainsaws: Gender in the Modern Horror Film.* Princeton: Princeton University Press, 1992.

Cohan, Steven. "Judy on the Net: Judy Garland Fandom and 'The Gay Thing' Revisited." In *Keyframes: Popular Cinema and Cultural Studies,* edited by Matthew Tinkcom and Amy Villarejo, 119–36. London and New York: Routledge, 2001.

Corliss, Richard. "A Screen Gem Turns Director." *Time,* 14 October 1991, 68–72.

Cornwell, Patricia D. *Point of Origin.* New York: Putnam, 1998.

———. *Scarpetta's Winter Table.* Charleston, S.C.: Wyrick, 1998.

———. *From Potter's Field.* New York: Scribner's 1995.

———. *The Body Farm.* New York: Scribner's, 1994.

———. *Cruel and Unusual.* New York: Scribner's, 1993.

Craig, Patricia, and Mary Cadogan. *The Lady Investigates: Women Detectives & Spies in Fiction.* New York: St. Martin's, 1981.

D'Acci, Julie. *Defining Women: Television and the Case of Cagney & Lacey.* Chapel Hill: University of North Carolina Press, 1994.

Deaver, Jeffery. *The Bone Collector.* New York: Viking, 1997.

Denby, David. "Dirty Harriett." *New York,* 26 March 1990, 76–77.

DiBattista, Maria. *Fast-Talking Dames.* New Haven: Yale University Press, 2001.

Dole, Carol M. "The Gun and the Badge: Hollywood and the Female Lawman." In *Reel Knockouts: Violent Women in the Movies,* edited by Martha McCaughey and Neal King, 78–105. Austin: University of Texas Press, 2001.

Doty, Alexander. "There's Something Queer Here." In *Making Things Perfectly Queer: Interpreting Mass Culture,* 1–16. Minneapolis: University of Minnesota Press, 1993.

Douglas, John, and Mark Olshaker. *Journey into Darkness.* New York: Scribner, 1997.

———. *Mind Hunter: Inside the FBI's Elite Serial Crime Unit.* New York: Scribner, 1995.

Douglas, Susan J. *Where the Girls Are: Growing Up Female with the Mass Media.* New York: Random House, 1995.

Dyer, Lucinda. "It's Not Whodunit, But How-Do-You-Do-It?" *Publishers Weekly,* 25 October 1999, 34–43.

Dyer, Richard. "Kill and Kill Again." *Sight and Sound* (September 1997): 14–17.

Evanovich, Janet. *One for the Money.* New York: Scribner, 1994.

Ferro, Christina. "How to Be Your Own Private Detective: Cunning Clues from a Bestselling Sleuth." *McCall's,* August 1991, 50+.

Fickling, G.G. *Dig a Dead Doll.* New York: Pyramid, 1960.

Fleming, Charles. "That's Why the Lady Is a Champ: Women in Action Roles." *Newsweek,* 7 June 1993, 66.

Francke, Lizzie. *Script Girls: Women Screenwriters in Hollywood.* London: British Film Institute, 1994.

Frederick, Heather Vogel. "Revisiting the Scene of the Crime." *Publishers Weekly,* 24 April 2000, 38–51.

Freud, Sigmund. " 'A Child Is Being Beaten': A Contribution to the Origin of Sexual Perversions." In *Sexuality and the Psychology of Love.* 1919. Reprint, New York: Collier, 1972.

Fuss, Diana. "Monsters of Perversion: Jeffrey Dahmer and *The Silence of the Lambs.*" In *Media Spectacles,* edited by Marjorie Garber et al., 181–205. New York and London: Routledge, 1993.

Gamman, Lorraine. "Watching the Detectives: The Enigma of the Female Gaze." In *The Female Gaze: Women as Viewers of Popular Culture,* edited by Lorraine Gamman and Margaret Marshment, 8–26. Seattle: Real Comet, 1989.

Gehring, Wes D. *Screwball Comedy: A Genre of Madcap Romance.* New York: Greenwood, 1986.

Gerosa, Melina. "Fascinating Mom." *Ladies Home Journal,* January 2000, 88+.

Gitlin, Todd. *Inside Prime Time.* New York: Panthcon, 1983; reprint, 1985.

Grafton, Sue. *Q Is for Quarry.* New York: Putnam, 2002.

———. *O Is for Outlaw.* New York: Henry Holt, 1999.

———. *K Is for Killer.* New York: Henry Holt, 1994.

———. *J Is for Judgment.* New York: Henry Holt, 1993.

———. *I Is for Innocent.* New York: Henry Holt, 1992.

———. *G Is for Gumshoe.* New York: Henry Holt, 1990.

———. *F Is for Fugitive.* New York: Henry Holt, 1989.

———. *D Is for Deadbeat.* New York: Henry Holt, 1987.

———. *C Is for Corpse.* New York: Henry Holt, 1986.

———. *B Is for Burglar.* New York: Henry, Holt, 1985.

———. *A Is for Alibi.* New York: Holt, Rinehart and Winston, 1982.

Grant, Barry Keith. *The Dread of Difference: Gender and the Horror Film.* Austin: University of Texas Press, 1996.

Greiner, Richard. "Killer Bimbos." *Commentary,* September 1991, 50–52.

Grimes, William. "Detective Tennison Returns to PBS." *New York Times,* 2 February 1993, B1–2.

Gross, Larry. *Contested Closets: The Politics and Ethics of Outing.* Minneapolis: University of Minnesota Press, 1993.

Halberstam, Judith. *Female Masculinity.* London: Duke University Press, 1998.

Hamer, Diane, and Belinda Budge, eds. *The Good, the Bad, and the Gorgeous: Popular Culture's Romance with Lesbianism.* London: Pandora, 1994.

Handelman, David. "The Dark Side of the Moon." *Rolling Stone,* 26 March 1987, 52+.

Hantke, Steffen. " 'The Kingdom of the Unimaginable': The Construction of Social Space and the Fantasy of Privacy in Serial Killer Narratives." *Literature/Film Quarterly 26,* no. 3 (1998): 178–95.

Harris, Cheryl, and Alison Alexander, eds. *Theorizing Fandom: Fans, Subculture, and Identity.* Cresskill, N.J.: Hampton Press, 1998.

Harris, Mark. "Body Double." *Entertainment Weekly,* 17 July 1998, 75–76.

Harris, Thomas. *Red Dragon.* New York: Putnam, 1981.

———. *The Silence of the Lambs.* New York: St. Martin's, 1988.

———. *Hannibal.* New York: Delacorte, 1999.

Hart, Lynda. *Fatal Women: Lesbian Sexuality and the Mark of Aggression.* Princeton: Princeton University Press, 1994.

Haskell, Molly. "Can 'Charlie's Angels' Still Fly in a 'G.I. Jane' World?" *New York Times,* 10 September 2000, 70+.

———. *From Reverence to Rape: The Treatment of Women in the Movies.* 1974; reprint, Chicago: University of Chicago Press, 1987.

Haycraft, Howard. *Murder for Pleasure: The Life and Times of the Detective Story.* 1941. Reprint, New York: Carroll and Graf, 1984.

Heller, Dana A. "Almost Blue: Policing Lesbian Desire in *Internal Affairs.*" In *The Lesbian Postmodern,* edited by Laura Doan, 173–88. New York: Columbia University Press, 1994.

"Her Big Little Drama 'Profiler' Gave Walker More Than She Expected." *USA Today,* 8 May 1997, 3D.

Holmlund, Chris. *Impossible Bodies: Femininity and Masculinity at the Movies.* London and New York: Routledge, 2002.

Horowitz, Joy. "The Madcap behind Moonlighting." *New York Times Magazine,* 30 March 1986, 24+.

Irons, Glenwood, ed. *Feminism in Women's Detective Fiction.* Toronto: University of Toronto Press, 1995.

James, Caryn. "Women Cops Can Be a Cliché in Blue." *New York Times*, 15 April 1990, sec. 2, p. 17+.

Jenkins, Henry. "Reception Theory and Audience Research: The Mystery of the Vampire's Kiss." In *Reinventing Film Studies*, edited by Christine Gledhill and Linda Williams, 165–82. London: Oxford University Press, 2000.

Johnson, Mandy. "Women as Action Heroes: Is Violence a Positive Direction for Females?" *Glamour*, March 1994, 153.

Kaplan, Cora. "Dirty Harriet/*Blue Steel*: Feminist Theory Goes to Hollywood." *Discourse* 16, no. 1 (Fall 1993): 50–70.

Karnick, Kristine Brunovska, and Henry Jenkins, eds. *Classical Hollywood Comedy*. New York and London: Routledge, 1995.

Kaufman, Natalie Hevener, and Carol McGinnis Kay. *G Is for Grafton: The World of Kinsey Millhone*. New York: Henry Holt, 1997.

Kennedy, Lisa. "Writers on the Lamb: Sorting Out the Sexual Politics of a Controversial Film." *Village Voice*, 5 March 1991, 49+.

Kinsman, Margaret. "A Question of Visibility: Paretsky and Chicago." In *Women Times Three: Writers, Detectives, Readers*, edited by Kathleen Gregory Klein, 15–28.

Klawans, Suart. "Films." Review of *The Silence of the Lambs*. *The Nation*, 25 February 1991, 246–47.

Klein, Kathleen Gregory. "*Habeas Corpus*: Feminism and Detective Fiction." In *Feminism in Women's Detective Fiction*, edited by Glenwood Irons, 171–90. Toronto: University of Toronto Press, 1995.

———. "Watching Warshawski." In *It's a Print! Detective Fiction from Page to Screen*, edited by William Reynolds and Elizabeth Trembley, 145–57. Bowling Green, Ohio: Popular Press, 1994.

———. *The Woman Detective: Gender and Genre*. Urbana: University of Illinois Press, 1988, reprint, 1995.

———, ed. *Woman Times Three: Writers, Detectives, Readers*. Bowling Green, Ohio: Popular Press, 1995.

Krutnik, John. *In a Lonely Street: Film Noir, Genre, Masculinity*. London and New York: Routledge, 1991.

Lane, Christina. *Feminist Hollywood: From 'Born in Flames' to 'Point Break.'* Detroit: Wayne State University Press, 2000.

LaPlanche, Jean, and Jean-Bertrand Pontalis. "Fantasy and the Origins of Sexuality." In *Formations of Fantasy*, edited by Victor Burgin et al., 5–34. 1964. Reprint, London: Methuen, 1986.

Lavery, David, et al., eds. *"Deny All Knowledge:" Reading the X-Files*. Syracuse: Syracuse University Press, 1996.

Linson, Art. "The $75 Million Difference." *New York Times Magazine*, 16 November 1997, 88–89.

Littlefield, Kinney. "In 'Profiler,' Ally Walker Boasts Intriguing Persona." *Seattle Times*, 4 May 1997, 59.

Lott, Eric. "The Whiteness of *Film Noir*." In *National Imaginaries, American Identities: The Cultural Work of American Iconography*, edited by Larry J. Reynolds and Gordon Hutner, 159–81. Princeton: Princeton University Press, 2000.

Malach, Michele. " 'I Want to Believe . . . in the FBI': The Special Agent and *The X-Files*." In *"Deny All Knowledge,"* edited by David Lavery, 63–76.

Mandel, Ernest. *Delightful Murder: A Social History of the Crime Story*. London: Pluto, 1984.

Mansfield, Stephanie. "Gillian Looks Like a Million." *TV Guide*, 6 July 1996, 6+.

Maples, William R. *Dead Men Do Tell Tales: The Strange and Fascinating Cases of a Forensic Anthropologist*. New York: Doubleday, 1994.

Maslin, Janet. "Cultural Cross-Pollination: A Thousand Markets Bloom." *New York Times*, 26 August 1999, B1+.

Mason, Bobbie Ann. *The Girl Sleuth: On the Trail of Nancy Drew, Judy Bolton, and Cherry Ames*. 1975. Reprint, Athens: University of Georgia Press, 1995.

Mayne, Judith. *Cinema and Spectatorship*. New York and London: Routledge, 1993.

———. *The Woman at the Keyhole: Feminism and Women's Cinema*. Bloomington: Indiana University Press, 1990.

McCaughey, Martha, and Neal King, eds. *Reel Knockouts: Violent Women in the Movies*. Austin: University of Texas Press, 2001.

McManus, Kevin. "Census of State and Local Law Enforcement." Washington, D.C., 1996.

——— *The G-Women*. Washington, D.C.: Department of the Treasury, 1989.

Meisler, Andy. "The Arbiters of TV Style: How to Fashion a Character." *New York Times*, 4 September 1994, sec. 4, p. 5.

Mellencamp, Patricia. *High Anxiety: Catastrophe, Scandal, Age, and Comedy*. Bloomington: University of Indiana Press, 1992.

Messent, Peter, ed. *Criminal Proceedings: The Contemporary American Crime Novel*. London: Pluto, 1997.

Meyers, Ric. *Murder on the Air: Television's Great Mystery Series*. New York: Mysterious Press, 1989.

Miller, Mark. "A League of Her Own: Patricia Cornwell Mines Her Dark Side." *Newsweek*, 22 July 1996.

Millman, Joyce. "Latest Cop Series Commits Serious Dramatic Felonies." *Vancouver Sun*, 20 September 1994, C10.

Mizejewski, Linda. "Bodies of Evidence: Patricia Cornwell and the Body Double." *South Central Review*, 18, nos. 3–4 (2001): 6–20.

———. "Stardom and Serial Fantasies: Thomas Harris's *Hannibal*." In *Keyframes: Popular Cinema and Cultural Studies*, edited by Matthew Tinkcom and Amy Villarejo, 159–70. London and New York: Routledge, 2001.

———. "Picturing the Female Dick: *Blue Steel* and *The Silence of the Lambs*." *Journal of Film and Video* 45, nos. 2–3 (1993): 6–23.

Modleski, Tania. *Loving with a Vengeance: Mass-Produced Fantasies for Women*. 1982. Reprint, New York: Methuen, 1984.

Morgan, Ted. "Women Make Good Cops." *New York Times Magazine*, 3 November 1974, 18+.

Nashawaty, Chris. "The Hunger." *Entertainment Weekly*, 7 May 1999, 24+.

Negra, Diane. *Off-White Hollywood: American Culture and Ethnic Female Stardom*. London and New York: Routledge, 2001.

Nicholls, Jane, and Bonnie Bell. "Banishing Old Ghosts: In Louisville, Novelist Sue Grafton Tries to Bury the Pain of Her Childhoood." *People*, 30 October 1995, 115–16.

Niebuhr, Gary Warren. *A Reader's Guide to the Private Eye Novel*. New York: G.K. Hall, 1993.

"No Longer Men or Women—Just Police Officers." *U.S. News and World Report*, 19 August 1974, 45–46.

Nollinger, Mark. "Twenty Things You Need to Know About *The X-Files*." *TV Guide*, 6 April 1996, 18+.

Nussbaum, Emily. "Misogyny Plus Girl Power: Original-Recipe Angels." *New York Times*, 29 June 2003, sec. 2, 26.

O'Briant, Don. "Pistol-packing Author's Dreams Are Just as Grisly as Her Thrillers." *Atlanta Journal and Constitution*, 2 August 1998.

O'Brien, Geoffrey. *Hardboiled America: The Lurid Years of Paperbacks*. New York: Van Nostrand Reinhold, 1981.

O'Connor, John J. "In a Season of Grays, One Show That's Noir." *New York Times*, 7 November 1996, 26C.

———. "A Woman Among Men: Just Call Her Phil." *New York Times*, 13 October 1994, C20.

———. "Feminism on the Force in a Three-Part 'Mystery' Tale," *New York Times*, 23 January 1992, 15C.

Palmer, Paulina. "The Lesbian Thriller: Transgressive Investigation." In *Criminal Proceedings*, edited by Peter Messent, 87–110.

Paretsky, Sara. *Bitter Medicine*. New York: William Morrow, 1987.

Parker, Robert B. *Family Honor*. New York: Putnam, 1999.

Passero, Kathy. "Stranger than Fiction: The True-life Drama of Novelist Patricia Cornwell." *Biography*, May 1998, 66.

Pavletich, Jo Ann. "Muscling the Mainstream: Lesbian Murder Mysteries and Fantasies of Justice." *Discourse* 15, no. 1 (1992): 94–111.

Phillips, Mike. "Chic and Beyond." *Sight and Sound* (August 1996): 25–27.

Pope, Rebecca A. " 'Friends Is a Weak Word for It': Female Friendship and the Spectre of Lesbianism in Sara Paretsky." In *Women's Detective Fiction*, edited by Glenwood Irons, 157–70.

Rabinowicz, Peter. " 'Reader, I blew him away': Convention and Transgression in Sue Grafton." In *Famous Last Words: Changes in Gender and Narrative Closure*, edited by Alison Booth, 326–46. Charlottesville: University of Virginia Press, 1993.

Radway, Janice A. *Reading the Romance: Women, Patriarchy, and Popular Literature*. Chapel Hill: University of North Carolina Press, 1984.

Reddy, Maureen T. "The Feminist Counter-Tradition in Crime: Cross, Grafton, Paretsky, and Wilson." In *The Cunning Craft: Original Essays on Detective Fiction and Contemporary Literary Theory*, edited by Ronald G. Walker and June M. Frazer, 174–87. Macomb: Western Illinois University Press, 1990.

———. *Sisters in Crime: Feminism and the Crime Novel*. New York: Continuum, 1988.

Redmann, J.M. *Death by the Riverside*. Norwich, Vt.: New Victoria, 1990.

Rehak, Melanie. "What Are Cops Afraid Of? Questions for Patricia Cornwell." *New York Times Magazine*, 21 February 1999, 17.

Review of *Charlie's Angels*. *Variety*, 18 September 1974.

Rhodes, Joe. "Profile: Karen Sillas." *Los Angeles Times*, 15 January 1995, 78.

Rich, B. Ruby. "Nobody's Handmaid." *Sight and Sound* (December 1991): 7–10.

———. "The Lady Dicks: Genre Benders Take the Case." *Village Voice Literary Supplement*, June 1989, 24–26.

Robbins, Bruce. "Murder and Mentorship: Advancement in *The Silence of the Lambs*." *UTS Review* 1, no. 1 (1995): 30–49.

Rosenberg, Howard. "Promising Series Still 'Under Suspicion.'" *Los Angeles Times*, 16 September 1994, F24.

Roush, Matt. " 'Anna Lee': Mystery with Unorthodox Energy," *USA Today*, 4 October 1994, 3D.

Rowe, Kathleen. "Comedy, Melodrama and Gender: Theorizing the Genres of Laughter." In *Classical Hollywood Comedy*, edited by Karnick and Jenkins, 39–59.

———. *The Unruly Woman: Gender and the Genres of Laughter*. Austin: University of Texas Press, 1995.

Salamon, Julie. "Weirdo Killer Shrink Meets the G-Girl." *Wall Street Journal*, 14 February 1991, A12.

Sands, Rich. "The Fans Are Out There." *TV Guide*, 6 July 1996, 10.

Schickel, Richard. "Viewpoints," *Time*, 21 October 1974, 126–27.

Scoppettone, Sandra. *My Sweet Untraceable You*. Boston: Little, Brown, 1994.

Seibel, Deborah Starr. "Gillian & Dave's Excellent Adventure." *TV Guide*, 11 March 1995, 8+.

Seltzer, Mark. *Serial Killers: Death and Life in America's Wound Culture*. New York and London: Routledge, 1998.

Shapiro, Laura. "Women Who Kill Too Much." *Newsweek*, 17 June 1991, 63.

Shuker-Haines, Timothy, and Martha M. Umphrey. "Gender (De)Mystified: Resistance and Recuperaton in Hard-Boiled Female Detective Fiction." In *The Detective in American Fiction, Film, and Television*, edited by Jerome H. Delameter and Ruth Prigozy, 71–82. Westport, Conn.: Greenwood, 1998.

Springer, Kimberly. "Waiting to Set It Off: African American Women and the Sapphire Fixation." In *Reel Knockouts: Violent Women in the Movies*, edited by Martha McCaughey and Neal King, 172–99. Austin: University of Texas Press, 2001.

Stabiner, Karen. "The Pregnant Detective." *New York Times Magazine*, 22 September 1985, 82+.

Stacey, Jackie. *Star Gazing: Hollywood Cinema and Female Spectatorship*. London and New York: Routledge, 1994.

Staiger, Janet. "Taboos and Totems: Cultural Meanings of *The Silence of the Lambs*." In *Film Theory Goes to the Movies*, edited by Jim Collins et al., 142–54. New York and London: Routledge, 1993.

Straayer, Chris. "*Femme Fatale* or Lesbian Femme: *Bound* in Sexual Difference." In *Women in Film Noir*, edited by E. Ann Kaplan, 151–62. London: British Film Institute, 1998.

Straub, Valerie. "The Ambiguities of 'Lesbian' Viewing Pleasure: The (Dis)articulations of *Black Widow*." In *Out in Culture: Gay, Lesbian, and Queer Essays on Popular Culture*, edited by Corey K. Creekmur and Alexander Doty, 115–36. London: Cassell, 1995.

Stuart, Andrea. "Making Whoopi." *Sight and Sound* (February 1993): 12–13.

Svetkey, Benjamin. "Xplanations." *Entertainment Weekly*, 10 July 1998, 24.

Swertlow, Frank. "CBS Alters 'Cagney,' Calling It 'Too Women's Lib,' " *TV Guide*, 12–18 June 1982, A-1.

Symons, Julian. *Bloody Murder: From the Detective Story to the Crime Novel*. 3rd rev. ed. 1972. Reprint, New York: Mysterious Press, 1992.

Tasker, Tvonne. *The Silence of the Lambs*. London: British Film Institute, 2002.

———. *Working Girls: Gender and Sexuality in Popular Cinema*. London and New York: Routledge, 1998.

———. "Pussy Galore: Lesbian Images and Lesbian Desire in the Popular Cinema." In *The Good, the Bad, and the Gorgeous: Popular Culture's Romance with Lesbianism*, edited by Hamer and Budge, 172–83.

Taubin, Amy. "Demme's Mode." *Village Voice*, 19 February 1991, 64.

Taylor, Bruce. "G Is for (Sue) Grafton: An Interview with the Creator of the Kinsey Millhone Private Eye Series Who Delights Mystery Fans as She Writes Her Way through the Alphabet." *Armchair Detective* 22, no. 1 (1989): 4–13.

Taylor, Verta, and Leila Rupp. "Women's Culture and Lesbian Feminist Activism: A Reconsideration of Cultural Feminism." *Signs: Journal of Women in Culture & Society* 19, no. 1 (1993): 32–62.

Tharp, Julie. "The Transvestite as Monster: Gender Horror in *The Silence of the Lambs* and *Psycho*." *Journal of Popular Film and Television* 19, no. 3 (1991): 106–13.

Thomas, Ronald R. *Detective Fiction and the Rise of Forensic Science*. Cambridge and New York: Cambridge University Press, 1999.

Todorov, Tzvetan. "The Typology of Detective Fiction." In *The Poetics of Prose*, translated by Richard Howard. Ithaca, N.Y.: Cornell University Press, 1977.

Tomasulo, Frank P. "The Maltese Phallcon: The Oedipal Trajectory of Classical Hollywood Cinema." In *Authority and Transgression in Literature and Film*, edited by Bonnie Braendlin and Hans Braendlin, 78–88. Gainesville: University of Florida Press, 1996.

Tomc, Sandra. "Questing Women: The Feminist Mystery after Feminism." In *Women's Detective Fiction*, edited by Glenwood Irons, 46–63.

Tresniowski, Alex, et al. "Stranger than Fiction: Novelist Patricia Cornwell Gets Caught Up in a Real-Life Crime." *People*, 22 July 1996, 44–46.

Tucker, Ken. "Spooky Kind of Love." *Entertainment Weekly*, 29 November 1996, 34.

Turnbull, Sue. "Bodies of Knowledge: Pleasure and Anxiety in the Detective Fiction of Patricia D. Cornwell." *Australian Journal of Law and Society* 9 (1993): 19–42.

"TV's Super Women." *Time*, 22 November 1976, 67–71.

Tyre, Peg. "Come Out, Kay Scarpetta." *Newsday*, 20 July 1997, G14.

Vanacker, Sabine. "V.I. Warshawski, Kinsey Millhone and Kay Scarpetta: Creating a Feminist Detective Hero." In *Criminal Proceedings*, edited by Peter Messent, 62–86.

Van Meter, Jan R. "Sophocles and the Rest of the Boys in the Pulps: Myth and the Detective Novel." In *Dimensions of Detective Fiction*, edited by Larry Landrum et al., 12–21. Bowling Green, Ohio: Popular Press, 1976.

Van Slyke, Helen. "Calling on a Lady Cop." *Saturday Evening Post*, 1 December 1975, 50–51.

Vernet, Marc. "*Film Noir* on the Edge of Doom." In *Shades of Noir*, edited by Joan Copjec, 1–32. London: Verso, 1993.

Walls, Jeanette. "Jodie, Jodie, Jodie." *Esquire*, January 1997, 14.

Walton, Priscilla L. " 'E' is for Engendered Readings." In *Women Times Three: Writers, Detectives, Readers*, edited by Kathleen Gregory Klein, 101–16.

Walton, Priscilla L., and Manina Jones. *Detective Agency: Women Rewriting the Hard-boiled Tradition*. Berkeley: University of California Press, 1999.

Waters, Harry F., and Nikki Finke Greenberg. "Sly and Sexy: TV's Fun Couple." *Newsweek*, 8 September 1986, 46–52.

Watson, Bret. "A Gillian to One." *Entertainment Weekly*, 9 February 1996, 20+.

Whatling, Clare. *Screen Dreams: Fantasizing Lesbians in Film*. Manchester: Manchester University Press, 1997.

———. "Fostering the Illusion: Stepping Out with Jodie." In *The Good, the Bad, and the Gorgeous*, edited by Hamer and Budge, 184–95.

White, Susan. "Veronica Clare and the *New Film Noir* Heroine." *Camera Obscura* 33–34 (1995): 77–100.

Whitlock, Gillian. " 'Cop it sweet': Lesbian Crime Fiction." In *The Good, the Bad, and the Gorgeous*, edited by Hamer and Budge, 96–118.

Wilcox, Rhonda, and J.P. Williams. " 'What Do You Think?' *The X-Files*, Liminality, and Gender Pleasure." In *"Deny All Knowledge:" Reading the X-Files*, edited by David Lavery et al., 99–120. Syracuse: Syracuse University Press, 1996.

Wild, David. "*The X Files* Undercover." *Rolling Stone*, 16 May 1996, 39.

Williams, Linda. "Film Bodies: Gender, Genre, and Excess." *Film Quarterly* 44, no. 4 (1991), 2–13.

———. "Melodrama Revised." In *Refiguring American Film Genres*. Berkeley: University of California Press, 1989.

Wilson, Ann. "The Female Dick and the Crisis of Heterosexuality." In *Feminism in Women's Detective Fiction*, edited by Glenwood Irons, 148–56.

Winks, Robin W., ed. *Detective Fiction: A Collection of Critical Essays*. Englewood Cliffs, N.J.: Prentice-Hall, 1980.

Wolcott, James. "Columbo in Furs." *New Yorker*, 25 January 1993, 102.

Wolfe, Cary, and Jonathan Elmer. "Subject to Sacrifice: Ideology, Psychoanalysis, and the Discourse of Species in Jonathan Demme's *Silence of the Lambs*." *boundary* 2 (Fall 1995): 141–70.

Wood, Robin. "Ideology, Genre, Auteur." *Film Comment* 13, no. 1 (1977).

Young, Elizabeth. "*The Silence of the Lambs* and the Flaying of Feminist Theory." *Camera Obscura* 27 (1991): 5–35.

INDEX